PENGUIN CLASS

RAGGED DICK and STRUG

Horatio Alger, Jr. was born in Chelsea, Massachusetts in 1832, the son of a Unitarian minister. He received a strict upbringing and was educated for a life in the church, graduating from Harvard in 1852.

After leaving Harvard, Alger, to his father's disappointment, took a job as a historian in Middlesex County, Massachusetts and later worked as a teacher at a boys' boarding school in East Greenwich, Rhode Island. He travelled in Europe for a year, and then returned to the United States in 1857 to complete his studies at the Cambridge Divinity School.

In 1864 Alger was ordained a minister at the First Parish Unitarian Church of Brewster on Cape Cod. Sixteen months later, however, he was dismissed from the pulpit after being accused of engaging in homosexual relations with two boys. After his dismissal, Alger began to focus on his writing career, which spanned more than three decades and 110 books. He wrote mainly children's books about boys and girls who rise from rags to riches through hard work and faith in the American dream. His first major success came with the publication of his eighth novel, *Ragged Dick*, in 1868. Other popular novels include *Luck and Pluck* (1869), *Tattered Tom* (1871), and *Strive and Succeed* (1872). Alger also wrote several adult novels, including *A Fancy of Her's* (first published as *The New Schoolma'am* in 1877) and *The Disagreeable Woman* (1895).

Alger, who never married, spent the last decades of his life living at his family home in South Natick, Massachusetts, where he died in 1899.

Carl Bode was founder and first president of the American Studies Association and past president of the Popular Culture Association. He was the author of two books on nineteenth-century social history, *The American Lyceum: Town Meeting of the Mind* and *Antebellum Culture*, and the editor of two more, *American Life in the 1840s* and *Midcentury America: Life in the 1850s*. He edited P. T. Barnum's *Struggles and Triumphs* for the Penguin American Library.

RAGGED DICK
and
STRUGGLING UPWARD

BY

HORATIO ALGER, JR.

EDITED AND WITH AN INTRODUCTION BY
CARL BODE

PENGUIN BOOKS

PENGUIN BOOKS
Published by the Penguin Group
Penguin Books USA Inc.,
375 Hudson Street, New York, New York 10014, U.S.A.
Penguin Books Ltd, 27 Wrights Lane, London W8 5TZ, England
Penguin Books Australia Ltd, Ringwood, Victoria, Australia
Penguin Books Canada Ltd, 10 Alcorn Avenue,
Toronto, Ontario, Canada M4V 3B2
Penguin Books (N.Z.) Ltd, 182–190 Wairau Road, Auckland 10, New Zealand

Penguin Books Ltd, Registered Offices:
Harmondsworth, Middlesex, England

Ragged Dick first published in the United States of America
by A. K. Loring 1868

Struggling Upward first published in the United States of America
by Porter & Coates 1890
This edition first published in The Penguin American Library 1985
Published simultaneously in Canada
Reprinted in Penguin Classics 1986

13 15 17 18 16 14

ISBN 0 14 03.9033 2

Printed in the United States of America
Set in Electra

Acknowledgments

For help while I worked on this volume I'm grateful to these colleagues of mine at the University of Maryland: Pamella Pressman and Sylvia Smith, my research assistants; Gordon Kelly, chairman of the American Studies department; Pearl Leopard and Katie Helene of the American Studies office; and Shirley Kenny, provost for Arts and Humanities.

I've always been fortunate in my editors at Viking Penguin, starting with Pascal Covici in 1946, when I began work on the *Portable Thoreau*. Anne-Marie Demetz, the editor for this project, was as helpful in 1984 as Mr. Covici was in 1946. And I'm much indebted to John Seelye, general editor of the Penguin American Library, for his encouragement and support in connection with my edition of Barnum's autobiography as well as this edition of a pair of Alger's novels.

C. B.

Contents

Introduction

I. MORE LITERATURE THAN LIFE

Horatio Alger, you look good to me. Stuns you, does it? You yourself conceded that the "higher walks of literature," as you put it, weren't your domain. But, like you, I believe that literature, high or low, can teach us a lesson. In your bouncy little books for boys you urged the merits of honesty, hard work, and cheerfulness in adversity. Nowadays we could use much more honesty and hard work. And the only cheerfulness in adversity comes from the White House; it isn't very catching. You emblematized those qualities in your young heroes, who were all poor on the first page but prospering on the last one. Not that you turned them into top-hatted millionaires, as the Alger myth has it. Your slogan wasn't rags to riches but, more sensibly, rags to respectability. And that was the kind of progress your readers had a chance to make.

My guess is that you were a good influence on the Gilded Age; it needed a touch of old-fashioned principle. You furnished it and displayed its benefits. From 1867 to 1899 you wrote a hundred novels whose aim was to teach young boys how to succeed by being good. Almost at once you found the right formula for your fiction and never had to alter it. You acknowledged toward the end of a long career that your novels all had a "family resemblance" but then added, with the comfortable assurance of an author who'd sold thousands and thousands of copies, that "this does not seem an objection to readers."

Of course this sameness irked the critics. One of them snapped in the *Literary World*, perhaps on reviewing your ninetieth novel, that the only thing new was the names of the characters. However, I'd argue that the critics demanded something you never pretended to provide. They wanted gourmet fare while you were running a fast-food restaurant, and you knew more about a boy's appetite than they did. You also knew more about the kind of book adults would buy for boys. At the same time that you were telling a tale to enthrall the boys, you were preaching a Protestant ethic endorsed by their parents.

Then, too, your fiction had its share of craftsmanship. Everyone agrees that your plots and characters were built alike, but it isn't everyone who notices how carefully you kept within your boundaries. Take the matter of tone. Yours was always optimistic and positive but seldom egregiously so. Or the matter of violence. It rarely appeared in your books; though the heroes were sturdy youngsters, they preferred to fend off a bully instead of knocking him flat. Or the matter of dramatic incident. Even while the wicked squire stormed, your readers realized that something would happen to keep him from foreclosing the widow's mortgage. You used suspense but never of the nail-biting sort—nobody wrestled at the edge of the abyss. The cosmos you created had to be narrow because it was basically benign.

You filled your plots with the problems attached to moving upward but never let them become insoluble. You called, loudly and frequently, on coincidence to help you. Coincidence took the shape of good luck for good people and bad luck for bad. Friend Horatio, I must say that nothing incensed your critics as much as your leaning on luck. You made their necks grow red and their mustaches bristle. It's true that your heroes were all too apt to rescue a rich man's child from drowning in the Hudson or from a careening carriage on Broadway, and so assure themselves of a lifetime of good wages and white collars. Correspondingly, bad luck dogged the footsteps of your villains, major or minor. Chance helped to foil the plotting lawyer.

Still, I'd like to plead mitigating circumstances on your behalf. I feel that this is actually another illustration of the fact that there's more to your fiction than we see at first. I think you struck a chord in the American character: our readiness to believe that good fortune awaits us. This belief explained the success of lotteries, among other things, when you were little, and explains it today. Another mitigating circumstance is that you never let success come through luck alone. It had to be a combination: as you phrased it in the title of one of your series of books, it had to be "Luck and Pluck." You made one of the first of many kindly rich men remark, after reflecting, "I generally find that luck comes oftenest to those who deserve it."

You created characters who are more convincing than your plots. You always prided yourself on providing us with a "real boy," active and enterprising, as the hero. You often gave him an endearing sense of humor that he could display even while standing on the bottom rung of the ladder. For his supporting cast you concocted three other characters, so that you had two pairs of foils. Against the hero you set a malicious young snob. Against the hero's worldly but warmhearted patron, often the father of the rescued child, you set a middle-aged rascal who schemed to do the hero in. You frequently added two minor characters: the hero's devoted and usually widowed mother and a rich, mysterious stranger who helped to thwart the rascal. You chose your remaining characters from a gallery of city and country types that you'd observed. Most were male. Though you were no American Dickens, you could paint a businessman, a bootblack, or a bartender in just a few broad strokes. Your female characters, I'm afraid, were all too often cut from cardboard.

I think you were shrewd—or lucky like your lads—in your choice of settings for your early and especially important fiction. Your favorite was Manhattan and not simply because you settled there. Despite the deductions for dirt and crime, New York was already our most exciting city. When you wrote your breakthrough book, *Ragged Dick*, you set the action in downtown and midtown Manhattan. A third of the way into the story you took your readers on a tour with your loquacious hero that must have widened their eyes; you made crossing Broadway against the clattering traffic an adventure.

You liked dialogue and learned to make yours brisk, particularly in the confrontation scenes, which you obviously relished. When good disputed with evil, good always won; the hero's patron always faced down the hero's enemy, leaving him muttering and discomfited. Also you made your dialogue the vehicle for your humor. A typical exchange would be between an Irish kitchen maid, speaking in the broadest of brogues, and the testy squire she worked for. Though no one ever accused you of being a wit, your efforts lightened your pages.

It wasn't in the dialogue alone that good triumphed in your abbreviated universe. In the end it won in deed as well as word, though evil had to win the preliminary skirmishes or there wouldn't have been a book. Beneath all your busyness—manipulating your characters, making things happen, shifting your scenery—you kept your ultimate purpose in mind. You were not merely telling a tale, you were giving golden instructions.

Out of the Protestant ethic you picked two related elements to emphasize. One was that, for young or old, honesty was the best policy; the other was that, besides being advantageous, honesty was right. The honesty you illustrated throughout your books was, both literally and figuratively, fiscal. After Ragged Dick repaid a customer the fifteen cents due him, the customer gave Ragged Dick a job. Not at once, naturally; you had to complicate the plot first. But by the end of the novel Ragged Dick was on his way to being Richard Hunter, Esquire.

You wrote as if your young audience sat spellbound before you, eager to be instructed. And you didn't hesitate to instruct. You wanted to inspire honesty above all in your boys, but you realized that there were other aids to respectability, temperance in particular. A dedicated foe of drinking and smoking, you could conjure up a lurid picture of the wreck that alcohol made of a man and then add, "Think of this picture, boy-reader, and resolve thus early that such a description shall never apply to you." And you seldom missed a chance to stigmatize tobacco as the "noxious weed."

Thanks to the hundred novels you ended up as an American legend. Today we have not only a flourishing Horatio Alger myth—which doesn't quite fit reality—but also a Horatio Alger Society, an annual Horatio Alger Award, and even a Horatio Alger postage stamp. Yet one thing is certain: you never dreamed of becoming legendary.

II. MORE LIFE THAN LITERATURE

Born on January 13, 1832, into a threadbare ministerial family—his father usually had to struggle to make ends meet—Horatio Alger spent his boyhood in the pleasant town of Marlborough, Massachusetts. His fiction would later mirror both the hard times his family knew and the pastoral atmosphere of Marlborough. Like a good many bright boys, he went to his local academy to prepare for college. He entered Harvard in the autumn of 1848, and the next four years were, he said once, the most enjoyable in his life.

After college he embarked on a career as a writer, not of boys' books but of literature for adults. However, he had to earn a living and, no matter how fast he pushed his pen, he stayed on the edge of genteel poverty. He turned to the ministry because it promised a decent income, but the ministry proved to be a disaster. It was only after that, when he was thirty-five, that he migrated to New York and quickly established himself as the nation's most notable author of juvenile fiction. Appropriately, good luck helped; but the important thing was that, once on top, he had the talent to stay there for three rewarding decades.

His shift to New York in 1866 was the pivotal point in his career. Just before that he'd served as minister of a little Unitarian church in Brewster, on Cape Cod. When he was chosen by the congregation late in 1864, the members must have had mixed emotions. He was short, barely over five feet, and slight, with a boyish look to him; in fact, he was the smallest man in his Harvard class. His manner was effusive and he stammered slightly in conversation, though he spoke easily enough in the pulpit. Anyone who yearned for a pulpit thunderer was going to be disappointed.

True enough, his college record had been one of the best in the class of '52. However, during the dozen years after graduation, he showed no evidence of the "call" that some church members considered indispensable for a minister. He plainly preferred writing to preaching, for he'd been writing since boyhood and he'd begun to publish as early as his sophomore year. It turned out that he housed a dynamo in his small frame. As the 1850s went along, he produced a prodigious amount of mildly sentimental, mildly didactic fiction for adults, fiction that was the 1850s equivalent of today's television serials. All this was for the popular magazines and newspapers, but he also published a respectfully received book. Its very title illuminates the gap between his time and ours. No reader today, however refined, could be lured into buying a volume entitled *Bertha's Christmas Vision: An Autumn Sheaf*. Yet the *Monthly Religious Magazine* for January 1856 recommended the book as a "collection of stories and verses, written in an uncommonly pure spirit."

Though purity of spirit was calculated to impress a congregation, the fact remained that Alger's interest in preparing for the ministry had been limited. As a graduate student in Harvard's Divinity School he performed only passably. His attendance was irregular and he didn't finish until July 1860. Meanwhile, he'd been winning his way into some of the better magazines such as *Harper's* and *Putnam's* and even, once, the prestigious *North American Review*. But he was still poorly paid. Writing to another author in later years, he reported wryly, "For an article in the *North American Review* on which I expended considerable labor I was paid at the rate of a dollar per printed page."

When the Civil War broke out he was rejected for military service as asthmatic; so, since he was a vigorous Unionist, he contributed his talent for writing to the Union cause. He produced much patriotic prose and verse, but the most significant result was his first boys' book. He called it *Frank's Campaign* and published it in 1864 with the Boston firm A. K. Loring. Though he'd composed nothing resembling it before, it proved to contain almost every element that he was to use during the rest of his career. The story centered on a hardy lad who volunteered to work the family farm so that his father could volunteer for the Union army. Alger made the mainspring of the plot the victory of good over evil, and he advised his young readers to apply the book's lessons to their lives. The cast of characters, from the hero to the mysterious but helpful stranger, made the first of a hundred appearances. The magazine *Student and Schoolmate* endorsed *Frank's Campaign* as a capital book for boys.

At intervals he put down his pen and looked around for a congregation. In Brewster he discovered one willing to pay $800 a year and still allow him almost as much freedom to write as he craved. When, after some debate, the congregation formally installed him, it was entitled to more misgivings than it realized. For it was installing a closet homosexual.

During his first year, most things went swimmingly. The better magazines accepted more of his writing and his second boys' book, *Paul Prescott's Charge*, came out. "Likely to prove a favorite," the *Nation* predicted. He performed his ministerial duties and even found time for joining organizations. But he also found time for his homosexuality.

Edwin Hoyt, in his *Horatio's Boys: The Life and Works of Horatio Alger, Jr.*, provides the fullest account of the affair, based on parish records. They show that by the start of Alger's second year rumors were circulating about his habits. In March 1866 the congregation set up an investigating committee. The evidence it found was shocking. The congregation hailed Alger before it, confronted him with the evidence, and then expelled him from his post. In a letter to the American Unitarian Association in Boston, the congregation charged that he'd been guilty of the "abominable and revolting crime of unnatural familiarity with *boys*." In outrage it underlined the word "boys." When confronted he'd merely admitted to being "imprudent," so the congregation added that he'd responded to the charge "with the apparent calmness of an old offender."

Perhaps so. But I believe it's much more likely that beneath his surface calmness lay profound shame and humiliation. In the eyes of nineteenth-century America he'd been guilty of an abomination. I believe that he soon felt deeply that his conduct cried for repentance and penance. One important index of this is a poem he composed shortly after his expulsion. I believe that, writer that he was, he coped with his emotions in part at least by putting them on paper. Composing the poem was an attempt at catharsis. It may well have worked, for he even submitted the poem for publication to a New York monthly, the *Galaxy*. He titled it "Friar Anselmo's Sin."

The opening couplet reads: "Friar Anselmo (God's grace may he win!) / Committed one sad day a deadly sin." It closes: "And many a soul, oppressed with pain and grief,/ Owed to the friar solace and relief." Early in the poem the friar yearns for death in order to expiate his unspecified sin. However, by chance a wounded traveler crawls to his door and Anselmo tends him. Thereafter an angel appears to Anselmo to assure him that he can erase his sin by serving others: "Thy guilty stains shall be washed white again,/ By noble service done thy fellow-men."

I believe that Alger meant what he implied in the poem, that he considered suicide but determined to live a life of penance. He reacted to the trauma of Brewster by sublimating his homosexuality into a permanent concern for the welfare not of his fellow men but of boys, particularly poor ones. I believe that he courted temptation and overcame it; I don't think that Brewster simply taught him to be more circumspect. There's no record of any overt sexual activity later on, and after the success of *Ragged Dick* he was enough of a public figure to make any deviation apt to be observed.

I think his conversion was so effective that in a few years he could look back on his earlier actions almost as if they were those of someone else. There's an interesting sign of this in a letter that Henry James, Sr., sent to his author son. He wrote in spring of 1870, "Alger talks freely about his own late insanity—which he in fact appears to enjoy as a subject of conversation." He added that Alger had interested William James in it, and we know that William had been doing some research on insanity. We can get an idea of how well Alger distanced himself by a comment he made in print two decades later. He noted, in a perfectly matter-of-fact way, that he had a "natural liking for boys." It's true that he may have written this with a wicked grin, but I doubt it. Even the hard-bitten publisher Frank Munsey eulogized him, after his death, for his purity of soul.

At any rate, he proceeded to do a double penance, through his writing and through personal philanthropy. He announced that he'd "leased [his] pen to the boys," and boys became both his permanent subject and the bulk of his public.

It was less than a month after Brewster that he surfaced in New York. He rented a dingy room and then gravitated toward the "street arabs" of Manhattan. There were thousands of them, runaways or orphans for the most part. Many had to live in the Five Points area, Manhattan's notorious slum. As early as summer 1866 he attended a children's church service at the Five Points mission. The first street arab he befriended was one Johnny Nolan, who worked as a bootblack and called every day at the office of an acquaintance of Alger's. Johnny's stories of street life excited Alger's interest and led him, as he wrote later, "to undertake the story of 'Ragged Dick,' in which Johnny figures."

Because the real-life Johnny was shiftless and no model for the hero Alger wanted, he levied on Johnny's peers and devised a rough diamond whom he christened Dick. Alger gave him, beneath his rags, decent instincts and innate honesty. Alger knew that boys in general wouldn't relish reading about a prig, so he made him wise in the ways of the street and allowed him a cocky sense of humor. He built a short serial out of Dick's experiences in Manhattan, using the techniques and structures he'd first employed in *Frank's Campaign*. He sold the serial to *Student and Schoolmate* and with each installment the enthusiasm of young readers grew. After expanding the serial he mailed the manuscript to his publisher, Mr. Loring.

The book was an instant hit. Nobody had written anything like it before. Boys, and no doubt numbers of girls, besieged their parents to buy it for them. Parents responded readily to the moral teachings so colorfully dressed. *Student and Schoolmate* overflowed with pride at *Ragged Dick*'s reception, prophesying that it would propel Alger into first place among authors of juvenile fiction. Its success persuaded even so solidly established a magazine for adults as *Putnam's* to term it very readable. And *Putnam's* was right. He'd given readers a lively, likable hero; a stage setting before which nothing stood still; and, quite probably, an inspiration to work hard and do well.

According to several accounts, the acclaim for *Ragged Dick* led to Alger's becoming acquainted with the New York philanthropist Charles L. Brace, whose chief concern was homeless boys. Brace had started the Children's Aid Society, which in turn had started the Newsboys' Lodging House. He introduced Alger to the Lodging House, and Alger found it the ideal headquarters. For several years he received a bed there to sleep in if he wished and even a desk where he could jot down his observations while they were fresh. He sallied out from the Lodging House in various directions, usually into Manhattan's meanest streets and onto the waterfront. The *Golden Argosy* recalled, in an issue in 1885, that he soon "became a familiar figure along the docks, and wherever the friendless urchins could be found."

He encountered an ample supply of boys to write about and to assist. I consider it a tribute to Alger that his assistance obviously wasn't resented. An elfin little man with big eyes and a soup-strainer mustache, he mingled comfortably with his boys. Grace Edes wrote of him in retrospect, in her *Annals of the Harvard Class of 1852*, "His genial manner, ready sympathy, and generous aid made him beloved" among the street arabs.

He did his double penance with such devotion that I can't escape thinking that it soon stopped being penance. During most of his career he enjoyed writing even though he occasionally complained about it. Similarly, he enjoyed helping boys even though at least once he had to move from bigger to smaller quarters to cut down on their clamorous company. Otherwise, he loved his chains. His best work, according to the *Argosy*, was often done when half a dozen boys were "making the liveliest kind of music" in his handsome rooms on West 26th Street.

In fact, he grew to believe that he had a genuine call to his kind of authorship. He never had a call to the ministry, and he once assured a correspondent that he'd studied theology mainly for its relation to literature. Authorship was something else, though. In a piece headed "Writing Stories for Boys" that he contributed to the *Writer* magazine of March 1896, he said firmly that "no writer should undertake to write for boys who does not feel that he has been called to that particular work."

$

No later novel aroused the excitement that *Ragged Dick* did, but Alger never quite lost the prestige it gave him. He went ahead, turning out page after foolscap page. Delighted by the sales of *Ragged Dick*, Loring contracted for the publication of five more novels in what became the Ragged Dick Series. Then came the Tattered Tom Series, followed by the Luck and Pluck Series, the Brave and Bold Series, and several more. The very titles of the books often told the tale and attested, incidentally, to the similarity of his stories. For instance, he produced *Mark the Match Boy*, *Ben the Luggage Boy*, and *Dan the Newsboy*; along with *The Young Bank Messenger*, *The Young Sales-*

man, and *The Young Miner*. He systematically altered the occupations while keeping the basic structure.

He shifted his settings less easily than his occupations, but shift them he did. However, he was happiest with Manhattan and, after that, a Massachusetts village much like the one he grew up in. In some novels he alternated between the city and the country. Gradually and a little reluctantly, he went further afield and in time ventured as far away as California. He exemplified his outreach in one of the novels of the mid-1870s, *Julius or The Street Boy Out West*. And later, after a trip to California, he tendered the public a whole Pacific Series.

Yet he did more than try to ring changes on *Ragged Dick*. For a time he improved as a writer. He widened his efforts at characterization and sharpened his dialogue. He developed the ability to manufacture suspense and improved at least slightly in integrating his lessons into the action. By the end of the 1870s his creativity waned, for even Alger's effervescent energy had its limits. Nevertheless, he worked along efficiently for at least another ten years, seasoned professional that he was. As late as 1890 he published a book that proved quite acceptable to his readers despite the cavils of the critics, *Struggling Upward or Luke Larkin's Luck*.

There he displayed his time-tested formula from the title page to the conclusion. *Struggling Upward* is the story of an honest, vigorous boy who lives in the village of Groveton. He is accused, falsely of course, of theft, but wins the confidence of two potential benefactors. After assorted adventures including a trip out west to the Black Hills, he sees his enemies confounded by his benefactors, his widowed mother relieved of want, and himself on the path to a promising position in New York.

In *Struggling Upward* Alger's cast of characters, like his plot, contains no surprises. Luke's foil, named Randolph Duncan, is a bully and a snob, much given to curling his lip. His father, Squire Duncan, shows an arrogance befitting his first name, which is Prince, and a greed that pushes him into crime. One of Luke's benefactors, Roland Reed, also plays the mysterious stranger. He appears at Luke's trial and dramatically establishes Luke's innocence. The other benefactor, John Armstrong, is an elderly businessman whose bonds Squire Duncan has stolen and whose office will later employ Luke.

Some of the dialogue assigned to his characters shows that Alger was tiring, for instance, when he has Luke say to a girl who's just invited him to a party: "Thank you, Florence. . . . You are very kind, and I shall have great pleasure in being present. Shall you have many?" But ordinarily his dialogue is much more animated, for example, in a tense cat-and-mouse conversation between the squire and the village saloonkeeper who has come to blackmail him.

Alger also left other hallmarks on *Struggling Upward*. He leaned so heavily on coincidence that it threatened to break under its own weight. For example, when Mr. Armstrong sends Luke out West to search for his former bookkeeper, Alger has the bookkeeper stay in the same hotel in Chicago where Luke will later stay. More than that, he has the hotel clerk find and show to Luke a diary which the bookkeeper has left behind. Astonishingly, it contains a clue to the bookkeeper's whereabouts. Even Alger admitted that this "was a little singular." When it comes to characterization, the squire is wicked as we'd expect him to be. When it comes to plot, it's the squire of course who threatens to foreclose the mortgage on Mrs. Larkin's cottage.

Also typically, Alger intervenes in the story, both in commenting on the action and in pointing a moral. When Luke accepts a tin box from the stranger, Alger breaks in to speculate about the event, "Was it for good or ill?" And he preaches with undiminished insistence. He has Mr. Reed assure Luke, "Do your duty, Luke, and your good fortune will continue." When Alger doesn't speak through his characters, he speaks directly as the author; for instance, "Debt is much more easily contracted than liquidated." He reemphasizes the merits of honesty, hard work, and cheerfulness in adversity. He has Mr. Armstrong announce that he'd begun as a poor boy, barefoot and in overalls; far from harming him, poverty has made him "industrious and self-reliant" and anxious to please his employer.

The rewards and punishments Alger parcels out in the final pages are all as should be. Squire Duncan flees Groveton in disgrace; Randolph has to go to work as an office boy at little more than 50 cents a day. Mr. Reed, who turns out to be a cousin of Luke's late father, gives Luke a nest egg of $10,000; Mr. Armstrong gives him a position "at a liberal salary." Mr. Reed also builds a new and better house for Luke's mother. What more could we ask?

$

Looking back we can see that Alger was an American accident and prospered for decades through the happiest of chances. He filled a void in our country's culture. When he began in the late 1860s, he had scant competition, direct or indirect. A handful of other authors were writing boys' books, chief among them the editor of *Student and Schoolmate*, but he generously granted Alger superiority. Throughout the years he overmatched all others by what he wrote, by how much he wrote, and by how long he wrote. Even in his final decade he hadn't lost all momentum: *Struggling Upward* was a token of this fact.

His indirect competition came from genres other than juvenile fiction. Being indirect they never threatened either his sales or his standing very much. The domestic novel, for one, appealed to adults with a liking for sentimentality. It often included children among its characters; but when they had a leading role they were invariably little girls who responded to mistreatment with tears or, occasionally, tantrums. Little boys were merely noisy and well fed. I can't recall an American domestic novel with a little boy as its hero, but I know of a dozen centering around a little girl. Susan Warner's *The Wide, Wide World*, about little Ellen's travails, is a classic of that genre. Its attraction for boy readers must have been zero.

I don't think that the manual of conduct for males cut into Alger's readership either. It was an era of manuals but most were addressed to young men rather than to boys. And anyway, they were too preachy to be appreciated by a young audience. While their sober and steady moralizing commended the manuals to parents, most boys must have read them with eyes glazed. It's true that a few alert authors, led by T. S. Arthur and W. A. Alcott, enlivened their manuals with made-up anecdotes, but their appeal didn't come close to Alger's.

The inspirational biography offered some, though not much, competition. The poet Longfellow spoke for his era in "The Psalm of Life" when he announced, to the beat of the metronome, "Lives of great men all remind us / We can make our lives sublime." The all too popular prototype was the work of the incredible Mason Locke Weems. The full title of one of the early nineteenth-century versions of "Parson" Weems's book makes the point: *The Life of George Washington; with Curious Anecdotes, Equally Honorable to Himself and Exemplary to His Young Countrymen*. The book remained popular throughout the century, and its success encouraged the production of a good many imitations. Understandably, though, they were about presidents or generals rather than about commercial or industrial leaders. An Andrew Jackson had far more appeal than a John

Jacob Astor but didn't provide much guidance for Alger's boys.

At the other extreme from the conduct manual and, inevitably, much more inviting, stood the dime novel. It developed during the latter part of Alger's career. Its plots were action-packed; its heroes were burly outdoor types with scant interest in upward mobility; and it favored frontier settings, the West above all. Its authors aimed as a rule at the adult market. However, knowing as well as the next man that the dime novel appealed to many boys, they aimed an occasional one straight at them. Alger recognized a threat when he saw one, so he fought back. "Such stories," he warned in "Writing Stories for Boys," "as 'The Boy Highwayman,' 'The Boy Pirate,' and books of that class, do incalculable mischief." Apparently large numbers of ministers, parents, and librarians felt the same way; anyhow, his books kept on selling, with never a "Young Gunslinger" among them.

If his efficiency was awesome, his modesty about his talent was admirable. To another author, E. C. Stedman, he admitted that when he devoted himself to juvenile fiction, the adult world was spared much poor poetry and high-flown prose. And when Alger published his March 1896 piece in the *Writer*, he showed a proper sense of proportion. He promised his fellow professionals that he wouldn't weary them "with a detailed account of [his] books and the circumstances under which they were written."

When he died three years later, the obituaries were more or less dismissive. On the other hand, by a turn of events so remarkable that even Alger wouldn't have dared to use it in his books, the early twentieth century took up those books and transformed them into a vogue. During the euphoric years before World War I, the Alger myth was perfected and his fiction sold better—by hundreds of thousands of copies—than it ever had while he was alive.

$

Right now I have a dog-eared, incomplete copy of *Ragged Dick* lying on my desk. It's one of those early twentieth-century reprints, and its condition reminds me that I've seldom noticed a copy of any of his novels that hasn't been read to tatters. Though no one can measure how much their young readers benefited, I like to think that the benefit was substantial. So I end as I began: Horatio Alger, you look good to me.

—C. B.

Suggestions for Further Reading

BIOGRAPHIES

Ralph D. Gardner, *Horatio Alger, or The American Hero Era* (Mendota, Ill.: Wayside Press, 1964). An enthusiastic biography and extensive bibliography by an Alger devotee.

Edwin P. Hoyt, *Horatio's Boys: The Life and Works of Horatio Alger, Jr.* (Radnor, Pa.: Chilton Book Co., 1974). An informative biography; somewhat flawed by occasional errors and a rather high-pitched tone but otherwise satisfactory.

Herbert R. Mayes, *Alger: A Biography Without a Hero* (New York: Macy-Masius, 1928). A hoax worthy of Barnum, complete with imaginary adventures such as a liaison in Paris and nonexistent books such as *Ben Barton's Battle*.

Gary Scharnhorst, *Horatio Alger, Jr.* (Boston: Twayne Publishers, 1980). The most reliable biography; marked by an austere attitude toward its subject but especially good in analyzing Alger's ideas.

BIBLIOGRAPHIES

Bob Bennett, *Horatio Alger, Jr.: A Comprehensive Bibliography* (Mt. Pleasant, Mich.: Flying Eagle Publishing Co., 1980).

Gary Scharnhorst and Jack Bales, *Horatio Alger, Jr.: An Annotated Bibliography of Comment and Criticism* (Metuchen, N.J.: Scarecrow Press, 1981).

A Note on the Text

Because of cheap paper and cheap bindings, copies of the original editions of *Ragged Dick* and *Struggling Upward* that can be reproduced today without damage are practically impossible to secure. Moved by that fact, plus considerations of economy, the publishers of the present volume have availed themselves of permission to reprint the texts used in *Struggling Upward and Other Works by Horatio Alger, Jr.*, which was issued by Crown in 1945 with an introduction by Russel Crouse.

RAGGED DICK

OR

STREET LIFE IN NEW YORK

CHAPTER I

RAGGED DICK IS INTRODUCED TO THE READER

"WAKE up there, youngster," said a rough voice.

Ragged Dick opened his eyes slowly, and stared stupidly in the face of the speaker, but did not offer to get up.

"Wake up, you young vagabond!" said the man a little impatiently; "I suppose you'd lay there all day, if I hadn't called you."

"What time is it?" asked Dick.

"Seven o'clock."

"Seven o'clock! I oughter've been up an hour ago. I know what 'twas made me so precious sleepy. I went to the Old Bowery last night, and didn't turn in till past twelve."

"You went to the Old Bowery? Where'd you get your money?" asked the man, who was a porter in the employ of a firm doing business on Spruce Street.

"Made it by shines, in course. My guardian don't allow me no money for theatres, so I have to earn it."

"Some boys get it easier than that," said the porter significantly.

"You don't catch me stealin', if that's what you mean," said Dick.

"Don't you ever steal, then?"

"No, and I wouldn't. Lots of boys does it, but I wouldn't."

"Well, I'm glad to hear you say that. I believe there's some good in you, Dick, after all."

"Oh, I'm a rough customer!" said Dick. "But I wouldn't steal. It's mean."

"I'm glad you think so, Dick," and the rough voice sounded gentler than at first. "Have you got any money to buy your breakfast?"

"No, but I'll soon get some."

While this conversation had been going on, Dick had got up. His bedchamber had been a wooden box half full of straw, on which the young bootblack had reposed his weary limbs, and slept as soundly as if it had been a bed of down. He dumped down into the straw without taking the trouble of undressing.

Getting up too was an equally short process. He jumped out of the box, shook himself, picked out one or two straws that had found their way into rents in his clothes, and, drawing a well-worn cap over his uncombed locks, he was all ready for the business of the day.

Dick's appearance as he stood beside the box was rather peculiar. His pants were torn in several places, and had apparently belonged in the first instance to a boy two sizes larger than himself. He wore a vest, all the buttons of which were gone except two, out of which peeped a shirt which looked as if it had been worn a month. To complete his costume he wore a coat too long for him, dating back, if one might judge from its general appearance, to a remote antiquity.

Washing the face and hands is usually considered proper in commencing the day, but Dick was above such refinement. He had no particular dislike to dirt, and did not think it necessary to remove several dark streaks on his face and hands. But in spite of his dirt and rags there was something about Dick that was attractive. It was easy to see that if he had been clean and well dressed he would have been decidedly good-looking. Some of his companions were sly, and their faces inspired distrust; but Dick had a frank, straight-forward manner that made him a favorite.

Dick's business hours had commenced. He had no office to open. His little blacking-box was ready for use, and he looked sharply in the faces of all who passed, addressing each with, "Shine yer boots, sir?"

"How much?" asked a gentleman on his way to his office.

"Ten cents," said Dick, dropping his box, and sinking upon his knees on the sidewalk, flourishing his brush with the air of one skilled in his profession.

"Ten cents! Isn't that a little steep?"

"Well, you know 'taint all clear profit," said Dick, who had already set to work. "There's the *blacking* costs something, and I have to get a new brush pretty often."

"And you have a large rent too," said the gentleman quizzically, with a glance at a large hole in Dick's coat.

"Yes, sir," said Dick, always ready to joke; "I have to pay such a big rent for my manshun up on Fifth Avenoo, that I can't afford to take less than ten cents a shine. I'll give you a bully shine, sir."

"Be quick about it, for I am in a hurry. So your house is on Fifth Avenue, is it?"

"It isn't anywhere else," said Dick, and Dick spoke the truth there.

"What tailor do you patronize?" asked the gentleman, surveying Dick's attire.

"Would you like to go to the same one?" asked Dick, shrewdly.

"Well, no; it strikes me that he didn't give you a very good fit."

"This coat once belonged to General Washington," said Dick, comically. "He wore it all through the Revolution, and it got torn some, 'cause he fit so hard. When he died he told his widder to give it to some smart young feller that hadn't got none of his own; so she gave it to me. But if you'd like it, sir, to remember General Washington by, I'll let you have it reasonable."

"Thank you, but I wouldn't want to deprive you of it. And did your pants come from General Washington too?"

"No, they was a gift from Lewis Napoleon. Lewis had outgrown 'em and sent 'em to me,—he's bigger than me, and that's why they don't fit."

"It seems you have distinguished friends. Now, my lad, I suppose you would like your money."

"I shouldn't have any objection," said Dick.

"I believe," said the gentleman, examining his pocket-book, "I haven't got anything short of twenty-five cents. Have you got any change?"

"Not a cent," said Dick. "All my money's invested in the Erie Railroad."

"That's unfortunate."

"Shall I get the money changed, sir?"

"I can't wait; I've got to meet an appointment immediately. I'll hand you twenty-five cents, and you can leave the change at my office any time during the day."

"All right, sir. Where is it?"

"No. 125 Fulton Street. Shall you remember?"

"Yes, sir. What name?"

"Greyson,—office on second floor."

"All right, sir; I'll bring it."

"I wonder whether the little scamp will prove honest," said Mr. Greyson to himself, as he walked away. "If he does, I'll give him my custom regularly. If he don't, as is most likely, I shan't mind the loss of fifteen cents."

Mr. Greyson didn't understand Dick. Our ragged hero wasn't a model boy in all respects. I am afraid he swore sometimes, and now and then he played tricks upon unsophisticated boys from the country, or gave a wrong direction to honest old gentlemen unused to the city. A clergyman in search of the Cooper Institute he once directed to the Tombs Prison, and, following him unobserved, was highly delighted when the unsuspicious stranger walked up the front steps of the great stone building on Centre Street, and tried to obtain admission.

"I guess he wouldn't want to stay long if he did get in," thought Ragged Dick, hitching up his pants. "Leastways I shouldn't. They're so precious glad to see you that they won't let you go, but board you gratooitous, and never send in no bills."

Another of Dick's faults was his extravagance. Being always wide-awake and ready for business, he earned enough to have supported him comfortably and respectably. There were not a few young clerks who employed Dick from time to time in his professional capacity, who scarcely earned as much as he, greatly as their style and dress exceeded his. But Dick was careless of his earnings. Where they went he could hardly have told himself. However much he managed to earn during the day, all was generally spent before morning. He was fond of going to the Old Bowery Theatre, and to Tony Pastor's, and if he had any money left afterwards, he would invite some of his friends in somewhere to have an oyster stew; so it seldom happened that he commenced the day with a penny.

Then I am sorry to add that Dick had formed the habit of smoking. This cost him considerable, for Dick was rather fastidious about his cigars, and wouldn't smoke the cheapest. Besides, having a liberal nature, he was generally ready to treat his companions. But of course the expense was the smallest objection. No boy of fourteen can smoke without being affected injuriously. Men are frequently injured by smoking, and boys always. But large numbers of the newsboys and boot-blacks form the habit. Exposed to the cold and wet they find that it warms them up, and the self-indulgence grows upon them. It is not uncommon to see a little boy, too young to be out of his mother's sight, smoking with all the apparent satisfaction of a veteran smoker.

There was another way in which Dick sometimes lost money.

There was a noted gambling-house on Baxter Street, which in the evening was sometimes crowded with these juvenile gamesters, who staked their hard earnings, generally losing of course, and refreshing themselves from time to time with a vile mixture of liquor at two cents a glass. Sometimes Dick strayed in here, and played with the rest.

I have mentioned Dick's faults and defects, because I want it understood, to begin with, that I don't consider him a model boy. But there were some good points about him nevertheless. He was above doing anything mean or dishonorable. He would not steal, or cheat, or impose upon younger boys, but was frank and straight-forward, manly and self-reliant. His nature was a noble one, and had saved him from all mean faults. I hope my young readers will like him as I do, without being blind to his faults. Perhaps, although he was only a boot-black, they may find something in him to imitate.

And now, having fairly introduced Ragged Dick to my young readers, I must refer them to the next chapter for his further adventures.

CHAPTER II

JOHNNY NOLAN

AFTER Dick had finished polishing Mr. Greyson's boots he was fortunate enough to secure three other customers, two of them reporters in the Tribune establishment, which occupies the corner of Spruce Street and Printing House Square.

When Dick had got through with his last customer the City Hall clock indicated eight o'clock. He had been up an hour, and hard at work, and naturally began to think of breakfast. He went up to the head of Spruce Street, and turned into Nassau. Two blocks further, and he reached Ann Street. On this street was a small, cheap restaurant, where for five cents Dick could get a cup of coffee, and for ten cents more, a plate of beefsteak with a plate of bread thrown in. These Dick ordered, and sat down at a table.

It was a small apartment with a few plain tables unprovided with cloths, for the class of customers who patronized it were not very particular. Our hero's breakfast was soon before him. Neither the coffee nor the steak were as good as can be bought at Delmonico's; but then it is very doubtful whether, in the present state of his wardrobe, Dick would have been received at that aristocratic restaurant, even if his means had admitted of paying the high prices there charged.

Dick had scarcely been served when he espied a boy about his own size standing at the door, looking wistfully into the restaurant. This was Johnny Nolan, a boy of fourteen, who was engaged in the same profession as Ragged Dick. His wardrobe was in very much the same condition as Dick's.

"Had your breakfast, Johnny?" inquired Dick, cutting off a piece of steak.

"No."

"Come in, then. Here's room for you."

"I ain't got no money," said Johnny, looking a little enviously at his more fortunate friend.

"Haven't you had any shines?"

"Yes, I had one, but I shan't get any pay till to-morrow."

"Are you hungry?"

"Try me, and see."

"Come in. I'll stand treat this morning."

Johnny Nolan was nowise slow to accept this invitation, and was soon seated beside Dick.

"What'll you have, Johnny?"

"Same as you."

"Cup o' coffee and beefsteak," ordered Dick.

These were promptly brought, and Johnny attacked them vigorously.

Now, in the boot-blacking business, as well as in higher avocations, the same rule prevails, that energy and industry are rewarded, and indolence suffers. Dick was energetic and on the alert for business, but Johnny the reverse. The consequence was that Dick earned probably three times as much as the other.

"How do you like it?" asked Dick, surveying Johnny's attacks upon the steak with evident complacency.

"It's hunky."

I don't believe "hunky" is to be found in either Webster's or Worcester's big dictionary; but boys will readily understand what it means.

"Do you come here often?" asked Johnny.

"Most every day. You'd better come too."

"I can't afford it."

"Well, you'd ought to, then," said Dick. "What do you do with your money, I'd like to know?"

"I don't get near as much as you, Dick."

"Well, you might if you tried. I keep my eyes open,—that's the way I get jobs. You're lazy, that's what's the matter."

Johnny did not see fit to reply to this charge. Probably he felt the justice of it, and preferred to proceed with the breakfast, which he enjoyed the more as it cost him nothing.

Breakfast over, Dick walked up to the desk, and settled the bill. Then, followed by Johnny, he went out into the street.

"Where are you going, Johnny?"

"Up to Mr. Taylor's, on Spruce Street, to see if he don't want a shine."

"Do you work for him reg'lar?"

"Yes. Him and his partner wants a shine most every day. Where are you goin'?"

"Down front of the Astor House. I guess I'll find some customers there."

At this moment Johnny started, and, dodging into an entry way, hid behind the door, considerably to Dick's surprise.

"What's the matter now?" asked our hero.

"Has he gone?" asked Johnny, his voice betraying anxiety.

"Who gone, I'd like to know?"

"That man in the brown coat."

"What of him. You ain't scared of him, are you?"

"Yes, he got me a place once."

"Where?"

"Ever so far off."

"What if he did?"

"I ran away."

"Didn't you like it?"

"No, I had to get up too early. It was on a farm, and I had to get up at five to take care of the cows. I like New York best."

"Didn't they give you enough to eat?"

"Oh, yes, plenty."

"And you had a good bed?"

"Yes."

"Then you'd better have stayed. You don't get either of them here. Where'd you sleep last night?"

"Up an alley in an old wagon."

"You had a better bed than that in the country, didn't you?"

"Yes, it was as soft as—as cotton."

Johnny had once slept on a bale of cotton, the recollection supplying him with a comparison.

"Why didn't you stay?"

"I felt lonely," said Johnny.

Johnny could not exactly explain his feelings, but it is often the case that the young vagabond of the streets, though his food is uncertain, and his bed may be any old wagon or barrel that he is lucky enough to find unoccupied when night sets in, gets so attached to his precarious but independent mode of life, that he feels discontented in any other. He is accustomed to the noise and bustle and ever-varied life of the streets, and in the quiet scenes of the country misses the excitement in the midst of which he has always dwelt.

Johnny had but one tie to bind him to the city. He had a father living, but he might as well have been without one. Mr. Nolan was a confirmed drunkard, and spent the greater part of his wages for liquor. His potations made him ugly, and inflamed a temper never very sweet, working him up sometimes to such a pitch of rage that Johnny's life was in danger. Some months before, he had thrown a flat-iron at his son's head with such terrific force that unless Johnny had dodged he would not have lived long enough to obtain a place in our story. He fled the house, and from that time had not dared to re-enter it. Somebody had given him a brush and box of blacking, and he had set up in business on his own account. But he had not energy enough to succeed, as has already been stated, and I am afraid the poor boy had met with many hardships, and suffered more than once from cold and hunger. Dick had befriended him more than once, and often given him a breakfast or dinner, as the case might be.

"How'd you get away?" asked Dick, with some curiosity. "Did you walk?"

"No, I rode on the cars."

"Where'd you get your money? I hope you didn't steal it."

"I didn't have none."

"What did you do, then?"

"I got up about three o'clock, and walked to Albany."

"Where's that?" asked Dick, whose ideas on the subject of geography were rather vague.

"Up the river."

"How far?"

"About a thousand miles," said Johnny, whose conceptions of distance were equally vague.

"Go ahead. What did you do then?"

"I hid on top of a freight car, and came all the way without their seeing me.* That man in the brown coat was the man that got me the place, and I'm afraid he'd want to send me back."

"Well," said Dick, reflectively, "I dunno as I'd like to live in the country. I couldn't go to Tony Pastor's or the Old Bowery. There wouldn't be no place to spend my evenings. But I say, it's tough in winter, Johnny, 'specially when your overcoat's at the tailor's, an' likely to stay there."

"That's so, Dick. But I must be goin', or Mr. Taylor'll get somebody else to shine his boots."

Johnny walked back to Nassau Street, while Dick kept on his way to Broadway.

"That boy," soliloquized Dick, as Johnny took his departure, "ain't got no ambition. I'll bet he won't get five shines to-day. I'm glad I ain't like him. I couldn't go to the theatre, nor buy no cigars, nor get half as much as I wanted to eat.—Shine yer boots, sir?"

Dick always had an eye to business, and this remark was addressed to a young man, dressed in a stylish manner, who was swinging a jaunty cane.

"I've had my boots blacked once already this morning, but this confounded mud has spoiled the shine."

"I'll make 'em all right, sir, in a minute."

"Go ahead, then."

The boots were soon polished in Dick's best style, which proved very satisfactory, our hero being a proficient in the art.

"I haven't got any change," said the young man, fumbling in his pocket, "but here's a bill you may run somewhere and get changed. I'll pay you five cents extra for your trouble."

He handed Dick a two-dollar bill, which our hero took into a store close by.

"Will you please change that, sir?" said Dick, walking up to the counter.

The salesman to whom he proffered it took the bill, and, slightly glancing at it, exclaimed angrily, "Be off, you young vagabond, or I'll have you arrested."

"What's the row?"

* A fact.

"You've offered me a counterfeit bill."

"I didn't know it," said Dick.

"Don't tell me. Be off, or I'll have you arrested."

CHAPTER III

DICK MAKES A PROPOSITION

THOUGH Dick was somewhat startled at discovering that the bill he had offered was counterfeit, he stood his ground bravely.

"Clear out of this shop, you young vagabond," repeated the clerk.

"Then give me back my bill."

"That you may pass it again? No, sir, I shall do no such thing."

"It doesn't belong to me," said Dick. "A gentleman that owes me for a shine gave it to me to change."

"A likely story," said the clerk; but he seemed a little uneasy.

"I'll go and call him," said Dick.

He went out, and found his late customer standing on the Astor House steps.

"Well, youngster, have you brought back my change? You were a precious long time about it. I began to think you had cleared out with the money."

"That ain't my style," said Dick, proudly.

"Then where's the change?"

"I haven't got it."

"Where's the bill then?"

"I haven't got that either."

"You young rascal!"

"Hold on a minute, mister," said Dick, "and I'll tell you all about it. The man what took the bill said it wasn't good, and kept it."

"The bill was perfectly good. So he kept it, did he? I'll go with you to the store, and see whether he won't give it back to me."

Dick led the way, and the gentleman followed him into the store. At the reappearance of Dick in such company, the clerk flushed a little, and looked nervous. He fancied that he could browbeat a ragged boot-black, but with a gentleman he saw that it would be a different matter. He did not seem to notice the newcomers, but began to replace some goods on the shelves.

"Now," said the young man, "point out the clerk that has my money."

"That's him," said Dick, pointing out the clerk.

The gentleman walked up to the counter.

"I will trouble you," he said a little haughtily, "for a bill which that boy offered you, and which you still hold in your possession."

"It was a bad bill," said the clerk, his cheek flushing, and his manner nervous.

"It was no such thing. I require you to produce it, and let the matter be decided."

The clerk fumbled in his vest-pocket, and drew out a bad-looking bill.

"This is a bad bill, but it is not the one I gave the boy."

"It is the one he gave me."

The young man looked doubtful.

"Boy," he said to Dick, "is this the bill you gave to be changed?"

"No, it isn't."

"You lie, you young rascal!" exclaimed the clerk, who began to find himself in a tight place, and could not see the way out.

This scene naturally attracted the attention of all in the store, and the proprietor walked up from the lower end, where he had been busy.

"What's all this, Mr. Hatch?" he demanded.

"That boy," said the clerk, "came in and asked change for a bad bill. I kept the bill, and told him to clear out. Now he wants it again to pass on somebody else."

"Show the bill."

The merchant looked at it. "Yes, that's a bad bill," he said. "There is no doubt about that."

"But it is not the one the boy offered," said Dick's patron. "It is one of the same denomination, but on a different bank."

"Do you remember what bank it was on?"

"It was on the Merchants' Bank of Boston."

"Are you sure of it?"

"I am."

"Perhaps the boy kept it and offered the other."

"You may search me if you want to," said Dick, indignantly.

"He doesn't look as if he was likely to have any extra bills. I suspect that your clerk pocketed the good bill, and has substituted the counterfeit note. It is a nice little scheme of his for making money."

"I haven't seen any bill on the Merchants' Bank," said the clerk, doggedly.

"You had better feel in your pockets."

"This matter must be investigated," said the merchant, firmly. "If you have the bill, produce it."

"I haven't got it," said the clerk; but he looked guilty notwithstanding.

"I demand that he be searched," said Dick's patron.

"I tell you I haven't got it."

"Shall I send for a police officer, Mr. Hatch, or will you allow yourself to be searched quietly?" said the merchant.

Alarmed at the threat implied in these words, the clerk put his hand into his vest-pocket, and drew out a two-dollar bill on the Merchants' Bank.

"Is this your note?" asked the shopkeeper, showing it to the young man.

"It is."

"I must have made a mistake," faltered the clerk.

"I shall not give you a chance to make such another mistake in my employ," said the merchant sternly. "You may go up to the desk and ask for what wages are due you. I shall have no further occasion for your services."

"Now, youngster," said Dick's patron, as they went out of the store, after he had finally got the bill changed. "I must pay you something extra for your trouble. Here's fifty cents."

"Thank you, sir," said Dick. "You're very kind. Don't you want some more bills changed?"

"Not to-day," said he with a smile. "It's too expensive."

"I'm in luck," thought our hero complacently. "I guess I'll go to Barnum's to-night, and see the bearded lady, the eight-foot giant, the two-foot dwarf, and the other curiosities, too numerous to mention."

Dick shouldered his box and walked up as far as the Astor House. He took his station on the sidewalk, and began to look about him.

Just behind him were two persons,—one, a gentleman of

fifty; the other, a boy of thirteen or fourteen. They were speaking together, and Dick had no difficulty in hearing what was said.

"I am sorry, Frank, that I can't go about, and show you some of the sights of New York, but I shall be full of business to-day. It is your first visit to the city, too."

"Yes, sir."

"There's a good deal worth seeing here. But I'm afraid you'll have to wait till next time. You can go out and walk by yourself, but don't venture too far, or you will get lost."

Frank looked disappointed.

"I wish Tom Miles knew I was here," he said. "He would go around with me."

"Where does he live?"

"Somewhere up town, I believe."

"Then, unfortunately, he is not available. If you would rather go with me than stay here, you can, but as I shall be most of the time in merchants' counting-rooms, I am afraid it would not be very interesting."

"I think," said Frank, after a little hesitation, "that I will go off by myself. I won't go very far, and if I lose my way, I will inquire for the Astor House."

"Yes, anybody will direct you here. Very well, Frank, I am sorry I can't do better for you."

"Oh, never mind, uncle, I shall be amused in walking around, and looking at the shop-windows. There will be a great deal to see."

Now Dick had listened to all this conversation. Being an enterprising young man, he thought he saw a chance for a speculation, and determined to avail himself of it.

Accordingly he stepped up to the two just as Frank's uncle was about leaving, and said, "I know all about the city, sir; I'll show him around, if you want me to."

The gentleman looked a little curiously at the ragged figure before him.

"So you are a city boy, are you?"

"Yes, sir," said Dick, "I've lived here ever since I was a baby."

"And you know all about the public buildings, I suppose?"

"Yes, sir."

"And the Central Park?"

"Yes, sir. I know my way all round."

The gentleman looked thoughtful.

"I don't know what to say, Frank," he remarked after a while. "It is rather a novel proposal. He isn't exactly the sort of guide I would have picked out for you. Still he looks honest. He has an open face, and I think can be depended upon."

"I wish he wasn't so ragged and dirty," said Frank, who felt a little shy about being seen with such a companion.

"I'm afraid you haven't washed your face this morning," said Mr. Whitney, for that was the gentleman's name.

"They didn't have no wash-bowls at the hotel where I stopped," said Dick.

"What hotel did you stop at?"

"The Box Hotel."

"The Box Hotel?"

"Yes, sir, I slept in a box on Spruce Street."

Frank surveyed Dick curiously.

"How did you like it?" he asked.

"I slept bully."

"Suppose it had rained."

"Then I'd have wet my best clothes," said Dick.

"Are these all the clothes you have?"

"Yes, sir."

Mr. Whitney spoke a few words to Frank, who seemed pleased with the suggestion.

"Follow me, my lad," he said.

Dick in some surprise obeyed orders, following Mr. Whitney and Frank into the hotel, past the office, to the foot of the staircase. Here a servant of the hotel stopped Dick, but Mr. Whitney explained that he had something for him to do, and he was allowed to proceed.

They entered a long entry, and finally paused before a door. This being opened a pleasant chamber was disclosed.

"Come in, my lad," said Mr. Whitney.

Dick and Frank entered.

CHAPTER IV

DICK'S NEW SUIT

"NOW," said Mr. Whitney to Dick, "my nephew here is on his way to a boarding-school. He has a suit of clothes in his trunk about half worn. He is willing to give them to you. I think they will look better than those you have on."

Dick was so astonished that he hardly knew what to say. Presents were something that he knew very little about, never having received any to his knowledge. That so large a gift should be made to him by a stranger seemed very wonderful.

The clothes were brought out, and turned out to be a neat gray suit.

"Before you put them on, my lad, you must wash yourself. Clean clothes and a dirty skin don't go very well together. Frank, you may attend to him. I am obliged to go at once. Have you got as much money as you require?"

"Yes, uncle."

"One more word, my lad," said Mr. Whitney, addressing Dick; "I may be rash in trusting a boy of whom I know nothing, but I like your looks, and I think you will prove a proper guide for my nephew."

"Yes, I will, sir," said Dick, earnestly. "Honor bright!"

"Very well. A pleasant time to you."

The process of cleansing commenced. To tell the truth Dick needed it, and the sensation of cleanliness he found both new and pleasant. Frank added to his gift a shirt, stockings, and an old pair of shoes. "I am sorry I haven't any cap," said he.

"I've got one," said Dick.

"It isn't so new as it might be," said Frank, surveying an old felt hat, which had once been black, but was now dingy, with a large hole in the top and a portion of the rim torn off.

"No," said Dick; "my grandfather used to wear it when he was a boy, and I've kep' it ever since out of respect for his memory. But I'll get a new one now. I can buy one cheap on Chatham Street."

"Is that near here?"

"Only five minutes' walk."

"Then we can get one on the way."

When Dick was dressed in his new attire, with his face and hands clean, and his hair brushed, it was difficult to imagine that he was the same boy.

He now looked quite handsome, and might readily have been taken for a young gentleman, except that his hands were red and grimy.

"Look at yourself," said Frank, leading him before the mirror.

"By gracious!" said Dick, starting back in astonishment, "that isn't me, is it?"

"Don't you know yourself?" asked Frank, smiling.

"It reminds me of Cinderella," said Dick, "when she was changed into a fairy princess. I see it one night at Barnum's. What'll Johnny Nolan say when he sees me? He won't dare to speak to such a young swell as I be now. Ain't it rich?" and Dick burst into a loud laugh. His fancy was tickled by the anticipation of his friend's surprise. Then the thought of the valuable gifts he had received occurred to him, and he looked gratefully at Frank.

"You're a brick," he said.

"A what?"

"A brick! You're a jolly good fellow to give me such a present."

"You're quite welcome, Dick," said Frank, kindly. "I'm better off than you are, and I can spare the clothes just as well as not. You must have a new hat though. But that we can get when we go out. The old clothes you can make into a bundle."

"Wait a minute till I get my handkercher," and Dick pulled from the pocket of the pants a dirty rag, which might have been white once, though it did not look like it, and had apparently once formed a part of a sheet or shirt.

"You mustn't carry that," said Frank.

"But I've got a cold," said Dick.

"Oh, I don't mean you to go without a handkerchief. I'll give you one."

Frank opened his trunk and pulled out two, which he gave to Dick.

"I wonder if I ain't dreamin'," said Dick, once more surveying himself doubtfully in the glass. "I'm afraid I'm dreamin', and shall wake up in a barrel, as I did night afore last."

"Shall I pinch you so you can wake here?" asked Frank, playfully.

"Yes," said Dick, seriously, "I wish you would."

He pulled up the sleeve of his jacket, and Frank pinched him pretty hard, so that Dick winced.

"Yes, I guess I'm awake," said Dick; "you've got a pair of nippers, you have. But what shall I do with my brush and blacking?" he asked.

"You can leave them here till we come back," said Frank. "They will be safe."

"Hold on a minute," said Dick, surveying Frank's boots with a professional eye, "you ain't got a good shine on them boots. I'll make 'em shine so you can see your face in 'em."

And he was as good as his word.

"Thank you," said Frank; "now you had better brush your own shoes."

This had not occurred to Dick, for in general the professional boot-black considers his blacking too valuable to expend on his own shoes or boots, if he is fortunate enough to possess a pair.

The two boys now went downstairs together. They met the same servant who had spoken to Dick a few minutes before, but there was no recognition.

"He don't know me," said Dick. "He thinks I'm a young swell like you."

"What's a swell?"

"Oh, a feller that wears nobby clothes like you."

"And you, too, Dick."

"Yes," said Dick, "who'd ever have thought as I should have turned into a swell?"

They had now got out on Broadway, and were slowly walking along the west side by the Park, when who should Dick see in front of him, but Johnny Nolan?

Instantly Dick was seized with a fancy for witnessing Johnny's amazement at his change in appearance. He stole up behind him, and struck him on the back.

"Hallo, Johnny, how many shines have you had?"

Johnny turned round expecting to see Dick, whose voice he recognized, but his astonished eyes rested on a nicely dressed boy (the hat alone excepted) who looked indeed like Dick, but so transformed in dress that it was difficult to be sure of his identity.

"What luck, Johnny?" repeated Dick.

Johnny surveyed him from head to foot in great bewilderment.

"Who be you?" he said.

"Well, that's a good one," laughed Dick; "so you don't know Dick?"

"Where'd you get all them clothes?" asked Johnny. "Have you been stealin'?"

"Say that again, and I'll lick you. No, I've lent my clothes to a young feller as was goin' to a party, and didn't have none fit to wear, and so I put on my second-best for a change."

Without deigning any further explanation, Dick went off, followed by the astonished gaze of Johnny Nolan, who could not quite make up his mind whether the neat-looking boy he had been talking with was really Ragged Dick or not.

In order to reach Chatham Street it was necessary to cross Broadway. This was easier proposed than done. There is always such a throng of omnibuses, drays, carriages, and vehicles of all kinds in the neighborhood of the Astor House, that the crossing is formidable to one who is not used to it. Dick made nothing of it, dodging in and out among the horses and wagons with perfect self-possession. Reaching the opposite sidewalk, he looked back, and found that Frank had retreated in dismay, and that the width of the street was between them.

"Come across!" called out Dick.

"I don't see any chance," said Frank, looking anxiously at the prospect before him. "I'm afraid of being run over."

"If you are, you can sue 'em for damages," said Dick.

Finally Frank got safely over after several narrow escapes, as he considered them.

"Is it always so crowded?" he asked.

"A good deal worse sometimes," said Dick. "I knowed a young man once who waited six hours for a chance to cross, and at last got run over by an omnibus, leaving a widder and a large family of orphan children. His widder, a beautiful young woman, was obliged to start a peanut and apple stand. There she is now."

"Where?"

Dick pointed to a hideous old woman, of large proportions, wearing a bonnet of immense size, who presided over an apple-stand close by.

Frank laughed.

"If that is the case," he said, "I think I will patronize her."

"Leave it to me," said Dick, winking.

He advanced gravely to the apple-stand, and said, "Old lady, have you paid your taxes?"

The astonished woman opened her eyes.

"I'm a gov'ment officer," said Dick, "sent by the mayor to collect your taxes. I'll take it in apples just to oblige. That big red one will about pay what you're owin' to the gov'ment."

"I don't know nothing about no taxes," said the old woman, in bewilderment.

"Then," said Dick, "I'll let you off this time. Give us two of your best apples, and my friend here, the President of the Common Council, will pay you."

Frank smiling, paid three cents apiece for the apples, and they sauntered on, Dick remarking, "If these apples ain't good, old lady, we'll return 'em, and get our money back." This would have been rather difficult in his case, as the apple was already half consumed.

Chatham Street, where they wished to go, being on the East side, the two boys crossed the Park. This is an enclosure of about ten acres, which years ago was covered with a green sward, but is now a great thoroughfare for pedestrians and contains several important public buildings. Dick pointed out the City Hall, the Hall of Records, and the Rotunda. The former is a white building of large size, and surmounted by a cupola.

"That's where the mayor's office is," said Dick. "Him and me are very good friends. I once blacked his boots by partic'lar appointment. That's the way I pay my city taxes."

CHAPTER V

CHATHAM STREET AND BROADWAY

THEY were soon in Chatham Street, walking between rows of ready-made clothing shops, many of which had half their stock in trade exposed on the sidewalk. The proprietors of these establishments stood at the doors, watching attentively the passersby, extending urgent invitations to any who even glanced at the goods, to enter.

"Walk in, young gentlemen," said a stout man, at the entrance of one shop.

"No, I thank you," replied Dick, "as the fly said to the spider."

"We're selling off at less than cost."

"Of course you be. That's where you makes your money," said Dick. "There ain't nobody of any enterprise that pretends to make any profit on his goods."

The Chatham Street trader looked after our hero as if he didn't quite comprehend him; but Dick, without waiting for a reply, passed on with his companion.

In some of the shops auctions seemed to be going on.

"I am only offered two dollars, gentlemen, for this elegant pair of doeskin pants, made of the very best of cloth. It's a frightful sacrifice. Who'll give an eighth? Thank you, sir. Only seventeen shillings! Why the cloth cost more by the yard!"

This speaker was standing on a little platform haranguing to three men, holding in his hand meanwhile a pair of pants very loose in the legs, and presenting a cheap Bowery look.

Frank and Dick paused before the shop door, and finally saw them knocked down to rather a verdant-looking individual at three dollars.

"Clothes seem to be pretty cheap here," said Frank.

"Yes, but Baxter Street is the cheapest place."

"Is it?"

"Yes. Johnny Nolan got a whole rig-out there last week, for a dollar,—coat, cap, vest, pants, and shoes. They was very good measure, too, like my best clothes that I took off to oblige you."

"I shall know where to come for clothes next time," said Frank, laughing. "I had no idea the city was so much cheaper than the country. I suppose the Baxter Street tailors are fashionable?"

"In course they are. Me and Horace Greeley always go there for clothes. When Horace gets a new suit, I always have one made just like it; but I can't go the white hat. It ain't becomin' to my style of beauty."

A little farther on a man was standing out on the sidewalk, distributing small printed handbills. One was handed to Frank, which he read as follows,—

"GRAND CLOSING-OUT SALE!—A variety of Beautiful and Costly Articles for Sale, at a Dollar apiece. Unparalleled Inducements! Walk in, Gentlemen!"

"Whereabouts is this sale?" asked Frank.

"In here, young gentlemen," said a black-whiskered individual, who appeared suddenly on the scene. "Walk in."

"Shall we go in, Dick?"

"It's a swindlin' shop," said Dick, in a low voice. "I've been there. That man's a reg'lar cheat. He's seen me before, but he don't know me coz of my clothes."

"Step in and see the articles," said the man, persuasively. "You needn't buy, you know."

"Are all the articles worth more'n a dollar?" asked Dick.

"Yes," said the other, "and some worth a great deal more."

"Such as what?"

"Well, there's a silver pitcher worth twenty dollars."

"And you sell it for a dollar. That's very kind of you," said Dick, innocently.

"Walk in, and you'll understand it."

"No, I guess not," said Dick. "My servants is so dishonest that I wouldn't like to trust 'em with a silver pitcher. Come along, Frank. I hope you'll succeed in your charitable enterprise of supplyin' the public with silver pitchers at nineteen dollars less than they are worth."

"How does he manage, Dick?" asked Frank, as they went on.

"All his articles are numbered, and he makes you pay a dollar, and then shakes some dice, and whatever the figgers come to, is the number of the article you draw. Most of 'em ain't worth sixpence."

A hat and cap store being close at hand, Dick and Frank went in. For seventy-five cents, which Frank insisted on paying, Dick succeeded in getting quite a neat-looking cap, which corresponded much better with his appearance than the one he had on. The last, not being considered worth keeping, Dick dropped on the sidewalk, from which, on looking back, he saw it picked up by a brother boot-black who appeared to consider it better than his own.

They retraced their steps and went up Chambers Street to Broadway. At the corner of Broadway and Chambers Street is a large white marble warehouse, which attracted Frank's attention.

"What building is that?" he asked, with interest.

"That belongs to my friend A. T. Stewart," said Dick. "It's the biggest store on Broadway.* If I ever retire from boot-

* Mr. Stewart's Tenth Street store was not open at the time Dick spoke.

blackin', and go into mercantile pursuits, I may buy him out, or build another store that'll take the shine off this one."

"Were you ever in the store?" asked Frank.

"No," said Dick; "but I'm intimate with one of Stewart's partners. He is a cash boy, and does nothing but take money all day."

"A very agreeable employment," said Frank, laughing.

"Yes," said Dick, "I'd like to be in it."

The boys crossed to the West side of Broadway, and walked slowly up the street. To Frank it was a very interesting spectacle. Accustomed to the quiet of the country, there was something fascinating in the crowds of people thronging the sidewalks, and the great variety of vehicles constantly passing and repassing in the street. Then again the shop-windows with their multifarious contents interested and amused him, and he was constantly checking Dick to look in at some well-stocked window.

"I don't see how so many shopkeepers can find people enough to buy of them," he said. "We haven't got but two stores in our village, and Broadway seems to be full of them."

"Yes," said Dick; "and its pretty much the same in the avenoos, 'specially the Third, Sixth, and Eighth avenoos. The Bowery, too, is a great place for shoppin'. There everybody sells cheaper'n anybody else, and nobody pretends to make no profit on their goods."

"Where's Barnum's Museum?" asked Frank.

"Oh, that's down nearly opposite the Astor House," said Dick. "Didn't you see a great building with lots of flags?"

"Yes."

"Well, that's Barnum's.* That's where the Happy Family live, and the lions, and bears, and curiosities generally. It's a tip-top place. Haven't you ever been there? It's most as good as the Old Bowery, only the plays isn't quite so excitin'."

"I'll go if I get time," said Frank. "There is a boy at home who came to New York a month ago, and went to Barnum's, and has been talking about it ever since, so I suppose it must be worth seeing."

"They've got a great play at the Old Bowery now," pursued Dick. " 'Tis called the 'Demon of the Danube.' The Demon falls

* Since destroyed by fire, and rebuilt farther up Broadway, and again burned down in February.

in love with a young woman, and drags her by the hair up to the top of a steep rock where his castle stands."

"That's a queer way of showing his love," said Frank, laughing.

"She didn't want to go with him, you know, but was in love with another chap. When he heard about his girl bein' carried off, he felt awful, and swore an oath not to rest till he had got her free. Well, at last he got into the castle by some underground passage, and he and the Demon had a fight. Oh, it was bully seein' 'em roll round on the stage, cuttin' and slashin' at each other."

"And which got the best of it?"

"At first the Demon seemed to be ahead, but at last the young Baron got him down, and struck a dagger into his heart, sayin', 'Die, false and perjured villain! The dogs shall feast upon thy carcass!' and then the Demon give an awful howl and died. Then the Baron seized his body, and threw it over the precipice."

"It seems to me the actor who plays the Demon ought to get extra pay, if he has to be treated that way."

"That's so," said Dick; "but I guess he's used to it. It seems to agree with his constitution."

"What building is that?" asked Frank, pointing to a structure several rods back from the street, with a large yard in front. It was an unusual sight for Broadway, all the other buildings in that neighborhood being even with the street.

"That is the New York Hospital," said Dick. "They're a rich institution, and take care of sick people on very reasonable terms."

"Did you ever go in there?"

"Yes," said Dick; "there was a friend of mine, Johnny Mullen, he was a newsboy, got run over by a omnibus as he was crossin' Broadway down near Park Place. He was carried to the Hospital, and me and some of his friends paid his board while he was there. It was only three dollars a week, which was very cheap, considerin' all the care they took of him. I got leave to come and see him while he was here. Everything looked so nice and comfortable, that I thought a little of coaxin' a omnibus driver to run over me, so I might go there too."

"Did your friend have to have his leg cut off?" asked Frank, interested.

"No," said Dick; "though there was a young student there

that was very anxious to have it cut off; but it wasn't done, and Johnny is around the streets as well as ever."

While this conversation was going on they reached No. 365, at the corner of Franklin Street.*

"That's Taylor's Saloon," said Dick. "When I come into a fortun' I shall take my meals there reg'lar."

"I have heard of it very often," said Frank. "It is said to be very elegant. Suppose we go in and take an ice-cream. It will give us a chance to see it to better advantage."

"Thank you," said Dick; "I think that's the most agreeable way of seein' the place myself."

The boys entered, and found themselves in a spacious and elegant saloon, resplendent with gilding, and adorned on all sides by costly mirrors. They sat down to a small table with a marble top, and Frank gave the order.

"It reminds me of Aladdin's palace," said Frank, looking about him.

"Does it?" said Dick; "he must have had plenty of money."

"He had an old lamp, which he had only to rub, when the Slave of the Lamp would appear, and do whatever he wanted."

"That must have been a valooable lamp. I'd be willin' to give all my Erie shares for it."

There was a tall, gaunt individual at the next table, who apparently heard this last remark of Dick's. Turning towards our hero, he said, "May I inquire, young man, whether you are largely interested in this Erie Railroad?"

"I haven't got no property except what's invested in Erie," said Dick, with a comical side-glance at Frank.

"Indeed! I suppose the investment was made by your guardian."

"No," said Dick; "I manage my property myself."

"And I presume your dividends have not been large?"

"Why, no," said Dick; "you're about right there. They haven't."

"As I supposed. It's poor stock. Now, my young friend, I can recommend a much better investment, which will yield you a large annual income. I am agent of the Excelsior Copper Mining Company, which possesses one of the most productive mines in the world. It's sure to yield fifty per cent. on the investment.

---

* Now the office of the Merchants' Union Express Company.

Now, all you have to do is to sell out your Erie shares, and invest in our stock, and I'll insure you a fortune in three years. How many shares did you say you had?"

"I didn't say, that I remember," said Dick. "Your offer is very kind and obligin', and as soon as I get time I'll see about it."

"I hope you will," said the stranger. "Permit me to give you my card. 'Samuel Snap, No.— Wall Street.' I shall be most happy to receive a call from you, and exhibit the maps of our mine. I should be glad to have you mention the matter also to your friends. I am confident you could do no greater service than to induce them to embark in our enterprise."

"Very good," said Dick.

Here the stranger left the table, and walked up to the desk to settle his bill.

"You see what it is to be a man of fortun', Frank," said Dick, "and wear good clothes. I wonder what that chap'll say when he sees me blackin' boots to-morrow in the street?"

"Perhaps you earn your money more honorably than he does, after all," said Frank. "Some of these mining companies are nothing but swindles, got up to cheat people out of their money."

"He's welcome to all he gets out of me," said Dick.

CHAPTER VI

UP BROADWAY TO MADISON SQUARE

AS THE boys pursued their way up Broadway, Dick pointed out the prominent hotels and places of amusement. Frank was particularly struck with the imposing fronts of the St. Nicholas and Metropolitan Hotels, the former of white marble, the latter of a subdued brown hue, but not less elegant in its internal appointments. He was not surprised to be informed that each of these splendid structures cost with the furnishing not far from a million dollars.

At Eighth Street Dick turned to the right, and pointed out the Clinton Hall Building now occupied by the Mercantile Library, comprising at that time over fifty thousand volumes.*

* Now not far from one hundred thousand.

A little farther on they came to a large building standing by itself just at the opening of Third and Fourth Avenues, and with one side on each.

"What is that building?" asked Frank.

"That's the Cooper Institute," said Dick; "built by Mr. Cooper, a particular friend of mine. Me and Peter Cooper used to go to school together."

"What is there inside?" asked Frank.

"There's a hall for public meetin's and lectures in the basement, and a readin' room and a picture gallery up above," said Dick.

Directly opposite Cooper Institute, Frank saw a very large building of brick, covering about an acre of ground.

"Is that a hotel?" he asked.

"No," said Dick; "that's the Bible House. It's the place where they make Bibles. I was in there once,—saw a big pile of 'em."

"Did you ever read the Bible?" asked Frank, who had some idea of the neglected state of Dick's education.

"No," said Dick; "I've heard it's a good book, but I never read one. I ain't much on readin'. It makes my head ache."

"I suppose you can't read very fast."

"I can read the little words pretty well, but the big ones is what stick me."

"If I lived in the city, you might come every evening to me, and I would teach you."

"Would you take so much trouble about me?" asked Dick, earnestly.

"Certainly; I should like to see you getting on. There isn't much chance of that if you don't know how to read and write."

"You're a good feller," said Dick, gratefully. "I wish you did live in New York. I'd like to know somethin'. Whereabouts do you live?"

"About fifty miles off, in a town on the left bank of the Hudson. I wish you'd come up and see me sometime. I would like to have you come and stop two or three days."

"Honor bright?"

"I don't understand."

"Do you mean it?" asked Dick, incredulously.

"Of course I do. Why shouldn't I?"

"What would your folks say if they knowed you asked a boot-black to visit you?"

"You are none the worse for being a boot-black, Dick."

"I ain't used to genteel society," said Dick. "I shouldn't know how to behave."

"Then I could show you. You won't be a boot-black all your life, you know."

"No," said Dick; "I'm goin' to knock off when I get to be ninety."

"Before that, I hope, said Frank, smiling.

"I really wish I could get somethin' else to do," said Dick, soberly. "I'd like to be a office boy, and learn business, and grow up 'spectable."

"Why don't you try, and see if you can't get a place, Dick?"

"Who'd take Ragged Dick?"

"But you ain't ragged now, Dick."

"No," said Dick; "I look a little better than I did in my Washington coat and Louis Napoleon pants. But if I got in a office, they wouldn't give me more'n three dollars a week, and I couldn't live 'spectable on that."

"No, I suppose not," said Frank, thoughtfully. "But you would get more at the end of the first year."

"Yes," said Dick; "but by that time I'd be nothin' but skin and bones."

Frank laughed. "That reminds me," he said, "of the story of an Irishman, who, out of economy, thought he would teach his horse to feed on shavings. So he provided the horse with a pair of green spectacles which made the shavings look eatable. But unfortunately, just as the horse got learned, he up and died."

"The hoss must have been a fine specimen of architectur' by the time he got through," remarked Dick.

"Whereabouts are we now?" asked Frank, as they emerged from Fourth Avenue into Union Square.

"That is Union Park," said Dick, pointing to a beautiful enclosure, in the centre of which was a pond, with a fountain playing.

"Is that the statue of General Washington?" asked Frank, pointing to a bronze equestrian statue, on a granite pedestal.

"Yes," said Dick; "he's growed some since he was President. If he'd been as tall as that when he fit in the Revolution, he'd have walloped the Britishers some, I reckon."

Frank looked up at the statue, which is fourteen and a half feet high, and acknowledged the justice of Dick's remark.

"How about the coat, Dick?" he asked. "Would it fit you?"

"Well, it might be rather loose," said Dick, "I ain't much more'n ten feet high with my boots off."

"No, I should think not," said Frank, smiling. "You're a queer boy, Dick."

"Well, I've been brought up queer. Some boys is born with a silver spoon in their mouth. Victoria's boys is born with a gold spoon, set with di'monds; but gold and silver was scarce when I was born, and mine was pewter."

"Perhaps the gold and silver will come by and by, Dick. Did you ever hear of Dick Whittington?"

"Never did. Was he a Ragged Dick?"

"I shouldn't wonder if he was. At any rate he was very poor when he was a boy, but he didn't stay so. Before he died, he became Lord Mayor of London."

"Did he?" asked Dick, looking interested. "How did he do it?"

"Why, you see, a rich merchant took pity on him, and gave him a home in his own house, where he used to stay with the servants, being employed in little errands. One day the merchant noticed Dick picking up pins and needles that had been dropped, and asked him why he did it. Dick told him he was going to sell them when he got enough. The merchant was pleased with his saving disposition, and when soon after, he was going to send a vessel to foreign parts, he told Dick he might send anything he pleased in it, and it should be sold to his advantage. Now Dick had nothing in the world but a kitten which had been given him a short time before."

"How much taxes did he have to pay on it?" asked Dick.

"Not very high, probably. But having only the kitten, he concluded to send it along. After sailing a good many months, during which the kitten grew up to be a strong cat, the ship touched at an island never before known, which happened to be infested with rats and mice to such an extent that they worried everybody's life out, and even ransacked the king's palace. To make a long story short, the captain, seeing how matters stood, brought Dick's cat ashore, and she soon made the rats and mice scatter. The king was highly delighted when he saw what havoc she made among the rats and mice, and resolved to have her at any price. So he offered a great quantity of gold for her, which, of course, the captain was glad to accept. It was faithfully carried back to Dick, and laid the foundation of his fortune. He prospered as he grew up, and in time became a very rich merchant, respected by all, and before he died was elected Lord Mayor of London."

"That's a pretty good story," said Dick; "but I don't believe all the cats in New York will ever make me mayor."

"No, probably not, but you may rise in some other way. A good many distinguished men have once been poor boys. There's hope for you, Dick, if you'll try."

"Nobody ever talked to me so before," said Dick. "They just called me Ragged Dick, and told me I'd grow up to be a vagabone (boys who are better educated need not be surprised at Dick's blunders) and come to the gallows."

"Telling you so won't make it turn out so, Dick. If you'll try to be somebody, and grow up into a respectable member of society, you will. You may not become rich,—it isn't everybody that becomes rich, you know,—but you can obtain a good position, and be respected."

"I'll try," said Dick, earnestly. "I needn't have been Ragged Dick so long if I hadn't spent my money in goin' to the theatre, and treatin' boys to oyster-stews, and bettin' money on cards, and such like."

"Have you lost money that way?"

"Lots of it. One time I saved up five dollars to buy me a new rig-out, cos my best suit was all in rags, when Limpy Jim wanted me to play a game with him."

"Limpy Jim?" said Frank, interrogatively.

"Yes, he's lame; that's what makes us call him Limpy Jim."

"I suppose you lost?"

"Yes, I lost every penny, and had to sleep out, cos I hadn't a cent to pay for lodgin'. 'Twas a awful cold night, and I got most froze."

"Wouldn't Jim let you have any of the money he had won to pay for a lodging?"

"No; I axed him for five cents, but he wouldn't let me have it."

"Can you get lodging for five cents?" asked Frank, in surprise.

"Yes," said Dick, "but not at the Fifth Avenue Hotel. That's it right out there."

CHAPTER VII

THE POCKET-BOOK

THEY had reached the junction of Broadway and of Fifth Avenue. Before them was a beautiful park of ten acres. On the left-hand side was a large marble building, presenting a fine appearance with its extensive white front. This was the building at which Dick pointed.

"Is that the Fifth Avenue Hotel?" asked Frank. "I've heard of it often. My Uncle William always stops there when he comes to New York."

"I once slept on the outside of it," said Dick. "They was very reasonable in their charges, and told me I might come again."

"Perhaps sometime you'll be able to sleep inside," said Frank.

"I guess that'll be when Queen Victoria goes to the Five Points to live."

"It looks like a palace," said Frank. "The queen needn't be ashamed to live in such a beautiful building as that."

Though Frank did not know it, one of the queen's palaces is far from being as fine a looking building as the Fifth Avenue Hotel. St. James' Palace is a very ugly-looking brick structure, and appears much more like a factory than like the home of royalty. There are few hotels in the world as fine-looking as this democratic institution.

At that moment a gentleman passed them on the sidewalk, who looked back at Dick, as if his face seemed familiar.

"I know that man," said Dick, after he had passed. "He's one of my customers."

"What is his name?"

"I don't know."

"He looked back as if he thought he knew you."

"He would have knowed me at once if it hadn't been for my new clothes," said Dick. "I don't look much like Ragged Dick now."

"I suppose your face looked familiar."

"All but the dirt," said Dick, laughing. "I don't always have the chance of washing my face and hands in the Astor House."

"You told me," said Frank, "that there was a place where you could get lodging for five cents. Where's that?"

"It's the News-boys' Lodgin' House, on Fulton Street," said Dick, "up over the 'Sun' office. It's a good place. I don't know what us boys would do without it. They give you supper for six cents, and a bed for five cents more."

"I suppose some boys don't even have the five cents to pay,—do they?"

"They'll trust the boys," said Dick. "But I don't like to get trusted. I'd be ashamed to get trusted for five cents, or ten either. One night I was comin' down Chatham Street, with fifty cents in my pocket. I was goin' to get a good oyster-stew, and then go to the lodgin' house; but somehow it slipped through a hole in my trowses-pocket, and I hadn't a cent left. If it had been summer I shouldn't have cared, but it's rather tough stayin' out winter nights."

Frank, who had always possessed a good home of his own, found it hard to realize that the boy who was walking at his side had actually walked the streets in the cold without a home, or money to procure the common comfort of a bed.

"What did you do?" he asked, his voice full of sympathy.

"I went to the 'Times' office. I knowed one of the press-men, and he let me set down in a corner, where I was warm, and I soon got fast asleep."

"Why don't you get a room somewhere, and so always have a home to go to?"

"I dunno," said Dick. "I never thought of it. P'rhaps I may hire a furnished house on Madison Square."

"That's where Flora McFlimsey lived."

"I don't know her," said Dick, who had never read the popular poem of which she is the heroine.

While this conversation was going on, they had turned into Twenty-fifth Street, and had by this time reached Third Avenue.

Just before entering it, their attention was drawn to the rather singular conduct of an individual in front of them. Stopping suddenly, he appeared to pick up something from the sidewalk, and then looked about him in rather a confused way.

"I know his game," whispered Dick. "Come along and you'll see what it is."

He hurried Frank forward until they overtook the man, who had come to a stand-still.

"Have you found anything?" asked Dick.

"Yes," said the man, "I've found this."

He exhibited a wallet which seemed stuffed with bills, to judge from its plethoric appearance.

"Whew!" exclaimed Dick; "you're in luck."

"I suppose somebody has lost it," said the man, "and will offer a handsome reward."

"Which you'll get."

"Unfortunately I am obliged to take the next train to Boston. That's where I live. I haven't time to hunt up the owner."

"Then I suppose you'll take the pocket-book with you," said Dick, with assumed simplicity.

"I should like to leave it with some honest fellow who would see it returned to the owner," said the man, glancing at the boys.

"I'm honest," said Dick.

"I've no doubt of it," said the other. "Well, young man, "I'll make you an offer. You take the pocket-book—"

"All right. Hand it over, then."

"Wait a minute. There must be a large sum inside. I shouldn't wonder if there might be a thousand dollars. The owner will probably give you a hundred dollars reward."

"Why don't you stay and get it?" asked Frank.

"I would, only there is sickness in my family, and I must get home as soon as possible. Just give me twenty dollars, and I'll hand you the pocket-book, and let you make whatever you can out of it. Come, that's a good offer. What do you say?"

Dick was well dressed, so that the other did not regard it as at all improbable that he might possess that sum. He was prepared, however, to let him have it for less, if necessary.

"Twenty dollars is a good deal of money," said Dick, appearing to hesitate.

"You'll get it back, and a good deal more," said the stranger, persuasively.

"I don't know but I shall. What would you do, Frank?"

"I don't know but I would," said Frank, "if you've got the money." He was not a little surprised to think that Dick had so much by him.

"I don't know but I will," said Dick, after some irresolution. "I guess I won't lose much."

"You can't lose anything," said the stranger briskly. "Only be quick, for I must be on my way to the cars. I am afraid I shall miss them now."

Dick pulled out a bill from his pocket, and handed it to the stranger, receiving the pocket-book in return. At that moment a policeman turned the corner, and the stranger, hurriedly thrusting the bill into his pocket, without looking at it, made off with rapid steps.

"What is there in the pocket-book, Dick?" asked Frank in some excitement. "I hope there's enough to pay you for the money you gave him."

Dick laughed.

"I'll risk that," said he.

"But you gave him twenty dollars. That's a good deal of money."

"If I had given him as much as that, I should deserve to be cheated out of it."

"But you did,—didn't you?"

"He thought so."

"What was it, then?"

"It was nothing but a dry-goods circular got up to imitate a bank-bill."

Frank looked sober.

"You ought not to have cheated him, Dick," he said, reproachfully.

"Didn't he want to cheat me?"

"I don't know."

"What do you s'pose there is in that pocket-book?" asked Dick, holding it up.

Frank surveyed its ample proportions, and answered sincerely enough, "Money, and a good deal of it."

"There ain't stamps enough in it to buy a oyster-stew," said Dick. "If you don't believe it, just look while I open it."

So saying he opened the pocket-book, and showed Frank that it was stuffed out with pieces of blank paper, carefully folded up in the shape of bills. Frank, who was unused to city life, and had never heard anything of the "drop-game" looked amazed at this unexpected development.

"I knowed how it was all the time," said Dick. "I guess I got the best of him there. This wallet's worth somethin'. I shall use it to keep my stiffkit's of Erie stock in, and all my other papers what ain't of no use to anybody but the owner."

"That's the kind of papers it's got in it now," said Frank, smiling.

"That's so!" said Dick.

"By hokey!" he exclaimed suddenly, "if there ain't the old chap comin' back ag'in. He looks as if he'd heard bad news from his sick family."

By this time the pocket-book dropper had come up.

Approaching the boys, he said in an undertone to Dick, "Give me back that pocket-book, you young rascal!"

"Beg your pardon, mister," said Dick, "but was you addressin' me?"

"Yes, I was."

"'Cause you called me by the wrong name. I've knowed some rascals, but I ain't the honor to belong to the family."

He looked significantly at the other as he spoke, which didn't improve the man's temper. Accustomed to swindle others, he did not fancy being practised upon in return.

"Give me back that pocket-book," he repeated in a threatening voice.

"Couldn't do it," said Dick, coolly. "I'm go'n' to restore it to the owner. The contents is so valooable that most likely the loss has made him sick, and he'll be likely to come down liberal to the honest finder."

"You gave me a bogus bill," said the man.

"It's what I use myself," said Dick.

"You've swindled me."

"I thought it was the other way."

"None of your nonsense," said the man angrily. "If you don't give up that pocket-book, I'll call a policeman."

"I wish you would," said Dick. "They'll know most likely whether it's Stewart or Astor that's lost the pocket-book, and I can get 'em to return it."

The "dropper," whose object it was to recover the pocket-book, in order to try the same game on a more satisfactory customer, was irritated by Dick's refusal, and above all by the coolness he displayed. He resolved to make one more attempt.

"Do you want to pass the night in the Tombs?" he asked.

"Thank you for your very obligin' proposal," said Dick; "but it ain't convenient to-day. Any other time, when you'd like to have me come and stop with you, I'm agreeable; but my two youngest children is down with the measles, and I expect I'll have to set up all night to take care of 'em. Is the Tombs, in gineral, a pleasant place of residence?"

Dick asked this question with an air of so much earnestness that Frank could scarcely forbear laughing, though it is hardly necessary to say that the dropper was by no means so inclined.

"You'll know sometime," he said, scowling.

"I'll make you a fair offer," said Dick. "If I get more'n fifty dollars as a reward for my honesty, I'll divide with you. But I say, ain't it most time to go back to your sick family in Boston?"

Finding that nothing was to be made out of Dick, the man strode away with a muttered curse.

"You were too smart for him, Dick," said Frank.

"Yes," said Dick, "I ain't knocked round the city streets all my life for nothin'."

CHAPTER VIII

DICK'S EARLY HISTORY

"HAVE you always lived in New York, Dick?" asked Frank, after a pause.

"Ever since I can remember."

"I wish you'd tell me a little about yourself. Have you got any father or mother?"

"I ain't got no mother. She died when I wasn't but three years old. My father went to sea; but he went off before mother died, and nothin' was ever heard of him. I expect he got wrecked, or died at sea."

"And what became of you when your mother died?"

"The folks she boarded with took care of me, but they was poor, and they couldn't do much. When I was seven the woman died, and her husband went out West, and then I had to scratch for myself."

"At seven years old!" exclaimed Frank, in amazement.

"Yes," said Dick, "I was a little feller to take care of myself, but," he continued with pardonable pride, "I did it."

"What could you do?"

"Sometimes one thing, and sometimes another," said Dick.

"I changed my business accordin' as I had to. Sometimes I was a newsboy, and diffused intelligence among the masses, as I heard somebody say once in a big speech he made in the Park. Them was the times when Horace Greeley and James Gordon Bennett made money."

"Through your enterprise?" suggested Frank.

"Yes," said Dick; "but I give it up after a while."

"What for?"

"Well, they didn't always put news enough in their papers, and people wouldn't buy 'em as fast as I wanted 'em to. So one mornin' I was stuck on a lot of Heralds, and I thought I'd make a sensation. So I called out 'GREAT NEWS! QUEEN VICTORIA ASSASSINATED!' All my Heralds went off like hot cakes, and I went off, too, but one of the gentlemen what got sold remembered me, and said he'd have me took up, and that's what made me change my business."

"That wasn't right, Dick," said Frank.

"I know it," said Dick; "but lots of boys does it."

"That don't make it any better."

"No," said Dick, "I was sort of ashamed at the time, 'specially about one poor old gentleman,—a Englishman he was. He couldn't help cryin' to think the queen was dead, and his hands shook when he handed me the money for the paper."

"What did you do next?"

"I went into the match business," said Dick; "but it was small sales and small profits. Most of the people I called on had just laid in a stock, and didn't want to buy. So one cold night, when I hadn't money enough to pay for a lodgin', I burned the last of my matches to keep me from freezin'. But it cost too much to get warm that way, and I couldn't keep it up."

"You've seen hard times, Dick," said Frank, compassionately.

"Yes," said Dick, "I've knowed what it was to be hungry and cold, with nothin' to eat or to warm me; but there's one thing I never could do," he added, proudly.

"What's that?"

"I never stole," said Dick. "It's mean and I wouldn't do it."

"Were you ever tempted to?"

"Lots of times. Once I had been goin' round all day, and hadn't sold any matches, except three cents' worth early in the mornin'. With that I bought an apple, thinkin' I should get some more bimeby. When evenin' come I was awful hungry. I went into a baker's just to look at the bread. It made me feel kind o' good just to look at the bread and cakes, and I thought maybe they would give me some. I asked 'em wouldn't they give me a loaf, and take their pay in matches. But they said they'd got enough matches to last three months; so there wasn't any chance for a trade. While I was standin' at the stove warmin' me, the baker went into a back room, and I felt so hungry I thought I would take just one loaf, and go off with it. There was such a big pile I don't think he'd have known it."

"But you didn't do it?"

"No, I didn't and I was glad of it, for when the man came in ag'in, he said he wanted some one to carry some cake to a lady in St. Mark's Place. His boy was sick, and he hadn't no one to send; so he told me he'd give me ten cents if I would go. My business wasn't very pressin' just then, so I went, and when I come back, I took my pay in bread and cakes. Didn't they taste good, though?"

"So you didn't stay long in the match business, Dick?"

"No, I couldn't sell enough to make it pay. Then there was some folks that wanted me to sell cheaper to them; so I couldn't make any profit. There was one old lady—she was rich, too, for she lived in a big brick house—beat me down so, that I didn't make no profit at all; but she wouldn't buy without, and I hadn't sold none that day; so I let her have them. I don't see why rich folks should be so hard upon a poor boy that wants to make a livin'."

"There's a good deal of meanness in the world, I'm afraid, Dick."

"If everybody was like you and your uncle," said Dick, "there would be some chance for poor people. If I was rich I'd try to help 'em along."

"Perhaps you will be rich sometime, Dick."

Dick shook his head.

"I'm afraid all my wallets will be like this," said Dick, indicating the one he had received from the dropper, "and will be full of papers what ain't of no use to anybody except the owner."

"That depends very much on yourself, Dick," said Frank. "Stewart wasn't always rich, you know."

"Wasn't he?"

"When he first came to New York as a young man he was a teacher, and teachers are not generally very rich. At last he went into business, starting in a small way, and worked his way up by degrees. But there was one thing he determined in the beginning: that he would be strictly honorable in all his dealings, and never overreach any one for the sake of making money. If there was a chance for him, Dick, there is a chance for you."

"He knowed enough to be a teacher, and I'm awful ignorant," said Dick.

"But you needn't stay so."

"How can I help it?"

"Can't you learn at school?"

"I can't go to school 'cause I've got my livin' to earn. It wouldn't do me much good if I learned to read and write, and just as I'd got learned I starved to death."

"But are there no night-schools?"

"Yes."

"Why don't you go? I suppose you don't work in the evenings."

"I never cared much about it," said Dick, "and that's the truth. But since I've got to talkin' with you, I think more about it. I guess I'll begin to go."

"I wish you would, Dick. You'll make a smart man if you only get a little education."

"Do you think so?" asked Dick, doubtfully.

"I know so. A boy who has earned his own living since he was seven years old must have something in him. I feel very much interested in you, Dick. You've had a hard time of it so far in life, but I think better times are in store. I want you to do well, and I feel sure you can if you only try."

"You're a good fellow," said Dick, gratefully. "I'm afraid I'm a pretty rough customer, but I ain't as bad as some. I mean to turn over a new leaf, and try to grow up 'spectable."

"There've been a great many boys begin as low down as you, Dick, that have grown up respectable and honored. But they had to work pretty hard for it."

"I'm willin' to work hard," said Dick.

"And you must not only work hard, but work in the right way."

"What's the right way?"

"You began in the right way when you determined never to steal, or do anything mean or dishonorable, however strongly tempted to do so. That will make people have confidence in you when they come to know you. But, in order to succeed well, you must manage to get as good an education as you can. Until you do, you cannot get a position in an office or counting-room, even to run errands."

"That's so," said Dick, soberly. "I never thought how awful ignorant I was till now."

"That can be remedied with perseverance," said Frank. "A year will do a great deal for you."

"I'll go to work and see what I can do," said Dick, energetically.

CHAPTER IX

A SCENE IN A THIRD AVENUE CAR

THE boys had turned into Third Avenue, a long street, which, commencing just below the Cooper Institute, runs out to Harlem. A man came out of a side street, uttering at intervals a monotonous cry which sounded like "glass puddin'."

"Glass pudding!" repeated Frank, looking in surprised wonder at Dick. "What does he mean?"

"Perhaps you'd like some," said Dick.

"I never heard of it before."

"Suppose you ask him what he charges for his puddin'."

Frank looked more narrowly at the man, and soon concluded that he was a glazier.

"Oh, I understand," he said. "He means 'glass put in.'"

Frank's mistake was not a singular one. The monotonous cry of these men certainly sounds more like "glass puddin'," than the words they intend to utter.

"Now," said Dick, "where shall we go?"

"I should like to see Central Park," said Frank. "Is it far off?"

"It is about a mile and a half from here," said Dick. "This is Twenty-ninth Street, and the Park begins at Fifty-ninth Street."

It may be explained, for the benefit of readers who have never visited New York, that about a mile from the City Hall the cross-streets begin to be numbered in regular order. There is a continuous line of houses as far as One Hundred and Thirtieth Street, where may be found the terminus of the Harlem line of horse-cars. When the entire island is laid out and settled, probably the numbers will reach two hundred or more. Central Park, which lies between Fifty-ninth Street on the south, and One Hundred and Tenth Street on the north, is true to its name, occupying about the centre of the island. The distance between two parallel streets is called a block, and twenty blocks make a mile. It will therefore be seen that Dick was exactly right, when he said they were a mile and a half from Central Park.

"That is too far to walk," said Frank.

" 'Twon't cost but six cents to ride," said Dick.

"You mean in the horse-cars?"

"Yes."

"All right then. We'll jump aboard the next car."

The Third Avenue and Harlem line of horse-cars is better patronized than any other in New York, though not much can be said for the cars, which are usually dirty and overcrowded. Still, when it is considered that only seven cents are charged for the entire distance to Harlem, about seven miles from the City Hall, the fare can hardly be complained of. But of course most of the profit is made from the way-passengers who only ride a short distance.

A car was at that moment approaching, but it seemed pretty crowded.

"Shall we take that, or wait for another?" asked Frank.

"The next'll most likely be as bad," said Dick.

The boys accordingly signalled to the conductor to stop, and got on the front platform. They were obliged to stand up till the car reached Fortieth Street, when so many of the passengers had got off that they obtained seats.

Frank sat down beside a middle-aged woman, or lady, as she probably called herself, whose sharp visage and thin lips did not seem to promise a very pleasant disposition. When the two gentlemen who sat beside her arose, she spread her skirts in the endeavor to fill two seats. Disregarding this, the boys sat down.

"There ain't room for two," she said, looking sourly at Frank.

"There were two here before."

"Well, there ought not to have been. Some people like to crowd in where they're not wanted."

"And some like to take up a double allowance of room," thought Frank; but he did not say so. He saw that the woman had a bad temper, and thought it wisest to say nothing.

Frank had never ridden up the city as far as this, and it was with much interest that he looked out of the car windows at the stores on either side. Third Avenue is a broad street, but in the character of its houses and stores it is quite inferior to Broadway, though better than some of the avenues further east. Fifth Avenue, as most of my readers already know, is the finest street in the city, being lined with splendid private residences, occupied by the wealthier classes. Many of the cross streets also boast houses which may be considered palaces, so elegant are they externally and internally. Frank caught glimpses of some of these as he was carried towards the Park.

After the first conversation, already mentioned, with the lady at his side, he supposed he should have nothing further to do with her. But in this he was mistaken. While he was busy looking out of the car window, she plunged her hand into her pocket in search of her purse, which she was unable to find. Instantly she jumped to the conclusion that it had been stolen, and her suspicions fastened upon Frank, with whom she was already provoked for "crowding her," as she termed it.

"Conductor!" she exclaimed in a sharp voice.

"What's wanted, ma'am?" returned that functionary.

"I want you to come here right off."

"What's the matter?"

"My purse has been stolen. There was four dollars and eighty cents in it. I know, because I counted it when I paid my fare."

"Who stole it?"

"That boy," she said pointing to Frank, who listened to the charge in the most intense astonishment. "He crowded in here on purpose to rob me, and I want you to search him right off."

"That's a lie!" exclaimed Dick, indignantly.

"Oh, you're in league with him, I dare say," said the woman spitefully. "You're as bad as he is, I'll be bound."

"You're a nice female, you be!" said Dick, ironically.

"Don't you dare to call me a female, sir," said the lady, furiously.

"Why, you ain't a man in disguise, be you?" said Dick.

"You are very much mistaken, madam," said Frank, quietly. "The conductor may search me, if you desire it."

A charge of theft, made in a crowded car, of course made quite a sensation. Cautious passengers instinctively put their hands on their pockets, to make sure that they, too, had not been robbed. As for Frank, his face flushed, and he felt very indignant that he should even be suspected of so mean a crime. He had been carefully brought up, and been taught to regard stealing as low and wicked.

Dick, on the contrary, thought it a capital joke that such a charge should have been made against his companion. Though he had brought himself up, and known plenty of boys and men, too, who would steal, he had never done so himself. He thought it mean. But he could not be expected to regard it as Frank did. He had been too familiar with it in others to look upon it with horror.

Meanwhile the passengers rather sided with the boys. Appearances go a great ways, and Frank did not look like a thief.

"I think you must be mistaken, madam," said a gentleman sitting opposite. "The lad does not look as if he would steal."

"You can't tell by looks," said the lady, sourly. "They're deceitful; villains are generally well dressed."

"Be they?" said Dick. "You'd ought to see me with my Washington coat on. You'd think I was the biggest villain ever you saw."

"I've no doubt you are," said the lady, scowling in the direction of our hero.

"Thank you, ma'am," said Dick. "'Tisn't often I get such fine compliments."

"None of your impudence," said the lady, wrathfully. "I believe you're the worst of the two."

Meanwhile the car had been stopped.

"How long are we going to stop here?" demanded a passenger, impatiently. "I'm in a hurry, if none of the rest of you are."

"I want my pocket-book," said the lady, defiantly.

"Well, ma'am, I haven't got it, and I don't see as it's doing you any good detaining us all here."

"Conductor, will you call a policeman to search that young scamp?" continued the aggrieved lady. "You don't expect I'm going to lose my money, and do nothing about it."

"I'll turn my pockets inside out if you want me to," said Frank, proudly. "There's no need of a policeman. The conductor, or any one else, may search me."

"Well, youngster," said the conductor, "if the lady agrees, I'll search you."

The lady signified her assent.

Frank accordingly turned his pockets inside out, but nothing was revealed except his own porte-monnaie and a penknife.

"Well, ma'am, are you satisfied?" asked the conductor.

"No, I ain't," said she, decidedly.

"You don't think he's got it still?"

"No, but he's passed it over to his confederate, that boy there that's so full of impudence."

"That's me," said Dick, comically.

"He confesses it," said the lady; "I want him searched."

"All right," said Dick, "I'm ready for the operation, only, as I've got valooable property about me, be careful not to drop any of my Erie Bonds."

The conductor's hand forthwith dove into Dick's pocket, and drew out a rusty jack-knife, a battered cent, about fifty cents in change, and the capacious pocket-book which he had received from the swindler who was anxious to get back to his sick family in Boston.

"Is that yours, ma'am?" asked the conductor, holding up the wallet which excited some amazement, by its size, among the other passengers.

"It seems to me you carry a large pocket-book for a young man of your age," said the conductor.

"That's what I carry my cash and valooable papers in," said Dick.

"I suppose that isn't yours, ma'am," said the conductor, turning to the lady.

"No," said she, scornfully. "I wouldn't carry round such a great wallet as that. Most likely he's stolen it from somebody else."

"What a prime detective you'd be!" said Dick. "P'rhaps you know who I took it from."

"I don't know but my money's in it," said the lady, sharply. "Conductor, will you open that wallet, and see what there is in it?"

"Don't disturb the valooable papers," said Dick, in a tone of pretended anxiety.

The contents of the wallet excited some amusement among the passengers.

"There don't seem to be much money here," said the conductor, taking out a roll of tissue paper cut out in the shape of bills, and rolled up.

"No," said Dick. "Didn't I tell you them were papers of no valoo to anybody but the owner? If the lady'd like to borrow, I won't charge no interest."

"Where is my money, then?" said the lady, in some discomfiture. "I shouldn't wonder if one of the young scamps had thrown it out of the window."

"You'd better search your pocket once more," said the gentleman opposite. "I don't believe either of the boys is in fault. They don't look to me as if they would steal."

"Thank you, sir," said Frank.

The lady followed out the suggestion, and, plunging her hand once more into her pocket, drew out a small porte-monnaie. She hardly knew whether to be glad or sorry at this discovery. It placed her in rather an awkward position after the fuss she had made, and the detention to which she had subjected the passengers, now, as it proved, for nothing.

"Is that the pocket-book you thought stolen?" asked the conductor.

"Yes," said she, rather confusedly.

"Then you've been keeping me waiting all this time for nothing," he said, sharply. "I wish you'd take care to be sure next time before you make such a disturbance for nothing. I've lost five minutes, and shall not be on time."

"I can't help it," was the cross reply; "I didn't know it was in my pocket."

"It seems to me you owe an apology to the boys you accused of a theft which they have not committed," said the gentleman opposite.

"I shan't apologize to anybody," said the lady, whose temper was not of the best; "least of all to such whipper-snappers as they are."

"Thank you, ma'am," said Dick, comically; "your handsome apology is accepted. It ain't of no consequence, only I didn't like to expose the contents of my valooable pocket-book, for fear it might excite the envy of some of my poor neighbors."

"You're a character," said the gentleman who had already spoken, with a smile.

"A bad character!" muttered the lady.

But it was quite evident that the sympathies of those present were against the lady, and on the side of the boys who had been falsely accused, while Dick's drollery had created considerable amusement.

The cars had now reached Fifty-ninth Street, the southern boundary of the Park, and here our hero and his companion got off.

"You'd better look out for pickpockets, my lad," said the conductor, pleasantly. "That big wallet of yours might prove a great temptation."

"That's so," said Dick. "That's the misfortin' of being rich. Astor and me don't sleep much for fear of burglars breakin' in and robbin' us of our valooable treasures. Sometimes I think I'll give all my money to an Orphan Asylum, and take it out in board. I guess I'd make money by the operation."

While Dick was speaking, the car rolled away, and the boys turned up Fifty-ninth Street, for two long blocks yet separated them from the Park.

CHAPTER X

INTRODUCES A VICTIM OF MISPLACED CONFIDENCE

"WHAT a queer chap you are, Dick!" said Frank, laughing. "You always seem to be in good spirits."

"No, I ain't always. Sometimes I have the blues."

"When?"

"Well, once last winter it was awful cold, and there was big holes in my shoes, and my gloves and all my warm clothes was at the tailor's. I felt as if life was sort of tough, and I'd like it if some rich man would adopt me, and give me plenty to eat and drink and wear, without my havin' to look so sharp after it. Then agin' when I've seen boys with good homes, and fathers, and mothers, I've thought I'd like to have somebody to care for me."

Dick's tone changed as he said this, from his usual levity, and there was a touch of sadness in it. Frank, blessed with a good home and indulgent parents, could not help pitying the friendless boy who had found life such up-hill work.

"Don't say you have no one to care for you, Dick," he said, lightly laying his hand on Dick's shoulder. "I will care for you."

"Will you?"

"If you will let me."

"I wish you would," said Dick, earnestly. "I'd like to feel that I have one friend who cares for me."

Central Park was now before them, but it was far from presenting the appearance which it now exhibits. It had not been long since work had been commenced upon it, and it was still very rough and unfinished. A rough tract of land, two miles and a half from north to south, and a half a mile broad, very rocky in parts, was the material from which the Park Commissioners have made the present beautiful enclosure. There were no houses of good appearance near it, buildings being limited mainly to rude temporary huts used by the workmen who were employed in improving it. The time will undoubtedly come when the Park will be surrounded by elegant residences, and compare favorably in this respect with the most attractive parts of any city in the world. But at the time when Frank and Dick visited it, not much could be said in favor either of the Park or its neighborhood.

"If this is Central Park," said Frank, who naturally felt disappointed, "I don't think much of it. My father's got a large pasture that is much nicer."

"It'll look better some time," said Dick. "There ain't much to see now but rocks. We will take a walk over it if you want to."

"No," said Frank, "I've seen as much of it as I want to. Besides, I feel tired."

"Then we'll go back. We can take the Sixth Avenue cars. They will bring us out at Vesey Street. just beside the Astor House."

"All right," said Frank. "That will be the best course. I hope," he added, laughing, "our agreeable lady friend won't be there. I don't care about being accused of *stealing* again."

"She was a tough one," said Dick. "Wouldn't she make a nice wife for a man that likes to live in hot water, and didn't mind bein' scalded two or three times a day?"

"Yes, I think she'd just suit him. Is that the right car, Dick?"

"Yes, jump in, and I'll follow."

The Sixth Avenue is lined with stores, many of them of very good appearance, and would make a very respectable principal street for a good-sized city. But it is only one of several long business streets which run up the island, and illustrate the extent and importance of the city to which they belong.

No incidents worth mentioning took place during their ride down town. In about three-quarters of an hour the boys got out of the car beside the Astor House.

"Are you goin' in now, Frank?" asked Dick.

"That depends upon whether you have anything else to show me."

"Wouldn't you like to go to Wall Street?"

"That's the street where there are so many bankers and brokers,—isn't it?"

"Yes, I s'pose you ain't afraid of bulls and bears,—are you?"

"Bulls and bears?" repeated Frank, puzzled.

"Yes."

"What are they?"

"The bulls is what tries to make the stocks go up, and the bears is what try to growl 'em down."

"Oh, I see. Yes, I'd like to go."

Accordingly they walked down on the west side of Broadway as far as Trinity Church, and then, crossing, entered a street not very wide or very long, but of very great importance. The reader would be astonished if he could know the amount of money involved in the transactions which take place in a single day in this street. It would be found that although Broadway is much greater in length, and lined with stores, it stands second to Wall Street in this respect.

"What is that large marble building?" asked Frank, pointing to a massive structure on the corner of Wall and Nassau Streets. It was in the form of a parallelogram, two hundred feet long by ninety wide, and about eighty feet in height, the ascent to the entrance being by eighteen granite steps.

"That's the Custom House," said Dick.

"It looks like pictures I've seen of the Parthenon at Athens," said Frank, meditatively.

"Where's Athens?" asked Dick. "It ain't in York State,—is it?"

"Not the Athens I mean, at any rate. It is in Greece, and was a famous city two thousand years ago."

"That's longer than I can remember," said Dick. "I can't remember distinctly more'n about a thousand years."

"What a chap you are, Dick! Do you know if we can go in?"

The boys ascertained, after a little inquiry, that they would be allowed to do so. They accordingly entered the Custom House and made their way up to the roof, from which they had a fine view of the harbor, the wharves crowded with shipping, and the neighboring shores of Long Island and New Jersey. Towards the north they looked down for many miles upon continuous lines of streets, and thousands of roofs, with here and there a church-spire rising above its neighbors. Dick had never before been up there, and he, as well as Frank, was interested in the grand view spread before them.

At length they descended, and were going down the granite steps on the outside of the building, when they were addressed by a young man, whose appearance is worth describing.

He was tall, and rather loosely put together, with small eyes and rather a prominent nose. His clothing had evidently not been furnished by a city tailor. He wore a blue coat with brass buttons, and pantaloons of rather scanty dimensions, which were several inches too short to cover his lower limbs. He held in his hand a piece of paper, and his countenance wore a look of mingled bewilderment and anxiety.

"Be they a-payin' out money inside there?" he asked, indicating the interior by a motion of his hand.

"I guess so," said Dick. "Are you a-goin' in for some?"

"Wal, yes. I've got an order here for sixty dollars,—made a kind of speculation this morning."

"How was it?" asked Frank.

"Wal, you see I brought down some money to put in the bank, fifty dollars it was, and I hadn't justly made up my mind what bank to put it into, when a chap came up in a terrible hurry, and said it was very unfortunate, but the bank wasn't open, and he must have some money right off. He was obliged to go out of the city by the next train. I asked him how much he wanted. He said fifty dollars. I told him I'd got that, and he offered me a check on the bank for sixty, and I let him have it. I thought that was a pretty easy way to earn ten dollars, so I counted out the money and he went off. He told me I'd hear a bell ring when they began to pay out money. But I've waited most two hours, and I hain't heard it yet. I'd ought to be goin', for I told dad I'd be home to-night. Do you think I can get the money now?"

"Will you show me the check?" asked Frank, who had listened attentively to the countryman's story, and suspected that he had been made the victim of a swindler. It was made out upon the "Washington Bank," in the sum of sixty dollars, and was signed "Ephraim Smith."

"Washington Bank!" repeated Frank. "Dick, is there such a bank in the city?"

"Not as I knows on," said Dick. "Leastways I don't own any shares in it."

"Ain't this the Washington Bank?" asked the countryman, pointing to the building on the steps of which the three were now standing.

"No, it's the Custom House."

"And won't they give me any money for this?" asked the young man, the perspiration standing on his brow.

"I am afraid the man who gave it to you was a swindler," said Frank, gently.

"And won't I ever see my fifty dollars again?" asked the youth in agony.

"I am afraid not."

"What'll dad say?" ejaculated the miserable youth. "It makes me feel sick to think of it. I wish I had the feller here. I'd shake him out of his boots."

"What did he look like? I'll call a policeman and you shall describe him. Perhaps in that way you can get track of your money."

Dick called a policeman, who listened to the description, and recognized the operator as an experienced swindler. He assured the countryman that there was very little chance of his ever seeing his money again. The boys left the miserable youth loudly bewailing his bad luck, and proceeded on their way down the street.

"He's a baby," said Dick, contemptuously. "He'd ought to know how to take care of himself and his money. A feller has to look sharp in this city, or he'll lose his eye-teeth before he knows it."

"I suppose you never got swindled out of fifty dollars, Dick?"

"No, I don't carry no such small bills. I wish I did," he added

"So do I, Dick. What's that building there at the end of the street?"

"That's the Wall-Street Ferry to Brooklyn."

"How long does it take to go across?"

"Not more'n five minutes."

"Suppose we just ride over and back."

"All right!" said Dick. "It's rather expensive; but if you don't mind, I don't."

"Why, how much does it cost?"

"Two cents apiece."

"I guess I can stand that. Let us go."

They passed the gate, paying the fare to a man who stood at the entrance, and were soon on the ferry-boat, bound for Brooklyn.

They had scarcely entered the boat, when Dick, grasping Frank by the arm, pointed to a man just outside of the gentlemen's cabin.

"Do you see that man, Frank?" he inquired.

"Yes, what of him?"

"He's the man that cheated the country chap out of his fifty dollars."

CHAPTER XI

DICK AS A DETECTIVE

DICK'S ready identification of the rogue who had cheated the countryman, surprised Frank.

"What makes you think it is he?" he asked.

"Because I've seen him before, and I know he's up to them kind of tricks. When I heard how he looked, I was sure I knowed him."

"Our recognizing him won't be of much use," said Frank. "It won't give back the countryman his money."

"I don't know," said Dick, thoughtfully. "May be I can get it."

"How?" asked Frank, incredulously.

"Wait a minute, and you'll see."

Dick left his companion, and went up to the man whom he suspected.

"Ephraim Smith," said Dick, in a low voice.

The man turned suddenly, and looked at Dick uneasily.

"What did you say?" he asked.

"I believe your name is Ephraim Smith," continued Dick.

"You're mistaken," said the man, and was about to move off.

"Stop a minute," said Dick. "Don't you keep your money in the Washington Bank?"

"I don't know any such bank. I'm in a hurry, young man, and I can't stop to answer any foolish questions."

The boat had by this time reached the Brooklyn pier, and Mr. Ephraim Smith seemed in a hurry to land.

"Look here," said Dick, significantly; "you'd better not go on shore unless you want to jump into the arms of a policeman."

"What do you mean?" asked the man, startled.

"That little affair of yours is known to the police," said Dick; "about how you got fifty dollars out of a greenhorn on a false check, and it mayn't be safe for you to go ashore."

"I don't know what you're talking about," said the swindler with affected boldness, though Dick could see that he was ill at ease.

"Yes you do," said Dick. "There isn't but one thing to do. Just give me back that money, and I'll see that you're not touched. If you don't, I'll give you up to the first p'liceman we meet."

Dick looked so determined, and spoke so confidently, that the other, overcome by his fears, no longer hesitated, but passed a roll of bills to Dick and hastily left the boat.

All this Frank witnessed with great amazement, not understanding what influence Dick could have obtained over the swindler sufficient to compel restitution.

"How did you do it?" he asked eagerly.

"I told him I'd exert my influence with the president to have him tried by *habeas corpus*," said Dick.

"And of course that frightened him. But tell me, without joking, how you managed."

Dick gave a truthful account of what occurred, and then said, "Now we'll go back and carry the money."

"Suppose we don't find the poor countryman?"

"Then the p'lice will take care of it."

They remained on board the boat, and in five minutes were again in New York. Going up Wall Street, they met the countryman a little distance from the Custom House. His face was marked with the traces of deep anguish; but in his case even grief could not subdue the cravings of appetite. He had purchased some cakes of one of the old women who spread out for the benefit of passers-by an array of apples and seed-cakes, and was munching them with melancholy satisfaction.

"Hilloa!" said Dick. "Have you found your money?"

"No," ejaculated the young man, with a convulsive gasp. "I sha'n't ever see it again. The mean skunk's cheated me out of it. Consarn his picter! It took me most six months to save it up. I was workin' for Deacon Pinkham in our place. Oh, I wish I'd never come to New York! The deacon, he told me he'd keep it for me; but I wanted to put it in the bank, and now it's all gone, boo hoo!"

And the miserable youth, having despatched his cakes, was so overcome by the thought of his loss that he burst into tears.

"I say," said Dick, "dry up, and see what I've got here."

The youth no sooner saw the roll of bills, and comprehended that it was indeed his lost treasure, than from the depths of anguish he was exalted to the most ecstatic joy. He seized Dick's hand, and shook it with so much energy that our hero began to feel rather alarmed for its safety.

"'Pears to me you take my arm for a pump-handle," said he. "Couldn't you show your gratitood some other way? It's just possible I may want to use my arm ag'in some time."

The young man desisted, but invited Dick most cordially to come up and stop a week with him at his country home, assuring him that he wouldn't charge him anything for board.

"All right!" said Dick. "If you don't mind I'll bring my wife along, too. She's delicate, and the country air might do her good."

Jonathan stared at him in amazement, uncertain whether to credit the fact of his marriage. Dick walked on with Frank, leaving him in an apparent state of stupefaction, and it is possible that he has not yet settled the affair to his satisfaction.

"Now," said Frank, "I think I'll go back to the Astor House. Uncle has probably got through his business and returned."

"All right," said Dick.

The two boys walked up to Broadway, just where the tall steeple of Trinity faces the street of bankers and brokers, and walked leisurely to the hotel. When they arrived at the Astor House, Dick said, "Good-by, Frank."

"Not yet," said Frank; "I want you to come in with me."

Dick followed his young patron up the steps. Frank went to the reading-room, where, as he had thought probable, he found his uncle already arrived, and reading a copy of "The Evening Post," which he had just purchased outside.

"Well, boys," he said, looking up, "have you had a pleasant jaunt?"

"Yes, sir," said Frank. "Dick's a capital guide."

"So this is Dick," said Mr. Whitney, surveying him with a smile. "Upon my word, I should hardly have known him. I must congratulate him on his improved appearance."

"Frank's been very kind to me," said Dick, who, rough street-boy as he was, had a heart easily touched by kindness, of which he had never experienced much. "He's a tip-top fellow."

"I believe he is a good boy," said Mr. Whitney. "I hope, my lad, you will prosper and rise in the world. You know in this free country poverty in early life is no bar to a man's advancement. I haven't risen very high myself," he added, with a smile, "but have met with moderate success in life; yet there was a time when I was as poor as you."

"Were you, sir," asked Dick, eagerly.

"Yes, my boy, I have known the time I have been obliged to go without my dinner because I didn't have enough money to pay for it."

"How did you get up in the world," asked Dick, anxiously.

"I entered a printing-office as an apprentice, and worked for some years. Then my eyes gave out and I was obliged to give that up. Not knowing what else to do, I went into the country, and worked on a farm. After a while I was lucky enough to invent a machine, which has brought me in a great deal of money. But there was one thing I got while I was in the printing-office which I value more than money."

"What was that, sir?"

"A taste for reading and study. During my leisure hours I improved myself by study, and acquired a large part of the knowledge which I now possess. Indeed, it was one of my books that first put me on the track of the invention, which I afterwards made. So you see, my lad, that my studious habits paid me in money, as well as in another way."

"I'm awful ignorant," said Dick, soberly.

"But you are young, and, I judge, a smart boy. If you try to learn, you can, and if you ever expect to do anything in the world, you must know something of books."

"I will," said Dick, resolutely. "I ain't always goin' to black boots for a livin'."

"All labor is respectable, my lad, and you have no cause to be ashamed of any honest business; yet when you can get something to do that promises better for your future prospects, I advise you to do so. Till then earn your living in the way you are accustomed to, avoid extravagance, and save up a little money if you can."

"Thank you for your advice," said our hero. "There aint many that takes an interest in Ragged Dick."

"So that's your name," said Mr. Whitney. "If I judge you

rightly, it won't be long before you change it. Save your money, my lad, buy books, and determine to be somebody, and you may yet fill an honorable position."

"I'll try," said Dick. "Good-night, sir."

"Wait a minute, Dick," said Frank. "Your blacking-box and old clothes are upstairs. You may want them."

"In course," said Dick. "I couldn't get along without my best clothes, and my stock in trade."

"You may go up to the room with him, Frank," said Mr. Whitney. "The clerk will give you the key. I want to see you, Dick, before you go."

"Yes, sir," said Dick.

"Where are you going to sleep to-night, Dick?" asked Frank, as they went upstairs together.

"P'r'aps at the Fifth Avenue Hotel—on the outside," said Dick.

"Haven't you any place to sleep, then?"

"I slept in a box, last night."

"In a box?"

"Yes, on Spruce Street."

"Poor fellow!" said Frank, compassionately.

"Oh, 'twas a bully bed—full of straw! I slept like a top."

"Don't you earn enough to pay for a room, Dick?"

"Yes," said Dick; "only I spend my money foolish, goin' to the Old Bowery, and Tony Pastor's, and sometimes gamblin' in Baxter Street."

"You won't gamble any more,—will you, Dick?" said Frank, laying his hand persuasively on his companion's shoulder.

"No, I won't," said Dick.

"You'll promise?"

"Yes, and I'll keep it. You're a good feller. I wish you was goin' to be in New York."

"I am going to a boarding-school in Connecticut. The name of the town is Barnton. Will you write to me, Dick?"

"My writing would look like hens' tracks," said our hero.

"Never mind. I want you to write. When you write you can tell me how to direct, and I will send you a letter."

"I wish you would," said Dick. "I wish I was more like you."

"I hope you will make a much better boy, Dick. Now we'll go in to my uncle. He wishes to see you before you go."

They went into the reading-room. Dick had wrapped up his

blacking-brush in a newspaper with which Frank had supplied him, feeling that a guest of the Astor House should hardly be seen coming out of the hotel displaying such a professional sign.

"Uncle, Dick's ready to go," said Frank.

"Good-by, my lad," said Mr. Whitney. "I hope to hear good accounts of you sometime. Don't forget what I have told you. Remember that your future position depends mainly upon yourself, and that it will be high or low as you choose to make it."

He held out his hand, in which was a five-dollar bill. Dick shrunk back.

"I don't like to take it," he said. "I haven't earned it."

"Perhaps not," said Mr. Whitney; "but I give it to you because I remember my own friendless youth. I hope it may be of service to you. Sometime when you are a prosperous man, you can repay it in the form of aid to some poor boy, who is struggling upward as you are now."

"I will, sir," said Dick, manfully.

He no longer refused the money, but took it gratefully, and, bidding Frank and his uncle good-by, went out into the street. A feeling of loneliness came over him as he left the presence of Frank, for whom he had formed a strong attachment in the few hours he had known him.

CHAPTER XII

DICK HIRES A ROOM ON MOTT STREET

GOING out into the fresh air Dick felt the pangs of hunger. He accordingly went to a restaurant and got a substantial supper. Perhaps it was the new clothes he wore, which made him feel a little more aristocratic. At all events, instead of patronizing the cheap restaurant where he usually procured his meals, he went into the refectory attached to Lovejoy's Hotel, where the prices were higher and the company more select. In his ordinary dress, Dick would have been excluded, but now he had the appearance of a very respectable, gentlemanly boy, whose presence would not discredit any establishment. His orders were therefore received with attention by the waiter and in due time a good supper was placed before him.

"I wish I could come here every day," thought Dick. "It seems kind o' nice and 'spectable, side of the other place. There's a gent at that other table that I've shined boots for more'n once. He don't know me in my new clothes. Guess he don't know his boot-black patronizes the same establishment."

His supper over, Dick went up to the desk, and, presenting his check, tendered in payment his five-dollar bill, as if it were one of a large number which he possessed. Receiving back his change he went out into the street.

Two questions now arose: How should he spend the evening, and where should he pass the night? Yesterday, with such a sum of money in his possession, he would have answered both questions readily. For the evening, he would have passed it at the Old Bowery, and gone to sleep in any out-of-the-way place that offered. But he had turned over a new leaf, or resolved to do so. He meant to save his money for some useful purpose,—to aid his advancement in the world. So he could not afford the theatre. Besides, with his new clothes, he was unwilling to pass the night out of doors.

"I should spile 'em," he thought, "and that wouldn't pay."

So he determined to hunt up a room which he could occupy regularly, and consider as his own, where he could sleep nights, instead of depending on boxes and old wagons for a chance shelter. This would be the first step towards respectability, and Dick determined to take it.

He accordingly passed through the City Hall Park, and walked leisurely up Centre Street.

He decided that it would hardly be advisable for him to seek lodgings in Fifth Avenue, although his present cash capital consisted of nearly five dollars in money, besides the valuable papers contained in his wallet. Besides, he had reason to doubt whether any in his line of business lived on that aristocratic street. He took his way to Mott Street, which is considerably less pretentious, and halted in front of a shabby brick lodging-house kept by a Mrs. Mooney, with whose son Tom, Dick was acquainted.

Dick rang the bell, which sent back a shrill metallic response.

The door was opened by a slatternly servant, who looked at him inquiringly, and not without curiosity. It must be remembered that Dick was well dressed, and that nothing in his appearance bespoke his occupation. Being naturally a good-looking boy, he might readily be mistaken for a gentleman's son.

"Well, Queen Victoria," said Dick, "is your missus at home?"

"My name's Bridget," said the girl.

"Oh, indeed!" said Dick. "You looked so much like the queen's picter what she gave me last Christmas in exchange for mine, that I couldn't help calling you by her name."

"Oh, go along wid ye!" said Bridget. "It's makin' fun ye are."

"If you don't believe me," said Dick, gravely, "all you've got to do is to ask my partic'lar friend, the Duke of Newcastle."

"Bridget!" called a shrill voice from the basement.

"The missus is calling me," said Bridget, hurriedly. "I'll tell her ye want her."

"All right!" said Dick.

The servant descended into the lower regions, and in a short time a stout, red-faced woman appeared on the scene.

"Well, sir, what's your wish?" she asked.

"Have you got a room to let?" asked Dick.

"Is it for yourself you ask?" questioned the woman, in some surprise.

Dick answered in the affirmative.

"I haven't got any very good rooms vacant. There's a small room in the third story."

"I'd like to see it," said Dick.

"I don't know as it would be good enough for you," said the woman, with a glance at Dick's clothes.

"I ain't very partic'lar about accommodations," said our hero. "I guess I'll look at it."

Dick followed the landlady up two narrow stair-cases, uncarpeted and dirty, to the third landing, where he was ushered into a room about ten feet square. It could not be considered a very desirable apartment. It had once been covered with an oilcloth carpet, but this was now very ragged, and looked worse than none. There was a single bed in the corner, covered with an indiscriminate heap of bed-clothing, rumpled and not over-clean. There was a bureau, with the veneering scratched and in some parts stripped off, and a small glass, eight inches by ten, cracked across the middle; also two chairs in rather a disjointed condition. Judging from Dick's appearance, Mrs. Mooney thought he would turn from it in disdain.

But it must be remembered that Dick's past experience had not been of a character to make him fastidious. In comparison with a box, or an empty wagon, even this little room seemed comfortable. He decided to hire it if the rent proved reasonable.

"Well, what's the tax?" asked Dick.

"I ought to have a dollar a week," said Mrs. Mooney, hesitatingly.

"Say seventy-five cents, and I'll take it," said Dick.

"Every week in advance?"

"Yes."

"Well, as times is hard, and I can't afford to keep it empty, you may have it. When will you come?"

"To-night," said Dick.

"It ain't lookin' very neat. I don't know as I can fix it up to-night."

"Well, I'll sleep here to-night, and you can fix it up to-morrow."

"I hope you'll excuse the looks. I'm a lone woman, and my help is so shiftless, I have to look after everything myself; so I can't keep things as straight as I want to."

"All right!" said Dick.

"Can you pay me the first week in advance?" asked the landlady, cautiously.

Dick responded by drawing seventy-five cents from his pocket, and placing it in her hand.

"What's your business, sir, if I may inquire?" said Mrs. Mooney.

"Oh, I'm professional!" said Dick.

"Indeed!" said the landlady, who did not feel much enlightened by this answer.

"How's Tom?" asked Dick.

"Do you know my Tom?" said Mrs. Mooney in surprise. "He's gone to sea,—to Californy. He went last week."

"Did he?" said Dick. "Yes, I knew him."

Mrs. Mooney looked upon her new lodger with increased favor, on finding that he was acquainted with her son, who, by the way, was one of the worst young scamps in Mott Street, which is saying considerable.

"I'll bring over my baggage from the Astor House this evening," said Dick in a tone of importance.

"From the Astor House!" repeated Mrs. Mooney, in fresh amazement.

"Yes, I've been stoppin' there a short time with some friends," said Dick.

Mrs. Mooney might be excused for a little amazement at finding that a guest from the Astor House was about to become one of her lodgers—such transfers not being common.

"Did you say you was purfessional?" she asked.

"Yes, ma'am," said Dick, politely.

"You ain't a—a—" Mrs. Mooney paused, uncertain what conjecture to hazard.

"Oh, no, nothing of the sort," said Dick, promptly. "How could you think so, Mrs. Mooney?"

"No offence, sir," said the landlady, more perplexed than ever.

"Certainly not," said our hero. "But you must excuse me now, Mrs. Mooney, as I have business of great importance to attend to."

"You'll come round this evening?"

Dick answered in the affirmative, and turned away.

"I wonder what he is!" thought the landlady, following him with her eyes as he crossed the street. "He's got good clothes on, but he don't seem very particular about his room. Well; I've got all my rooms full now. That's one comfort."

Dick felt more comfortable now that he had taken the decisive step of hiring a lodging, and paying a week's rent in advance. For seven nights he was sure of a shelter and a bed to sleep in. The thought was a pleasant one to our young vagrant, who hitherto had seldom known when he rose in the morning where he should find a resting-place at night.

"I must bring my traps round," said Dick to himself. "I guess I'll go to bed early to-night. It'll feel kinder good to sleep in a reg'lar bed. Boxes is rather hard to the back, and ain't comfortable in case of rain. I wonder what Johnny Nolan would say if he knew I'd got a room of my own."

CHAPTER XIII

MICKY MAGUIRE

ABOUT nine o'clock Dick sought his new lodgings. In his hands he carried his professional wardrobe, namely, the clothes which he had worn at the commencement of the day, and the implements of his business. These he stowed away in the bureau drawers, and by the light of a flickering candle took off his clothes and went to bed. Dick had a good digestion and a reasonably good conscience; consequently he was a good sleeper. Perhaps, too, the soft feather bed conduced to slumber. At any rate his eyes were soon closed, and he did not awake until half-past six the next morning.

He lifted himself on his elbow, and stared around him in transient bewilderment.

"Blest if I hadn't forgot where I was," he said to himself. "So this is my room, is it? Well, it seems kind of 'spectable to have a room and a bed to sleep in. I'd orter be able to afford seventy-five cents a week. I've throwed away more money than that in one evenin'. There ain't no reason why I shouldn't live 'spectable. I wish I knowed as much as Frank. He's a tip-top feller. Nobody ever cared enough for me before to give me good advice. It was kicks, and cuffs, and swearin' at me all the time. I'd like to show him I can do something."

While Dick was indulging in these reflections, he had risen from bed, and, finding an accession to the furniture of his room, in the shape of an ancient wash-stand bearing a cracked bowl and broken pitcher, indulged himself in the rather unusual ceremony of a good wash. On the whole, Dick preferred to be clean, but it was not always easy to gratify his desire. Lodging in the street as he had been accustomed to do, he had had no opportunity to perform his toilet in the customary manner. Even now he found himself unable to arrange his dishevelled locks, having neither comb nor brush. He determined to purchase a comb, at least, as soon as possible, and a brush too, if he could get one cheap. Meanwhile he combed his hair with his fingers as well as he could, though the result was not quite so satisfactory as it might have been.

A question now came up for consideration. For the first time in his life Dick possessed two suits of clothes. Should he put on the clothes Frank had given him, or resume his old rags?

Now, twenty-four hours before, at the time Dick was introduced to the reader's notice, no one could have been less fastidious as to his clothing than he. Indeed, he had rather a contempt for good clothes, or at least he thought so. But now, as he surveyed the ragged and dirty coat and the patched pants, Dick felt ashamed of them. He was unwilling to appear in the streets with them. Yet, if he went to work in his new suit, he was in danger of spoiling it, and he might not have it in his power to purchase a new one. Economy dictated a return to the old garments. Dick tried them on, and surveyed himself in the cracked glass; but the reflection did not please him.

"They don't look 'spectable," he decided; and, forthwith taking them off again, he put on the new suit of the day before.

"I must try to earn a little more," he thought, "to pay for my room, and to buy some new clo'es when these is wore out."

He opened the door of his chamber, and went downstairs and into the street, carrying his blacking-box with him.

It was Dick's custom to commence his business before breakfast; generally it must be owned, because he began the day penniless, and must earn his meal before he ate it. To-day it was different. He had four dollars left in his pocket-book; but this he had previously determined not to touch. In fact he had formed the ambitious design of starting an account at a savings' bank, in order to have something to fall back upon in case of sickness or any other emergency, or at any rate as a reserve fund to expend in clothing or other necessary articles when he required them. Hitherto he had been content to live on from day to day without a penny ahead; but the new vision of respectability which now floated before Dick's mind, owing to his recent acquaintance with Frank, was beginning to exercise a powerful effect upon him.

In Dick's profession as in others there are lucky days, when everything seems to flow prosperously. As if to encourage him in his new-born resolution, our hero obtained no less than six jobs in the course of an hour and a half. This gave him sixty cents, quite abundant to purchase his breakfast, and a comb besides. His exertions made him hungry, and, entering a small eating-house he ordered a cup of coffee and a beefsteak. To this he added a couple of rolls. This was quite a luxurious breakfast for Dick, and more expensive than he was accustomed to indulge himself with. To gratify the curiosity of my young readers, I will put down the items with their cost,—

Coffee, ...	5 cts.
Beefsteak, ...	15
A couple of rolls, ...	5
	—25 cts.

It will thus be seen that our hero had expended nearly one-half of his morning's earnings. Some days he had been compelled to breakfast on five cents, and then he was forced to content himself with a couple of apples, or cakes. But a good breakfast is a good preparation for a busy day, and Dick sallied forth from the restaurant lively and alert, ready to do a good stroke of business.

Dick's change of costume was liable to lead to one result of which he had not thought. His brother boot-blacks might think he had grown aristocratic, and was putting on airs,—that, in fact, he was getting above his business, and desirous to outshine his associates. Dick had not dreamed of this, because in fact, in spite of his new-born ambition, he entertained no such feelings. There was nothing of what boys call "big-feeling" about him. He was a thorough democrat, using the word not politically, but in its proper sense, and was disposed to fraternize with all whom he styled "good fellows," without regard to their position. It may seem a little unnecessary to some of my readers to make this explanation; but they must remember that pride and "big-feeling" are confined to no age or class, but may be found in boys as well as men, and in boot-blacks as well as those of a higher rank.

The morning being a busy time with the boot-blacks, Dick's changed appearance had not as yet attracted much attention. But when business slackened a little, our hero was destined to be reminded of it.

Among the down-town boot-blacks was one hailing from the Five Points,—a stout, red-haired, freckled-faced boy of fourteen, bearing the name of Micky Maguire. This boy, by his boldness and recklessness, as well as by his personal strength, which was considerable, had acquired an ascendency among his fellow professionals, and had a gang of subservient followers, whom he led on to acts of ruffianism, not unfrequently terminating in a month or two at Blackwell's Island. Micky himself had served two terms there; but the confinement appeared to have had very little effect in amending his conduct, except, perhaps, in making him a little more cautious about an encounter with the "copps," as the members of the city police are, for some unknown reason, styled among the Five-Point boys.

Now Micky was proud of his strength, and of the position of leader which it had secured him. Moreover he was democratic in his tastes, and had a jealous hatred of those who wore good clothes and kept their faces clean. He called it putting on airs, and resented the implied superiority. If he had been fifteen years older, and had a trifle more education, he would have interested himself in politics, and been prominent at ward meetings, and a terror to respectable voters on election day. As it was, he contented himself with being the leader of a gang of young ruffians, over whom he wielded a despotic power.

Now it is only justice to Dick to say that, so far as wearing good clothes was concerned, he had never hitherto offended the eyes of Micky Maguire. Indeed, they generally looked as if they patronized the same clothing establishment. On this particular morning it chanced that Micky had not been very fortunate in a business way, and, as a natural consequence, his temper, never very amiable, was somewhat ruffled by the fact. He had had a very frugal breakfast,—not because he felt abstemious, but owing to the low state of his finances. He was walking along with one of his particular friends, a boy nicknamed Limpy Jim, so called from a slight peculiarity in his walk, when all at once he espied our friend Dick in his new suit.

"My eyes!" he exclaimed, in astonishment; "Jim, just look at Ragged Dick. He's come into a fortun', and turned gentleman. See his new clothes."

"So he has," said Jim. "Where'd he get 'em, I wonder?"

"Hooked 'em, p'raps. Let's go and stir him up a little. We don't want no gentlemen on our beat. So he's puttin' on airs,—is he? I'll give him a lesson."

So saying the two boys walked up to our hero, who had not observed them, his back being turned, and Micky Maguire gave him a smart slap on the shoulder.

Dick turned round quickly.

CHAPTER XIV

A BATTLE AND A VICTORY

"WHAT'S that for?" demanded Dick, turning round to see who had struck him.

"You're gettin' mighty fine!" said Micky Maguire, surveying Dick's new clothes with a scornful air.

There was something in his words and tone, which Dick, who was disposed to stand up for his dignity, did not at all relish.

"Well, what's the odds if I am?" he retorted. "Does it hurt you any?"

"See him put on airs, Jim," said Micky, turning to his companion. "Where'd you get them clo'es?"

"Never mind where I got 'em. Maybe the Prince of Wales gave 'em to me."

"Hear him, now, Jim," said Micky. "Most likely he stole 'em."

"Stealin' ain't in *my* line."

It might have been unconscious the emphasis which Dick placed on the word "my." At any rate Micky chose to take offence.

"Do you mean to say *I* steal?" he demanded, doubling up his fist, and advancing towards Dick in a threatening manner.

"I don't say anything about it," answered Dick, by no means alarmed at this hostile demonstration. "I know you've been to the Island twice. P'r'aps 'twas to make a visit along of the Mayor and Aldermen. Maybe you was a innocent victim of oppression. I ain't a goin' to say."

Micky's freckled face grew red with wrath, for Dick had only stated the truth.

"Do you mean to insult me?" he demanded shaking the fist already doubled up in Dick's face. "Maybe you want a lickin'?"

"I ain't partic'larly anxious to get one," said Dick, coolly. "They don't agree with my constitution which is nat'rally delicate. I'd rather have a good dinner than a lickin' any time."

"You're afraid," sneered Micky. "Isn't he, Jim?"

"In course he is."

"P'r'aps I am," said Dick, composedly, "but it don't trouble me much."

"Do you want to fight?" demanded Micky, encouraged by Dick's quietness, fancying he was afraid to encounter him.

"No, I don't," said Dick. "I ain't fond of fightin'. It's a very poor amusement, and very bad for the complexion, 'specially for the eyes and nose, which is apt to turn red, white, and blue."

Micky misunderstood Dick, and judged from the tenor of his speech that he would be an easy victim. As he knew, Dick very seldom was concerned in any street fight,—not from cowardice, as he imagined, but because he had too much good sense to do so. Being quarrelsome, like all bullies, and supposing that he was more than a match for our hero, being about two inches taller, he could no longer resist an inclination to assault him, and tried to plant a blow in Dick's face which would have hurt him considerably if he had not drawn back just in time.

Now, though Dick was far from quarrelsome, he was ready to defend himself on all occasions, and it was too much to expect that he would stand quiet and allow himself to be beaten.

He dropped his blacking-box on the instant, and returned Micky's blow with such good effect that the young bully staggered back, and would have fallen, if he had not been propped up by his confederate, Limpy Jim.

"Go in, Micky!" shouted the latter, who was rather a coward on his own account, but liked to see others fight. "Polish him off, that's a good feller."

Micky was now boiling over with rage and fury, and required no urging. He was fully determined to make a terrible example of poor Dick. He threw himself upon him, and strove to bear him to the ground; but Dick, avoiding a close hug, in which he might possibly have got the worst of it, by an adroit movement, tripped up his antagonist, and stretched him on the sidewalk.

"Hit him, Jim!" exclaimed Micky, furiously.

Limpy Jim did not seem inclined to obey orders. There was a quiet strength and coolness about Dick, which alarmed him. He preferred that Micky should incur all the risks of battle, and accordingly set himself to raising his fallen comrade.

"Come, Micky," said Dick, quietly, "you'd better give it up. I wouldn't have touched you if you hadn't hit me first. I don't want to fight. It's low business."

"You're afraid of hurtin' your clo'es," said Micky, with a sneer.

"Maybe I am," said Dick. "I hope I haven't hurt yours."

Micky's answer to this was another attack, as violent and impetuous as the first. But his fury was in the way. He struck wildly, not measuring his blows, and Dick had no difficulty in turning aside, so that his antagonist's blow fell upon the empty air, and his momentum was such that he nearly fell forward headlong. Dick might readily have taken advantage of his unsteadiness, and knocked him down; but he was not vindictive, and chose to act on the defensive, except when he could not avoid it.

Recovering himself, Micky saw that Dick was a more formidable antagonist than he had supposed, and was meditating another assault, better planned, which by its impetuosity might bear our hero to the ground. But there was an unlooked-for interference.

"Look out for the 'copp,' " said Jim, in a low voice.

Micky turned round and saw a tall policeman heading towards him, and thought it might be prudent to suspend hostilities. He accordingly picked up his black-box, and, hitching up his pants, walked off, attended by Limpy Jim.

"What's that chap been doing?" asked the policeman of Dick.

"He was amoosin' himself by pitchin' into me," replied Dick.

"What for?"

"He didn't like it 'cause I patronized a different tailor from him."

"Well, it seems to me you *are* dressed pretty smart for a boot-black," said the policeman.

"I wish I wasn't a boot-black," said Dick.

"Never mind, my lad. It's an honest business," said the policeman, who was a sensible man and a worthy citizen. "It's an honest business. Stick to it till you get something better."

"I mean to," said Dick. "It ain't easy to get out of it, as the prisoner remarked, when he was asked how he liked his residence."

"I hope you don't speak from experience."

"No," said Dick; "I don't mean to get into prison if I can help it."

"Do you see that gentleman over there?" asked the officer, pointing to a well-dressed man who was walking on the other side of the street.

"Yes."

"Well, he was once a newsboy."

"And what is he now?"

"He keeps a bookstore, and is quite prosperous."

Dick looked at the gentleman with interest, wondering if he should look as respectable when he was a grown man.

It will be seen that Dick was getting ambitious. Hitherto he had thought very little of the future, but was content to get along as he could, dining as well as his means would allow, and spending the evenings in the pit of the Old Bowery, eating peanuts between the acts if he was prosperous, and if unlucky supping on dry bread or an apple, and sleeping in an old box or a wagon. Now, for the first time, he began to reflect that he could not black boots all his life. In seven years he would be a man, and, since his meeting with Frank, he felt that he would like to be a respectable man. He could see and appreciate the difference between Frank and such a boy as Micky Maguire, and it was not strange that he preferred the society of the former.

In the course of the next morning, in pursuance of his new resolutions for the future, he called at a savings bank, and held out four dollars in bills besides another dollar in change. There was a high railing, and a number of clerks busily writing at desks behind it. Dick, never having been in a bank before, did not know where to go. He went, by mistake, to the desk where money was paid out.

"Where's your book?" asked the clerk.

"I haven't got any."

"Have you any money deposited here?"

"No, sir, I want to leave some here."

"Then go to the next desk."

Dick followed directions, and presented himself before an elderly man with gray hair, who looked at him over the rims of his spectacles.

"I want you to keep that for me," said Dick, awkwardly emptying his money out on the desk.

"How much is there?"

"Five dollars."

"Have you got an account here?"

"No, sir."

"Of course you can write?"

The "of course" was said on account of Dick's neat dress.

"Have I got to do any writing?" asked our hero, a little embarrassed.

"We want you to sign your name in this book," and the old gentleman shoved round a large folio volume containing the names of depositors.

Dick surveyed the book with some awe.

"I ain't much on writin'," he said.

"Very well; write as well as you can."

The pen was put into Dick's hand, and, after dipping it in the inkstand, he succeeded after a hard effort, accompanied by many contortions of the face, in inscribing upon the book of the bank the name

DICK HUNTER.

"Dick!—that means Richard, I suppose," said the bank officer, who had some difficulty in making out the signature.

"No; Ragged Dick is what folks call me."

"You don't look very ragged."

"No, I've left my rags to home. They might get wore out if I used 'em too common."

"Well, my lad, I'll make out a book in the name of Dick Hunter, since you seem to prefer Dick to Richard. I hope you will save up your money and deposit more with us."

Our hero took his bank-book, and gazed on the entry "Five Dollars" with a new sense of importance. He had been accustomed to joke about Erie shares, but now, for the first time, he felt himself a capitalist; on a small scale, to be sure, but still it was no small thing for Dick to have five dollars which he could call his own. He firmly determined that he would lay by every cent he could spare from his earnings towards the fund he hoped to accumulate.

But Dick was too sensible not to know that there was something more than money needed to win a respectable position in the world. He felt that he was very ignorant. Of reading and writing he only knew the rudiments, and that, with a slight acquaintance with arithmetic, was all he did know of books. Dick knew he must study hard, and he dreaded it. He looked upon learning as attended with greater difficulties than it really possesses. But Dick had good pluck. He meant to learn, nevertheless, and resolved to buy a book with his first spare earnings.

When Dick went home at night he locked up his bank-book in one of the drawers of the bureau. It was wonderful how much more independent he felt whenever he reflected upon the contents of that drawer, and with what an important air of joint ownership he regarded the bank building in which his small savings were deposited.

CHAPTER XV

DICK SECURES A TUTOR

THE next morning Dick was unusually successful, having plenty to do, and receiving for one job twenty-five cents,—the gentleman refusing to take change. Then flashed upon Dick's mind the thought that he had not yet returned the change due to the gentleman whose boots he had blacked on the morning of his introduction to the reader.

"What'll he think of me?" said Dick to himself. "I hope he won't think I'm mean enough to keep the money."

Now Dick was scrupulously honest, and though the temptation to be otherwise had often been strong, he had always resisted it. He was not willing on any account to keep money which did not belong to him, and he immediately started for 125 Fulton Street (the address which had been given him) where he found Mr. Greyson's name on the door of an office on the first floor.

The door being open, Dick walked in.

"Is Mr. Greyson in?" he asked of a clerk who sat on a high stool before a desk.

"Not just now. He'll be in soon. Will you wait?"

"Yes," said Dick.

"Very well; take a seat then."

Dick sat down and took up the morning "Tribune," but presently came to a word of four syllables. which he pronounced to himself a "sticker," and laid it down. But he had not long to wait, for five minutes later Mr. Greyson entered.

"Did you wish to speak to me, my lad?" said he to Dick, whom in his new clothes he did not recognize.

"Yes, sir," said Dick. "I owe you some money."

"Indeed!" said Mr. Greyson, pleasantly; "that's an agreeable surprise. I didn't know but you had come for some. So you are a debtor of mine, and not a creditor?"

"I b'lieve that's right," said Dick, drawing fifteen cents from his pocket, and placing in Mr. Greyson's hand.

"Fifteen cents!" repeated he, in some surprise. "How do you happen to be indebted to me in that amount?"

"You gave me a quarter for a-shinin' your boots, yesterday mornin', and couldn't wait for the change. I meant to have brought it before, but I forgot all about it till this mornin'."

"It had quite slipped my mind also. But you don't look like the boy I employed. If I remember rightly he wasn't as well dressed as you."

"No," said Dick. "I was dressed for a party, then, but the clo'es was too well ventilated to be comfortable in cold weather."

"You're an honest boy," said Mr. Greyson. "Who taught you to be honest?"

"Nobody," said Dick. "But it's mean to cheat and steal. I've always knowed that."

"Then you've got ahead of some of our business men. Do you read the Bible?"

"No," said Dick. "I've heard it's a good book, but I don't know much about it."

"You ought to go to some Sunday School. Would you be willing?"

"Yes," said Dick, promptly. "I want to grow up 'spectable. But I don't know where to go."

"Then I'll tell you. The church I attend is at the corner of Fifth Avenue and Twenty-first Street."

"I've seen it," said Dick.

"I have a class in the Sunday School there. If you'll come next Sunday, I'll take you into my class, and do what I can to help you."

"Thank you," said Dick, "but p'r'aps you'll get tired of teaching me. I'm awful ignorant."

"No, my lad," said Mr. Greyson, kindly. "You evidently have some good principles to start with, as you have shown by your scorn of dishonesty. I shall hope good things of you in the future."

"Well, Dick," said our hero, apostrophizing himself, as he left the office; "you're gettin' up in the world. You've got money invested, and are goin' to attend church, by partic'lar invitation, on Fifth Avenue. I shouldn't wonder much if you should find cards, when you get home, from the Mayor, requestin' the honor of your company to dinner, along with other distinguished guests."

Dick felt in very good spirits. He seemed to be emerging from the world in which he had hitherto lived, into a new atmosphere of respectability, and the change seemed very pleasant to him.

At six o'clock Dick went into a restaurant on Chatham Street, and got a comfortable supper. He had been so successful during the day that, after paying for this, he still had ninety cents left. While he was despatching his supper, another boy came in, smaller and slighter than Dick, and sat down beside him. Dick recognized him as a boy who three months before had entered the ranks of the boot-blacks, but who, from a natural timidity, had not been able to earn much. He was ill-fitted for the coarse companionship of the street boys, and shrank from the rude jokes of his present associates. Dick had never troubled him; for our hero had a certain chivalrous feeling which would not allow him to bully or disturb a younger and weaker boy than himself.

"How are you, Fosdick?" said Dick, as the other seated himself.

"Pretty well," said Fosdick. "I suppose you're all right."

"Oh, yes, I'm right side up with care. I've been havin' a bully supper. What are you goin' to have?"

"Some bread and butter."

"Why don't you get a cup o' coffee?"

"Why," said Fosdick, reluctantly, "I haven't got money enough to-night."

"Never mind," said Dick; "I'm in luck to-day, I'll stand treat."

"That's kind in you," said Fosdick, gratefully.

"Oh, never mind that," said Dick.

Accordingly he ordered a cup of coffee, and a plate of beef-steak, and was gratified to see that his young companion partook of both with evident relish. When the repast was over, the boys went out into the street together, Dick pausing at the desk to settle for both suppers.

"Where are you going to sleep to-night, Fosdick?" asked Dick, as they stood on the sidewalk.

"I don't know," said Fosdick, a little sadly. "In some door-way, I expect. But I'm afraid the police will find me out, and make me move on."

"I'll tell you what," said Dick, "you must go home with me. I guess my bed will hold two."

"Have you got a room?" asked the other, in surprise.

"Yes," said Dick, rather proudly, and with a little excusable exultation. "I've got a room over in Mott Street; there I can receive my friends. That'll be better than sleepin' in a door-way,—won't it?"

"Yes, indeed it will," said Fosdick. "How lucky I was to come across you! It comes hard to me living as I do. When my father was alive I had every comfort."

"That's more'n I ever had," said Dick. "But I'm goin' to try to live comfortable now. Is your father dead?"

"Yes," said Fosdick, sadly. "He was a printer; but he was drowned one dark night from a Fulton ferry-boat, and, as I had no relations in the city, and no money, I was obliged to go to work as quick as I could. But I don't get on very well."

"Didn't you have no brothers nor sisters?" asked Dick.

"No," said Fosdick; "father and I used to live alone. He was always so much company to me that I feel very lonesome without him. There's a man out West somewhere that owes him two thousand dollars. He used to live in the city, and father lent him all his money to help him go into business; but he failed, or pretended to, and went off. If father hadn't lost that money he would have left me well off; but no money would have made up his loss to me."

"What's the man's name that went off with your father's money?"

"His name is Hiram Bates."

"P'r'aps you'll get the money again, sometime."

"There isn't much chance of it," said Fosdick. "I'd sell out my chances of that for five dollars."

"Maybe I'll buy you out sometime," said Dick. "Now, come round and see what sort of a room I've got. I used to go to the theatre evenings, when I had money; but now I'd rather go to bed early, and have a good sleep."

"I don't care much about theatres," said Fosdick. "Father didn't use to let me go very often. He said it wasn't good for boys."

"I like to go to the Old Bowery sometimes. They have tip-top plays there. Can you read and write well?" he asked, as a sudden thought came to him.

"Yes," said Fosdick. "Father always kept me at school when he was alive, and I stood pretty well in my classes. I was expecting to enter at the Free Academy * next year."

"Then I'll tell you what," said Dick; "I'll make a bargain with you. I can't read much more'n a pig; and my writin' looks like hens' tracks. I don't want to grow up knowin' no more'n a four-year-old boy. If you'll teach me readin' and writin' evenin's, you shall sleep in my room every night. That'll be better'n door-steps or old boxes, where I've slept many a time."

"Are you in earnest?" said Fosdick, his face lighting up hopefully.

"In course I am," said Dick. "It's fashionable for young gentlemen to have private tootors to introduct 'em into the flower-beds of literatoor and science, and why shouldn't I foller the fash-

---

* Now the college of the city of New York.

ion? You shall be my perfessor; only you must promise not to be very hard if my writin' looks like a rail-fence on a bender."

"I'll try not to be too severe," said Fosdick, laughing. "I shall be thankful for such a chance to get a place to sleep. Have you got anything to read out of?"

"No," said Dick. "My extensive and well-selected library was lost overboard in a storm, when I was sailin' from the Sandwich Islands to the desert of Sahara. But I'll buy a paper. That'll do me a long time."

Accordingly Dick stopped at a paper-stand, and bought a copy of a weekly paper, filled with the usual variety of reading matter,—stories, sketches, poems, etc.

They soon arrived at Dick's lodging-house. Our hero, procuring a lamp from the landlady, led the way into his apartment, which he entered with the proud air of a proprietor.

"Well, how do you like it, Fosdick?" he asked, complacently.

The time was when Fosdick would have thought it untidy and not particularly attractive. But he had served a severe apprenticeship in the streets, and it was pleasant to feel himself under shelter, and he was not disposed to be critical.

"It looks very comfortable, Dick," he said.

"The bed ain't very large," said Dick; "but I guess we can get along."

"Oh, yes," said Fosdick, cheerfully. "I don't take up much room."

"Then that's all right. There's two chairs, you see, one for you and one for me. In case the mayor comes in to spend the evenin' socially, he can sit on the bed."

The boys seated themselves, and five minutes later, under the guidance of his young tutor, Dick had commenced his studies.

CHAPTER XVI

THE FIRST LESSON

FORTUNATELY for Dick, his young tutor was well qualified to instruct him. Henry Fosdick, though only twelve years old, knew as much as many boys of fourteen. He had always been studious and ambitious to excel. His father, being a printer, employed in an office where books were printed, often brought home new books in sheets, which Henry was always glad to read. Mr. Fosdick had been, besides, a subscriber to the Mechanics' Apprentices' Library, which contains many thousands of well-selected and instructive books. Thus Henry had acquired an amount of general information, unusual in a boy of his age. Perhaps he had devoted too much time to study, for he was not naturally robust. All this, however, fitted him admirably for the office to which Dick had appointed him,—that of his private instructor.

The two boys drew up their chairs to the rickety table, and spread out the paper before them.

"The exercises generally commence with ringin' the bell," said Dick; "but as I ain't got none, we'll have to do without."

"And the teacher is generally provided with a rod," said Fosdick. "Isn't there a poker handy, that I can use in case my scholar doesn't behave well?"

" 'Tain't lawful to use fire-arms," said Dick.

"Now, Dick," said Fosdick, "before we begin, I must find out how much you already know. Can you read any?"

"Not enough to hurt me," said Dick. "All I know about readin' you could put in a nutshell, and there'd be room left for a small family."

"I suppose you know your letters?"

"Yes," said Dick, "I know 'em all, but not intimately. I guess I can call 'em all by name."

"Where did you learn them? Did you ever go to school?"

"Yes; I went two days."

"Why did you stop?"

"It didn't agree with my constitution."

"You don't look very delicate," said Fosdick.

"No," said Dick, "I ain't troubled much that way; but I found lickin's didn't agree with me."

"Did you get punished?"

"Awful," said Dick.

"What for?"

"For indulgin' in a little harmless amoosement," said Dick. "You see the boy that was sittin' next to me fell asleep, which I considered improper in school-time; so I thought I'd help the teacher a little by wakin' him up. So I took a pin and stuck into him; but I guess it went a little too far, for he screeched awful. The teacher found out what it was that made him holler, and whipped me with a ruler till I was black and blue. I thought 'twas about time to take a vacation; so that's the last time I went to school."

"You didn't learn to read in that time, of course?"

"No," said Dick; "but I was a newsboy a little while; so I learned a little, just so's to find out what the news was. Sometimes I didn't read straight and called the wrong news. One mornin' I asked another boy what the paper said, and he told me the King of Africa was dead. I thought it was all right till folks began to laugh."

"Well, Dick, if you'll only study well, you won't be liable to make such mistakes."

"I hope so," said Dick. "My friend Horace Greeley told me the other day that he'd get me to take his place now and then when he was off makin' speeches if my edication hadn't been neglected."

"I must find a good piece for you to begin on," said Fosdick, looking over the paper.

"Find an easy one," said Dick, "with words of one story."

Fosdick at length found a piece which he thought would answer. He discovered on trial that Dick had not exaggerated his deficiencies. Words of two syllables he seldom pronounced right, and was much surprised when he was told how "through" was sounded.

"Seems to me it's throwin' away letters to use all them," he said.

"How would you spell it?" asked his young teacher.

"T-h-r-u," said Dick.

"Well," said Fosdick, "there's a good many other words that are spelt with more letters than they need to have. But it's the fashion, and we must follow it."

But if Dick was ignorant, he was quick, and had an excellent capacity. Moreover he had perseverance, and was not easily discouraged. He had made up his mind he must know more, and was not disposed to complain of the difficulty of his task. Fosdick had occasion to laugh more than once at his ludicrous mistakes; but Dick laughed too, and on the whole both were quite interested in the lesson.

At the end of an hour and a half the boys stopped for the evening.

"You're learning fast, Dick," said Fosdick. "At this rate you will soon learn to read well."

"Will I?" asked Dick with an expression of satisfaction. "I'm glad of that. I don't want to be ignorant. I didn't use to care, but I do now. I want to grow up 'spectable."

"So do I, Dick. We will both help each other, and I am sure we can accomplish something. But I am beginning to feel sleepy."

"So am I," said Dick. "Them hard words make my head ache. I wonder who made 'em all?"

"That's more than I can tell. I suppose you've seen a dictionary."

"That's another of 'em. No, I can't say I have, though I may have seen him in the street without knowin' him."

"A dictionary is a book containing all the words in the language."

"How many are there?"

"I don't rightly know; but I think there are about fifty thousand."

"It's a pretty large family," said Dick. "Have I got to learn 'em all?"

"That will not be necessary. There are a large number which you would never find occasion to use."

"I'm glad of that," said Dick; "for I don't expect to live to be more'n a hundred, and by that time I wouldn't be more'n half through."

By this time the flickering lamp gave a decided hint to the boys that unless they made haste they would have to undress in the dark. They accordingly drew off their clothes, and Dick jumped into bed. But Fosdick, before doing so, knelt down by the side of the bed, and said a short prayer.

"What's that for?" asked Dick, curiously.

"I was saying my prayers," said Fosdick, as he rose from his knees. "Don't you ever do it?"

"No," said Dick. "Nobody ever taught me."

"Then I'll teach you. Shall I?"

"I don't know," said Dick, dubiously. "What's the good?"

Fosdick explained as well as he could, and perhaps his simple explanation was better adapted to Dick's comprehension than one from an older person would have been. Dick felt more free to ask questions, and the example of his new friend, for whom he was beginning to feel a warm attachment, had considerable effect upon him. When, therefore, Fosdick asked again if he should teach him a prayer, Dick consented, and his young bedfellow did so.

Dick was not naturally irreligious. If he had lived without a knowledge of God and of religious things, it was scarcely to be wondered at in a lad who, from an early age, had been thrown upon his own exertions for the means of living, with no one to care for him or give him good advice. But he was so far good that he could appreciate goodness in others, and this it was that had drawn him to Frank in the first place, and now to Henry Fosdick. He did not, therefore, attempt to ridicule his companion, as some boys better brought up might have done, but was willing to follow his example in what something told him was right. Our young hero had taken an important step toward securing that genuine respectability which he was ambitious to attain.

Weary with the day's work, and Dick perhaps still more fatigued by the unusual mental effort he had made, the boys soon sank into a deep and peaceful slumber, from which they did not awaken till six o'clock the next morning. Before going out Dick sought Mrs. Mooney, and spoke to her on the subject of taking Fosdick as a room-mate. He found that she had no objection, provided he would allow her twenty-five cents a week extra, in consideration of the extra trouble which his companion might be expected to make. To this Dick assented, and the arrangement was definitely concluded.

This over, the two boys went out and took stations near each other. Dick had more of a business turn than Henry, and less shrinking from publicity, so that his earnings were greater. But he had undertaken to pay the entire expenses of the room, and needed to earn more. Sometimes, when two customers presented themselves at the same time, he was able to direct one to his friend. So at the end of the week both boys found themselves with surplus earnings. Dick had the satisfaction of adding two dollars and a half to his deposits in the Savings Bank, and Fosdick commenced an account by depositing seventy-five cents.

On Sunday morning Dick bethought himself of his promise to Mr. Greyson to come to the church on Fifth Avenue. To tell the truth, Dick recalled it with some regret. He had never been inside a church since he could remember, and he was not much attracted by the invitation he had received. But Henry, finding him wavering, urged him to go, and offered to go with him. Dick gladly accepted the offer, feeling that he required someone to lend him countenance under such unusual circumstances.

Dick dressed himself with scrupulous care, giving his shoes a "shine" so brilliant that it did him great credit in a professional point of view, and endeavored to clean his hands thoroughly; but, in spite of all he could do, they were not so white as if his business had been of a different character.

Having fully completed his preparations, he descended into the street, and, with Henry by his side, crossed over to Broadway.

The boys pursued their way up Broadway, which on Sunday presents a striking contrast in its quietness to the noise and confusion of ordinary week-days, as far as Union Square, then turned down Fourteenth Street, which brought them to Fifth Avenue.

"Suppose we dine at Delmonico's," said Fosdick, looking towards that famous restaurant.

"I'd have to sell some of my Erie shares," said Dick.

A short walk now brought them to the church of which mention has already been made. They stood outside, a little abashed, watching the fashionably attired people who were entering, and were feeling a little undecided as to whether they had better enter also, when Dick felt a light touch upon his shoulder.

Turning round, he met the smiling glance of Mr. Greyson.

"So, my young friend, you have kept your promise," he said. "And whom have you brought with you?"

"A friend of mine," said Dick. "His name is Henry Fosdick."

"I am glad you have brought him. Now follow me, and I will give you seats."

CHAPTER XVII

DICK'S FIRST APPEARANCE IN SOCIETY

IT WAS the hour for morning service. The boys followed Mr. Greyson into the handsome church, and were assigned seats in his own pew.

There were two persons already seated in it,—a good-looking lady of middle age, and a pretty little girl of nine. They were Mrs. Greyson and her only daughter Ida. They looked pleasantly at the boys as they entered, smiling a welcome to them.

The morning service commenced. It must be acknowledged that Dick felt rather awkward. It was an unusual place for him, and it need not be wondered at that he felt like a cat in a strange garret. He would not have known when to rise if he had not taken notice of what the rest of the audience did, and followed their example. He was sitting next to Ida, and as it was the first time he had ever been near so well-dressed a young lady, he naturally felt bashful. When the hymns were announced, Ida found the place, and offered a hymn-book to our hero. Dick took it awkwardly, but his studies had not yet been pursued far enough for him to read the words readily. However, he resolved to keep up appearances, and kept his eyes fixed steadily on the hymn-book.

At length the service was over. The people began to file slowly out of church, and among them, of course, Mr. Greyson's family and the two boys. It seemed very strange to Dick to find himself in such different companionship from what he had been accustomed, and he could not help thinking, "Wonder what Johnny Nolan 'ould say if he could see me now!"

But Johnny's business engagements did not often summon him to Fifth Avenue, and Dick was not likely to be seen by any of his friends in the lower part of the city.

"We have our Sunday school in the afternoon," said Mr. Greyson. "I suppose you live at some distance from here?"

"In Mott Street, sir," answered Dick.

"That is too far to go and return. Suppose you and your friend come and dine with us, and then we can come here together in the afternoon."

Dick was as much astonished at this invitation as if he had really been invited by the Mayor to dine with him and the Board of Aldermen. Mr. Greyson was evidently a rich man, and yet he had actually invited two boot-blacks to dine with him.

"I guess we'd better go home, sir," said Dick, hesitating.

"I don't think you can have any very pressing engagements to interfere with your accepting my invitation," said Mr. Greyson, good-humoredly, for he understood the reason of Dick's hesitation. "So I take it for granted that you both accept."

Before Dick fairly knew what he intended to do, he was walking down Fifth Avenue with his new friends.

Now, our young hero was not naturally bashful; but he certainly felt so now, especially as Miss Ida Greyson chose to walk by his side, leaving Henry Fosdick to walk with her father and mother.

"What is your name?" asked Ida, pleasantly.

Our hero was about to answer "Ragged Dick," when it occurred to him that in the present company he had better forget his old nickname.

"Dick Hunter," he answered.

"Dick!" repeated Ida. "That means Richard, doesn't it?"

"Everybody calls me Dick."

"I have a cousin Dick," said the young lady, sociably. "His name is Dick Wilson. I suppose you don't know him?"

"No," said Dick.

"I like the name of Dick," said the young lady, with charming frankness.

Without being able to tell why, Dick felt rather glad she did. He plucked up courage to ask her name.

"My name is Ida," answered the young lady. "Do you like it?"

"Yes," said Dick. "It's a bully name."

Dick turned red as soon as he had said it, for he felt that he had not used the right expression.

The little girl broke into a silvery laugh.

"What a funny boy you are!" she said.

"I didn't mean it," said Dick, stammering. "I meant it's a tip-top name."

Here Ida laughed again, and Dick wished himself back in Mott Street.

"How old are you?" inquired Ida, continuing her examination.

"I'm fourteen,—goin' on fifteen," said Dick.

"You're a big boy of your age," said Ida. "My cousin Dick is a year older than you, but he isn't as large."

Dick looked pleased. Boys generally like to be told that they are large of their age.

"How old be you?" asked Dick, beginning to feel more at his ease.

"I'm nine years old," said Ida. "I go to Miss Jarvis's school. I've just begun to learn French. Do you know French?"

"Not enough to hurt me," said Dick.

Ida laughed again, and told him that he was a droll boy.

"Do you like it?" asked Dick.

"I like it pretty well, except the verbs. I can't remember them well. Do you go to school?"

"I'm studying with a private tutor," said Dick.

"Are you? So is my cousin Dick. He's going to college this year. Are you going to college?"

"Not this year."

"Because, if you did, you know you'd be in the same class with my cousin. It would be funny to have two Dicks in one class."

They turned down Twenty-fourth Street, passing the Fifth Avenue Hotel on the left, and stopped before an elegant house with a brown stone front. The bell was rung, and the door being opened, the boys, somewhat abashed, followed Mr. Greyson into a handsome hall. They were told where to hang their hats, and a moment afterwards were ushered into a comfortable dining-room, where a table was spread for dinner.

Dick took his seat on the edge of a sofa, and was tempted to rub his eyes to make sure that he was really awake. He could hardly believe that he was a guest in so fine a mansion.

Ida helped to put the boys at their ease.

"Do you like pictures?" she asked.

"Very much," answered Henry.

The little girl brought a book of handsome engravings, and, seating herself beside Dick, to whom she seemed to have taken a decided fancy, commenced showing them to him.

"There are the Pyramids of Egypt," she said, pointing to one engraving.

"What are they for?" asked Dick, puzzled. "I don't see any winders."

"No," said Ida, "I don't believe anybody lives there. Do they, papa?"

"No, my dear. They were used for the burial of the dead. The largest of them is said to be the loftiest building in the world with one exception. The spire of the Cathedral of Strasburg is twenty-four feet higher, if I remember rightly."

"Is Egypt near here?" asked Dick.

"Oh, no, it's ever so many miles off; about four or five hundred. Didn't you know?"

"No," said Dick. "I never heard."

"You don't appear to be very accurate in your information, Ida," said her mother. "Four or five thousand miles would be considerably nearer the truth."

After a little more conversation they sat down to dinner. Dick seated himself in an embarrassed way. He was very much afraid of doing or saying something which would be considered an impropriety, and had the uncomfortable feeling that everybody was looking at him, and watching his behavior.

"Where do you live, Dick?" asked Ida, familiarly.

"In Mott Street."

"Where is that?"

"More than a mile off."

"Is it a nice street?"

"Not very," said Dick. "Only poor folks live there."

"Are you poor?"

"Little girls should be seen and not heard," said her mother, gently.

"If you are," said Ida, "I'll give you the five-dollar gold-piece aunt gave me for a birthday present."

"Dick cannot be called poor, my child," said Mrs. Greyson, "since he earns his living by his own exertions."

"Do you earn your living?" asked Ida, who was a very inquisitive young lady, and not easily silenced. "What do you do?"

Dick blushed violently. At such a table, and in presence of the servant who was standing at that moment behind his chair, he did not like to say that he was a shoe-black, although he well knew that there was nothing dishonorable in the occupation.

Mr. Greyson perceived his feelings, and to spare them, said, "You are too inquisitive, Ida. Sometime Dick may tell you, but you know we don't talk of business on Sundays."

Dick in his embarrassment had swallowed a large spoonful of hot soup, which made him turn red in the face. For the second time, in spite of the prospect of the best dinner he had ever eaten, he wished himself back in Mott Street. Henry Fosdick was more easy and unembarrassed than Dick, not having led such a vagabond and neglected life. But it was to Dick that Ida chiefly directed her conversation, having apparently taken a fancy to his frank and handsome face. I believe I have already said that Dick was a very good-looking boy, especially now since he kept his face clean. He had a frank, honest expression, which generally won its way to the favor of those with whom he came in contact.

Dick got along pretty well at the table by dint of noticing how the rest acted, but there was one thing he could not manage, eating with his fork, which, by the way, he thought a very singular arrangement.

At length they arose from the table, somewhat to Dick's relief.

Again Ida devoted herself to the boys, and exhibited a profusely illustrated Bible for their entertainment. Dick was interested in looking at the pictures, though he knew very little of their subjects. Henry Fosdick was much better informed, as might have been expected.

When the boys were about to leave the house with Mr. Greyson for the Sunday school, Ida placed her hand in Dick's, and said persuasively. "You'll come again, Dick, won't you?"

"Thank you," said Dick, "I'd like to," and he could not help thinking Ida the nicest girl he had ever seen.

"Yes," said Mrs. Greyson, hospitably, "we shall be glad to see you both here again."

"Thank you very much," said Henry Fosdick, gratefully. "We shall like very much to come."

I will not dwell upon the hour spent in Sunday school, nor upon the remarks of Mr. Greyson to his class. He found Dick's ignorance of religious subjects so great that he was obliged to begin at the beginning with him. Dick was interested in hearing the children sing, and readily promised to come again the next Sunday.

When the service was over Dick and Henry walked homewards. Dick could not help letting his thoughts rest on the sweet little girl who had given him so cordial a welcome, and hoping that he might meet her again.

"Mr. Greyson is a nice man,—isn't he, Dick?" asked Henry, as they were turning into Mott Street, and were already in sight of their lodging-house.

"Ain't he, though?" said Dick. "He treated us just as if we were young gentlemen."

"Ida seemed to take a great fancy to you."

"She's a tip-top girl," said Dick, "but she asked so many questions that I didn't know what to say."

He had scarcely finished speaking, when a stone whizzed by his head, and, turning quickly, he saw Micky Maguire running round the corner of the street which they had just passed.

CHAPTER XVIII

MICKY MAGUIRE'S SECOND DEFEAT

DICK was no coward. Nor was he in the habit of submitting passively to an insult. When, therefore, he recognized Micky Maguire as his assailant, he instantly turned and gave chase. Micky anticipated pursuit, and ran at his utmost speed. It is doubtful if Dick would have overtaken him, but Micky had the ill luck to trip just as he had entered a narrow alley, and, falling with some violence, received a sharp blow from the hard stones, which made him scream with pain.

"Ow!" he whined. "Don't you hit a feller when he's down."

"What made you fire that stone at me?" demanded our hero, looking down at the fallen bully.

"Just for fun," said Micky.

"It would have been a very agreeable s'prise if it had hit me," said Dick. "S'posin' I fire a rock at you jest for fun."

"Don't!" exclaimed Micky, in alarm.

"It seems you don't like agreeable s'prises," said Dick, "any more'n the man did what got hooked by a cow one mornin', before breakfast. It didn't improve his appetite much."

"I've most broke my arm," said Micky, ruefully, rubbing the affected limb.

"If it's broke you can't fire no more stones, which is a very cheerin' reflection," said Dick. "Ef you haven't money enough to buy a wooden one I'll lend you a quarter. There's one good thing about wooden ones, they ain't liable to get cold in winter, which is another cheerin' reflection."

"I don't want none of yer cheerin' reflections," said Micky, sullenly. "Yer company ain't wanted here."

"Thank you for your polite invitation to leave," said Dick, bowing ceremoniously. "I'm willin' to go, but ef you throw any more stones at me, Micky Maguire, I'll hurt you worse than the stones did."

The only answer made to this warning was a scowl from his fallen opponent. It was quite evident that Dick had the best of it, and he thought it prudent to say nothing.

"As I've got a friend waitin' outside, I shall have to tear

myself away," said Dick. "You'd better not throw any more stones, Micky Maguire, for it don't seem to agree with your constitution."

Micky muttered something which Dick did not stay to hear. He backed out of the alley, keeping a watchful eye on his fallen foe, and rejoined Henry Fosdick, who was awaiting his return.

"Who was it, Dick?" he asked.

"A partic'lar friend of mine, Micky Maguire," said Dick. "He playfully fired a rock at my head as a mark of his 'fection. He loves me like a brother, Micky does."

"Rather a dangerous kind of a friend, I should think," said Fosdick. "He might have killed you."

"I've warned him not to be so 'fectionate another time," said Dick.

"I know him," said Henry Fosdick. "He's at the head of a gang of boys living at the Five-Points. He threatened to whip me once because a gentleman employed me to black his boots instead of him."

"He's been at the Island two or three times for stealing," said Dick. "I guess he won't touch me again. He'd rather get hold of small boys. If he ever does anything to you, Fosdick, just let me know, and I'll give him a thrashing."

Dick was right. Micky Maguire was a bully, and like most bullies did not fancy tackling boys whose strength was equal or superior to his own. Although he hated Dick more than ever, because he thought our hero was putting on airs, he had too lively a remembrance of his strength and courage to venture upon another open attack. He contented himself, therefore, whenever he met Dick, with scowling at him. Dick took this very philosophically, remarking that, "if it was soothin' to Micky's feelings, he might go ahead, as it didn't hurt him much."

It will not be necessary to chronicle the events of the next few weeks. A new life had commenced for Dick. He no longer haunted the gallery of the Old Bowery; and even Tony Pastor's hospitable doors had lost their old attractions. He spent two hours every evening in study. His progress was astonishingly rapid. He was gifted with a natural quickness; and he was stimulated by the desire to acquire a fair education as a means of "growin' up 'spectable," as he termed it. Much was due also to the patience and perseverance of Henry Fosdick, who made a capital teacher.

"You're improving wonderfully, Dick," said his friend, one evening, when Dick had read an entire paragraph without a mistake.

"Am I?" said Dick, with satisfaction.

"Yes. If you'll buy a writing-book to-morrow, we can begin writing to-morrow evening."

"What else do you know, Henry?" asked Dick.

"Arithmetic, and geography, and grammar."

"What a lot you know!" said Dick, admiringly.

"I don't *know* any of them," said Fosdick. "I've only studied them. I wish I knew a great deal more."

"I'll be satisfied when I know as much as you," said Dick.

"It seems a great deal to you now, Dick, but in a few months you'll think differently. The more you know, the more you'll want to know."

"Then there ain't any end to learnin'?" said Dick.

"No."

"Well," said Dick, "I guess I'll be as much as sixty before I know everything."

"Yes; as old as that, probably," said Fosdick, laughing.

"Anyway, you know too much to be blackin' boots. Leave that to ignorant chaps like me."

"You won't be ignorant long, Dick."

"You'd ought to get into some office or countin'-room."

"I wish I could," said Fosdick, earnestly. "I don't succeed very well at blacking boots. You make a great deal more than I do."

"That's cause I ain't troubled with bashfulness," said Dick. "Bashfulness ain't as natural to me as it is to you. I'm always on hand, as the cat said to the milk. You'd better give up shines, Fosdick, and give your 'tention to mercantile pursuits."

"I've thought of trying to get a place," said Fosdick; "but no one would take me with these clothes;" and he directed his glance to his well-worn suit, which he kept as neat as he could, but which, in spite of all his care, began to show decided marks of use. There was also here and there a stain of blacking upon it, which, though an advertisement of his profession, scarcely added to its good appearance.

"I almost wanted to stay at home from Sunday school last Sunday," he continued, "because I thought everybody would notice how dirty and worn my clothes had got to be."

"If my clothes wasn't two sizes too big for you," said Dick, generously, "I'd change. You'd look as if you'd got into your great-uncle's suit by mistake."

"You're very kind, Dick, to think of changing," said Fosdick, "for your suit is much better than mine; but I don't think that mine would suit you very well. The pants would show a little more of your ankles than is the fashion, and you couldn't eat a very hearty dinner without bursting the buttons off the vest."

"That wouldn't be very convenient," said Dick. "I ain't fond of lacin' to show my elegant figger. But I say," he added with a sudden thought, "how much money have we got in the savings' bank?"

Fosdick took a key from his pocket, and went to the drawer in which the bank-books were kept, and, opening it, brought them out for inspection.

It was found that Dick had the sum of eighteen dollars and ninety cents placed to his credit, while Fosdick had six dollars and forty-five cents. To explain the large difference, it must be remembered that Dick had deposited five dollars before Henry deposited anything, being the amount he had received as a gift from Mr. Whitney.

"How much does that make, the lot of it?" asked Dick. "I ain't much on figgers yet, you know."

"It makes twenty-five dollars and thirty-five cents, Dick," said his companion, who did not understand the thought which suggested the question.

"Take it, and buy some clothes, Henry," said Dick, shortly.

"What, your money too?"

"In course."

"No, Dick, you are too generous. I couldn't think of it. Almost three-quarters of the money is yours. You must spend it on yourself."

"I don't need it," said Dick.

"You may not need it now, but you will some time."

"I shall have some more then."

"That may be; but it wouldn't be fair for me to use your money, Dick. I thank you all the same for your kindness."

"Well, I'll lend it to you, then," persisted Dick, "and you can pay me when you get to be a rich merchant."

"But it isn't likely I ever shall be one."

"How d'you know? I went to a fortun' teller once, and she

told me I was born under a lucky star with a hard name, and I should have a rich man for my particular friend, who would make my fortun'. I guess you are going to be the rich man."

Fosdick laughed, and steadily refused for some time to avail himself of Dick's generous proposal; but at length, perceiving that our hero seemed much disappointed, and would be really glad if his offer were accepted, he agreed to use as much as might be needful.

This at once brought back Dick's good-humor, and he entered with great enthusiasm into his friend's plans.

The next day they withdrew the money from the bank, and, when business got a little slack, in the afternoon set out in search of a clothing store. Dick knew enough of the city to be able to find a place where a good bargain could be obtained. He was determined that Fosdick should have a good serviceable suit, even if it took all the money they had. The result of their search was that for twenty-three dollars Fosdick obtained a very neat outfit, including a couple of shirts, a hat, and a pair of shoes, besides a dark mixed suit, which appeared stout and of good quality.

"Shall I sent the bundle home?" asked the salesman, impressed by the off-hand manner in which Dick drew out the money in payment for the clothes.

"Thank you," said Dick, "you're very kind, but I'll take it home myself, and you can allow me something for my trouble."

"All right," said the clerk, laughing; "I'll allow it on your next purchase."

Proceeding to their apartment in Mott Street, Fosdick at once tried on his new suit, and it was found to be an excellent fit. Dick surveyed his new friend with much satisfaction.

"You look like a young gentleman of fortun'," he said, "and do credit to your governor."

"I suppose that means you, Dick," said Fosdick, laughing.

"In course it does."

"You should say *of* course," said Fosdick, who, in virtue of his position as Dick's tutor, ventured to correct his language from time to time.

"How dare you correct your gov'nor?" said Dick, with comic indignation. " 'I'll cut you off with a shillin', you young dog,' as the Markis says to his nephew in the play at the Old Bowery."

CHAPTER XIX

FOSDICK CHANGES HIS BUSINESS

FOSDICK did not venture to wear his new clothes while engaged in his business. This he felt would have been wasteful extravagance. About ten o'clock in the morning, when business slackened, he went home, and dressing himself went to a hotel where he could see copies of the "Morning Herald" and "Sun," and, noting down the places where a boy was wanted, went on a round of applications. But he found it no easy thing to obtain a place. Swarms of boys seemed to be out of employment, and it was not unusual to find from fifty to a hundred applicants for a single place.

There was another difficulty. It was generally desired that the boy wanted should reside with his parents. When Fosdick, on being questioned, revealed the fact of his having no parents, and being a boy of the street, this was generally sufficient of itself to insure a refusal. Merchants were afraid to trust one who had led such a vagabond life. Dick, who was always ready for an emergency, suggested borrowing a white wig, and passing himself off for Fosdick's father or grandfather. But Henry thought this might be rather a difficult character for our hero to sustain. After fifty applications and as many failures, Fosdick began to get discouraged. There seemed to be no way out of his present business, for which he felt unfitted.

"I don't know but I shall have to black boots all my life," he said, one day, despondently, to Dick.

"Keep a stiff upper lip," said Dick. "By the time you get to be a gray-headed veteran, you may get a chance to run errands for some big firm on the Bowery, which is a very cheerin' reflection."

So Dick by his drollery and perpetual good spirits kept up Fosdick's courage.

"As for me," said Dick, "I expect by that time to lay up a colossal fortun' out of shines, and live in princely style on the Avenoo."

But one morning, Fosdick, straying into French's Hotel, discovered the following advertisement in the columns of "The Herald,"—

"WANTED—A smart, capable boy to run errands, and make himself generally useful in a hat and cap store. Salary three dollars a week at first. Inquire at No. — Broadway, after ten o'clock, A.M."

He determined to make application, and, as the City Hall clock just then struck the hour indicated, lost no time in proceeding to the store, which was only a few blocks distant from the Astor House. It was easy to find the store, as from a dozen to twenty boys were already assembled in front of it. They surveyed each other askance, feeling that they were rivals, and mentally calculating each other's chances.

"There isn't much chance for me," said Fosdick to Dick, who had accompanied him. "Look at all these boys. Most of them have good homes, I suppose, and good recommendations, while I have nobody to refer to."

"Go ahead," said Dick. "Your chance is as good as anybody's."

While this was passing between Dick and his companion, one of the boys, a rather supercilious-looking young gentleman, genteelly dressed, and evidently having a very high opinion of his dress and himself turned suddenly to Dick, and remarked,—

"I've seen you before."

"Oh, have you?" said Dick, whirling round; "then p'r'aps you'd like to see me behind."

At this unexpected answer all the boys burst into a laugh with the exception of the questioner, who, evidently, considered that Dick had been disrespectful.

"I've seen you somewhere," he said, in a surly tone, correcting himself.

"Most likely you have," said Dick. "That's where I generally keep myself."

There was another laugh at the expense of Roswell Crawford, for that was the name of the young aristocrat. But he had his revenge ready. No boy relishes being an object of ridicule, and it was with a feeling of satisfaction that he retorted,—

"I know you for all your impudence. You're nothing but a boot-black."

This information took the boys who were standing around by surprise, for Dick was well-dressed, and had none of the implements of his profession with him.

"S'pose I be," said Dick. "Have you got any objection?"

"Not at all," said Roswell, curling his lip; "only you'd better stick to blacking boots, and not try to get into a store."

"Thank you for your kind advice," said Dick. "Is it gratooitous, or do you expect to be paid for it?"

"You're an impudent fellow."

"That's a very cheerin' reflection," said Dick, good-naturedly.

"Do you expect to get this place when there's gentlemen's sons applying for it? A boot-black in a store! That would be a good joke."

Boys as well as men are selfish, and, looking upon Dick as a possible rival, the boys who listened seemed disposed to take the same view of the situation.

"That's what I say," said one of them, taking sides with Roswell.

"Don't trouble yourselves," said Dick. "I ain't agoin' to cut you out. I can't afford to give up a independent and loocrative purfession for a salary of three dollars a week."

"Hear him talk!" said Roswell Crawford, with an unpleasant sneer. "If you are not trying to get the place, what are you here for?"

"I came with a friend of mine," said Dick, indicating Fosdick, "who's goin' in for the situation."

"Is he a boot-black, too?" demanded Roswell, superciliously.

"He!" retorted Dick, loftily. "Didn't you know his father was a member of Congress, and intimately acquainted with all the biggest men in the State?"

The boys surveyed Fosdick as if they did not quite know whether to credit this statement, which, for the credit of Dick's veracity, it will be observed he did not assert, but only propounded in the form of a question. There was no time for comment, however, as just then the proprietor of the store came to the door, and, casting his eyes over the waiting group, singled out Roswell Crawford, and asked him to enter.

"Well, my lad, how old are you?"

"Fourteen years old," said Roswell, consequentially.

"Are your parents living?"

"Only my mother. My father is dead. He was a gentleman," he added, complacently.

"Oh, was he?" said the shop-keeper. "Do you live in the city?"

"Yes, sir. In Clinton Place."

"Have you ever been in a situation before?"

"Yes, sir," said Roswell, a little reluctantly.

"Where was it?"

"In an office on Dey Street."

"How long were you there?"

"A week."

"It seems to me that was a short time. Why did you not stay longer?"

"Because," said Roswell, loftily, "the man wanted me to get to the office at eight o'clock, and make the fire. I'm a gentleman's son, and am not used to such dirty work."

"Indeed!" said the shop-keeper. "Well, young gentleman, you may step aside a few minutes. I will speak with some of the other boys before making my selection."

Several other boys were called in and questioned. Roswell stood by and listened with an air of complacency. He could not help thinking his chances the best. "The man can see I'm a gentleman, and will do credit to his store," he thought.

At length it came to Fosdick's turn. He entered with no very sanguine anticipations of success. Unlike Roswell, he set a very low estimate upon his qualifications when compared with those of other applicants. But his modest bearing, and quiet, gentlemanly manner, entirely free from pretension, prepossessed the shop-keeper, who was a sensible man, in his favor.

"Do you reside in the city?" he asked.

"Yes, sir," said Henry.

"What is your age?"

"Twelve."

"Have you ever been in any situation?"

"No, sir."

"I should like to see a specimen of your handwriting. Here, take the pen and write your name."

Henry Fosdick had a very handsome handwriting for a boy of his age, while Roswell, who had submitted to the same test, could do little more than scrawl.

"Do you reside with your parents?"

"No, sir, they are dead."

"Where do you live, then?"

"In Mott Street."

Roswell curled his lip when this name was pronounced, for Mott Street, as my New York readers know, is in the immediate neighborhood of the Five-Points, and very far from a fashionable locality.

"Have you any testimonials to present?" asked Mr. Henderson, for that was his name.

Fosdick hesitated. This was the question which he had foreseen would give him trouble.

But at this moment it happened most opportunely that Mr. Greyson entered the shop with the intention of buying a hat.

"Yes," said Fosdick, promptly; "I will refer to this gentleman."

"How do you do, Fosdick?" asked Mr. Greyson, noticing him for the first time. "How do you happen to be here?"

"I am applying for a place, sir," said Fosdick. "May I refer the gentleman to you?"

"Certainly, I shall be glad to speak a good word for you. Mr. Henderson, this is a member of my Sunday-school class, of whose good qualities and good abilities I can speak confidently."

"That will be sufficient," said the shop-keeper, who knew Mr. Greyson's high character and position. "He could have no better recommendation. You may come to the store to-morrow morning at half past seven o'clock. The pay will be three dollars a week for the first six months. If I am satisfied with you, I shall then raise it to five dollars."

The other boys looked disappointed, but none more so than Roswell Crawford. He would have cared less if any one else had obtained the situation; but for a boy who lived in Mott Street to be preferred to him, a gentleman's son, he considered indeed humiliating. In a spirit of petty spite, he was tempted to say, "He's a boot-black. Ask him if he isn't."

"He's an honest and intelligent lad," said Mr. Greyson. "As for you, young man, I only hope you have one-half his good qualities."

Roswell Crawford left the store in disgust, and the other unsuccessful applicants with him.

"What luck, Fosdick?" asked Dick, eagerly, as his friend came out of the store.

"I've got the place," said Fosdick, in accents of satisfaction; "but it was only because Mr. Greyson spoke up for me."

"He's a trump," said Dick, enthusiastically.

The gentleman, so denominated, came out before the boys went away, and spoke with them kindly.

Both Dick and Henry were highly pleased at the success of the application. The pay would indeed be small, but, expended economically, Fosdick thought he could get along on it, receiving his room rent, as before, in return for his services as Dick's private tutor. Dick determined, as soon as his education would permit, to follow his companion's example.

"I don't know as you'll be willin' to room with a boot-black," he said, to Henry, "now you're goin' into business."

"I couldn't room with a better friend, Dick," said Fosdick, affectionately, throwing his arm round our hero. "When we part, it'll be because you wish it."

So Fosdick entered upon a new career.

CHAPTER XX

NINE MONTHS LATER

THE next morning Fosdick rose early, put on his new suit, and, after getting breakfast, set out for the Broadway store in which he had obtained a position. He left his little blacking-box in the room.

"It'll do to brush my own shoes," he said. "Who knows but I may have to come back to it again?"

"No danger," said Dick; "I'll take care of the feet, and you'll have to look after the heads, now you're in a hat-store."

"I wish you had a place too," said Fosdick.

"I don't know enough yet," said Dick. "Wait till I've gradooated."

"And can put A.B. after your name."

"What's that?"

"It stands for Bachelor of Arts. It's a degree that students get when they graduate from college."

"Oh," said Dick, "I didn't know but it meant A Boot-black. I can put that after my name now. Wouldn't Dick Hunter, A.B., sound tip-top?"

"I must be going," said Fosdick. "It won't do for me to be late the very first morning."

"That's the difference between you and me," said Dick. "I'm my own boss, and there ain't no one to find fault with me if I'm late. But I might as well be goin' too. There's a gent as comes down to his store pretty early that generally wants a shine."

The two boys parted at the Park. Fosdick crossed it, and proceeded to the hat-store, while Dick, hitching up his pants, began to look about him for a customer. It was seldom that Dick had to wait long. He was always on the alert, and if there was any business to do he was always sure to get his share of it. He had now a stronger inducement than ever to attend strictly to business; his little stock of money in the savings bank having been nearly exhausted by his liberality to his room-mate. He determined to be as economical as possible, and moreover to study as hard as he could, that he might be able to follow Fosdick's example, and obtain a place in a store or counting-room. As there were no striking incidents occurring in our hero's history within the next nine months, I propose to pass over that period, and recount the progress he made in that time.

Fosdick was still at the hat-store, having succeeded in giving perfect satisfaction to Mr. Henderson. His wages had just been raised to five dollars a week. He and Dick still kept house together at Mrs. Mooney's lodging-house, and lived very frugally, so that both were able to save up money. Dick had been unusually successful in business. He had several regular patrons, who had been drawn to him by his ready wit, and quick humor, and from two of them he had received presents of clothing, which had saved him any expense on that score. His income had averaged quite seven dollars a week in addition to this. Of this amount he was now obliged to pay one dollar weekly for the room which he and Fosdick occupied, but he was still able to save one half the remainder. At the end of nine months therefore, or thirty-nine weeks, it will be seen that he had accumulated no less a sum than one hundred and seventeen dollars. Dick may be excused for feeling like a capitalist when he looked at the long row of deposits in his little bank-book. There were other boys in the same business who had earned as much money, but they had had little care for the future, and spent as they went along, so that few could boast a bank-account, however small.

"You'll be a rich man some time, Dick," said Henry Fosdick, one evening."

"And live on Fifth Avenoo," said Dick.

"Perhaps so. Stranger things have happened."

"Well," said Dick, "if such a misfortin' should come upon me

I should bear it like a man. When you see a Fifth Avenoo manshun for sale for a hundred and seventeen dollars, just let me know and I'll buy it as an investment."

"Two hundred and fifty years ago you might have bought one for that price, probably. Real estate wasn't very high among the Indians."

"Just my luck," said Dick; "I was born too late. I'd orter have been an Indian, and lived in splendor on my present capital."

"I'm afraid you'd have found your present business rather unprofitable at that time."

But Dick had gained something more valuable than money. He had studied regularly every evening, and his improvement had been marvellous. He could now read well, write a fair hand, and had studied arithmetic as far as Interest. Besides this he had obtained some knowledge of grammar and geography. If some of my boy readers, who have been studying for years, and got no farther than this, should think it incredible that Dick, in less than a year, and studying evenings only, should have accomplished it, they must remember that our hero was very much in earnest in his desire to improve. He knew that, in order to grow up respectable, he must be well advanced, and he was willing to work. But then the reader must not forget that Dick was naturally a smart boy. His street education had sharpened his faculties, and taught him to rely upon himself. He knew that it would take him a long time to reach the goal which he had set before him, and he had patience to keep on trying. He knew that he had only himself to depend upon, and he determined to make the most of himself,—a resolution which is the secret of success in nine cases out of ten.

"Dick," said Fosdick, one evening, after they had completed their studies, "I think you'll have to get another teacher soon."

"Why?" asked Dick, in some surprise. "Have you been offered a more loocrative position?"

"No," said Fosdick, "but I find I have taught you all I know myself. You are now as good a scholar as I am."

"Is that true?" said Dick, eagerly, a flush of gratification coloring his brown cheek.

"Yes," said Fosdick. "You've made wonderful progress. I propose, now that evening schools have begun, that we join one, and study together through the winter."

"All right," said Dick. "I'd be willin' to go now; but when

I first began to study I was ashamed to have anybody know that I was so ignorant. Do you really mean, Fosdick, that I know as much as you?"

"Yes, Dick, it's true."

"Then I've got you to thank for it," said Dick, earnestly. "You've made me what I am."

"And haven't you paid me, Dick?"

"By payin' the room-rent," said Dick, impulsively. "What's that? It isn't half enough. I wish you'd take half my money; you deserve it."

"Thank you, Dick, but you're too generous. You've more than paid me. Who was it took my part when all the other boys imposed upon me? And who gave me money to buy clothes, and so got me my situation?"

"Oh, that's nothing!" said Dick.

"It's a great deal, Dick. I shall never forget it. But now it seems to me you might try to get a situation yourself."

"Do I know enough?"

"You know as much as I do."

"Then I'll try," said Dick, decidedly.

"I wish there was a place in our store," said Fosdick. "It would be pleasant for us to be together."

"Never mind," said Dick; "there'll be plenty of other chances. P'r'aps A. T. Stewart might like a partner. I wouldn't ask more'n a quarter of the profits."

"Which would be a very liberal proposal on your part," said Fosdick, smiling. "But perhaps Mr. Stewart might object to a partner living on Mott Street."

"I'd just as lieves move to Fifth Avenoo," said Dick. "I ain't got no prejudices in favor of Mott Street."

"Nor I," said Fosdick, "and in fact I have been thinking it might be a good plan for us to move as soon as we could afford. Mrs. Mooney doesn't keep the room quite so neat as she might."

"No," said Dick. "She ain't got no prejudices against dirt. Look at that towel."

Dick held up the article indicated, which had now seen service nearly a week, and hard service at that,—Dick's avocation causing him to be rather hard on towels.

"Yes," said Fosdick, "I've got about tired of it. I guess we can find some better place without having to pay much more.

When we move, you must let me pay my share of the rent."

"We'll see about that," said Dick. "Do you propose to move to Fifth Avenoo?"

"Not just at present, but to some more agreeable neighborhood than this. We'll wait till you get a situation, and then we can decide."

A few days later, as Dick was looking about for customers in the neighborhood of the Park, his attention was drawn to a fellow boot-black, a boy about a year younger than himself, who appeared to have been crying.

"What's the matter, Tom?" asked Dick. "Haven't you had luck to-day?"

"Pretty good," said the boy; "but we're havin' hard times at home. Mother fell last week and broke her arm, and to-morrow we've got to pay the rent, and if we don't the landlord says he'll turn us out."

"Haven't you got anything except what you earn?" asked Dick.

"No," said Tom, "not now. Mother used to earn three or four dollars a week; but she can't do nothin' now, and my little sister and brother are too young."

Dick had quick sympathies. He had been so poor himself, and obliged to submit to so many privations that he knew from personal experience how hard it was. Tom Wilkins he knew as an excellent boy who never squandered his money, but faithfully carried it home to his mother. In the days of his own extravagance and shiftlessness he had once or twice asked Tom to accompany him to the Old Bowery or Tony Pastor's, but Tom had always steadily refused.

"I'm sorry for you, Tom," he said. "How much do you owe for rent?"

"Two weeks now," said Tom.

"How much is it a week?"

"Two dollars a week—that makes four."

"Have you got anything towards it?"

"No; I've had to spend all my money for food for mother and the rest of us. I've had pretty hard work to do that. I don't know what we'll do. I haven't any place to go to, and I'm afraid mother'll get cold in her arm."

"Can't you borrow the money somewhere?" asked Dick.

Tom shook his head despondingly.

"All the people I know are as poor as I am," said he. "They'd help me if they could, but it's hard work for them to get along themselves."

"I'll tell you what, Tom," said Dick, impulsively, "I'll stand your friend."

"Have you got any money?" asked Tom, doubtfully.

"Got any money!" repeated Dick. "Don't you know that I run a bank on my own account? How much is it you need?"

"Four dollars," said Tom. "If we don't pay that before to-morrow night, out we go. You haven't got as much as that, have you?"

"Here are three dollars," said Dick, drawing out his pocket-book. "I'll let you have the rest to-morrow, and maybe a little more."

"You're a right down good fellow, Dick," said Tom; "but won't you want it yourself?"

"Oh, I've got some more," said Dick.

"Maybe I'll never be able to pay you."

"S'pose you don't," said Dick; "I guess I won't fail."

"I won't forget it, Dick. I hope I'll be able to do somethin' for you sometime."

"All right," said Dick. "I'd ought to help you. I haven't got no mother to look out for. I wish I had."

There was a tinge of sadness in his tone, as he pronounced the last four words; but Dick's temperament was sanguine, and he never gave way to unavailing sadness. Accordingly he began to whistle as he turned away, only adding, "I'll see you to-morrow, Tom."

The three dollars which Dick had handed to Tom Wilkins were his savings for the present week. It was now Thursday afternoon. His rent, which amounted to a dollar, he expected to save out of the earnings of Friday and Saturday. In order to give Tom the additional assistance he had promised, Dick would be obliged to have recourse to his bank-savings. He would not have ventured to trench upon it for any other reason but this. But he felt that it would be selfish to allow Tom and his mother to suffer when he had it in his power to relieve them. But Dick was destined to be surprised, and that in a disagreeable manner, when he reached home.

CHAPTER XXI

DICK LOSES HIS BANK-BOOK

IT WAS hinted at the close of the last chapter that Dick was destined to be disagreeably surprised on reaching home.

Having agreed to give further assistance to Tom Wilkins, he was naturally led to go to the drawer where he and Fosdick kept their bank-books. To his surprise and uneasiness *the drawer proved to be empty!*

"Come here a minute, Fosdick," he said.

"What's the matter, Dick?"

"I can't find my bank-book, nor yours either. What's 'come of them?"

"I took mine with me this morning, thinking I might want to put in a little more money. I've got it in my pocket, now."

"But where's mine?" asked Dick, perplexed.

"I don't know. I saw it in the drawer when I took mine this morning."

"Are you sure?"

"Yes, positive, for I looked into it to see how much you had got."

"Did you lock it again?" asked Dick.

"Yes; didn't you have to unlock it just now?"

"So I did," said Dick. "But it's gone now. Somebody opened it with a key that fitted the lock, and then locked it ag'in."

"That must have been the way."

"It's rather hard on a feller," said Dick, who, for the first time since we became acquainted with him, began to feel down-hearted.

"Don't give it up, Dick. You haven't lost the money, only the bank-book."

"Ain't that the same thing?"

"No. You can go to the bank to-morrow morning, as soon as it opens, and tell them you have lost the book, and ask them not to pay the money to any one except yourself."

"So I can," said Dick, brightening up. "That is, if the thief hasn't been to the bank to-day."

"If he has, they might detect him by his handwriting."

"I'd like to get hold of the one that stole it," said Dick, indignantly. "I'd give him a good lickin'."

"It must have been somebody in the house. Suppose we go and see Mrs. Mooney. She may know whether anybody came into our room to-day."

The two boys went downstairs, and knocked at the door of a little back sitting-room where Mrs. Mooney generally spent her evenings. It was a shabby little room, with a threadbare carpet on the floor, the walls covered with a certain large-figured paper, patches of which had been stripped off here and there, exposing the plaster, the remainder being defaced by dirt and grease. But Mrs. Mooney had one of those comfortable temperaments which are tolerant of dirt, and didn't mind it in the least. She was seated beside a small pine work-table, industriously engaged in mending stockings.

"Good-evening, Mrs. Mooney," said Fosdick, politely.

"Good-evening," said the landlady. "Sit down, if you can find chairs. I'm hard at work as you see, but a poor lone widder can't afford to be idle."

"We can't stop long, Mrs. Mooney, but my friend here has had something taken from his room to-day, and we thought we'd come and see you about it."

"What is it?" asked the landlady. "You don't think I'd take anything? If I am poor, it's an honest name I've always had, as all my lodgers can testify."

"Certainly not, Mrs. Mooney; but there are others in the house that may not be honest. My friend has lost his bank-book. It was safe in the drawer this morning, but to-night it is not to be found."

"How much money was there in it?" asked Mrs. Mooney.

"Over a hundred dollars," said Fosdick.

"It was my whole fortun'," said Dick. "I was goin' to buy a house next year."

Mrs. Mooney was evidently surprised to learn the extent of Dick's wealth, and was disposed to regard him with increased respect.

"Was the drawer locked?" she asked.

"Yes."

"Then it couldn't have been Bridget. I don't think she has any keys."

"She wouldn't know what a bank-book was," said Fosdick.

"You didn't see any of the lodgers go into our room to-day, did you?"

"I shouldn't wonder if it was Jim Travis," said Mrs. Mooney, suddenly.

This James Travis was a bar-tender in a low groggery in Mulberry Street, and had been for a few weeks an inmate of Mrs. Mooney's lodging-house. He was a coarse-looking fellow who, from his appearance, evidently patronized liberally the liquor he dealt out to others. He occupied a room opposite Dick's, and was often heard by the two boys reeling upstairs in a state of intoxication, uttering shocking oaths.

This Travis had made several friendly overtures to Dick and his room-mate, and had invited them to call round at the bar-room where he tended, and take something. But this invitation had never been accepted, partly because the boys were better engaged in the evening, and partly because neither of them had taken a fancy to Mr. Travis; which certainly was not strange, for nature had not gifted him with many charms, either of personal appearance or manners. The rejection of his friendly proffers had caused him to take a dislike to Dick and Henry, whom he considered stiff and unsocial.

"What makes you think it was Travis?" asked Fosdick. "He isn't at home in the daytime."

"But he was to-day. He said he had got a bad cold, and had to come home for a clean handkerchief."

"Did you see him?" asked Dick.

"Yes," said Mrs. Mooney. "Bridget was hanging out clothes, and I went to the door to let him in."

"I wonder if he had a key that would fit our drawer," said Fosdick.

"Yes," said Mrs. Mooney. "The bureaus in the two rooms are just alike. I got 'em at auction, and most likely the locks is the same."

"It must have been he," said Dick, looking towards Fosdick.

"Yes," said Fosdick, "it looks like it."

"What's to be done? That's what I'd like to know," said Dick. "Of course he'll say he hasn't got it; and he won't be such a fool as to leave it in his room."

"If he hasn't been to the bank, it's all right," said Fosdick. "You can go there the first thing to-morrow morning, and stop their paying any money on it."

"But I can t get any money on it myself," said Dick. "I told Tom Wilkins I'd let him have some more money to-morrow, or his sick mother'll have to turn out of their lodgin's."

"How much money were you going to give him?"

"I gave him three dollars to-day, and was goin' to give him two dollars to-morrow."

"I've got the money, Dick. I didn't go to the bank this morning."

"All right. I'll take it, and pay you back next week."

"No, Dick; if you've given three dollars, you must let me give two."

"No, Fosdick, I'd rather give the whole. You know I've got more money than you. No, I haven't, either," said Dick, the memory of his loss flashing upon him. "I thought I was rich this morning, but now I'm in destitoot circumstances."

"Cheer up, Dick; you'll get your money back."

"I hope so," said our hero, rather ruefully.

The fact was, that our friend Dick was beginning to feel what is so often experienced by men who do business of a more important character and on a larger scale than he, the bitterness of a reverse of circumstances. With one hundred dollars and over carefully laid away in the savings bank, he had felt quite independent. Wealth is comparative, and Dick probably felt as rich as many men who are worth a hundred thousand dollars. He was beginning to feel the advantages of his steady self-denial, and to experience the pleasures of property. Not that Dick was likely to be unduly attached to money. Let it be said to his credit that it had never given him so much satisfaction as when it enabled him to help Tom Wilkins in his trouble.

Besides this, there was another thought that troubled him. When he obtained a place he could not expect to receive as much as he was now making from blacking boots,—probably not more than three dollars a week,—while his expenses without clothing would amount to four dollars. To make up the deficiency he had confidently relied upon his savings, which would be sufficient to carry him along for a year, if necessary. If he should not recover his money, he would be compelled to continue a boot-black for at least six months longer; and this was rather a discouraging reflection. On the whole it is not to be wondered at that Dick felt unusually sober this evening, and that neither of the boys felt much like studying.

The two boys consulted as to whether it would be best to speak to Travis about it. It was not altogether easy to decide. Fosdick was opposed to it.

"It will only put him on his guard," said he, "and I don't see as it will do any good. Of course he will deny it. We'd better keep quiet, and watch him, and, by giving notice at the bank, we can make sure that he doesn't get any money on it. If he does present himself at the bank, they will know at once that he is a thief, and he can be arrested."

This view seemed reasonable, and Dick resolved to adopt it. On the whole, he began to think prospects were brighter than he had at first supposed, and his spirits rose a little.

"How'd he know I had any bank-book? That's what I can't make out," he said.

"Don't you remember?" said Fosdick, after a moment's thought, "we were speaking of our savings, two or three evenings since?"

"Yes," said Dick.

"Our door was a little open at the time, and I heard somebody come upstairs, and stop a minute in front of it. It must have been Jim Travis. In that way he probably found out about your money, and took the opportunity to-day to get hold of it."

This might or might not be the correct explanation. At all events it seemed probable.

The boys were just on the point of going to bed, later in the evening, when a knock was heard at the door, and, to their no little surprise, their neighbor, Jim Travis, proved to be the caller. He was a sallow-complexioned young man, with dark hair and bloodshot eyes.

He darted a quick glance from one to the other as he entered, which did not escape the boys' notice.

"How are ye, to-night?" he said, sinking into one of the two chairs with which the room was scantily furnished.

"Jolly," said Dick. "How are you?"

"Tired as a dog," was the reply. "Hard work and poor pay; that's the way with me. I wanted to go to the theater, to-night, but I was hard up, and couldn't raise the cash."

Here he darted another quick glance at the boys; but neither betrayed anything.

"You don't go out much, do you?" he said.

"Not much," said Fosdick. "We spend our evenings in study."

"That's precious slow," said Travis, rather contemptuously. "What's the use of studying so much? You don't expect to be a lawyer, do you, or anything of that sort?"

"Maybe," said Dick. "I haven't made up my mind yet. If my feller-citizens should want me to go to Congress some time, I shouldn't want to disapp'int 'em; and then readin' and writin' might come handy."

"Well," said Travis, rather abruptly, "I'm tired and I guess I'll turn in."

"Good-night," said Fosdick.

The boys looked at each other as their visitor left the room.

"He came in to see if we'd missed the bank-book," said Dick.

"And to turn off suspicion from himself, by letting us know he had no money," added Fosdick.

"That's so," said Dick. "I'd like to have searched them pockets of his."

CHAPTER XXII

TRACKING THE THIEF

FOSDICK was right in supposing that Jim Travis had stolen the bank-book. He was also right in supposing that that worthy young man had come to the knowledge of Dick's savings by what he had accidentally overheard. Now, Travis, like a very large number of young men of his class, was able to dispose of a larger amount of money than he was able to earn. Moreover, he had no great fancy for work at all, and would have been glad to find some other way of obtaining money enough to pay his expenses. He had recently received a letter from an old companion, who had strayed out to California, and going at once to the mines had been lucky enough to get possession of a very remunerative claim. He wrote to Travis that he had already realized two thousand dollars from it, and expected to make his fortune within six months.

Two thousand dollars! This seemed to Travis a very large

sum, and quite dazzled his imagination. He was at once inflamed with the desire to go out to California and try his luck. In his present situation he only received thirty dollars a month, which was probably all that his services were worth, but went a very little way towards gratifying his expensive tastes. Accordingly he determined to take the next steamer to the land of gold, if he could possibly manage to get money enough to pay the passage.

The price of a steerage passage at that time was seventy-five dollars,—not a large sum, certainly,—but it might as well have been seventy-five hundred for any chance James Travis had of raising the amount at present. His available funds consisted of precisely two dollars and a quarter; of which sum, one dollar and a half was due to his washerwoman. This, however, would not have troubled Travis much, and he would conveniently have forgotten all about it; but, even leaving this debt unpaid, the sum at his command would not help him materially towards paying his passage money.

Travis applied for help to two or three of his companions; but they were all of that kind who never keep an account with savings banks, but carry all their spare cash about with them. One of these friends offered to lend him thirty-seven cents, and another a dollar; but neither of these offers seemed to encourage him much. He was about giving up his project in despair, when he learned, accidentally, as we have already said, the extent of Dick's savings.

One hundred and seventeen dollars! Why, that would not only pay his passage, but carry him up to the mines, after he had arrived in San Francisco. He could not help thinking it over, and the result of this thinking was that he determined to borrow it of Dick without leave. Knowing that neither of the boys were in their room in the daytime, he came back in the course of the morning, and, being admitted by Mrs. Mooney herself, said, by way of accounting for his presence, that he had a cold, and had come back for a handkerchief. The landlady suspected nothing, and, returning at once to her work in the kitchen, left the coast clear.

Travis at once entered Dick's room, and, as there seemed to be no other place for depositing money, tried the bureau-drawers. They were all readily opened, except one, which proved to be locked. This he naturally concluded must contain the money, and going back to his own chamber for the key of the bureau, tried it on his return, and found to his satisfaction that it would fit. When he discovered the bank-book, his joy was mingled with disappointment. He had expected to find bank-bills instead. This would have saved all further trouble, and would have been immediately available. Obtaining money at the savings bank would involve fresh risk. Travis hesitated whether to take it or not; but finally decided that it would be worth the trouble and hazard.

He accordingly slipped the book into his pocket, locked the drawer again, and, forgetting all about the handkerchief for which he had come home, went downstairs, and into the street.

There would have been time to go to the savings bank that day, but Travis had already been absent from his place of business some time, and did not venture to take the additional time required. Besides, not being very much used to savings banks, never having had occasion to use them, he thought it would be more prudent to look over the rules and regulations, and see if he could not get some information as to the way he ought to proceed. So the day passed, and Dick's money was left in safety at the bank.

In the evening, it occurred to Travis that it might be well to find out whether Dick had discovered his loss. This reflection it was that induced the visit which is recorded at the close of the last chapter. The result was that he was misled by the boys' silence on the subject, and concluded that nothing had yet been discovered.

"Good!" thought Travis, with satisfaction. "If they don't find out for twenty-four hours, it'll be too late, then, and I shall be all right."

There being a possibility of the loss being discovered before the boys went out in the morning, Travis determined to see them at that time, and judge whether such was the case. He waited, therefore, until he heard the boys come out, and then opened his own door.

"Morning, gents," said he, sociably. "Going to business?"

"Yes," said Dick. "I'm afraid my clerks'll be lazy if I ain't on hand."

"Good joke!" said Travis. "If you pay good wages, I'd like to speak for a place."

"I pay all I get myself," said Dick. "How's business with you?"

"So so. Why don't you call round, some time?"

"All my evenin's is devoted to literatoor and science," said Dick. "Thank you all the same."

"Where do you hang out?" inquired Travis, in choice language, addressing Fosdick.

"At Henderson's hat and cap store, on Broadway."

"I'll look in upon you some time when I want a tile," said Travis. "I suppose you sell cheaper to your friends."

"I'll be as reasonable as I can," said Fosdick, not very cordially; for he did not much fancy having it supposed by his employer that such a disreputable-looking person as Travis was a friend of his.

However, Travis had no idea of showing himself at the Broadway store, and only said this by way of making conversation, and encouraging the boys to be social.

"You haven't any of you gents seen a pearl-handled knife, have you?" he asked.

"No," said Fosdick; "have you lost one?"

"Yes," said Travis, with unblushing falsehood. "I left it on my bureau a day or two since. I've missed one or two other little matters. Bridget don't look to me any too honest. Likely she's got 'em."

"What are you goin' to do about it?" said Dick.

"I'll keep mum unless I lose something more, and then I'll kick up a row, and haul her over the coals. Have you missed anything?"

"No," said Fosdick, answering for himself, as he could do without violating the truth.

There was a gleam of satisfaction in the eyes of Travis, as he heard this.

"They haven't found it out yet," he thought. "I'll bag the money to-day, and then they may whistle for it."

Having no further object to serve in accompanying the boys, he bade them good-morning, and turned down another street.

"He's mighty friendly all of a sudden," said Dick.

"Yes," said Fosdick; "it's very evident what it all means. He wants to find out whether you have discovered your loss or not."

"But he didn't find out."

"No; we've put him on the wrong track. He means to get his money to-day, no doubt."

"My money," suggested Dick.

"I accept the correction," said Fosdick.

"Of course, Dick, you'll be on hand as soon as the bank opens."

"In course I shall. Jim Travis'll find he's walked into the wrong shop."

"The bank opens at ten o'clock, you know."

"I'll be there on time."

The two boys separated.

"Good luck, Dick," said Fosdick, as he parted from him. "It'll all come out right, I think."

"I hope 'twill," said Dick.

He had recovered from his temporary depression, and made up his mind that the money would be recovered. He had no idea of allowing himself to be outwitted by Jim Travis, and enjoyed already, in anticipation, the pleasure of defeating his rascality.

It wanted two hours and a half yet to ten o'clock, and this time to Dick was too precious to be wasted. It was the time of his greatest harvest. He accordingly repaired to his usual place of business, succeeded in obtaining six customers, which yielded him sixty cents. He then went to a restaurant, and got some breakfast. It was now half-past nine, and Dick, feeling that it wouldn't do to be late, left his box in charge of Johnny Nolan, and made his way to the bank.

The officers had not yet arrived, and Dick lingered on the outside, waiting till they should come. He was not without a little uneasiness, fearing that Travis might be as prompt as himself, and finding him there, might suspect something, and so escape the snare. But, though looking cautiously up and down the street, he could discover no traces of the supposed thief. In due time ten o'clock struck, and immediately afterwards the doors of the bank were thrown open, and our hero entered.

As Dick had been in the habit of making a weekly visit for the last nine months, the cashier had come to know him by sight.

"You're early, this morning, my lad," he said, pleasantly. "Have you got some more money to deposit? You'll be getting rich, soon."

"I don't know about that," said Dick. "My bank-book's been stole."

"Stolen!" echoed the cashier. "That's unfortunate. Not

so bad as it might be, though. The thief can't collect the money."

"That's what I came to see about," said Dick. "I was afraid he might have got it already."

"He hasn't been here yet. Even if he had, I remember you, and should have detected him. When was it taken?"

"Yesterday," said Dick. "I missed it in the evenin' when I got home."

"Have you any suspicion as to the person who took it?" asked the cashier.

Dick thereupon told all he knew as to the general character and suspicious conduct of Jim Travis, and the cashier agreed with him that he was probably the thief. Dick also gave his reason for thinking that he would visit the bank that morning, to withdraw the funds.

"Very good," said the cashier. "We'll be ready for him. What is the number of your book?"

"No. 5,678," said Dick.

"Now give me a litttle description of this Travis whom you suspect."

Dick accordingly furnished a brief outline sketch of Travis, not particularly complimentary to the latter.

"That will answer. I think I shall know him," said the cashier. "You may depend upon it that he shall receive no money on your account."

"Thank you," said Dick.

Considerably relieved in mind, our hero turned towards the door, thinking that there would be nothing gained by his remaining longer, while he would of course lose time.

He had just reached the doors, which were of glass, when through them he perceived James Travis himself just crossing the street, and apparently coming towards the bank. It would not do, of course, for him to be seen.

"Here he is," he exclaimed, hurrying back. "Can't you hide me somewhere? I don't want to be seen."

The cashier understood at once how the land lay. He quickly opened a little door, and admitted Dick behind the counter.

"Stoop down," he said, "so as not to be seen."

Dick had hardly done so when Jim Travis opened the outer door, and, looking about him in a little uncertainty, walked up to the cashier's desk.

CHAPTER XXIII

TRAVIS IS ARRESTED

JIM TRAVIS advanced into the bank with a doubtful step, knowing well that he was on a dishonest errand, and heartily wishing that he were well out of it. After a little hesitation, he approached the paying-teller, and, exhibiting the bank-book, said, "I want to get my money out."

The bank-officer took the book, and, after looking at it a moment, said, "How much do you want?"

"The whole of it," said Travis.

"You can draw out any part of it, but to draw out the whole requires a week's notice."

"Then I'll take a hundred dollars."

"Are you the person to whom the book belongs?"

"Yes, sir," said Travis, without hesitation.

"Your name is—"

"Hunter."

The bank-clerk went to a large folio volume, containing the names of depositors, and began to turn over the leaves. While he was doing this, he managed to send out a young man connected with the bank for a policeman. Travis did not perceive this, or did not suspect that it had anything to do with himself. Not being used to savings banks, he supposed the delay only what was usual. After a search, which was only intended to gain time that a policeman might be summoned, the cashier came back, and, sliding out a piece of paper to Travis, said, "It will be necessary for you to write an order for the money."

Travis took a pen, which he found on the ledge outside, and wrote the order, signing his name "Dick Hunter," having observed that name on the outside of the book.

"Your name is Dick Hunter, then?" said the cashier, taking the paper, and looking at the thief over his spectacles.

"Yes," said Travis, promptly.

"But," continued the cashier, "I find Hunter's age is put down on the bank-book as fourteen. Surely you must be more than that."

Travis would gladly have declared that he was only fourteen;

but, being in reality twenty-three, and possessing a luxuriant pair of whiskers, this was not to be thought of. He began to feel uneasy.

"Dick Hunter's my younger brother," he said. "I'm getting out the money for him."

"I thought you said your own name was Dick Hunter," said the cashier.

"I said my name was Hunter," said Travis, ingeniously. "I didn't understand you."

"But you've signed the name of Dick Hunter to this order. How is that?" questioned the troublesome cashier.

Travis saw that he was getting himself into a tight place; but his self-possession did not desert him.

"I thought I must give my brother's name," he answered.

"What is your own name?"

"Henry Hunter."

"Can you bring any one to testify that the statement you are making is correct?"

"Yes, a dozen if you like," said Travis, boldly. "Give me the book, and I'll come back this afternoon. I didn't think there'd be such a fuss about getting out a little money."

"Wait a moment. Why don't your brother come himself?"

"Because he's sick. He's down with the measles," said Travis.

Here the cashier signed to Dick to rise and show himself. Our hero accordingly did so.

"You will be glad to find that he has recovered," said the cashier, pointing to Dick.

With an exclamation of anger and dismay, Travis, who saw the game was up, started for the door, feeling that safety made such a course prudent. But he was too late. He found himself confronted by a burly policeman, who seized him by the arm, saying, "Not so fast, my man. I want you."

"Let me go," exclaimed Travis, struggling to free himself.

"I'm sorry I can't oblige you," said the officer. "You'd better not make a fuss, or I may have to hurt you a little."

Travis sullenly resigned himself to his fate, darting a look of rage at Dick, whom he considered the author of his present misfortune.

"This is your book," said the cashier, handing back his rightful property to our hero. "Do you wish to draw out any money?"

"Two dollars," said Dick.

"Very well. Write an order for the amount."

Before doing so, Dick, who now that he saw Travis in the power of the law began to pity him, went up to the officer, and said,—

"Won't you let him go? I've got my bank-book back, and I don't want anything done to him."

"Sorry I can't oblige you," said the officer; "but I'm not allowed to do it. He'll have to stand his trial."

"I'm sorry for you, Travis," said Dick. "I didn't want you arrested. I only wanted my bank-book back."

"Curse you!" said Travis, scowling vindictively. "Wait till I get free. See if I don't fix you."

"You needn't pity him too much," said the officer. "I know him now. He's been to the Island before."

"It's a lie," said Travis, violently.

"Don't be too noisy, my friend," said the officer. "If you've got no more business here, we'll be going."

He withdrew with the prisoner in charge, and Dick, having drawn his two dollars, left the bank. Notwithstanding the violent words the prisoner had used towards himself, and his attempted robbery, he could not help feeling sorry that he had been instrumental in causing his arrest.

"I'll keep my book a little safer hereafter," thought Dick. "Now I must go and see Tom Wilkins."

Before dismissing the subject of Travis and his theft, it may be remarked that he was duly tried, and, his guilt being clear, was sent to Blackwell's Island for nine months. At the end of that time, on his release, he got a chance to work his passage on a ship to San Francisco, where he probably arrived in due time. At any rate, nothing more has been heard of him, and probably his threat of vengence against Dick will never be carried into effect.

Returning to the City Hall Park, Dick soon fell in with Tom Wilkins.

"How are you, Tom?" he said. "How's your mother?"

"She's better, Dick, thank you. She felt worried about bein' turned out into the street; but I gave her that money from you, and now she feels a good deal easier."

"I've got some more for you, Tom," said Dick, producing a two-dollar bill from his pocket.

"I ought not to take it from you, Dick."

"Oh, it's all right, Tom. Don't be afraid."

"But you may need it yourself."

"There's plenty more where that came from."

"Any way, one dollar will be enough. With that we can pay the rent."

"You'll want the other to buy something to eat."

"You're very kind, Dick."

"I'd ought to be. I've only got myself to take care of."

"Well, I'll take it for my mother's sake. When you want anything done just call on Tom Wilkins."

"All right. Next week, if your mother doesn't get better, I'll give you some more."

Tom thanked our hero very gratefully, and Dick walked away, feeling the self-approval which always accompanies a generous and disinterested action. He was generous by nature, and, before the period at which he is introduced to the reader's notice, he frequently treated his friends to cigars and oyster-stews. Sometimes he invited them to accompany him to the theatre at his expense. But he never derived from these acts of liberality the same degree of satisfaction as from this timely gift to Tom Wilkins. He felt that his money was well bestowed, and would save an entire family from privation and discomfort. Five dollars would, to be sure, make something of a difference in the amount of his savings. It was more than he was able to save up in a week. But Dick felt fully repaid for what he had done, and he felt prepared to give as much more, if Tom's mother should continue to be sick, and should appear to him to need it.

Besides all this, Dick felt a justifiable pride in his financial ability to afford so handsome a gift. A year before, however much he might have desired to give, it would have been quite out of his power to give five dollars. His cash balance never reached that amount. It was seldom, indeed, that it equalled one dollar. In more ways than one Dick was beginning to reap the advantage of his self-denial and judicious economy.

It will be remembered that when Mr. Whitney at parting with Dick presented him with five dollars, he told him that he might repay it to some other boy who was struggling upward. Dick thought of this, and it occurred to him that after all he was only paying up an old debt.

When Fosdick came home in the evening, Dick announced his success in recovering his lost money, and described the manner it had been brought about.

"You're in luck," said Fosdick. "I guess we'd better not trust the bureau-drawer again."

"I mean to carry my book round with me," said Dick.

"So shall I, as long as we stay at Mrs. Mooney's. I wish we were in a better place."

"I must go down and tell her she needn't expect Travis back. Poor chap, I pity him!"

Travis was never more seen in Mrs. Mooney's establishment. He was owing that lady for a fortnight's rent of his room, which prevented her feeling much compassion for him. The room was soon after let to a more creditable tenant who proved a less troublesome neighbor than his predecessor.

CHAPTER XXIV

DICK RECEIVES A LETTER

IT WAS about a week after Dick's recovery of his bank-book, that Fosdick brought home with him in the evening a copy of the "Daily Sun."

"Would you like to see your name in print, Dick?" he asked.

"Yes," said Dick, who was busy at the wash-stand, endeavoring to efface the marks which his day's work had left upon his hands. "They haven't put me up for mayor, have they? 'Cause if they have, I shan't accept. It would interfere too much with my private business."

"No," said Fosdick, "they haven't put you up for office yet, though that may happen sometime. But if you want to see your name in print, here it is."

Dick was rather incredulous, but, having dried his hands on the towel, took the paper, and following the directions of Fosdick's finger, observed in the list of advertised letters the name of "RAGGED DICK."

"By gracious, so it is," said he. "Do you s'pose it means me?"

"I don't know of any other Ragged Dick,—do you?"

"No," said Dick, reflectively; "it must be me. But I don't know of anybody that would be likely to write to me."

"Perhaps it is Frank Whitney," suggested Fosdick, after a little reflection. "Didn't he promise to write to you?"

"Yes," said Dick, "and he wanted me to write to him."

"Where is he now?"

"He was going to a boarding-school in Connecticut, he said. The name of the town was Barnton."

"Very likely the letter is from him."

"I hope it is. Frank was a tip-top boy, and he was the first that made me ashamed of bein' so ignorant and dirty."

"You had better go to the post-office to-morrow morning, and ask for the letter."

"P'r'aps they won't give it to me."

"Suppose you wear the old clothes you used to a year ago, when Frank first saw you? They won't have any doubt of your being Ragged Dick then."

"I guess I will. I'll be sort of ashamed to be seen in 'em though," said Dick, who had considerable more pride in a neat personal appearance than when we were first introduced to him.

"It will be only for one day, or one morning," said Fosdick.

"I'd do more'n that for the sake of gettin' a letter from Frank. I'd like to see him."

The next morning, in accordance with the suggestion of Fosdick, Dick arrayed himself in the long disused Washington coat and Napoleon pants, which he had carefully preserved, for what reason he could hardly explain.

When fairly equipped, Dick surveyed himself in the mirror,—if the little seven-by-nine-inch looking-glass, with which the room was furnished, deserved the name. The result of the survey was not on the whole a pleasing one. To tell the truth, Dick was quite ashamed of his appearance, and, on opening the chamber-door, looked around to see that the coast was clear, not being willing to have any of his fellow-boarders see him in his present attire.

He managed to slip out into the street unobserved, and, after attending to two or three regular customers who came down-town early in the morning, he made his way down Nassau Street to the post-office. He passed along until he came to a compartment on which he read ADVERTISED LETTERS, and, stepping up to the little window, said,—

"There's a letter for me. I saw it advertised in the 'Sun' yesterday."

"What name?" demanded the clerk.

"Ragged Dick," answered our hero.

"That's a queer name," said the clerk, surveying him a little curiously. "Are you Ragged Dick?"

"If you don't believe me, look at my clo'es," said Dick.

"That's pretty good proof, certainly," said the clerk, laughing. "If that isn't your name, it deserves to be."

"I believe in dressin' up to your name," said Dick.

"Do you know any one in Barnton, Connecticut?" asked the clerk, who had by this time found the letter.

"Yes," said Dick. "I know a chap that's at boardin'-school there."

"It appears to be in a boy's hand. I think it must be yours."

The letter was handed to Dick through the window. He received it eagerly, and drawing back so as not to be in the way of the throng who were constantly applying for letters, or slipping them into the boxes provided for them, hastily opened it, and began to read. As the reader may be interested in the contents of the letter as well as Dick, we transcribe it below.

It was dated Barnton, Conn., and commenced thus,—

"DEAR DICK,—You must excuse my addressing this letter to 'Ragged Dick'; but the fact is, I don't know what your last name is, nor where you live. I am afraid there is not much chance of your getting this letter; but I hope you will. I have thought of you very often, and wondered how you were getting along, and I should have written to you before if I had known where to direct.

"Let me tell you a little about myself. Barnton is a very pretty country town, only about six miles from Hartford. The boarding-school which I attend is under the charge of Ezekiel Munroe, A.M. He is a man of about fifty, a graduate of Yale College, and has always been a teacher. It is a large two-story house, with an addition containing a good many small bed-chambers for the boys. There are about twenty of us, and there is one assistant teacher who teaches the English branches. Mr. Munroe, or Old Zeke, as we call him behind his back, teaches Latin and Greek. I am studying both these languages, because father wants me to go to college.

"But you won't be interested in hearing about our studies. I will tell you how we amuse ourselves. There are about fifty acres of land belonging to Mr. Munroe; so that we have plenty of room for play. About a quarter of a mile from the house there is a good-sized pond. There is a large, round-bottomed boat, which is stout and strong. Every Wednesday and Saturday afternoon, when the weather is good, we go out rowing on the pond. Mr. Barton, the assistant teacher, goes with us, to look after us. In the summer we are allowed to go in bathing. In the winter there is splendid skating on the pond.

"Besides this, we play ball a good deal, and we have various other plays. So we have a pretty good time, although we study pretty hard too. I am getting on very well in my studies. Father has not decided yet where he will send me to college.

"I wish you were here, Dick. I should enjoy your company, and besides I should like to feel that you were getting an education. I think you are naturally a pretty smart boy; but I suppose, as you have to earn your own living, you don't get much chance to learn. I only wish I had a few hundred dollars of my own. I would have you come up here, and attend school with us. If I ever have a chance to help you in any way, you may be sure that I will.

"I shall have to wind up my letter now, as I have to hand in a composition to-morrow, on the life and character of Washington. I might say that I have a friend who wears a coat that once belonged to the general. But I suppose that coat must be worn out by this time. I don't much like writing compositions. I would a good deal rather write letters.

"I have written a longer letter than I meant to. I hope you will get it, though I am afraid not. If you do, you must be sure to answer it, as soon as possible. You needn't mind if your writing does look like 'hens-tracks,' as you told me once.

"Good-by, Dick. You must always think of me, as your very true friend,

"FRANK WHITNEY."

Dick read this letter with much satisfaction. It is always pleasant to be remembered, and Dick had so few friends that it was more to him than to boys who are better provided. Again, he felt a new sense of importance in having a letter addressed to him. It was the first letter he had ever received. If it had been sent to him a year before, he would not have been able to read it. But now, thanks to Fosdick's instructions, he could not only read writing, but he could write a very good hand himself.

There was one passage in the letter which pleased Dick. It

was where Frank said that if he had the money he would pay for his education himself.

"He's a tip-top feller," said Dick. "I wish I could see him ag'in."

There were two reasons why Dick would like to have seen Frank. One was, the natural pleasure he would have in meeting a friend; but he felt also that he would like to have Frank witness the improvement he had made in his studies and mode of life.

"He'd find me a little more 'spectable than when he first saw me," thought Dick.

Dick had by this time got up to Printing House Square. Standing on Spruce Street, near the "Tribune" office, was his old enemy, Micky Maguire.

It has already been said that Micky felt a natural enmity towards those in his own condition in life who wore better clothes than himself. For the last nine months, Dick's neat appearance had excited the ire of the young Philistine. To appear in neat attire and with a clean face Micky felt was a piece of presumption, and an assumption of superiority on the part of our hero, and he termed it "tryin' to be a swell."

Now his astonished eyes rested on Dick in his ancient attire, which was very similar to his own. It was a moment of triumph to him. He felt that "pride had had a fall," and he could not forbear reminding Dick of it.

"Them's nice clo'es you've got on," said he, sarcastically, as Dick came up.

"Yes," said Dick, promptly. "I've been employin' your tailor. If my face was only dirty we'd be taken for twin brothers."

"So you've give up tryin' to be a swell?"

"Only for this partic'lar occasion," said Dick. "I wanted to make a fashionable call, so I put on my regimentals."

"I don't b'lieve you've got any better clo'es," said Micky.

"All right," said Dick, "I won't charge you nothin' for what you believe."

Here a customer presented himself for Micky, and Dick went back to his room to change his clothes, before resuming business.

CHAPTER XXV

DICK WRITES HIS FIRST LETTER

WHEN Fosdick reached home in the evening, Dick displayed his letter with some pride.

"It's a nice letter," said Fosdick, after reading it. "I should like to know Frank."

"I'll bet you would," said Dick. "He's a trump."

"When are you going to answer it?"

"I don't know," said Dick, dubiously. "I never writ a letter."

"That's no reason why you shouldn't. There's always a first time, you know."

"I don't know what to say," said Dick.

"Get some paper and sit down to it, and you'll find enough to say. You can do that this evening instead of studying."

"If you'll look it over afterwards, and shine it up a little."

"Yes, if it needs it; but I rather think Frank would like it best just as you wrote it."

Dick decided to adopt Fosdick's suggestion. He had very serious doubts as to his ability to write a letter. Like a good many other boys, he looked upon it as a very serious job, not reflecting that, after all, letter-writing is nothing but talking upon paper. Still, in spite of his misgivings, he felt that the letter ought to be answered, and he wished Frank to hear from him. After various preparations, he at last got setttled down to his task, and, before the evening was over, a letter was written. As the first letter which Dick had ever produced, and because it was characteristic of him, my readers may like to read it.

Here it is,—

"DEAR FRANK,—I got your letter this mornin', and was very glad to hear you hadn't forgotten Ragged Dick. I ain't so ragged as I was. Openwork coats and trowsers has gone out of fashion. I put on the Washington coat and Napoleon pants to go to the post-office, for fear they wouldn't think I was the boy that was meant. On my way back I received the congratulations of my intimate friend, Micky Maguire, on my improved appearance.

"I've give up sleepin' in boxes, and old wagons, findin' it didn't agree with my constitution. I've hired a room in Mott Street, and have got a private tooter, who rooms with me and looks after my studies in the evenin'. Mott Street ain't very fashionable; but my manshun on Fifth Avenoo isn't finished yet, and I'm afraid it won't be till I'm a gray-haired veteran. I've got a hundred dollars towards it, which I've saved up from my earnin's. I haven't forgot what you and your uncle said to me, and I'm tryin' to grow up 'spectable. I haven't been to Tony Pastor's, or the Old Bowery, for ever so long. I'd rather save up my money to support me in my old age. When my hair gets gray, I'm goin' to knock off blackin' boots, and go into some light, genteel employment, such as keepin' an apple-stand, or disseminatin' pea-nuts among the people.

"I've got so as to read pretty well, so my tooter says. I've been studyin' geography and grammar also. I've made such astonishin' progress that I can tell a noun from a conjunction as far away as I can see 'em. Tell Mr. Munroe that if he wants an accomplished teacher in his school, he can send for me, and I'll come on by the very next train. Or, if he wants to sell out for a hundred dollars, I'll buy the whole concern, and agree to teach the scholars all I know myself in less than six months. Is teachin' as good business, generally speakin', as blackin' boots? My private tooter combines both, and is makin' a fortun' with great rapidity. He'll be as rich as Astor some time, *if he only lives long enough.*

"I should think you'd have a bully time at your school. I should like to go out in the boat, or play ball with you. When are you comin' to the city? I wish you'd write and let me know when you do, and I'll call and see you. I'll leave my business in the hands of my numerous clerks, and go round with you. There's lots of things you didn't see when you was here before. They're getting on fast at the Central Park. It looks better than it did a year ago.

"I ain't much used to writin' letters. As this is the first one I ever wrote, I hope you'll excuse the mistakes. I hope you'll write to me again soon. I can't write so good a letter as you; but I'll do my best, as the man said when he was asked if he could swim over to Brooklyn backwards. Good-by, Frank. Thank you for all your kindness. Direct your next letter to No. — Mott Street.

"Your true friend,

"DICK HUNTER."

When Dick had written the last word, he leaned back in his chair, and surveyed the letter with much satisfaction.

"I didn't think I could have wrote such a long letter, Fosdick," said he.

"Written would be more grammatical, Dick," suggested his friend.

"I guess there's plenty of mistakes in it," said Dick. "Just look at it, and see."

Fosdick took the letter, and read it over carefully.

"Yes, there are some mistakes," he said; "but it sounds so much like you that I think it would be better to let it go just as it is. It will be more likely to remind Frank of what you were when he first saw you."

"Is it good enough to send?" asked Dick, anxiously.

"Yes; it seems to me to be quite a good letter. It is written just as you talk. Nobody but you could have written such a letter, Dick. I think Frank will be amused at your proposal to come up there as teacher."

"P'r'aps it would be a good idea for us to open a seleck school here in Mott Street," said Dick, humorously. "We could call it 'Professor Fosdick and Hunter's Mott Street Seminary.' Boot-blackin' taught by Professor Hunter."

The evening was so far advanced that Dick decided to postpone copying his letter till the next evening. By this time he had come to have a very fair handwriting, so that when the letter was complete it really looked quite creditable, and no one would have suspected that it was Dick's first attempt in this line. Our hero surveyed it with no little complacency. In fact, he felt rather proud of it, since it reminded him of the great progress he had made. He carried it down to the post-office, and deposited it with his own hands in the proper box. Just on the steps of the building, as he was coming out, he met Johnny Nolan, who had been sent on an errand to Wall Street by some gentleman, and was just returning.

"What are you doin' down nere, Dick?" asked Johnny.

"I've been mailin' a letter."

"Who sent you?"

"Nobody."

"I mean, who writ the letter?"

"I wrote it myself."

"Can you write letters?" asked Johnny, in amazement.

"Why shouldn't I?"

"I didn't know you could write. I can't."

"Then you ought to learn."

"I went to school once; but it was too hard work, so I give it up."

"You're lazy, Johnny,—that's what's the matter. How'd you ever expect to know anything, if you don't try?"

"I can't learn."

"You can, if you want to."

Johnny Nolan was evidently of a different opinion. He was a good-natured boy, large of his age, with nothing particularly bad about him, but utterly lacking in that energy, ambition, and natural sharpness, for which Dick was distinguished. He was not adapted to succeed in the life which circumstances had forced upon him; for in the street-life of the metropolis a boy needs to be on the alert, and have all his wits about him, or he will find himself wholly distanced by his more enterprising competitors for popular favor. To succeed in his profession, humble as it is, a boot-black must depend upon the same qualities which gain success in higher walks in life. It was easy to see that Johnny, unless very much favored by circumstances, would never rise much above his present level. For Dick, we cannot help hoping much better things.

CHAPTER XXVI

AN EXCITING ADVENTURE

DICK now began to look about for a position in a store or counting-room. Until he should obtain one he determined to devote half the day to blacking boots, not being willing to break in upon his small capital. He found that he could earn enough in half a day to pay all his necessary expenses, including the entire rent of the room. Fosdick desired to pay his half; but Dick steadily refused, insisting upon paying so much as compensation for his friend's services as instructor.

It should be added that Dick's peculiar way of speaking and use of slang terms had been somewhat modified by his education and his intimacy with Henry Fosdick. Still he continued to indulge in them to some extent, especially when he felt like joking, and it was natural to Dick to joke, as my readers have probably found out by this time. Still his manners were considerably improved, so that he was more likely to obtain a situation than when first introduced to our notice.

Just now, however, business was very dull, and merchants, instead of hiring new assistants, were disposed to part with those already in their employ. After making several ineffectual applications, Dick began to think he should be obliged to stick to his profession until the next season. But about this time something occurred which considerably improved his chances of preferment.

This is the way it happened.

As Dick, with a balance of more than a hundred dollars in the savings bank, might fairly consider himself a young man of property, he thought himself justified in occasionally taking a half holiday from business, and going on an excursion. On Wednesday afternoon Henry Fosdick was sent by his employer on an errand to that part of Brooklyn near Greenwood Cemetery. Dick hastily dressed himself in his best, and determined to accompany him.

The two boys walked down to the South Ferry, and, paying their two cents each, entered the ferry boat. They remained at the stern, and stood by the railing, watching the great city, with its crowded wharves, receding from view. Beside them was a gentleman with two children,—a girl of eight and a little boy of six. The children were talking gayly to their father. While he was pointing out some object of interest to the little girl, the boy managed to creep, unobserved, beneath the chain that extends across the boat, for the protection of passengers, and, stepping incautiously to the edge of the boat, fell over into the foaming water.

At the child's scream, the father looked up, and, with a cry of horror, sprang to the edge of the boat. He would have plunged in, but, being unable to swim, would only have endangered his own life, without being able to save his child.

"My child!" he exclaimed in anguish,—"who will save my child? A thousand—ten thousand dollars to any one who will save him!"

There chanced to be but rew passengers on board at the time, and nearly all these were either in the cabins or standing forward. Among the few who saw the child fall was our hero.

Now Dick was an expert swimmer. It was an accomplishment which he had possessed for years, and he no sooner saw the boy fall than he resolved to rescue him. His determination was formed before he heard the liberal offer made by the boy's father. Indeed, I must do Dick the justice to say that, in the excitement of the moment, he did not hear it at all, nor would it have stimulated the alacrity with which he sprang to the rescue of the little boy.

Little Johnny had already risen once, and gone under for the second time, when our hero plunged in. He was obliged to strike out for the boy, and this took time. He reached him none too soon. Just as he was sinking for the third and last time, he caught him by the jacket. Dick was stout and strong, but Johnny clung to him so tightly, that it was with great difficulty he was able to sustain himself.

"Put your arms round my neck," said Dick.

The little boy mechanically obeyed, and clung with a grasp strengthened by his terror. In this position Dick could bear his weight better. But the ferry-boat was receding fast. It was quite impossible to reach it. The father, his face pale with terror and anguish, and his hands clasped in suspense, saw the brave boy's struggles, and prayed with agonizing fervor that he might be successful. But it is probable, for they were now midway of the river, that both Dick and the little boy whom he had bravely undertaken to rescue would have been drowned, had not a row-boat been fortunately near. The two men who were in it witnessed the accident, and hastened to the rescue of our hero.

"Keep up a little longer," they shouted, bending to their oars, "and we will save you."

Dick heard the shout, and it put fresh strength into him. He battled manfully with the treacherous sea, his eyes fixed longingly upon the approaching boat.

"Hold on tight, little boy," he said. "There's a boat coming."

The little boy did not see the boat. His eyes were closed to shut out the fearful water, but he clung the closer to his young preserver. Six long, steady strokes, and the boat dashed along side. Strong hands seized Dick and his youthful burden, and drew them into the boat, both dripping with water.

"God be thanked!" exclaimed the father, as from the steamer he saw the child's rescue. "That brave boy shall be rewarded, if I sacrifice my whole fortune to compass it."

"You've had a pretty narrow escape, young chap," said one of the boatmen to Dick. "It was a pretty tough job you undertook."

"Yes," said Dick. "That's what I thought when I was in the water. If it hadn't been for you, I don't know what would have 'come of us."

"Anyhow you're a plucky boy, or you wouldn't have dared to jump into the water after this little chap. It was a risky thing to do."

"I'm used to the water," said Dick, modestly. "I didn't stop to think of the danger, but I wasn't going to see that little fellow drown without tryin' to save him."

The boat at once headed for the ferry wharf on the Brooklyn side. The captain of the ferry-boat, seeing the rescue, did not think it necessary to stop his boat, but kept on his way. The whole occurrence took place in less time than I have occupied in telling it.

The father was waiting on the wharf to receive his little boy, with what feelings of gratitude and joy can be easily understood. With a burst of happy tears he clasped him to his arms. Dick was about to withdraw modestly, but the gentleman perceived the movement, and, putting down the child, came forward, and, clasping his hand, said with emotion, "My brave boy, I owe you a debt I can never repay. But for your timely service I should now be plunged into an anguish which I cannot think of without a shudder."

Our hero was ready enough to speak on most occasions, but always felt awkward when he was praised.

"It wasn't any trouble," he said, modestly. "I can swim like a top."

"But not many boys would have risked their lives for a stranger," said the gentleman. "But," he added with a sudden thought, as his glance rested on Dick's dripping garments, "both you and my little boy will take cold in wet clothes. Fortunately I have a friend living close at hand, at whose house you will have an opportunity of taking off your clothes, and having them dried."

Dick protested that he never took cold; but Fosdick, who had now joined them, and who, it is needless to say. had been greatly alarmed at Dick's danger, joined in urging compliance with the gentleman's proposal, and in the end our hero had to yield. His new friend secured a hack, the driver of which agreed for extra recompense to receive the dripping boys into his carriage, and they were whirled rapidly to a pleasant house in a side street, where matters were quickly explained, and both boys were put to bed.

"I ain't used to goin' to bed quite so early," thought Dick. "This is the queerest excursion I ever took."

Like most active boys Dick did not enjoy the prospect of spending half a day in bed; but his confinement did not last as long as he anticipated.

In about an hour the door of his chamber was opened, and a servant appeared, bringing a new and handsome suit of clothes throughout.

"You are to put on these," said the servant to Dick; "but you needn't get up till you feel like it."

"Whose clothes are they?" asked Dick.

"They are yours."

"Mine! Where did they come from?"

"Mr. Rockwell sent out and bought them for you. They are the same size as your wet ones."

"Is he here now?"

"No. He bought another suit for the little boy, and has gone back to New York. Here's a note he asked me to give you."

Dick opened the paper, and read as follows,—

"Please accept this outfit of clothes as the first instalment of a debt which I can never repay. I have asked to have your wet suit dried, when you can reclaim it. Will you oblige me by calling to-morrow at my counting room, No. —, Pearl Street.

"Your friend,

"JAMES ROCKWELL."

CHAPTER XXVII

CONCLUSION

WHEN Dick was dressed in his new suit, he surveyed his figure with pardonable complacency. It was the best he had ever worn, and fitted him as well as if it had been made expressly for him.

"He's done the handsome thing," said Dick to himself; "but there wasn't no 'casion for his givin' me these clothes. My lucky stars are shinin' pretty bright now. Jumpin' into the water pays better than shinin' boots; but I don't think I'd like to try it more'n once a week."

About eleven o'clock the next morning Dick repaired to Mr. Rockwell's counting-room on Pearl Street. He found himself in front of a large and handsome warehouse. The counting-room was on the lower floor. Our hero entered, and found Mr. Rockwell sitting at a desk. No sooner did that gentleman see him than he arose, and, advancing, shook Dick by the hand in the most friendly manner.

"My young friend," he said, "you have done me so great service that I wish to be of some service to you in return. Tell me about yourself, and what plans or wishes you have formed for the future."

Dick frankly related his past history, and told Mr. Rockwell of his desire to get into a store or counting-room, and of the failure of all his applications thus far. The merchant listened attentively to Dick's statement, and, when he had finished, placed a sheet of paper before him, and, handing him a pen, said, "Will you write your name on this piece of paper?"

Dick wrote in a free, bold hand, the name Richard Hunter. He had very much improved in his penmanship, as has already been mentioned, and now had no cause to be ashamed of it.

Mr. Rockwell surveyed it approvingly.

"How would you like to enter my counting-room as clerk, Richard?" he asked.

Dick was about to say "Bully," when he recollected himself, and answered, "Very much."

"I suppose you know something of arithmetic, do you not?"

"Yes, sir."

"Then you may consider yourself engaged at a salary of ten dollars a week. You may come next Monday morning."

"Ten dollars!" repeated Dick, thinking he must have misunderstood.

"Yes; will that be sufficient?"

"It's more than I can earn," said Dick, honestly.

"Perhaps it is at first," said Mr. Rockwell, smiling; "but I am willing to pay you that. I will besides advance you as fast as your progress will justify it."

Dick was so elated that he hardly restrained himself from some demonstration which would have astonished the merchant; but he exercised self-control, and only said, "I'll try to serve you so faithfully, sir, that you won't repent having taken me into your service."

"And I think you will succeed," said Mr. Rockwell, encouragingly. "I will not detain you any longer, for I have some important business to attend to. I shall expect to see you on Monday morning."

Dick left the counting-room, hardly knowing whether he stood on his head or his heels, so overjoyed was he at the sudden change in his fortunes. Ten dollars a week was to him a fortune, and three times as much as he had expected to obtain at first. Indeed he would have been glad, only the day before, to get a place at three dollars a week. He reflected that with the stock of clothes which he had now on hand, he could save up at least half of it, and even then live better than he had been accustomed to do; so that his little fund in the savings bank, instead of being diminished, would be steadily increasing. Then he was to be advanced if he deserved it. It was indeed a bright prospect for a boy who, only a year before, could neither read nor write, and depended for a night's lodging upon the chance hospitality of an alley-way or old wagon. Dick's great ambition to "grow up 'spectable" seemed likely to be accomplished after all.

"I wish Fosdick was as well off as I am," he thought generously. But he determined to help his less fortunate friend, and assist him up the ladder as he advanced himself.

When Dick entered his room on Mott Street, he discovered that some one else had been there before him, and two articles of wearing apparel had disappeared.

"By gracious!" he exclaimed; "somebody's stole my Washington coat and Napoleon pants. Maybe it's an agent of Barnum's, who expects to make a fortun' by exhibitin' the valooable wardrobe of a gentleman of fashion."

Dick did not shed many tears over his loss, as, in his present circumstances, he never expected to have any further use for the well-worn garments. It may be stated that he afterwards saw them adorning the figure of Micky Maguire; but whether that estimable young man stole them himself, he never ascertained. As to the loss, Dick was rather pleased that it had occurred. It seemed to cut him off from the old vagabond life which he hoped never to resume. Henceforward he meant to press onward, and rise as high as possible.

Although it was yet only noon, Dick did not go out again with his brush. He felt that it was time to retire from business. He would leave his share of the public patronage to other boys less fortunate than himself. That evening Dick and Fosdick had a long conversation. Fosdick rejoiced heartily in his friend's success, and on his side had the pleasant news to communicate that his pay had been advanced to six dollars a week.

"I think we can afford to leave Mott Street now," he continued. "This house isn't as neat as it might be, and I shall like to live in a nicer quarter of the city."

"All right," said Dick. "We'll hunt up a new room tomorrow. I shall have plenty of time, having retired from business. I'll try to get my reg'lar customers to take Johnny Nolan in my place. That boy hasn't any enterprise. He needs somebody to look out for him."

"You might give him your box and brush, too, Dick."

"No," said Dick; "I'll give him some new ones, but mine I want to keep, to remind me of the hard times I've had, when I was an ignorant boot-black, and never expected to be anything better."

"When, in short, you were 'Ragged Dick.' You must drop that name, and think of yourself now as"—

"Richard Hunter, Esq.," said our hero, smiling.

"A young gentleman on the way to fame and fortune," added Fosdick.

Here ends the story of Ragged Dick. As Fosdick said, he is Ragged Dick no longer. He has taken a step upward, and is determined to mount still higher. There are fresh adventures in store for him, and for others who have been introduced in these pages. Those who have felt interested in his early life will find his history continued in a new volume, forming the second of the series, to be called,—

FAME AND FORTUNE;
OR,
THE PROGRESS OF RICHARD HUNTER.

STRUGGLING UPWARD

OR

LUKE LARKIN'S LUCK

CHAPTER I

THE WATERBURY WATCH

ONE Saturday afternoon in January a lively and animated group of boys were gathered on the western side of a large pond in the village of Groveton. Prominent among them was a tall, pleasant-looking young man of twenty-two, the teacher of the Center Grammar School, Frederic Hooper, A.B., a recent graduate of Yale College. Evidently there was something of importance on foot. What it was may be learned from the words of the teacher.

"Now, boys," he said, holding in his hand a Waterbury watch, of neat pattern, "I offer this watch as a prize to the boy who will skate across the pond and back in the least time. You will all start together, at a given signal, and make your way to the mark which I have placed at the western end of the lake, skate around it, and return to this point. Do you fully understand?"

"Yes, sir!" exclaimed the boys, unanimously.

Before proceeding, it may be well to refer more particularly to some of the boys who were to engage in the contest.

First, in his own estimation, came Randolph Duncan, son of Prince Duncan, president of the Groveton Bank, and a prominent town official. Prince Duncan was supposed to be a rich man, and lived in a style quite beyond that of his neighbors. Randolph was his only son, a boy of sixteen, and felt that in social position and blue blood he was without a peer in the village. He was a tall, athletic boy, and disposed to act the part of boss among the Groveton boys.

Next came a boy similar in age and physical strength, but in other respects very different from the young aristocrat. This was Luke Larkin, the son of a carpenter's widow, living on narrow means, and so compelled to exercise the strictest economy. Luke worked where he could, helping the farmers in hay-time, and ready to do odd jobs for any one in the village who desired his services. He filled the position of janitor at the school which he attended, sweeping out twice a week and making the fires. He had a pleasant expression, and a bright, resolute look, a warm heart, and a clear intellect, and was probably, in spite of his poverty, the most popular boy in Groveton. In this respect he was the opposite of Randolph Duncan, whose assumption of superiority and desire to "boss" the other boys prevented him from having any real friends. He had two or three companions, who flattered him and submitted to his caprices because they thought it looked well to be on good terms with the young aristocrat.

These two boys were looked upon as the chief contestants for the prize offered by their teacher. Opinions differed as to which would win.

"I think Luke will get the watch," said Fred Acken, a younger boy.

"I don't know about that," said Tom Harper. "Randolph skates just as well, and he has a pair of club skates. His father sent to New York for them last week. They're beauties, I tell you. Randolph says they cost ten dollars."

"Of course that gives him the advantage," said Percy Hall. "Look at Luke's old-fashioned wooden skates! They would be dear at fifty cents!"

"It's a pity Luke hasn't a better pair," said Harry Wright. "I don't think the contest is a fair one. Luke ought to have an allowance of twenty rods, to make up for the difference in skates."

"He wouldn't accept it," said Linton Tomkins, the son of a manufacturer in Groveton, who was an intimate friend of Luke, and preferred to associate with him, though Randolph had made advances toward intimacy, Linton being the only boy in the village whom he regarded as his social equal. "I offered him my club skates, but he said he would take the chances with his own."

Linton was the only boy who had a pair of skates equal to Randolph's. He, too, was a contestant, but, being three years younger than Luke and Randolph, had no expectation of rivaling them.

Randolph had his friends near him, administering the adulation he so much enjoyed.

"I have no doubt you'll get the watch, Randolph," said Sam Noble. "You're a better skater any day than Luke Larkin."

"Of course you are!" chimed in Tom Harper.

"The young janitor doesn't think so," said Randolph, his lips curling.

"Oh, he's conceited enough to think he can beat you, I make no doubt," said Sam.

"On those old skates, too! They look as if Adam might have used them when he was a boy!"

This sally of Tom's created a laugh.

"His skates are old ones, to be sure," said Randolph, who was quick-sighted enough to understand that any remark of this kind might dim the luster of his expected victory. "His skates are old enough, but they are just as good for skating as mine."

"They won't win him the watch, though," said Sam.

"I don't care for the watch myself," said Randolph, loftily. "I've got a silver one now, and am to have a gold one when I'm eighteen. But I want to show that I am the best skater. Besides, father has promised me ten dollars if I win."

"I wish I had ten dollars," said Sam, enviously.

He was the son of the storekeeper, and his father allowed him only ten cents a week pocket-money, so that ten dollars in his eyes was a colossal fortune.

"I have no doubt you would, Sam," said Tom, joyously; "but you couldn't be trusted with so much money. You'd go down to New York and try to buy out A. T. Stewart."

"Are you ready, boys?" asked Mr. Hooper.

Most of the boys responded promptly in the affirmative; but Luke, who had been tightening his straps, said quickly: "I am not ready, Mr. Hooper. My strap has broken!"

"Indeed, Luke, I am sorry to hear it," said the teacher, approaching and examining the fracture. "As matters stand, you can't skate."

Randolph's eyes brightened. Confident as he professed to feel, he knew that his chances of success would be greatly increased by Luke's withdrawal from the list.

"The prize is yours now," whispered Tom.

"It was before," answered Randolph, conceitedly.

Poor Luke looked disappointed. He knew that he had at least an even chance of winning, and he wanted the watch. Several of his friends of his own age had watches, either silver or Waterbury, and this seemed, in his circumstances, the only chance of securing one. Now he was apparently barred out.

"It's a pity you shouldn't skate, Luke," said Mr. Hooper, in a tone of sympathy. "You are one of the best skaters, and had an excellent chance of winning the prize. Is there any boy willing to lend Luke his skates?"

"I will," said Frank Acken.

"My dear boy," said the teacher, "you forget that your feet are several sizes smaller than Luke's."

"I didn't think of that," replied Frank, who was only twelve years old.

"You may use my skates, Luke," said Linton Tomkins. "I think they will fit you."

Linton was only thirteen, but he was unusually large for his age.

"You are very kind, Linton," said Luke, "but that will keep you out of the race."

"I stand no chance of winning," said Linton, "and I will do my skating afterward."

"I don't think that fair," said Randolph, with a frown. "Each boy ought to use his own skates."

"There is nothing unfair about it," said the teacher, "except that Luke is placed at disadvantage in using a pair of skates he is unaccustomed to."

Randolph did not dare gainsay the teacher, but he looked sullen.

"Mr. Hooper is always favoring that beggar!" he said in a low voice, to Tom Harper.

"Of course he is!" chimed in the toady.

"You are very kind, Linny," said Luke, regarding his friend affectionately. "I won't soon forget it."

"Oh, it's all right, Luke," said Linton. "Now go in and win!"

CHAPTER II

TOM HARPER'S ACCIDENT

TOM HARPER and Sam Noble were not wholly disinterested in their championship of Randolph. They were very ordinary skaters, and stood no chance of winning the match themselves. They wished Randolph to win, for each hoped, as he had a silver watch himself already, he might give the Waterbury to his faithful friend and follower. Nothing in Randolph's character warranted such a hope, for he was by no means generous or openhanded, but each thought that he might open his heart on this occasion. Indeed, Tom ventured to hint as much.

"I suppose, Randolph," he said, "if you win the watch you will give it to me?"

"Why should I?" asked Randolph, surveying Tom with a cold glance.

"You've got a nice silver watch yourself, you know."

"I might like to have two watches."

"You'll have the ten dollars your father promised you."

"What if I have? What claim have you on me?"

Tom drew near and whispered something in Randolph's ear.

"I'll see about it," said Randolph, nodding.

"Are you ready?" asked the teacher, once more.

"Aye, aye!" responded the boys.

"One—two—three—go!"

The boys darted off like arrows from a bow. Luke made a late start, but before they were half across the pond he was even with Randolph, and both were leading. Randolph looked sidewise, and shut his mouth tight as he saw his hated rival on equal terms with him and threatening to pass him. It would be humiliating in the extreme, he thought, to be beaten by such a boy.

But beaten he seemed likely to be, for Luke was soon a rod in advance and slowly gaining. Slowly, for Randolph was really a fine skater and had no rival except Luke. But Luke was his superior, as seemed likely to be proved.

Though only these two stood any chance of final success, all the boys kept up the contest.

A branch of a tree had been placed at the western end of the pond, and this was the mark around which the boys were to skate. Luke made the circuit first, Randolph being about half a dozen rods behind. After him came the rest of the boys in procession, with one exception. This exception was Tom Harper, who apparently gave up the contest when half-way across, and began skating about, here and there, apparently waiting for his companions to return.

"Tom Harper has given up his chance," said Linton to the teacher.

"So it seems," replied Mr. Hooper, "but he probably had no expectation of succeeding."

"I should think he would have kept on with the rest. I would have done so, though my chance would have been no better than his."

Indeed, it seemed strange that Tom should have given up

so quickly. It soon appeared that it was not caprice, but that he had an object in view, and that a very discreditable one.

He waited till the boys were on their way back. By this time Luke was some eight rods in advance of his leading competitor. Then Tom began to be on the alert. As Luke came swinging on to victory he suddenly placed himself in his way. Luke's speed was so great that he could not check himself. He came into collision with Tom, and in an instant both were prostrate. Tom, however, got the worst of it. He was thrown violently backward, falling on the back of his head, and lay stunned and motionless on the ice. Luke fell over him, but was scarcely hurt at all. He was up again in an instant, and might still have kept the lead, but instead he got down on his knees beside Tom and asked anxiously: "Are you much hurt, Tom?"

Tom didn't immediately answer, but lay breathing heavily, with his eyes still closed.

Meanwhile, Randolph, with a smile of triumph, swept on to his now assured victory. Most of the boys, however, stopped and gathered round Luke and Tom.

This accident had been watched with interest and surprise from the starting-point.

"Tom must be a good deal hurt," said Linton. "What could possibly have made him get in Luke's way?"

"I don't know," said the teacher, slowly; "it looks strange."

"It almost seemed as if he got in the way on purpose," Linton continued.

"He is a friend of Randolph Duncan, is he not?" asked the teacher, abruptly.

"They are together about all the time."

"Ha!" commented the teacher, as if struck by an idea. He didn't, however, give expression to the thought in his mind.

A minute more, and Randolph swept into the presence of the teacher.

"I believe I have won?" he said, with a smile of gratification on his countenance.

"You have come in first," said the teacher coldly.

"Luke was considerably ahead when he ran into Tom," suggested Linton.

"That's not my lookout," said Randolph, shrugging his shoulders. "The point is that I have come in first."

"Tom Harper is a friend of yours, is he not?" asked the teacher.

"Oh, yes!" answered Randolph, indifferently.

"He seems to be a good deal hurt. It was very strange that he got in Luke's way."

"So it was," said Randolph, without betraying much interest.

"Will you lend me your skates, Randolph?" asked Linton. "I should like to go out and see if I can help Tom in any way."

If any other boy than Linton had made the request, Randolph would have declined, but he wished, if possible, to add Linton to his list of friends, and graciously consented.

Before Linton could reach the spot, Tom had been assisted to his feet, and, with a dazed expression, assisted on either side by Luke and Edmund Blake, was on his way back to the starting-point.

"What made you get in my way, Tom?" asked Luke, puzzled.

"I don't know," answered Tom, sullenly.

"Are you much hurt?"

"I think my skull must be fractured," moaned Tom.

"Oh, not so bad as that," said Luke, cheerfully. "I've fallen on my head myself, but I got over it."

"You didn't fall as hard as I did," groaned Tom.

"No, I presume not; but heads are hard, and I guess you'll be all right in a few days."

Tom had certainly been severely hurt. There was a swelling on the back of his head almost as large as a hen's egg.

"You've lost the watch, Luke," said Frank Acken. "Randolph has got in first."

"Yes, I supposed he would," answered Luke, quietly.

"And there is Linton Tomkins coming to meet us on Randolph's skates."

"Randolph is sitting down on a log taking it easy. What is your loss, Luke, is his gain."

"Yes."

"I think he might have come back to inquire after you, Tom, as you are a friend of his."

Tom looked resentfully at Randolph, and marked his complacent look, and it occurred to him also that the friend he had risked so much to serve was very ungrateful. But he hoped now, at any rate, to get the watch, and thought it prudent to say nothing.

The boys had now reached the shore.

"Hope you're not much hurt, Tom?" said Randolph, in a tone of mild interest.

"I don't know but my skull is fractured," responded Tom, bitterly.

"Oh, I guess not. It's the fortune of war. Well, I got in first."

Randolph waited for congratulations, but none came. All the boys looked serious, and more than one suspected that there had been foul play. They waited for the teacher to speak.

CHAPTER III

RANDOLPH GETS THE WATCH

"IT IS true," said the teacher, slowly. "Randolph has won the race."

Randolph's face lighted up with exultation.

"But it is also evident," continued Mr. Hooper, "that he would not have succeeded but for the unfortunate collision between Luke Larkin and Tom Harper."

Here some of Luke's friends brightened up.

"I don't know about that," said Randolph. "At any rate, I came in first."

"I watched the race closely," said the teacher, "and I have no doubt on the subject. Luke had so great a lead that he would surely have won the race."

"But he didn't," persisted Randolph, doggedly

"He did not, as we all know. It is also clear that had he not stopped to ascertain the extent of Tom's injuries he still might have won."

"That's so!" said half a dozen boys.

"Therefore I cannot accept the result as indicating the superiority of the successful contestant."

"I think I am entitled to the prize," said Randolph.

"I concede that; but, under the circumstances, I suggest to you that it would be graceful and proper to waive your claim and try the race over again."

The boys applauded, with one or two exceptions.

"I won't consent to that, Mr. Hooper," said Randolph, frowning. "I've won the prize fairly and I want it."

"I am quite willing Randolph should have it, sir," said Luke. "I think I should have won it if I had not stopped with Tom, but that doesn't affect the matter one way or the other. Randolph came in first, as he says, and I think he is entitled to the watch."

"Then," said Mr. Hooper, gravely, "there is nothing more to be said. Randolph, come forward and receive the prize."

Randolph obeyed with alacrity, and received the Waterbury watch from the hands of Mr. Hooper. The boys stood in silence and offered no congratulations.

"Now, let me say," said the teacher, "that I cannot understand why there was any collision at all. Tom Harper, why did you get in Luke's way?"

"Because I was a fool, sir," answered Tom, smarting from his injuries, and the evident indifference of Randolph, in whose cause he had incurred them.

"That doesn't answer my question. Why did you act like a fool, as you expressed it?"

"I thought I could get out of the way in time," stammered Tom, who did not dare to tell the truth.

"You had no other reason?" asked the teacher, searchingly.

"No, sir. What other reason could I have?" said Tom, but his manner betrayed confusion.

"Indeed, I don't know," returned the teacher, quietly. "Your action, however, spoiled Luke's chances and insured the success of Randolph."

"And got me a broken head," muttered Tom, placing his hand upon the swelling at the back of his head.

"Yes, you got the worst of it. I advise you to go home and apply cold water or any other remedy your mother may suggest."

Randolph had already turned away, meaning to return home. Tom joined him. Randolph would gladly have dispensed with his company, but had no decent excuse, as Tom's home lay in the same direction as his.

"Well, Randolph, you've won the watch," said Tom, when they were out of hearing of the other boys.

"Yes," answered Randolph, indifferently. "I don't care so much for that as for the ten dollars my father is going to give me."

"That's what I thought. You've got another watch, you know—more valuable."

"Well, what of it?" said Randolph, suspiciously.

"I think you might give me the Waterbury. I haven't got any."

"Why should I give it to you?" answered Randolph, coldly.

"Because but for me you wouldn't have won it, nor the ten dollars, neither."

"How do you make that out?"

"The teacher said so himself."

"I don't agree to it."

"You can't deny it. Luke was seven or eight rods ahead when I got in his way."

"Then it was lucky for me."

"It isn't lucky for me. My head hurts awfully."

"I'm very sorry, of course."

"That won't do me any good. Come, Randolph, give me the watch, like a good fellow."

"Well, you've got cheek, I must say. I want the watch myself."

"And is that all the satisfaction I am to get for my broken head?" exclaimed Tom, indignantly.

Randolph was a thoroughly mean boy, who, if he had had a dozen watches, would have wished to keep them all for himself.

"I've a great mind to tell Luke and the teacher of the arrangement between us."

"There wasn't any arrangement," said Randolph, sharply. "However, as I'm really sorry for you, I am willing to give you a quarter. There, now, don't let me hear any more about the matter."

He drew a silver quarter from his vest pocket and tendered it to Tom.

Tom Harper was not a sensitive boy, but his face flushed with indignation and shame, and he made no offer to take the money.

"Keep your quarter, Randolph Duncan," he said scornfully. "I think you're the meanest specimen of a boy that I ever came across. Any boy is a fool to be your friend. I don't care to keep company with you any longer."

"This to me!" exclaimed Randolph, angrily. "This is the pay I get for condescending to let you go with me."

"You needn't condescend any longer," said Tom, curtly, and he crossed to the other side of the street.

Randolph looked after him rather uneasily. After all, he was sorry to lose his humble follower.

"He'll be coming round in a day or two to ask me to take him back," he reflected. "I would be willing to give him ten cents more, but as for giving him the watch, he must think me a fool to part with that."

CHAPTER IV

LUKE'S NIGHT ADVENTURE

"I AM sorry you have lost the watch, Luke," said the teacher, after Randolph's departure. "You will have to be satisfied with deserving it."

"I am reconciled to the disappointment, sir," answered Luke. "I can get along for the present without a watch."

Nevertheless, Luke did feel disappointed. He had fully expected to have the watch to carry home and display to his mother. As it was, he was in no hurry to go home, but remained for two hours skating with the other boys. He used his friend Linton's skates, Linton having an engagement which prevented his remaining.

It was five o'clock when Luke entered the little cottage which he called home. His mother, a pleasant woman of middle age, was spreading the cloth for supper. She looked up as he entered.

"Well, Luke?" she said inquiringly.

"I haven't brought home the watch, mother," he said. "Randolph Duncan won it by accident. I will tell you about it."

After he had done so, Mrs. Larkin asked thoughtfully: "Isn't it a little singular that Tom should have got in your way?"

"Yes; I thought so at the time."

"Do you think there was any arrangement between him and Randolph?"

"As you ask me, mother, I am obliged to say that I do."

"It was a very mean trick!" said Mrs. Larkin, resentfully.

"Yes, it was; but poor Tom was well punished for it. Why, he's got a bunch on the back of his head almost as large as a hen's egg."

"I don't pity him," said Mrs. Larkin.

"I pity him, mother, for I don't believe Randolph will repay him for the service done him. If Randolph had met with the same accident I am not prepared to say that I should have pitied him much."

"You might have been seriously injured yourself, Luke."

"I might, but I wasn't, so I won't take that into consideration. However, mother, watch or no watch, I've got a good appetite. I shall be ready when supper is."

Luke sat down to the table ten minutes afterward and proved his words good, much to his mother's satisfaction.

While he is eating we will say a word about the cottage. It was small, containing only four rooms, furnished in the plainest fashion. The rooms, however, were exceedingly neat, and presented an appearance of comfort. Yet the united income of Mrs. Larkin and Luke was very small. Luke received a dollar a week for taking care of the schoolhouse, but this income only lasted forty weeks in the year. Then he did odd jobs for the neighbors, and picked up perhaps as much more. Mrs. Larkin had some skill as a dressmaker, but Groveton was a small village, and there was another in the same line, so that her income from this source probably did not average more than three dollars a week. This was absolutely all that they had to live on, though there was no rent to pay; and the reader will not be surprised to learn that Luke had no money to spend for watches.

"Are you tired, Luke?" asked his mother, after supper.

"No, mother. Can I do anything for you?"

"I have finished a dress for Miss Almira Clark. I suppose she will want to wear it to church tomorrow. But she lives so far away, I don't like to ask you to carry it to her."

"Oh, I don't mind. It won't do me any harm."

"You will get tired."

"If I do, I shall sleep the better for it."

"You are a good son, Luke."

"I ought to be. Haven't I got a good mother?"

So it was arranged. About seven o'clock, after his chores were done—for there was some wood to saw and split—Luke set out, with the bundle under his arm, for the house of Miss Clark, a mile and a half away.

It was a commonplace errand, that on which Luke had started, but it was destined to be a very important day in his life. It was to be a turning-point, and to mark the beginning of a new chapter of experiences. Was it to be for good or ill? That we are not prepared to reveal. It will be necessary for the reader to follow his career, step by step, and decide for himself.

Of course, Luke had no thought of this when he set out. To him it had been a marked day on account of the skating match, but this had turned out a disappointment. He accomplished his errand, which occupied a considerable time, and then set out on his return. It was half-past eight, but the moon had risen and diffused a mild radiance over the landscape. Luke thought he would shorten his homeward way by taking a path through the woods. It was not over a quarter of a mile, but would shorten the distance by as much more. The trees were not close together, so that it was light enough to see. Luke had nearly reached the edge of the wood, when he overtook a tall man, a stranger in the neighborhood, who carried in his hand a tin box. Turning, he eyed Luke sharply.

"Boy, what's your name?" he asked.

"Luke Larkin," our hero answered, in surprise.

"Where do you live?"

"In the village yonder."

"Will you do me a favor?"

"What is it, sir?"

"Take this tin box and carry it to your home. Keep it under lock and key till I call for it."

"Yes, sir, I can do that. But how shall I know you again?"

"Take a good look at me, that you may remember me."

"I think I shall know you again, but hadn't you better give me a name?"

"Well, perhaps so," answered the other, after a moment's thought. "You may call me Roland Reed. Will you remember?"

"Yes, sir."

"I am obliged to leave this neighborhood at once, and can't conveniently carry the box," explained the stranger. "Here's something for your trouble."

Luke was about to say that he required no money, when it occurred to him that he had no right to refuse, since money was so scarce at home. He took the tin box and thrust the bank-bill into his vest pocket. He wondered how much it was, but it was too dark to distinguish.

"Good night!" said Luke, as the stranger turned away.

"Good night!" answered his new acquaintance, abruptly.

If Luke could have foreseen the immediate consequences of this apparently simple act, and the position in which it would soon place him, he would certainly have refused to take charge of the box. And yet in so doing it might have happened that he had made a mistake. The consequences of even our simple acts are oftentimes far-reaching and beyond the power of human wisdom to foreknow.

Luke thought little of this as, with the box under his arm, he trudged homeward.

CHAPTER V

LUKE RECEIVES AN INVITATION

"WHAT have you there, Luke?" asked Mrs. Larkin, as Luke entered the little sitting-room with the tin box under his arm.

"I met a man on my way home, who asked me to keep it for him."

"Do you know the man?" asked his mother, in surprise.

"No," answered Luke.

"It seems very singular. What did he say?"

"He said that he was obliged to leave the neighborhood at once, and could not conveniently carry the box."

"Do you think it contains anything of value?"

"Yes, mother. It is like the boxes rich men have to hold their stocks and bonds. I was at the bank one day, and saw a gentleman bring in one to deposit in the safe."

"I can't understand that at all, Luke. You say you did not know this man?"

"I never met him before."

"And, of course, he does not know you?"

"No, for he asked my name."

"Yet he put what may be valuable property in your possession."

"I think," said Luke, shrewdly, "he had no one else to trust it to. Besides, a country boy wouldn't be very likely to make use of stocks and bonds."

"No, that is true. I suppose the tin box is locked?"

"Yes, mother. The owner—he says his name is Roland Reed—wishes it put under lock and key."

"I can lock it up in my trunk, Luke."

"I think that will be a good idea."

"I hope he will pay you for your trouble when he takes away the tin box."

"He has already; I forgot to mention it," and Luke drew from his vest pocket the bank-note he had thrust in as soon as received. "Why, it's a ten-dollar bill!" he exclaimed. "I wonder whether he knew he was giving me as much?"

"I presume so, Luke," said his mother, brightening up. "You are in luck!"

"Take it, mother. You will find a use for it."

"But, Luke, this money is yours."

"No, it is yours, for you are going to take care of the box."

It was, indeed, quite a windfall, and both mother and son retired to rest in a cheerful frame of mind, in spite of Luke's failure in the race.

"I have been thinking, Luke," said his mother, at the breakfast-table, "that I should like to have you buy a Waterbury watch out of this money. It will only cost three dollars and a half, and that is only one-third."

"Thank you, mother, but I can get along without the watch. I cared for it chiefly because it was to be a prize given to the best skater. All the boys know that I would have won but for the accident, and that satisfies me."

"I should like you to have a watch, Luke."

"There is another objection, mother. I don't want any one to know about the box or the money. If it were known that we had so much property in the house, some attempt might be made to rob us."

"That is true, Luke. But I hope it won't be long before you have a watch of your own."

When Luke was walking, after breakfast, he met Randolph Duncan, with a chain attached to the prize watch ostentatiously displayed on the outside of his vest. He smiled complacently, and rather triumphantly, when he met Luke. But Luke looked neither depressed nor angry.

"I hope your watch keeps good time, Randolph," he said.

"Yes; it hasn't varied a minute so far. I think it will keep as good time as my silver watch."

"You are fortunate to have two watches."

"My father has promised me a gold watch when I am eighteen," said Randolph, pompously.

"I don't know if I shall have any watch at all when I am eighteen."

"Oh, well, you are a poor boy. It doesn't matter to you."

"I don't know about that, Randolph. Time is likely to be of as much importance to a poor boy as to a rich boy."

"Oh, ah! yes, of course, but a poor boy isn't expected to wear a watch."

Here the conversation ended. Luke walked on with an amused smile on his face.

"I wonder how it would seem to be as complacent and self-satisfied as Randolph?" he thought. "On the whole, I would rather be as I am."

"Good morning, Luke!"

It was a girl's voice that addressed him. Looking up, he met the pleasant glance of Florence Grant, considered by many the prettiest girl in Groveton. Her mother was a widow in easy circumstances, who had removed from Chicago three years before, and occupied a handsome cottage nearly opposite Mr. Duncan's residence. She was a general favorite, not only for her good looks, but on account of her pleasant manner and sweet disposition.

"Good morning, Florence," said Luke, with an answering smile.

"What a pity you lost the race yesterday!"

"Randolph doesn't think so."

"No; he is a very selfish boy, I am afraid."

"Did you see the race?" asked Luke.

"No, but I heard all about it. If it hadn't been for Tom Harper you would have won, wouldn't you?"

"I think so."

"All the boys say so. What could have induced Tom to get in the way?"

"I don't know. It was very foolish, however. He got badly hurt."

"Tom is a friend of Randolph," said Florence significantly.

"Yes," answered Luke; "but I don't think Randolph would stoop to such a trick as that."

"You wouldn't, Luke, but Randolph is a different boy. Besides, I hear he was trying for something else."

"I know; his father offered him ten dollars besides."

"I don't see why it is that some fare so much better than

others," remarked Florence, thoughtfully. "The watch and the money would have done you more good."

"So they would, Florence, but I don't complain. I may be better off some day than I am now."

"I hope you will, Luke," said Florence, cordially.

"I am very much obliged to you for your good wishes," said Luke, warmly.

"That reminds me, Luke, next week, Thursday, is my birthday, and I am to have a little party in the evening. Will you come?"

Luke's face flushed with pleasure. Though he knew Florence very well from their being schoolfellows, he had never visited the house. He properly regarded the invitation as a compliment, and as a mark of friendship from one whose good opinion he highly valued.

"Thank you, Florence," he said. "You are very kind, and I shall have great pleasure in being present. Shall you have many?"

"About twenty. Your friend Randolph will be there."

"I think there will be room for both of us," said Luke, with a smile.

The young lady bade him good morning and went on her way.

Two days later Luke met Randolph at the dry-goods store in the village.

"What are you buying?" asked Randolph, condescendingly.

"Only a spool of thread for my mother."

"I am buying a new necktie to wear to Florence Grant's birthday party," said Randolph, pompously.

"I think I shall have to do the same," said Luke, enjoying the surprise he saw expressed on Randolph's face.

"Are you going?" demanded Randolph, abruptly.

"Yes."

"Have you been invited?"

"That is a strange question," answered Luke, indignantly. "Do you think I would go without an invitation?"

"Really, it will be quite a mixed affair," said Randolph, shrugging his shoulders.

"If you think so, why do you go?"

"I don't want to disappoint Florence."

Luke smiled. He was privately of the opinion that the disappointment wouldn't be intense.

CHAPTER VI

PREPARING FOR THE PARTY

THE evening of the party arrived. It was quite a social event at Groveton, and the young people looked forward to it with pleasant anticipation. Randolph went so far as to order a new suit for the occasion. He was very much afraid it would not be ready in time, but he was not to be disappointed. At five o'clock on Thursday afternoon it was delivered, and Randolph, when arrayed in it, surveyed himself with great satisfaction. He had purchased a handsome new necktie, and he reflected with pleasure that no boy present—not even Linton—would be so handsomely dressed as himself. He had a high idea of his personal consequence, but he was also of the opinion that "fine feathers make fine birds," and his suit was of fine cloth and stylish make.

"I wonder what the janitor will wear?" he said to himself, with a curl of the lip. "A pair of overalls, perhaps. They would be very appropriate, certainly."

This was just the question which was occupying Luke's mind. He did not value clothes as Randolph did, but he liked to look neat. Truth to tell, he was not very well off as to wardrobe. He had his every-day suit, which he wore to school, and a better suit, which he had worn for over a year. It was of mixed cloth, neat in appearance, though showing signs of wear; but there was one trouble. During the past year Luke had grown considerably, and his coat-sleeves were nearly two inches too short, and the legs of his trousers deficient quite as much. Nevertheless, he dressed himself, and he, too, surveyed himself, not before a pier-glass, but before the small mirror in the kitchen.

"Don't my clothes look bad, mother?" he asked anxiously.

"They are neat and clean, Luke," said his mother, hesitatingly.

"Yes, I know; but they are too small."

"You have been growing fast in the last year, Luke," said his mother, looking a little disturbed. "I suppose you are not sorry for that?"

"No," answered Luke, with a smile, "but I wish my coat and trousers had grown, too."

"I wish, my dear boy, I could afford to buy you a new suit."

"Oh, never mind, mother," said Luke, recovering his cheerfulness. "They will do for a little while yet. Florence didn't invite me for my clothes."

"No; she is a sensible girl. She values you for other reasons."

"I hope so, mother. Still, when I consider how handsomely Randolph will be dressed, I can't help thinking that there is considerable difference in our luck."

"Would you be willing to exchange with him, Luke?"

"There is one thing I wouldn't like to exchange."

"And what is that?"

"I wouldn't exchange my mother for his," said Luke, kissing the widow affectionately. "His mother is a cold, proud, disagreeable woman, while I have the best mother in the world."

"Don't talk foolishly, Luke," said Mrs. Larkin; but her face brightened, and there was a warm feeling in her heart, for it was very pleasant to her to hear Luke speak of her in this way.

"I won't think any more about it, mother," said Luke. "I've got a new necktie, at any rate, and I will make that do."

Just then there was a knock at the door, and Linton entered.

"I thought I would come round and go to the party with you, Luke," he said.

Linton was handsomely dressed, though he had not bought a suit expressly, like Randolph. He didn't appear to notice Luke's scant suit. Even if he had, he would have been too much of a gentleman to refer to it.

"I think we shall have a good time," he said. "We always do at Mrs. Grant's. Florence is a nice girl, and they know how to make it pleasant. I suppose we shall have dancing."

"I don't know how to dance," said Luke, regretfully. "I should like to have taken lessons last winter when Professor Bent had a class, but I couldn't afford it."

"You have seen dancing?"

"Oh, yes."

"It doesn't take much knowledge to dance a quadrille, particularly if you get on a side set. Come, we have an hour before it is time to go. Suppose I give you a lesson?"

"Do you think I could learn enough in that time to venture?"

"Yes, I do. If you make an occasional mistake it won't matter. So, if your mother will give us the use of the sitting-room, I will commence instructions."

Luke had looked at some dancers in the dining-room at the hotel, and was not wholly a novice, therefore. Linton was an excellent dancer, and was clear in his directions. It may also be said that Luke was a ready learner. So it happened at the end of the hour that the pupil had been initiated not only in the ordinary changes of the quadrille, but also in one contra dance, the Virginia Reel, which was a great favorite among the young people of Groveton.

"Now, I think you'll do, Luke," said Linton, when the lesson was concluded. "You are very quick to learn."

"You think I won't be awkward, Linton?"

"No, if you keep cool and don't get flustered."

"I am generally pretty cool. But I shall be rather surprised to see myself on the floor," laughed Luke.

"No doubt others will be, but you'll have a great deal more fun."

"So I shall. I don't like leaning against the wall while others are having a good time."

"If you could dance as well as you can skate you would have no trouble, Luke."

"No; that is where Randolph has the advantage of me."

"He is a very great dancer, though he can't come up to you in skating. However, dancing isn't everything. Dance as well as he may, he doesn't stand as high in the good graces of Florence Grant as he would like to do."

"I always noticed that he seemed partial to Florence."

"Yes, but it isn't returned. How about yourself, Luke?"

Luke, being a modest boy, blushed.

"I certainly think Florence a very nice girl," he said.

"I was sure of that," said Linton, smiling.

"But I don't want to stand in your way, Linton," continued Luke, with a smile.

"No danger, Luke. Florence is a year older than I am. Now, you are nearly two years older than she, and are better matched. So you needn't consider me in the matter."

Of course, this was all a joke. It was true, however, that of all the girls in Groveton, Luke was more attracted by Florence Grant than by any other, and they had always been excellent friends. It was well known that Randolph also was partial to the young lady, but he certainly had never received much encouragement.

Finally the boys got out, and were very soon at the door of

Mrs. Grant's handsome cottage. It was large upon the ground, with a broad veranda, in the Southern style. In fact, Mrs. Grant was Southern by birth, and, erecting the house herself, had it built after the fashion of her Southern birthplace.

Most of the young visitors had arrived when Luke and Linton put in an appearance. They had been detained longer than they were aware by the dancing-lesson.

Randolph and Sam Noble were sitting side by side at one end of the room, facing the entrance.

"Look," said Randolph, with a satirical smile, to his companion, "there comes the young janitor in his dress suit. Just look at his coat-sleeves and the legs of his trousers. They are at least two inches too short. Any other boy would be ashamed to come to a party in such ridiculous clothes."

Sam looked and tittered. Luke's face flushed, for, though he did not hear the words, he guessed their tenor. But he was made to forget them when Florence came forward and greeted Linton and himself with unaffected cordiality.

CHAPTER VII

FLORENCE GRANT'S PARTY

LUKE'S uncomfortable consciousness of his deficiencies in dress soon passed off. He noticed the sneer on Randolph's face and heard Sam's laugh, but he cared very little for the opinion of either of them. No other in the company appeared to observe his poor dress, and he was cordially greeted by them all, with the two exceptions already named.

"The janitor ought to know better than to intrude into the society of his superiors," said Randolph to Sam.

"He seems to enjoy himself," said Sam.

This was half an hour after the party had commenced, when all were engaged in one of the plays popular at a country party.

"I am going to have a party myself in a short time," continued Randolph, "but I shall be more select than Florence in my invitations. I shall not invite any working boys."

"Right you are, Randolph," said the subservient Sam. "I hope you won't forget me."

"Oh, no; I shall invite you. Of course, you don't move exactly in my circle, but, at any rate, you dress decently."

If Sam Noble had had proper pride he would have resented the insolent assumption of superiority in this speech, but he was content to play second fiddle to Randolph Duncan. His family, like himself, were ambitious to be on good terms with the leading families in the village, and did not mind an occasional snub.

"Shall you invite Tom Harper?" he asked.

He felt a little jealous of Tom, who had vied with him in flattering attentions to Randolph.

"No, I don't think so. Tom isn't here, is he?"

"He received an invitation, but ever since his accident he has been troubled with severe headaches, and I suppose that keeps him away."

"He isn't up to my standard," said Randolph, consequentially. "He comes of a low family."

"You and he have been together a good deal."

"Oh, I have found him of some service, but I have paid for it."

Yet this was the boy who, at his own personal risk, had obtained for Randolph the prize at the skating-match. Privately, Sam thought Randolph ungrateful, but he was, nevertheless, pleased at having distanced Tom in the favor of the young aristocrat.

After an hour, spent in various amusements, one of the company took her place at the piano, and dancing began.

"Now is your time, Luke," said Linton. "Secure a partner. It is only a quadrille."

"I feel a little nervous," said Luke. "Perhaps I had better wait till the second dance."

"Oh, nonsense! Don't be afraid."

Meanwhile, Randolph, with a great flourish, had invited Florence to dance.

"Thank you," she answered, taking his arm.

Randolph took his place with her as head couple. Linton and Annie Comray faced them. To Randolph's amazement, Luke and Fanny Pratt took their places as one of the side couples. Randolph, who was aware that Luke had never taken lessons, remarked this with equal surprise and disgust. His lip curled as he remarked to his partner: "Really, I didn't know that Luke Larkin danced."

"Nor I," answered Florence.

"I am sorry he is in our set."

"Why?" asked Florence, regarding him attentively.

"He will probably put us out by his clownish performance."

"Wouldn't it be well to wait and see whether he does or not?" responded Florence, quietly.

Randolph shrugged his shoulders.

"I pity his partner, at any rate," he said.

"I can't join in any such conversation about one of my guests," said Florence, with dignity.

Here the first directions were given, and the quadrille commenced.

Luke felt a little nervous, it must be confessed, and for that reason he watched with unusual care the movements of the head couples. He was quick to learn, and ordinarily cool and self-possessed. Besides, he knew that no one was likely to criticize him except Randolph. He saw the latter regarding him with a mocking smile, and this stimulated him to unusual carefulness. The result was that he went through his part with quite as much ease and correctness as any except the most practiced dancers. Florence said nothing, but she turned with a significant smile to Randolph. The latter looked disappointed and mortified. His mean disposition would have been gratified by Luke's failure, but this was a gratification he was not to enjoy.

The dance was at length concluded, and Luke, as he led his partner to a seat, felt that he had scored a success.

"May I have the pleasure of dancing with you next time, Florence?" asked Randolph.

"Thank you, but I should not think it right to slight my other guests," said the young lady.

Just then Luke came up and preferred the same request. He would not have done so if he had not acquitted himself well in the first quadrille.

Florence accepted with a smile.

"I was not aware that dancing was one of your accomplishments, Luke," she said.

"Nor I, till this evening," answered Luke. "There stands my teacher," and he pointed to Linton.

"You do credit to your teacher," said Florence. "I should not have known you were such a novice."

Luke was pleased with this compliment, and very glad that

he had been spared the mortification of breaking down before the eyes of his ill-wisher, Randolph Duncan. It is hardly necessary to say that he did equally well in the second quadrille, though he and Florence were head couple.

The next dance was the Virginia Reel. Here Florence had Linton for a partner, and Luke secured as his own partner a very good dancer. From prudence, however, he took his place at some distance from the head, and by dint of careful watching he acquitted himself as well as in the quadrilles.

"Really, Luke, you are doing wonderfully well," said Linton, when the dance was over. "I can hardly believe that you have taken but one lesson, and that from so poor a teacher as I am."

"I couldn't have had a better teacher, Lin," said Luke. "I owe my success to you."

"Didn't you say Luke couldn't dance?" asked Sam Noble of Randolph, later in the evening.

"He can't," answered Randolph, irritably.

"He gets along very well, I am sure. He dances as well as I do."

"That isn't saying much," answered Randolph, with a sneer. He could not help sneering even at his friends, and this was one reason why no one was really attached to him.

Sam walked away offended.

The party broke up at half-past ten. It was an early hour, but late enough considering the youth of the participants. Luke accompanied home one of the girls who had no brother present, and then turned toward his own home.

He had nearly reached it, when a tall figure, moving from the roadside, put a hand on his shoulder.

"You are Luke Larkin?" said the stranger, in questioning tone.

"Yes, sir."

"Is the tin box safe?"

"Yes, sir."

"That is all—for the present," and the stranger walked quickly away.

"Who can he be," thought Luke, in wonder, "and why should he have trusted a complete stranger—and a boy?"

Evidently there was some mystery about the matter. Had the stranger come honestly by the box, or was Luke aiding and abetting a thief? He could not tell.

CHAPTER VIII

MISS SPRAGUE DISCOVERS A SECRET

ABOUT this time it became known to one person in the village that the Larkins had in their possession a tin box, contents unknown.

This is the way it happened:

Among the best-known village residents was Miss Melinda Sprague, a maiden lady, who took a profound interest in the affairs of her neighbors. She seldom went beyond the limits of Groveton, which was her world. She had learned the business of dressmaking, and often did work at home for her customers. She was of a curious and prying disposition, and nothing delighted her more than to acquire the knowledge of a secret.

One day—a few days after Florence Grant's party—Mrs. Larkin was in her own chamber. She had the trunk open, having occasion to take something from it, when, with a light step, Miss Sprague entered the room. The widow, who was on her knees before the trunk, turning, recognized the intruder, not without displeasure.

"I hope you'll excuse my coming in so unceremoniously, Mrs. Larkin," said Melinda, effusively. "I knocked, but you didn't hear it, being upstairs, and I took the liberty, being as we were so well acquainted, to come upstairs in search of you."

"Yes, certainly," answered Mrs. Larkin, but her tone was constrained.

She quickly shut the lid of the trunk. There was only one thing among its contents which she was anxious to hide, but that Miss Melinda's sharp eyes had already discovered. Unfortunately, the tin box was at one side, in plain sight.

"What on earth does Mrs. Larkin do with a tin box?" she asked herself, with eager curiosity. "Can she have property that people don't know of? I always thought she was left poor."

Melinda asked no questions. The sudden closing of the trunk showed her that the widow would not be inclined to answer any questions.

"I won't let her think I saw anything," she said to herself. "Perhaps she'll get anxious and refer to it."

"We will go downstairs, Melinda," said Mrs. Larkin. "It will be more comfortable."

"If you have anything to do up here, I beg you won't mind me," said the spinster.

"No, I have nothing that won't wait."

So the two went down into the sitting-room.

"And how is Luke?" asked Miss Sprague, in a tone of friendly interest.

"Very well, thank you."

"Luke was always a great favorite of mine," continued the spinster. "Such a manly boy as he is!"

"He is a great help to me," said Mrs. Larkin.

"No doubt he is. He takes care of the schoolhouse, doesn't he?"

"Yes."

"How much pay does he get?"

"A dollar a week."

"I hope he will be able to keep the position."

"What do you mean, Melinda?" asked the widow, not without anxiety.

"You know Doctor Snodgrass has resigned on the school committee, and Squire Duncan has been elected in his place."

"Well?"

"Mrs. Flanagan went to him yesterday to ask to have her son Tim appointed janitor in place of Luke, and I heard that she received considerable encouragement from the squire."

"Do they find any fault with Luke?" asked Mrs. Larkin, jealously.

"No, not as I've heard; but Mrs. Flanagan said Luke had had it for a year, and now some one else ought to have the chance."

"Are you quite sure of this, Melinda?"

Miss Sprague, though over forty, was generally called by her first name, not as a tribute to her youth, but to the fact of her being still unmarried.

"Yes, I am; I had it from Mrs. Flanagan herself."

"I don't think Tim would do as well as Luke. He has never been able to keep a place yet."

"Just so; but, of course, his mother thinks him a polygon."

Probably Miss Sprague meant a paragon—she was not very careful in her speech, but Mrs. Larkin did not smile at her mistake. She was too much troubled at the news she had just heard. A dollar a week may seem a ridiculous trifle to some of my readers, but, where the entire income of the family was so small, it was a matter of some consequence.

"I don't think Luke has heard anything of this," said the widow. "He has not mentioned it to me."

"Perhaps there won't be any change, after all," said Melinda. "I am sure Tim Flanagan wouldn't do near as well as Luke."

Miss Melinda was not entirely sincere. She had said to Mrs. Flanagan that she quite agreed with her that Luke had been janitor long enough, and hoped Tim would get the place. She was in the habit of siding with the person she chanced to be talking with at the moment, and this was pretty well understood.

Luke, however, had heard of this threatened removal. For this, it may be said, Randolph was partly responsible. Just after Mrs. Flanagan's call upon the squire to solicit his official influence, Prince Duncan mentioned the matter to his son.

"How long has Luke Larkin been janitor at the schoolhouse?" he asked.

"About a year. Why do you ask?"

"Does he attend to the duties pretty well?"

"I suppose so. He's just fit to make fires and sweep the floor," answered Randolph, his lip curling.

"Mrs. Flanagan has been here to ask me to appoint her son Tim in Luke's place."

"You'd better do it, pa," said Randolph, quickly.

"Why? You say Luke is well fitted for the position."

"Oh, anybody could do as well, but Luke puts on airs. He feels too big for his position."

"I suppose Mrs. Larkin needs the money."

"So does Mrs. Flanagan," said Randolph.

"What sort of a boy is Tim? I have heard that he is lazy."

"Oh, I guess he'll do. Of course, I am not well acquainted with a boy like him," said the young aristocrat. "But I'm quite disgusted with Luke. He was at Florence Grant's party the other evening, and was cheeky enough to ask her to dance with him."

"Did she do so?"

"Yes; I suppose it was out of pity. He ought to have known better than to attend a party with such a suit. His coat and pantaloons were both too small for him, but he flourished around as if he were fashionably dressed."

Squire Duncan made no reply to his son's comments, but he

felt disposed, for reasons of his own, to appoint Tim Flanagan. He was hoping to be nominated for representative at the next election, and thought the appointment might influence the Irish vote in his favor.

"Shall you appoint Tim, pa?" asked Randolph.

"I think it probable. It seems only right to give him a chance. Rotation in office is a principle of which I approve."

"That's good!" thought Randolph, with a smile of gratification. "It isn't a very important place, but Luke will be sorry to lose it. The first time I see him I will give him a hint of it."

Randolph met Luke about an hour later in the village street. He did not often stop to speak with our hero, but this time he had an object in doing so.

CHAPTER IX

LUKE LOSES HIS POSITION

"LUKE LARKIN!"

Luke turned, on hearing his name called, and was rather surprised to see Randolph hastening toward him.

"How are you, Randolph?" he said politely.

"Where are you going?" asked Randolph, not heeding the inquiry.

"To the schoolhouse, to sweep out."

"How long have you been janitor?" asked Randolph, abruptly.

"About a year," Luke answered, in surprise.

"That's a good while."

Luke was puzzled. Why should Randolph feel such an interest, all at once, in his humble office?

"I suppose you know that my father is now on the school committee?" Randolph continued.

"Yes; I heard so."

"He thinks of appointing Tim Flanagan janitor in your place."

Luke's face showed his surprise and concern. The loss of his modest income would, as he knew, be severely felt by his mother and himself. The worst of it was, there seemed no chance in Groveton of making it up in any other way.

"Did your father tell you this?" he asked, after a pause.

"Yes; he just told me," answered Randolph, complacently.

"Why does he think of removing me? Are there any complaints of the way I perform my duties?"

"Really, my good fellow," said Randolph, languidly, "I can't enlighten you on that point. You've held the office a good while, you know."

"You are very kind to tell me—this bad news," said Luke, pointedly.

"Oh, don't mention it. Good morning. Were you fatigued after your violent exercise at Florence Grant's party?"

"No. Were you?"

"I didn't take any," said Randolph, haughtily. "I danced—I didn't jump round."

"Thank you for the compliment. Is there anything more you wish to say to me?"

"No."

"Then good morning."

When Luke was left alone he felt serious. How was he going to make up the dollar a week of which he was to be deprived? The more he considered the matter the further he was from thinking anything. He was not quite sure whether the news was reliable, or merely invented by Randolph to tease and annoy him. Upon this point, however, he was soon made certain. The next day, as he was attending to his duties in the schoolhouse, Tim Flanagan entered.

"Here's a note for you, Luke," he said.

Luke opened the note and found it brief but significant. It ran thus:

"LUKE LARKIN: I have appointed the bearer, Timothy Flanagan, janitor in your place. You will give him the key of the schoolhouse, and he will at once assume your duties.

"PRINCE DUNCAN."

"Well, Tim," said Luke, calmly, "it appears that you are going to take my place."

"Yes, Luke, but I don't care much about it. My mother went to the squire and got me the job. The pay's a dollar a week, isn't it?"

"Yes."

"That isn't enough."

"It isn't very much, but there are not many ways of earning money here in Groveton."

"What do you have to do?"

"Make the fire every morning and sweep out twice a week. Then there's dusting, splitting up kindlings, and so on."

"I don't think I'll like it. I ain't good at makin' fires."

"Squire Duncan writes you are to begin at once."

"Shure, I'm afraid I won't succeed."

"I'll tell you what, Tim. I'll help you along till you've got used to the duties. After a while they'll get easy for you."

"Will you now? You're a good feller, Luke. I thought you would be mad at losin' the job."

"I am not mad, but I am sorry. I needed the money, but no doubt you do, also. I have no grudge against you."

Luke had just started in his work. He explained to Tim how to do it, and remained with him till it was done.

"I'll come again to-morrow, Tim," he said. "I will get you well started, for I want to make it easy for you."

Tim was by no means a model boy, but he was warm-hearted, and he was touched by Luke's generous treatment.

"I say, Luke," he exclaimed, "I don't want to take your job. Say the word, and I'll tell mother and the squire I don't want it."

"No, Tim, it's your duty to help your mother. Take it and do your best."

On his way home Luke chanced to meet the squire, walking in his usual dignified manner toward the bank, of which he was president.

"Squire Duncan," he said, walking up to him in a manly way, "I would like to speak a word to you."

"Say on, young man."

"Tim Flanagan handed me a note from you this morning ordering me to turn over my duties as janitor to him."

"Very well?"

"I have done so, but I wish to ask you if I have been removed on account of any complaints that my work was not well done?"

"I have heard no complaints," answered the squire. "I appointed Timothy in your place because I approved of rotation in office. It won't do any good for you to make a fuss about it."

"I don't intend to make a fuss, Squire Duncan," said Luke, proudly. "I merely wished to know if there were any charges against me."

"There are none."

"Then I am satisfied. Good morning, sir."

"Stay, young man. Is Timothy at the schoolhouse?"

"Yes, sir. I gave him some instruction about the work, and promised to go over to-morrow to help him."

"Very well."

Squire Duncan was rather relieved to find that Luke did not propose to make any fuss. His motive, as has already been stated, was a political one. He wished to ingratiate himself with Irish voters and obtain an election as representative; not that he cared so much for this office, except as a stepping-stone to something higher.

Luke turned his steps homeward. He dreaded communicating the news to his mother, for he knew that it would depress her, as it had him. However, it must be known sooner or later, and he must not shrink from telling her.

"Mother," he said, as he entered the room where she was sewing, "I have lost my job as janitor."

"I expected you would, Luke," said his mother, soberly.

"Who told you?" asked Luke, in surprise.

"Melinda Sprague was here yesterday and told me Tim Flanagan was to have it."

"Miss Sprague seems to know everything that is going on."

"Yes, she usually hears everything. Have you lost the place already?"

"Tim brought me a note this morning from Squire Duncan informing me that I was removed and he was put in my place."

"It is going to be a serious loss to us, Luke," said Mrs. Larkin, gravely.

"Yes, mother, but I am sure something will turn up in its place."

Luke spoke confidently, but it was a confidence he by no means felt.

"It is a sad thing to be so poor as we are," said Mrs. Larkin, with a sigh.

"It is very inconvenient, mother, but we ought to be glad that we have perfect health. I am young and strong, and I am sure I can find some other way of earning a dollar a week."

"At any rate, we will hope so, Luke."

Luke went to bed early that night. The next morning, as they were sitting at breakfast, Melinda Sprague rushed into the house and sank into a chair, out of breath.

"Have you heard the news?"

"No. What is it?"

"The bank has been robbed! A box of United States bonds has been taken, amounting to thirty or forty thousand dollars!"

Luke and his mother listened in amazement.

CHAPTER X

MELINDA MAKES MISCHIEF

"WHERE did you hear this, Melinda?" asked Mrs. Larkin.

"I called on Mrs. Duncan just now—I was doing some work for her—and she told me. Isn't it awful?"

"Was the bank broken open last night, Miss Sprague?" asked Luke.

"I don't know when it was entered."

"I don't understand it at all," said Luke, looking puzzled.

"All I know is that, on examining the safe, the box of bonds was missing."

"Then it might have been taken some time since?"

"Yes, it might."

The same thought came to Luke and his mother at once. Was the mysterious stranger the thief, and had he robbed the bank and transferred the tin box to Luke? It might be so, but, as this happened more than a fortnight since, it would have been strange in that case that the box had not been missed sooner at the bank. Luke longed to have Miss Sprague go, that he might confer with his mother on this subject. He had been told to keep the possession of the box secret, and therefore he didn't wish to reveal the fact that he had it unless it should prove to be necessary.

"Were any traces of the robber discovered?" he added.

"Not that I heard of; but I pity the thief, whoever he is," remarked Melinda. "When he's found out he will go to jail, without any doubt."

"I can't understand, for my part, how an outside party could open the safe," said Mrs. Larkin. "It seems very mysterious."

"There's many things we can't understand," said Melinda, shaking her head sagely. "All crimes are mysterious."

"I hope they'll find out who took the bonds," said the widow. "Did they belong to the bank?"

"No, they belonged to a gentleman in Cavendish, who kept them in the bank, thinking they would be safer than in his own house. Little did he know what iniquity there was even in quiet country places like Groveton."

"Surely, Melinda, you don't think any one in Groveton robbed the bank?" said Mrs. Larkin.

"There's no knowing!" said Miss Sprague, solemnly. "There's those that we know well, or think we do, but we cannot read their hearts and their secret ways."

"Have you any suspicions, Miss Sprague?" asked Luke, considerably amused at the portentous solemnity of the visitor.

"I may and I may not, Luke," answered Melinda, with the air of one who knew a great deal more than she chose to tell; "but it isn't proper for me to speak at present."

Just then Miss Sprague saw some one passing who, she thought, had not heard of the robbery, and, hastily excusing herself, she left the house.

"What do you think, Luke?" asked his mother, after the spinster had gone. "Do you think the box we have was taken from the bank?"

"No, I don't, mother. I did think it possible at first, but it seems very foolish for the thief, if he was one, to leave the box in the same village, in the charge of a boy. It would have been more natural and sensible for him to open it, take out the bonds, and throw it away or leave it in the woods."

"There is something in that," said Mrs. Larkin, thoughtfully. "There is certainly a mystery about our box, but I can't think it was stolen from the bank."

Meanwhile, Miss Sprague had formed an important resolve. The more she thought of it, the more she believed the missing box was the one of which she had caught a glimpse of in Mrs. Larkin's trunk. True, Luke and the widow had not betrayed that confusion and embarrassment which might have been anticipated when the theft was announced, but she had noticed the look exchanged between them, and she was sure it meant something. Above all, her curiosity was aroused to learn how it happened that a woman as poor as the Widow Larkin should have a tin box in her trunk, the contents of which might be presumed to be valuable.

"I don't like to get Luke and his mother into trouble," Melinda said to herself, "but I think it my duty to tell all I know. At any rate, they will have to tell how the box came into their possession, and what it contains. I'll go to the bank and speak to Squire Duncan."

Prince Duncan had called an extra meeting of the directors to consider the loss which had been discovered, and they were now seated in the bank parlor. There were three of them present, all of whom resided in Groveton—Mr. Manning, the hotelkeeper; Mr. Bailey, a storekeeper, and Mr. Beane, the Groveton lawyer.

Miss Sprague entered the bank and went up to the little window presided over by the paying-teller.

"Is Squire Duncan in the bank?" she asked.

"Yes, Miss Sprague."

"I would like to speak with him."

"That is impossible. He is presiding at a directors' meeting."

"Still, I would like to see him," persisted Melinda.

"You will have to wait," said the paying-teller, coldly. He had no particular respect or regard for Miss Sprague, being quite familiar with her general reputation as a gossip and busybody.

"I think he would like to see me," said Melinda, nodding her head with mysterious significance. "There has been a robbery at the bank, hasn't there?"

"Do you know anything about it, Miss Sprague?" demanded the teller, in surprise.

"Maybe I do, and maybe I don't; but I've got a secret to tell to Squire Duncan."

"I don't believe it amounts to anything," thought the teller. "Well, I will speak to Squire Duncan," he said aloud.

He went to the door of the directors' room, and after a brief conference with Prince Duncan he returned with the message, "You may go in, Miss Sprague."

She nodded triumphantly, and with an air of conscious importance walked to the bank parlor.

Prince Duncan and his associates were sitting round a mahogany table.

Melinda made a formal curtsy and stood facing them.

"I understand, Miss Sprague, that you have something to communicate to us in reference to the loss the bank has just sustained," said the squire, clearing his throat.

"I thought it my duty to come and tell you all I knew, Squire Duncan and gentlemen," said Melinda.

"Quite right, Miss Sprague. Now, what can you tell us?"

"The article lost was a tin box, was it not?"

"Yes."

"About so long?" continued Miss Sprague, indicating a length of about fifteen inches.

"Yes."

"What was there in it?"

"Government bonds."

"I know where there is such a box," said Miss Sprague, slowly.

"Where? Please be expeditious, Miss Sprague."

"A few days since I was calling on Mrs. Larkin—Luke's mother—just happened in, as I may say, and, not finding her downstairs, went up into her chamber. I don't think she heard me, for when I entered the chamber and spoke to her she seemed quite flustered. She was on her knees before an open trunk, and in that trunk I saw the tin box."

The directors looked at each other in surprise, and Squire Duncan looked undeniably puzzled.

"I knew the box was one such as is used to hold valuable papers and bonds," proceeded Melinda, "and, as I had always looked on the widow as very poor, I didn't know what to make of it."

"Did you question Mrs. Larkin about the tin box?" asked Mr. Beane.

"No; she shut the trunk at once, and I concluded she didn't want me to see it."

"Then you did not say anything about it?"

"No; but I went in just now to tell her about the bank being robbed."

"How did it seem to affect her?" asked Mr. Bailey.

"She and Luke—Luke was there, too—looked at each other in dismay. It was evident that they were thinking of the box in the trunk."

Melinda continued her story, and the directors were somewhat impressed.

"I propose," said Mr. Manning, "that we get out a search-warrant and search Mrs. Larkin's cottage. That box may be the one missing from the bank."

CHAPTER XI

LUKE IS ARRESTED

JUST after twelve o'clock, when Luke was at home eating dinner, a knock was heard at the front door.

"I'll go, mother," said Luke, and he rose from the table, and, going into the entry, opened the outer door.

His surprise may be imagined when he confronted Squire Duncan and the gentlemen already mentioned as directors of the Groveton bank.

"Did you wish to see mother?" he asked.

"Yes; we have come on important business," said Squire Duncan, pompously.

"Walk in, if you please."

Luke led the way into the little sitting-room, followed by the visitors. The dinner-table was spread in the kitchen adjoining. The room looked very much filled up with the unwonted company, all being large men.

"Mother," called Luke, "here are some gentlemen who wish to see you."

The widow entered the room, and looked with surprise from one to another. All waited for Squire Duncan, as the proper person, from his official position, to introduce the subject of their visit.

"Mrs. Larkin," said the squire, pompously, "it has possibly come to your ears that the Groveton Bank, of which you are aware that I am the president, has been robbed of a box of bonds?"

"Yes, sir. I was so informed by Miss Melinda Sprague this morning."

"I am also informed that you have in your custodv a tin box similar to the one that has been taken."

He expected to see Mrs. Larkin show signs of confusion, but she answered calmly: "I have a box in my custody, but whether it resembles the one lost I can't say."

"Ha! you admit that you hold such a box?" said the squire, looking significantly at his companions.

"Certainly. Why should I not?"

"Are you willing to show it to us?"

"Yes, we are willing to show it," said Luke, taking it upon himself to answer, "but I have no idea that it will do you any good."

"That is for us to decide, young man," said Squire Duncan.

"Do you suppose it is the box missing from the bank, sir?"

"It may be."

"When did you miss the box?"

"Only this morning, but it may have been taken a month ago."

"This box has been in our possession for a fortnight."

"Such is your statement, Luke."

"It is the truth," said Luke, flushing with indignation.

"My boy," said Mr. Beane, "don't be angry. I, for one, have no suspicion that you have done anything wrong, but it is our duty to inquire into this matter."

"Who told you that we had such a box, Mr. Beane?"

"Miss Melinda Sprague was the informant."

"I thought so, mother," said Luke. "She is a prying old maid, and it is just like her."

"Miss Sprague only did her duty," said the squire. "But we are losing time. We require you to produce the box."

"I will get it, gentlemen," said the widow, calmly.

While she was upstairs, Mr. Manning inquired: "Where did you get the box, Luke?"

"If you identify it as the box taken from the bank," answered Luke, "I will tell you. Otherwise I should prefer to say nothing, for it is a secret of another person."

"Matters look very suspicious, in my opinion, gentlemen," said Squire Duncan, turning to his associates.

"Not necessarily," said Mr. Beane, who seemed inclined to favor our hero. "Luke may have a good reason for holding his tongue."

Here Mrs. Larkin presented herself with the missing box. Instantly it became an object of attention.

"It looks like the missing box," said the squire.

"Of course, I can offer no opinion," said Mr. Beane, "not having seen the one lost. Such boxes, however, have a general resemblance to each other."

"Have you the key that opens it?" asked the squire.

"No, sir."

"Squire Duncan," asked Mr. Beane, "have you the key unlocking the missing box?"

"No, sir," answered Squire Duncan, after a slight pause.

"Then I don't think we can decide as to the identity of the two boxes."

The trustees looked at each other in a state of indecision. No one knew what ought to be done.

"What course do you think we ought to take, Squire Duncan?" asked Mr. Bailey.

"I think," said the bank president, straightening up, "that there is sufficient evidence to justify the arrest of this boy Luke."

"I have done nothing wrong, sir," said Luke, indignantly. "I am no more of a thief than you are."

"Do you mean to insult me, you young jackanapes?" demanded Mr. Duncan, with an angry flush on his face.

"I intend to insult no one, but I claim that I have done nothing wrong."

"That is what all criminals say," sneered the squire.

Luke was about to make an angry reply, but Mr. Beane, waving his hand as a signal for our hero to be quiet, remarked calmly: "I think, Duncan, in justice to Luke, we ought to hear his story as to how the box came into his possession."

"That is my opinion," said Mr. Bailey. "I don't believe Luke is a bad boy."

Prince Duncan felt obliged to listen to that suggestion, Mr. Bailey and Mr. Beane being men of consideration in the village.

"Young man," he said, "we are ready to hear your story. From whom did you receive this box?"

"From a man named Roland Reed," answered Luke.

The four visitors looked at each other in surprise.

"And who is Roland Reed?" asked the president of the bank. "It seems very much like a fictitious name."

"It may be, for aught I know," said Luke, "but it is the name given me by the person who gave me the box to keep for him."

"State the circumstances," said Mr. Beane.

"About two weeks since I was returning from the house of Miss Almira Clark, where I had gone on an errand for my mother. To shorten my journey, I took my way through the woods. I had nearly passed through to the other side, when a tall man, dark complexioned, whom I had never seen before stepped up to me. He asked me my name, and, upon my telling him, asked if I would do him a favor. This was to take charge of a tin box, which he carried under his arm."

"The one before us?" asked Mr. Manning.

"Yes, sir."

"Did he give any reason for making this request?"

"He said he was about to leave the neighborhood, and wished it taken care of. He asked me to put it under lock and key."

"Did he state why he selected you for this trust?" asked Mr. Beane.

"No, sir; he paid me for my trouble, however. He gave me a bank-note, which, when I reached home, I found to be a ten-dollar bill."

"And you haven't seen him since?"

"Once only."

"When was that?"

"On the evening of Florence Grant's party. On my way home the same man came up to me and asked if the box was safe. I answered, 'Yes.' He said, 'That is all—for the present,' and disappeared. I have not seen him since."

"That is a very pretty romance," said Prince Duncan, with a sneer.

"I can confirm it," said Mrs. Larkin, calmly. "I saw Luke bring in the box, and at his request I took charge of it. The story he told at that time is the same that he tells now."

"Very possibly," said the bank president. "It was all cut and dried."

"You seem very much prejudiced against Luke," said Mrs. Larkin, indignantly.

"By no means, Mrs. Larkin. I judge him and his story from the standpoint of common sense. Gentlemen, I presume this story makes the same impression on you as on me?"

Mr. Beane shook his head. "It may be true; it is not impossible," he said.

"You believe, then, there is such a man as Roland Reed?"

"There may be a man who calls himself such."

"If there is such a man, he is a thief."

"It may be so, but that does not necessarily implicate Luke."

"He would be a receiver of stolen property."

"Not knowing it to be such."

"At all events, I feel amply justified in causing the arrest of Luke Larkin on his own statement."

"Surely you don't mean this?" exclaimed Mrs. Larkin, in dismay.

"Don't be alarmed, mother," said Luke, calmly. "I am innocent of wrong, and no harm will befall me."

CHAPTER XII

LUKE AS A PRISONER

PRINCE DUNCAN, who was a magistrate, directed the arrest of Luke on a charge of robbing the Groveton Bank. The constable who was called upon to make the arrest performed the duty unwillingly.

"I don't believe a word of it, Luke," he said. "It's perfect nonsense to say you have robbed the bank. I'd as soon believe myself guilty."

Luke was not taken to the lock-up, but was put in the personal custody of Constable Perkins, who undertook to be responsible for his appearance at the trial.

"You mustn't run away, or you'll get me into trouble, Luke," said the good-natured constable.

"It's the last thing I'd be willing to do, Mr. Perkins," said Luke, promptly. "Then everybody would decide that I was guilty. I am innocent, and want a chance to prove it."

What was to be done with the tin box, was the next question.

"I will take it over to my house," said Squire Duncan.

"I object," said Mr. Beane.

"Do you doubt my integrity?" demanded the bank president, angrily.

"No; but it is obviously improper that any one of us should take charge of the box before it has been opened and its contents examined. We are not even certain that it is the one missing from the bank."

As Mr. Beane was a lawyer, Prince Duncan, though unwillingly, was obliged to yield. The box, therefore, was taken to the bank and locked up in the safe till wanted.

It is hardly necessary to say that the events at the cottage of Mrs. Larkin, and Luke's arrest, made a great sensation in the village. The charge that Luke had robbed the bank was received not only with surprise, but with incredulity. The boy was so well and so favorably known in Groveton that few could be found to credit the charge. There were exceptions, however. Melinda Sprague enjoyed the sudden celebrity she had achieved as the original discoverer of the thief who had plundered the bank. She was inclined to believe that Luke was guilty, because it enhanced her own importance.

"Most people call Luke a good boy," she said, "but there was always something about him that made me suspicious.

"There was something in his expression—I can't tell you what—that set me to thinkin' all wasn't right. Appearances are deceitful, as our old minister used to say."

"They certainly are, if Luke is a bad boy and a thief," retorted the other, indignantly. "You might be in better business, Melinda, than trying to take away the character of a boy like Luke."

"I only did my duty," answered Melinda, with an air of superior virtue. "I had no right to keep secret what I knew about the robbery."

"You always claimed to be a friend of the Larkins. Only last week you took tea there."

"That's true. I am a friend now, but I can't consent to cover up inquiry. Do you know whether the bank has offered any reward for the detection of the thief?"

"No," said the other, shortly, with a look of contempt at the eager spinster. "Even if it did, and poor Luke were found guilty, it would be blood-money that no decent person would accept."

"Really, Mrs. Clark, you have singular ideas," said the discomfited Melinda. "I ain't after no money. I only mean to do my duty, but if the bank should recognize the value of my services, it would be only right and proper."

There was another who heard with great satisfaction of Luke's arrest. This was Randolph Duncan. As it happened, he was late in learning that his rival had got into trouble, not having seen his father since breakfast.

"This is great news about Luke," said his friend Sam Noble, meeting him on the street.

"What news? I have heard nothing," said Randolph, eagerly.

"He has been arrested."

"You don't say so!" exclaimed Randolph. "What has he done?"

"Robbed the bank of a tin box full of bonds. It was worth an awful lot of money."

"Well, well!" ejaculated Randolph. "I always thought he was a boy of no principle."

"The tin box was found in his mother's trunk."

"What did Luke say? Did he own up?"

"No; he brazened it out. He said the box was given him to take care of by some mysterious stranger."

"That's too thin. How was it traced to Luke?"

"It seems Old Maid Sprague"—it was lucky for Melinda's peace of mind that she did not hear this contemptuous reference to her—"went to the Widow Larkin's house one day and saw the tin box in her trunk."

"She didn't leave the trunk open, did she?"

"No; but she had it open, looking into it, when old Melinda crept upstairs softly and caught her at it."

"I suppose Luke will have to go to State's prison," said Randolph, with a gratified smile.

"I hope it won't be quite so bad as that," said Sam, who was not equal in malice to his aristocratic friend.

"I haven't any pity for him," said Randolph, decidedly. "If he chooses to steal, he must expect to be punished."

Just then Mr. Hooper, the grammer-school teacher, came up.

"Mr. Hooper," said Randolph, eagerly, "have you heard about Luke?"

"I have heard that he has been removed from his janitorship, and I'm sorry for it."

"If he goes to jail he wouldn't be able to be janitor," said Randolph.

"Goes to jail! What do you mean?" demanded the teacher, sharply.

Hereupon Randolph told the story, aided and assisted by Sam Noble, to whom he referred as his authority.

"This is too ridiculous!" said Mr. Hooper, contemptuously. "Luke is no thief, and if he had the tin box he has given the right explanation of how he came by it."

"I know he is a favorite of yours, Mr. Hooper, but that won't save him from going to jail," said Randolph, tartly.

"If he is a favorite of mine," said the teacher, with dignity, "it is for a very good reason. I have always found him to be a high-minded, honorable boy, and I still believe him to be so, in spite of the grave accusation that has been brought against him."

There was something in the teacher's manner that deterred Randolph from continuing his malicious attack upon Luke. Mr. Hooper lost no time in inquiring into the facts of the case, and then in seeking out Luke, whom he found in the constable's house.

"Luke," he said, extending his hand, "I have heard that you were in trouble, and I have come to see what I can do for you."

"You are very kind, Mr. Hooper," said Luke, gratefully. "I hope you don't believe me guilty."

"I would as soon believe myself guilty of the charge, Luke."

"That's just what I said, Mr. Hooper," said Constable Perkins. "Just as if there wasn't more than one tin box in the world."

"You never told any one that you had a tin box in your custody, I suppose, Luke?"

"No, sir; the man who asked me to take care of it especially cautioned me to say nothing about it."

"What was his name?"

"Roland Reed."

"Do you know where to find him? It would be of service to you if you could obtain his evidence. It would clear you at once."

"I wish I could, sir, but I have no idea where to look for him."

"That is unfortunate," said the teacher, knitting his brows in perplexity. "When are you to be brought to trial?"

"To-morrow, I hear."

"Well, Luke, keep up a good heart and hope for the best."

"I mean to, sir."

CHAPTER XIII

IN THE COURT-ROOM

IT WAS decided that Luke should remain until his trial in the personal custody of Constable Perkins. Except for the name of it, his imprisonment was not very irksome, for the Perkins family treated him as an honored guest, and Mrs. Perkins prepared a nicer supper than usual. When Mr. Perkins went out he said to his wife, with a quizzical smile: "I leave Luke in your charge. Don't let him run away."

"I'll look out for that," said Mrs. Perkins, smiling.

"Perhaps I had better leave you a pistol, my dear?"

"I am afraid I should not know how to use it."

"You might tie my hands," suggested Luke.

"That wouldn't prevent your walking away."

"Then my feet."

"It won't be necessary, husband," said Mrs. Perkins. "I've got the poker and tongs ready."

But, though treated in this jesting manner, Luke could not help feeling a little anxious. For aught he knew, the tin box taken from his mother's trunk might be the same which had been stolen from the bank. In that case Roland Reed was not likely to appear again, and his story would be disbelieved. It was a strange one, he could not help admitting to himself. Yet he could not believe that the mysterious stranger was a burglar. If he were, it seemed very improbable that he would have left his booty within half a mile of the bank, in the very village where the theft had been committed. It was all very queer, and he could not see into the mystery.

"I should like to do something," thought Luke. "It's dull work sitting here with folded hands."

"Isn't there something I can do, Mrs. Perkins?" he said. "I am not used to sitting about the house idle."

"Well, you might make me some pies," said Mrs. Perkins.

"You'd never eat them if I did. I can boil eggs and fry potatoes. Isn't there some wood to saw and split?"

"Plenty out in the shed."

"I understand that, at any rate. Have you any objection to my setting to work?"

"No, if you won't run away."

"Send out Charlie to watch me."

Charlie was a youngster about four years of age, and very fond of Luke, who was a favorite with most young children.

"Yes, that will do. Charlie, go into the shed and see Luke saw wood."

"Yes, mama."

"Don't let him run away."

"No, I won't," said Charlie, gravely.

Luke felt happier when he was fairly at work. It took his mind off his troubles, as work generally does, and he spent a couple of hours in the shed. Then Mrs. Perkins came to the door and called him.

"Luke," she said, "a young lady has called to see the prisoner."

"A young lady! Who is it?"

"Florence Grant."

Luke's face brightened up with pleasure; he put on his coat and went into the house.

"Oh, Luke, what a shame!" exclaimed Florence, hastening to him with extended hand. "I only just heard of it."

"Then you're not afraid to shake hands with a bank burglar?" said Luke.

"No, indeed! What nonsense it is! Who do you think told me of your arrest?"

"Randolph Duncan."

"You have guessed it."

"What did he say? Did he seem to be shocked at my iniquity?"

"I think he seemed glad of it. Of course, he believes you guilty."

"I supposed he would, or pretend to, at any rate. I think his father is interested to make me out guilty. I hope you don't think there is any chance of it?"

"Of course not, Luke. I know you too well. I'd sooner suspect Randolph. He wanted to know what I thought of you now."

"And what did you answer?"

"That I thought the same as I always had—that you were one of the best boys in the village. 'I admire your taste,' said Randolph, with a sneer. Then I gave him a piece of my mind."

"I should like to have heard you, Florence."

"I don't know; you have no idea what a virago I am when I am mad. Now sit down and tell me all about it."

Luke obeyed, and the conversation was a long one, and seemed interesting to both. In the midst of it Linton Tomkins came in.

"Have you come to see the prisoner, also, Linton?" asked Florence.

"Yes, Florence. What a desperate-looking ruffian he is! I don't dare to come too near. How did you break into the bank, Luke?"

First Luke smiled, then he became grave. "After all, it is no joke to me, Linny," he said. "Think of the disgrace of being arrested on such a charge."

"The disgrace is in being a burglar, not in being arrested for one, Luke. Of course, it's absurd. Father wants me to say that if you are bound over for trial he will go bail for you to any amount."

"Your father is very kind, Linny. I may need to avail myself of his kindness."

The next day came, and at ten o'clock, Luke, accompanied by Constable Perkins, entered the room in which Squire Duncan sat as trial justice. A considerable number of persons were gathered, for it was a trial in which the whole village was interested. Among them was Mrs. Larkin, who wore an anxious, perturbed look.

"Oh, Luke," she said sorrowfully, "how terrible it is to have you here!"

"Don't be troubled, mother," said Luke. "We both know that I am innocent, and I rely on God to stand by me."

"Luke," said Mr. Beane, "though I am a bank trustee, I am your friend and believe you innocent. I will act as your lawyer."

"Thank you, Mr. Beane. I shall be very glad to accept your services."

The preliminary proceedings were of a formal character. Then Miss Melinda Sprague was summoned to testify. She professed to be very unwilling to say anything likely to injure her good friends, Luke and his mother, but managed to tell, quite dramatically, how she first caught a glimpse of the tin box.

"Did Mrs. Larkin know that you saw it?" asked the squire.

"She didn't know for certain," answered Melinda, "but she was evidently afraid I would, for she shut the trunk in a hurry, and seemed very much confused. I thought of this directly when I heard of the bank robbery, and I went over to tell Luke and his mother."

"How did they receive your communication?"

"They seemed very much frightened."

"And you inferred that they had not come honestly by the tin box?"

"It grieves me to say that I did," said Melinda, putting her handkerchief to her eyes to brush away an imaginary tear.

Finally Melinda sat down, and witnesses were called to testify to Luke's good character. There were more who wished to be sworn than there was time to hear. Mr. Beane called only Mr. Hooper, Mr. Tomkins and Luke's Sunday-school teacher. Then he called Luke to testify in his own defense.

Luke told a straightforward story—the same that he had told before—replying readily and easily to any questions that were asked him.

"I submit, Squire Duncan," said Mr. Beane, "that my client's statement is plain and frank and explains everything. I hold that it exonerates him from all suspicion of complicity with the robbery."

"I differ with you," said Squire Duncan, acidly. "It is a wild, improbable tale, that does not even do credit to the prisoner's invention. In my opinion, this mysterious stranger has no existence. Is there any one besides himself who has seen this Roland Reed?"

At this moment there was a little confusion at the door. A tall, dark-complexioned stranger pushed his way into the courtroom. He advanced quickly to the front.

"I heard my name called," he said. "There is no occasion to doubt my existence. I am Roland Reed!"

CHAPTER XIV

AN IMPORTANT WITNESS

THE effect of Roland Reed's sudden appearance in the courtroom, close upon the doubt expressed as to his existence, was electric. Every head was turned, and every one present looked with eager curiosity at the mysterious stranger. They saw a dark-complexioned, slender, but wiry man, above the middle height, with a pair of keen black eyes scanning, not without sarcastic amusement, the faces turned toward him.

Luke recognized him at once.

"Thank God!" he ejaculated, with a feeling of intense relief. "Now my innocence will be made known."

Squire Duncan was quite taken aback. His face betrayed his surprise and disappointment.

"I don't know you," he said, after a pause.

"Perhaps not, Mr. Duncan," answered the stranger, in a significant tone, "but I know you."

"Were you the man who gave this tin box to the defendant?"

"Wouldn't it be well, since this is a court, to swear me as a witness?" asked Roland Reed, quietly.

"Of course, of course," said the squire, rather annoyed to be reminded of his duty by this stranger.

This being done, Mr. Beane questioned the witness in the interest of his client.

"Do you know anything about the tin box found in the possession of Luke Larkin?" he asked.

"Yes, sir."

"Did you commit it to his charge for safe-keeping?"

"I did."

"Were you previously acquainted with Luke?"

"I was not."

"Was it not rather a singular proceeding to commit what is presumably of considerable value to an unknown boy?"

"It would generally be considered so, but I do many strange things. I had seen the boy by daylight, though he had never seen me, and I was sure I could trust him."

"Why, if you desired a place of safe-keeping for your box, did you not select the bank vaults?"

Roland Reed laughed, and glanced at the presiding justice.

"It might have been stolen," he said.

"Does the box contain documents of value?"

"The contents are valuable to me, at any rate."

"Mr. Beane," said Squire Duncan, irritably, "I think you are treating the witness too indulgently. I believe this box to be the one taken from the bank."

"You heard the remark of the justice," said the lawyer. "Is this the box taken from the bank?"

"It is not," answered the witness, contemptuously, "and no one knows this better than Mr. Duncan."

The justice flushed angrily.

"You are impertinent, witness," he said. "It is all very well to claim this box as yours, but I shall require you to prove ownership."

"I am ready to do so," said Roland Reed, quietly. "Is that the box on the table?"

"It is."

"Has it been opened?"

"No; the key has disappeared from the bank."

"The key is in the hands of the owner, where it properly belongs. With the permission of the court, I will open the box."

"I object," said Squire Duncan, quickly.

"Permit me to say that your refusal is extraordinary," said

Mr. Beane, pointedly. "You ask the witness to prove property, and then decline to allow him to do so."

Squire Duncan, who saw that he had been betrayed into a piece of folly, said sullenly: "I don't agree with you, Mr. Beane, but I withdraw my objection. The witness may come forward and open the box, if he can."

Roland Reed bowed slightly, advanced to the table, took a bunch of keys from his pocket, and inserting one of the smallest in the lock easily opened the box.

Those who were near enough, including the justice, craned their necks forward to look into the box.

The box contained papers, certificates of stock, apparently, and a couple of bank-books.

"The box missing from the vault contained government bonds, as I understand, Squire Duncan?" said the lawyer.

"Yes," answered the justice, reluctantly.

"Are there any government bonds in the box, Mr. Reed."

"You can see for yourself, sir."

The manner of the witness toward the lawyer was courteous, though in the tone in which he addressed the court there had been a scarcely veiled contempt.

"I submit, then, that my young client has been guilty of no wrong. He accepted the custody of the box from the rightful owner, and this he had a clear right to do."

"How do you know that the witness is the rightful owner of the box?" demanded the justice, in a cross tone. "He may have stolen it from some other quarter."

"There is not a shadow of evidence of this," said the lawyer, in a tone of rebuke.

"I am not sure but that he ought to be held."

"You will hold me at your peril, Mr. Duncan," said the witness, in clear, resolute tones. "I have a clear comprehension of my rights, and I do not propose to have them infringed."

Squire Duncan bit his lips. He had only a smattering of law, but he knew that the witness was right, and that he had been betrayed by temper into making a discreditable exhibition of himself.

"I demand that you treat me with proper respect," he said angrily.

"I am ready to do that," answered the witness, in a tone whose meaning more than one understood. It was not an apology calculated to soothe the ruffled pride of the justice.

"I call for the discharge of my young client, Squire Duncan," said the lawyer. "The case against him, as I hardly need say, has utterly failed."

"He is discharged," said the justice, unwillingly.

Instantly Luke's friends surrounded him and began to shower congratulations upon him. Among them was Roland Reed.

"My young friend," he said, "I am sincerely sorry that by any act of mine I have brought anxiety and trouble upon you. But I can't understand how the fact that you had the box in your possession became known."

This was explained to him.

"I have a proposal to make to you and your mother," said Roland Reed, "and with your permission I will accompany you home."

"We shall be glad to have you, sir," said Mrs. Larkin, cordially.

As they were making their way out of the court-room, Melinda Sprague, the cause of Luke's trouble, hurried to meet them. She saw by this time that she had made a great mistake, and that her course was likely to make her generally unpopular. She hoped to make it up with the Larkins.

"I am so glad you are acquitted, Luke," she began effusively. "I hope, Mrs. Larkin, you won't take offense at what I did. I did what I thought to be my duty, though with a bleeding heart. No one is more rejoiced at dear Luke's vindication."

"Miss Sprague," said she, "if you think you did your duty, let the consciousness of that sustain you. I do not care to receive any visits from you hereafter."

"How cruel and unfeeling you are, Mrs. Larkin," said the spinster, putting her handkerchief to her eyes.

Mrs. Larkin did not reply.

Miss Sprague found herself so coldly treated in the village that she shortly left Groveton on a prolonged visit to some relatives in a neighboring town. It is to be feared that the consciousness of having done her duty did not wholly console her. What she regretted most, however, was the loss of the reward which she had hoped to receive from the bank.

CHAPTER XV

THE LARKINS ARE IN LUCK

LUKE and his mother, accompanied by Roland Reed, took their way from the court-room to the widow's modest cottage.

"You may take the tin box, Luke," said the stranger, "if you are not afraid to keep in your charge what has given you so much trouble."

"All's well that ends well!" said Luke.

"Yes; I don't think it will occasion you any further anxiety."

Roland Reed walked in advance with Mrs. Larkin, leaving Luke to follow.

"What sort of a man is this Mr. Duncan?" he asked abruptly.

"Squire Duncan?"

"Yes, if that is his title."

"He is, upon the whole, our foremost citizen," answered the widow, after a slight hesitation.

"Is he popular?"

"I can hardly say that."

"He is president of the bank, is he not?"

"Yes."

"How long has he lived in Groveton?"

"Nearly twenty years."

"Was he born in this neighborhood?"

"I think he came from the West."

"Does he say from what part of the western country?"

"He says very little about his past life."

Roland Reed smiled significantly.

"Perhaps he has his reasons," he said meditatively.

"Is he thought to be rich?" he asked, after a pause.

"Yes, but how rich no one knows. He is taxed for his house and grounds, but he may have a good deal of property besides. It is generally thought he has."

"He does not appear to be friendly toward your son."

"No," answered Mrs. Larkin, with a trace of indignation, "though I am sure he has no cause to dislike him. He seemed convinced that Luke had come by your tin box dishonestly."

"It seemed to me that he was prejudiced against Luke. How do you account for it?"

"Perhaps his son, Randolph, has influenced him."

"So he has a son—how old?"

"Almost Luke's age. He thinks Luke beneath him, though why he should do so, except that Luke is poor, I can't understand. Not long since there was a skating match for a prize of a Waterbury watch, offered by the grammar-school teacher, which Luke would have won had not Randolph arranged with another boy to get in his way and leave the victory to him."

"So Randolph won the watch?"

"Yes."

"I suppose he had a watch of his own already."

"Yes, a silver one, while Luke had none. This makes it meaner in him."

"I don't mind it now, mother," said Luke, who had overheard the last part of the conversation. "He is welcome to his watches—I can wait."

"Has Squire Duncan shown his hostility to Luke in any other way?" inquired the stranger.

"Yes; Luke has for over a year been janitor at the schoolhouse. It didn't bring much—only a dollar a week—but it was considerable to us. Lately Squire Duncan was appointed on the school committee to fill a vacancy, and his first act was to remove Luke from his position."

"Not in favor of his son, I conclude."

Luke laughed.

"Randolph would be shocked at the mere supposition," he said. "He is a young man who wears kid gloves, and the duties of a school janitor he would look upon as degrading."

"I really think, Luke, you have been badly treated," said Roland Reed, with a friendly smile.

"I have thought so, too, sir, but I suppose I have no better claim to the office than any other boy."

"You needed the income, however."

"Yes, sir."

By this time they were at the door of the cottage.

"Won't you come in, sir?" asked Mrs. Larkin, cordially.

"Thank you. I will not only do so, but as I don't care to stay at the hotel, I will even crave leave to pass the night under your roof."

"If you don't mind our poor accommodations, you will be very welcome."

"I am not likely to complain, Mrs. Larkin. I have not been nursed in the lap of luxury. For two years I was a California miner, and camped out. For that long period I did not know what it was to sleep in a bed. I used to stretch myself in a blanket, and lie down on the ground."

"You won't have to do that here, Mr. Reed," said Luke, smiling. "But it must have been great fun."

"How can you say so, Luke?" expostulated his mother. "It must have been very uncomfortable, and dangerous to the health."

"I wouldn't mind it a bit, mother," said Luke, stoutly.

Roland Reed smiled.

"I am not surprised that you and your mother regard the matter from different points of view," he said. "It is only natural. Women are not adapted to roughing it. Boys like nothing better, and so with young men. But there comes a time—when a man passes forty—when he sets a higher value on the comforts of life. I don't mind confessing that I wouldn't care to repeat my old mining experiences."

"I hope you were repaid for your trouble and privations, sir."

"Yes, I was handsomely repaid. I may soon be as rich as your local magnate, Prince Duncan, but I have had to work harder for it, probably."

"So you know the squire's name?" said Mrs. Larkin, in some surprise.

"I must have heard it somewhere," remarked Roland Reed. "Have I got it right?"

"Yes; it's a peculiar name."

When they reached the cottage Mrs. Larkin set about getting supper. In honor of her guest she sent out for some steak, and baked some biscuit, so that the table presented an inviting appearance when the three sat down to it. After supper was over, Roland Reed said: "I told you that I wished to speak to you on business, Mrs. Larkin. It is briefly this: Are you willing to receive a boarder?"

"I am afraid, sir, that you would hardly be satisfied with our humble accommodations."

"Oh, I am not speaking of myself, but of a child. I am a widower, Mrs. Larkin, and have a little daughter eight years of age. She is now boarding in New York, but I do not like the people with whom I have placed her. She is rather delicate, also, and I think a country town would suit her better than the city air. I should like to have her under just such nice motherly care as I am sure you would give her."

"I shall be very glad to receive her," said Mrs. Larkin, with a flush of pleasure.

"And for the terms?"

"I would rather you would name them, sir."

"Then I will say ten dollars a week."

"Ten dollars!" exclaimed the widow, in amazement. "It won't be worth half that."

"I don't pay for board merely, but for care and attendance as well. She may be sick, and that would increase your trouble."

"She would in that case receive as much care as if she were my own daughter; but I don't ask such an exorbitant rate of board."

"It isn't exorbitant if I choose to pay it, Mrs. Larkin," said Mr. Reed, smiling. "I am entirely able to pay that price, and prefer to do so."

"It will make me feel quite rich, sir," said the widow, gratefully. "I shall find it useful, especially as Luke has lost his situation."

"Luke may find another position."

"When do you wish your daughter to come?" asked Mrs. Larkin.

"Luke will accompany me to the city to-morrow, and bring her back with him. By the way, I will pay you four weeks in advance."

He drew four ten-dollar bills from his pocket and put them into the widow's hand.

"I am almost afraid this is a dream," said Mrs. Larkin. "You have made me very happy."

"You mustn't become purse-proud, mother," said Luke, "because you have become suddenly rich."

"Can you be ready to take the first train to New York with me in the morning, Luke?" asked Roland Reed.

"Yes, sir; it starts at half-past seven."

"Your breakfast will be ready on time," said the widow, "and Luke will call you."

CHAPTER XVI

LUKE'S VISIT TO NEW YORK

THE morning train to New York carried among its passengers Luke and his new friend. The distance was thirty-five miles, and the time occupied was a trifle over an hour. The two sat together, and Luke had an opportunity of observing his companion more closely. He was a man of middle age, dark complexion, with keen black eyes, and the expression of one who understood the world and was well fitted to make his way in it. He had already given the Larkins to understand that he had been successful in accumulating money.

As for Luke, he felt happy and contented. The tide of fortune seemed to have turned in his favor, or rather in favor of his family. The handsome weekly sum which would be received for the board of Mr. Reed's little daughter would be sufficient of itself to defray the modest expenses of their household. If he, too, could obtain work, they would actually feel rich.

"Luke," said his companion, "does your mother own the cottage where you live?"

"Yes, sir."

"Free of incumbrance?"

"Not quite. There is a mortgage of three hundred dollars held by Squire Duncan. It was held by Deacon Tibbetts, but about three months since Squire Duncan bought it."

"What could be his object in buying it?"

"I don't know, sir. Perhaps the deacon owed him money."

"I am surprised, then, that he deprived you of your position as janitor, since it would naturally make it more difficult for you to meet the interest."

"That is true, sir. I wondered at it myself."

"Your house is a small one, but the location is fine. It would make a building lot suitable for a gentleman's summer residence."

"Yes, sir; there was a gentleman in the village last summer who called upon mother and tried to induce her to sell."

"Did he offer her a fair price?"

"No, sir; he said he should have to take down the cottage, and he only offered eight hundred dollars. Mother would have sold for a thousand."

"Tell her not to accept even that offer, but to hold on to the property. Some day she can obtain considerably more."

"She won't sell unless she is obliged to," replied Luke. "A few days since I thought we might have to do it. Now, with the generous sum which you allow for your little girl's board there will be no necessity."

"Has Squire Duncan broached the subject to your mother?"

"He mentioned it one day, but he wanted her to sell for seven hundred dollars."

"He is evidently sharp at a bargain."

"Yes, sir; he is not considered liberal."

There was one thing that troubled Luke in spite of the pleasure he anticipated from his visit to New York. He knew very well that his clothes were shabby, and he shrank from the idea of appearing on Broadway in a patched suit too small for him. But he had never breathed a word of complaint to his mother, knowing that she could not afford to buy him another suit, and he did not wish to add to her troubles. It might have happened that occasionally he fixed a troubled look on his clothes, but if Roland Reed noticed it he did not make any comment.

But when they reached New York, and found themselves on Broadway, his companion paused in front of a large clothing store with large plate-glass windows, and said, quietly: "Come in, Luke. I think you need some new clothes."

Luke's face flushed with pleasure, but he said, "I have no money, Mr. Reed."

"I have," said Roland Reed, significantly.

"You are very kind, sir," said Luke, gratefully.

"It costs little to be kind when you have more money than you know what to do with," said Reed. "I don't mean that I am a Vanderbilt or an Astor, but my income is much greater than I need to spend on myself."

A suit was readily found which fitted Luke as well as if it had been made for him. It was of gray mixed cloth, made in fashionable style.

"You may as well keep it on, Luke." Then to the shopman: "Have you a nice suit of black cloth, and of the same size?"

"Yes, sir," answered the salesman, readily.

"He may as well have two while we are about it. As to the

old suit, it is too small, and we will leave it here to be given away to some smaller boy."

Luke was quite overwhelmed by his new friend's munificence.

"I don't think mother will know me," he said, as he surveyed himself in a long mirror.

"Then I will introduce you or give you a letter of introduction. Have you a watch, Luke?"

"No, sir; you know I did not get the prize at the skating match."

"True; then I must remedy the deficiency."

They took the roadway stage down below the Astor House—it was before the days of Jacob Sharp's horse railway—and got out at Benedict's. There Mr. Reed made choice of a neat silver watch, manufactured at Waltham, and bought a plated chain to go with it.

"Put that in your vest pocket," he said. "It may console you for the loss of the Waterbury."

"How can I ever repay you for your kindness, Mr. Reed?" said Luke, overjoyed.

"I have taken a fancy to you, Luke," said his companion. "I hope to do more for you soon. Now we will go uptown, and I will put my little girl under your charge."

Luke had dreaded making a call at a nice city house in his old suit. Now he looked forward to it with pleasure, especially after his new friend completed his benefactions by buying him a new pair of shoes and a hat.

"Luke," asked his companion, as they were on their way uptown in a Sixth Avenue car, "do you know who owned the box of bonds taken from the Groveton Bank?"

"I have heard that it was a Mr. Armstrong, now traveling in Europe."

"How did he come to leave the box in a village bank?"

"He is some acquaintance of Squire Duncan, and spent some weeks last summer at the village hotel."

"Then probably he left the box there at the suggestion of Duncan, the president."

"I don't know, sir, but I think it very likely."

"Humph! This is getting interesting. The contents of the box were government bonds, I have heard."

"I heard Squire Duncan say so."

"Were they coupon or registered?"

"What difference would that make, sir?"

"The first could be sold without trouble by the thief, while the last could not be disposed of without a formal transfer from the owner."

"Then it would not pay to steal them?"

"Just so. Luke, do you know, a strange idea has come into my head."

"What is it, sir?"

"I think Prince Duncan knows more about how those bonds were spirited away than is suspected."

Luke was greatly surprised.

"You don't think he took them himself, do you?" he asked.

"That remains to be seen. It is a curious affair altogether. I may have occasion to speak of it another time. Are you a good writer?"

"Fair, I believe, sir."

"I have recently come into possession of a business in a city in Ohio, which I carry on through a paid agent. Among other things, I have bought out the old accounts. I shall need to have a large number of bills made out, covering a series of years, which I shall then put into the hands of a collector and realize so far as I can. This work, with a little instruction, I think you can do."

"I shall be very glad to do it, sir."

"You will be paid fairly for the labor."

"I don't need any pay, Mr. Reed. You have already paid me handsomely."

"You refer to the clothing and the watch? Those are gifts. I will pay you thirty cents an hour for the time employed, leaving you to keep the account. The books of the firm I have at the house where my daughter is boarding. You will take them back to Groveton with you."

"This is a fortunate day for me," said Luke. "It will pay me much better than the janitorship."

"Do your duty, Luke, and your good fortune will continue. But here is our street."

They left the car at the corner of Fourteenth Street and Sixth Avenue, and turning westward, paused in front of a four-story house of good appearance.

CHAPTER XVII

RANDOLPH IS MYSTIFIED

IN AN hour, Luke, with the little girl under his charge, was on his way to the depot, accompanied by Mr. Reed, who paid for their tickets, and bade them good-bye, promising to communicate with Luke.

Rosa Reed was a bright little girl of about eight years of age. She made no opposition to going with Luke, but put her hand confidently in his, and expressed much pleasure at the prospect of living in the country. She had been under the care of two maiden ladies, the Misses Graham, who had no love for children, and had merely accepted the charge on account of the liberal terms paid them by the father. They seemed displeased at the withdrawal of Rosa, and clearly signified this by their cold, stiff reception of Mr. Reed and Luke.

"The old girls don't like to part with Rosa," he said, with a smile, as they emerged into the street.

"Are you sorry to leave them, Rosa?" he inquired.

"No; they ain't a bit pleasant," answered the little girl, decidedly.

"Were they strict with you?" asked Luke.

"Yes; they were always saying, 'Little girls should be seen and not heard!' They didn't want me to make a bit of noise, and wouldn't let me have any little girls in to play with me. Are there any little girls at your home?"

"No, but there are some living near by, and they will come to see you."

"That will be nice," said Rosa, with satisfaction.

Directions were left to have the little girl's trunk go to Groveton by express, and, therefore, Luke was encumbered only by a small satchel belonging to his new charge.

Of the details of the journey it is unnecessary to speak. The two young travelers arrived at Groveton, and, as it chanced, reached Luke's cottage without attracting much observation. The door was opened by the widow, whose kind manner at once won the favor of the child.

"I like you much better than Miss Graham," she said, with childish frankness.

"I am glad of that, my child," said Mrs. Larkin. "I will try to make this a pleasant home for you."

"I like Luke, too," said Rosa.

"Really, Rosa, you make me blush," said Luke. "I am not used to hearing young ladies say they like me."

"I think he is a good boy," said Rosa, reflectively. "Isn't he, Mrs. Larkin?"

"I think so, my dear," said the widow, smiling.

"Then I suppose I shall have to behave like one," said Luke. "Do you think I have improved in appearance, mother?"

"I noticed your new suit at once, Luke."

"I have another in this bundle, mother; and that isn't all. Do you see this watch? I sha'n't mourn the loss of the Waterbury any longer."

"Mr. Reed is certainly proving a kind friend, Luke. We have much reason to be grateful."

"He has also provided me with employment for a time, mother." And then Luke told his mother about the copying he had engaged to do.

It is hardly necessary to say that the heart of the widow was unfeignedly thankful for the favorable change in their fortunes, and she did not omit to give thanks to Providence for raising up so kind and serviceable a friend.

About the middle of the afternoon Luke made his appearance in the village street. Though I hope my readers will not suspect him of being a dude, he certainly did enjoy the consciousness of being well dressed. He hoped he should meet Randolph, anticipating the surprise and disappointment of the latter at the evidence of his prosperity.

When Luke was arrested, Randolph rejoiced as only a mean and spiteful boy would be capable of doing at the humiliation and anticipated disgrace of a boy whom he disliked. He had indulged in more than one expression of triumph, and sought every opportunity of discussing the subject, to the disgust of all fair-minded persons. Even Sam Noble protested, though a toady of Randolph.

"Look here, Randolph," he said, "I don't like Luke overmuch, and I know he doesn't like me, but I don't believe he's a thief, and I am sorry he is in trouble."

"Then you are no friend of mine," said Randolph, looking black.

"Oh, I say, Randolph, you know better than that. Haven't I always stood up for you, and done whatever you wanted me to?"

"If you were my friend you wouldn't stand up for Luke."

"I am not a friend of his, and I am a friend of yours, but I don't want him to go to prison."

"I do, if he deserves it."

"I don't believe he does deserve it."

"That is what I complain of in you."

"The fact is, Randolph, you expect too much. If you want to break friendship, all right."

Randolph was amazed at this unexpected independence on the part of one whom he regarded as his bond slave; but, being hardly prepared to part with him, especially as his other follower, Tom Harper, had partially thrown off his allegiance, thought it prudent to be satisfied with Sam's expressions of loyalty, even if they did not go as far as he wished.

Randolph missed Luke at school on the day after the trial. Of course, he had no idea that our hero was out of school, and hastily concluded that on account of his trial he was ashamed to show himself.

"I don't wonder he doesn't want to show himself," he remarked to Tom Harper.

"Why not? He has been acquitted."

"Never mind. He has been under arrest, and may yet be guilty in spite of his acquittal. Have you seen him to-day?"

"No."

"Probably he is hiding at home. Well, it shows some sort of shame."

On his way home from school Randolph was destined to be surprised. Not far from his own house he met Luke, arrayed in his new suit, with a chain that looked like gold crossing his waistcoat. Instead of looking confused and ashamed, Luke looked uncommonly bright and cheerful.

Randolph was amazed. What could it all mean? He had intended not to notice Luke, but to pass him with a scornful smile, but his curiosity got the better of him.

"Why were you not at school to-day?" he asked, abruptly.

Luke smiled.

"I didn't think you would miss me, Randolph."

"I didn't, but wondered at your absence."

"I was detained by business. I expect to have the pleasure of seeing you there to-morrow."

"Humph! You seem to have invested in a new suit."

"Yes; my old suit was getting decidedly shabby, as you kindly remarked at Florence Grant's party."

"Where did you get them?"

"In New York."

"In New York!" repeated Randolph, in surprise. "When did you go there?"

"This morning. It was that which detained me from school."

"I see you've got a new watch-chain, too."

Randolph emphasized the word "chain" satirically, being under the impression that no watch was attached.

"Yes; you may like to see my new watch." And Luke, with pardonable triumph, produced his new watch, which was a stem-winder, whereas Randolph's was only a key-winder.

Randolph condescended to take the watch in his hands and examine it.

"Where was this bought?" he asked.

"At Benedict's."

"You seem to have plenty of money," he said, with unpleasant significance.

"I should like more."

"Only you are rather imprudent in making such extensive purchases so soon after your trial."

"What do you mean?" demanded Luke quickly.

"What should I mean? It is evident that you robbed the bank, after all. I shall tell my father, and you may find your trouble is not over."

"Look here, Randolph Duncan!" said Luke sternly, "I look upon that as an insult, and I don't mean to be insulted. I am no more a thief than you are, and that you know."

"Do you mean to charge me with being a thief?" fumed Randolph.

"No; I only say you are as much a thief as I am. If you repeat your insult, I shall be obliged to knock you down."

"You impudent loafer!" screamed Randolph. "You'll be sorry for this. I'll have you arrested over again."

"I have no doubt you would if you had the power. I sha'n't lie awake nights thinking of it. If you have nothing more to say I will leave you."

Randolph did not reply, probably because he was at a loss

what to say, but went home angry and mystified. Where could Luke have got his watch and new suit? He asked himself this many times, but no possible explanation suggested itself.

Scarcely had Luke parted with Randolph when he met his friend Linton, who surveyed Luke's improved appearance with pleasure and surprise.

"I say, Luke, are you setting up for a dude?"

"I thought a little of it," answered Luke, with a smile—and then he explained the cause of his good fortune. "I have only one regret," he added, "Randolph seems to be grieved over it. He liked me better in my old suit. Besides, I have a new watch, and it turns out to be better than his."

Here he displayed his new silver watch. Linton felt a generous pleasure in Luke's luck, and it may truly be said rejoiced more at it than he would at any piece of good fortune to himself.

"By the way, Luke," he said, "I am going to give a party next Thursday evening, and I give you the very first invitation. It is my birthday, you know."

"I accept with pleasure, sir. I look upon you as my warmest friend, and as long as I retain your friendship I shall not care for Randolph's malice."

CHAPTER XVIII

MR. DUNCAN'S SECRET

ABOUT two weeks later, Prince Duncan sat at his desk with a troubled look. Open before him were letters. One was postmarked London, and ran as follows:

"MY DEAR SIR: I have decided to shorten my visit, and shall leave Liverpool next Saturday en route for New York. You will see, therefore, that I shall arrive nearly as soon as the letter I am now writing. I have decided to withdraw the box of securities I deposited in your bank, and shall place it in a safe-deposit vault in New York. You may expect to see me shortly.

"Yours in haste,

"JOHN ARMSTRONG."

Drops of perspiration gathered on the brow of Prince Duncan as he read this letter. What would Mr. Armstrong say when he learned that the box had mysteriously disappeared? That he would be thoroughly indignant, and make it very unpleasant for the president of Groveton Bank, was certain. He would ask, among other things, why Mr. Duncan had not informed him of the loss by cable, and no satisfactory explanation could be given. He would ask, furthermore, why detectives had not been employed to ferret out the mystery, and here again no satisfactory explanation could be given. Prince Duncan knew very well that he had a reason, but it was not one that could be disclosed.

He next read the second letter, and his trouble was not diminished. It was from a Wall Street broker, informing him that the Erie shares bought for him on a margin had gone down two points, and it would be necessary for him to deposit additional margin, or be sold out.

"Why did I ever invest in Erie?" thought Duncan ruefully. "I was confidently assured that it would go up—that it must go up—and here it is falling, and Heaven knows how much lower it will go."

At this point the door opened, and Randolph entered. He had a special favor to ask. He had already given his father several hints that he would like a gold watch, being quite dissatisfied with his silver watch now that Luke Larkin possessed one superior to his. He had chosen a very unfavorable moment for his request, as he soon found out.

"Father," he said, "I have a favor to ask."

"What is it?" asked Prince Duncan, with a frown.

"I wish you would buy me a gold watch."

"Oh, you do!" sneered his father. "I was under the impression that you had two watches already."

"So I have, but one is a Waterbury, and the other a cheap silver one."

"Well, they keep time, don't they?"

"Yes."

"Then what more do you want?"

"Luke Larkin has a silver watch better than mine—a stem-winder."

"Suppose he has?"

"I don't want a working boy like him to outshine me."

"Where did he get his watch?"

"I don't know; he won't tell. Will you buy me a gold one, father? Then I can look down upon him again."

"No, I can't. Money is very scarce with me just now."

"Then I don't want to wear a watch at all," said Randolph pettishly.

"Suit yourself," said his father coldly. "Now you may leave the room. I am busy."

Randolph left the room. He would have slammed the door behind him, but he knew his father's temper, and he did not dare to do so.

"What am I to do?" Prince Duncan asked himself anxiously. "I must send money to the brokers, or they will sell me out, and I shall meet with a heavy loss."

After a little thought he wrote a letter enclosing a check, but dated it two days ahead.

"They will think it a mistake," he thought, "and it will give me time to turn around. Now for money to meet the check when it arrives."

Prince Duncan went up-stairs, and, locking the door of his chamber, opened a large trunk in one corner of the room. From under a pile of clothing he took out a tin box, and with hands that trembled with excitement he extracted therefrom a dozen government bonds. One was for ten thousand dollars, one for five, and the remainder were for one thousand dollars each.

"If they were only sold, and the money deposited in the bank to my credit," he thought. "I am almost sorry I started in this thing. The risk is very great, but—but I must have money."

At this moment some one tried the door.

Prince Duncan turned pale, and the bonds nearly fell from his hands.

"Who's there?" he asked.

"It is I, papa," answered Randolph.

"Then you may go down-stairs again," answered his father angrily. "I don't want to be disturbed."

"Won't you open the door a minute? I just want to ask a question."

"No, I won't. Clear out!" exclaimed the bank president angrily.

"What a frightful temper father has!" thought the discomfited Randolph.

There was nothing for it but to go down-stairs, and he did so in a very discontented frame of mind.

"It seems to me that something is going contrary," said Duncan to himself. "It is clear that it won't do to keep these bonds here any longer. I must take them to New York to-morrow—and raise money on them."

On second thought, to-morrow he decided only to take the five-thousand-dollar bond, and five of the one thousand, fearing that too large a sale at one time might excite suspicion.

Carefully selecting the bonds referred to, he put them away in a capacious pocket, and, locking the trunk, went down-stairs again.

"There is still time to take the eleven-o'clock train," he said, consulting his watch. "I must do it."

Seeking his wife, he informed her that he would take the next train for New York.

"Isn't this rather sudden?" she asked, in surprise.

"A little, perhaps, but I have a small matter of business to attend to. Besides, I think the trip will do me good. I am not feeling quite as well as usual."

"I believe I will go, too," said Mrs. Duncan unexpectedly. "I want to make some purchases at Stewart's."

This suggestion was very far from agreeable to her husband.

"Really—I am"—he said, "I must disappoint you. My time will be wholly taken up by matters of business, and I can't go with you."

"You don't need to. I can take care of myself, and we can meet at the depot at four o'clock."

"Besides, I can't supply you with any money for shopping."

'I have enough. I might have liked a little more, but I can make it do."

"Perhaps it will look better if we go in company," thought Prince Duncan. "She needn't be in my way, for we can part at the station."

"Very well, Jane," he said quietly. "If you won't expect me to dance attendance upon you, I withdraw my objections."

The eleven-o'clock train for New York had among its passengers Mr. and Mrs. Duncan.

There was another passenger whom neither of them noticed—a small, insignificant-looking man—who occasionally directed a quick glance at the portly bank president.

CHAPTER XIX

EFFECTING A LOAN

PRINCE DUNCAN was unusually taciturn during the railroad journey—so much so that his wife noticed it, and inquired the reason.

"Business, my dear," answered the bank president. "I am rather perplexed by a matter of business."

"Business connected with the bank, Mr. Duncan?" asked his wife.

"No, private business."

"Have you heard anything yet of the stolen bonds?"

"Not yet."

"Have you any suspicion?"

"None that I am at liberty to mention," answered Duncan, looking mysterious.

"I suppose you no longer suspect that boy Luke?"

"I don't know. The man who owns to having given him the tin box for safe-keeping is, in my opinion, a suspicious character. I shouldn't be at all surprised if he were a jailbird."

The small man already referred to, who occupied a seat just across the aisle, here smiled slightly, but whether at the president's remark, is not clear.

"What did he call himself?"

"Roland Reed—no doubt an alias."

"It seems to me you ought to follow him up, and see if you can't convict him of the theft."

"You may be sure, Jane, that the president and directors of the Groveton Bank will do their duty in this matter," said Mr. Duncan rather grandiloquently. "By the way, I have received this morning a letter from Mr. Armstrong, the owner of the stolen bonds, saying that he will be at home in a few days."

"Does he know of the loss?"

"Not yet."

"How will he take it?"

"Really, Jane, you are very inquisitive this morning. I presume he will be very much annoyed."

The car had become quite warm, and Mr. Duncan, who had

hitherto kept on his overcoat, rose to take it off. Unfortunately for him he quite forgot the bonds he had in the inside pocket, and in his careless handling of the coat the package fell upon the floor of the car, one slipping out of the envelope—a bond for one thousand dollars.

Prince Duncan turned pale, and stooped to pick up the package. But the small man opposite was too quick for him. He raised the package from the floor, and handing it to the bank president with a polite bow, said, with a smile: "You wouldn't like to lose this, sir."

"No," answered Duncan gruffly, angry with the other for anticipating him, "it was awkward of me."

Mrs. Duncan also saw the bond, and inquired with natural curiosity: "Do they belong to the bank, Mr. Duncan?"

"No; they are my own."

"I am glad of that. What are you going to do with them?"

"Hush! It is dangerous to speak of them here. Some one might hear, and I might be followed. I am very much annoyed that they have been seen at all."

This closed Mrs. Duncan's mouth, but she resolved to make further inquiries when they were by themselves.

Prince Duncan looked askance at his opposite neighbor. He was a man who had come to Groveton recently, and had opened a billiard saloon and bar not far from the bank. He was not regarded as a very desirable citizen, and had already excited the anxiety of parents by luring into the saloon some of the boys and young men of the village. Among them, though Squire Duncan did not know it, was his own son Randolph, who had already developed quite a fondness for playing pool, and even occasionally patronized the bar. This, had he known it, would have explained Randolph's increased applications for money.

Whether Tony Denton—his full name was Anthony Denton—had any special object in visiting New York, I am unable to state. At all events it appeared that his business lay in the same direction as that of Prince Duncan, for on the arrival of the train at the New York depot, he followed the bank president at a safe distance, and was clearly bent upon keeping him in view.

Mr. Duncan walked slowly, and appeared to be plunged in anxious thought. His difficulties were by no means over. He had the bonds to dispose of, and he feared the large amount might occasion suspicion. They were coupon bonds, and bore no name or other evidence of ownership. Yet the mere fact of having such a large amount might occasion awkward inquiries.

"Here's yer mornin' papers!" called a negro newsboy, thrusting his bundle in front of the country banker.

"Give me a *Herald*," said Mr. Duncan. Opening the paper, his eye ran hastily over the columns. It lighted up as he saw a particular advertisement.

"The very thing," he said to himself.

This was the advertisement:

"LOAN OFFICE—We are prepared to loan sums to suit, on first-class security, at a fair rate of interest. Call or address Sharp & Ketchum, No. — Wall Street. Third floor."

"I will go there," Prince Duncan suddenly decided. "I will borrow what I can on these bonds, and being merely held on collateral, they will be kept out of the market. At the end of six months, say, I will redeem them, or order them sold, and collect the balance, minus the interest."

Having arrived at this conclusion, he quickened his pace, his expression became more cheerful, and he turned his steps toward Wall Street.

"What did the old fellow see in the paper?" thought Tony Denton, who, still undiscovered, followed Mr. Duncan closely. "It is something that pleased him, evidently."

He beckoned the same newsboy, bought a *Herald* also, and turning to that part of the paper on which the banker's eyes had been resting, discovered Sharp & Ketchum's advertisement.

"That's it, I'll bet a hat," he decided. "He is going to raise money on the bonds. I'll follow him."

When Duncan turned into Wall Street, Tony Denton felt that he had guessed correctly. He was convinced when the bank president paused before the number indicated in the advertisement.

"It won't do for me to follow him in," he said to himself, "nor will it be necessary—I can remember the place and turn it to my own account by and by."

Prince Duncan went up-stairs, and paused before a door on which was inscribed:

SHARP & KETCHUM
BANKERS
LOANS NEGOTIATED

He opened the door, and found the room furnished in the style of a private banking-office.

"Is Mr. Sharp or Mr. Ketchum in?" he inquired of a sharp-faced young clerk, the son, as it turned out, of the senior partner.

"Yes, sir, Mr. Sharp is in."

"Is he at leisure? I wish to see him on business."

"Go in there, sir," said the clerk, pointing to a small private room in the corner of the office. Following the directions, Mr. Duncan found himself in the presence of a man of about fifty, with a hatchet face, much puckered with wrinkles, and a very foxy expression.

"I am Mr. Sharp," he said, in answer to an inquiry.

Prince Duncan unfolded his business. He wished to borrow eight or nine thousand dollars on ten thousand dollars' worth of United States Government bonds.

"Why don't you sell at once?" asked Sharp keenly.

"Because I wish, for special reasons, to redeem these identical bonds, say six months hence."

"They are your own?" asked Mr. Sharp.

"They are a part of my wife's estate, of which I have control. I do not, however, wish her to know that I have raised money on them," answered Duncan, with a smooth falsehood.

"Of course, that makes a difference. However, I will loan you seven thousand dollars, and you will give me your note for seven thousand five hundred, at the usual interest, with permission to sell the bonds at the end of six months if the note remains unpaid then, I to hand you the balance."

Prince Duncan protested against these terms as exorbitant, but was finally obliged to accede to them. On the whole, he was fairly satisfied. The check would relieve him from all his embarrassments and give him a large surplus.

"So far so good!" said Tony Denton, as he saw Mr. Duncan emerge into the street. "If I am not greatly mistaken this will prove a lucky morning for me."

CHAPTER XX

LUKE TALKS WITH A CAPITALIST

LUKE worked steadily on the task given him by his new patron. During the first week he averaged three hours a day, with an additional two hours on Saturday, making, in all, twenty hours, making, at thirty cents per hour, six dollars. This Luke considered fair pay, considering that he was attending school and maintaining good rank in his classes.

"Why don't we see more of you, Luke?" asked his friend Linton one day. "You seem to stay in the house all the time."

"Because I am at work, Linny. Last week I made six dollars."

"How?" asked Linton, surprised.

"By copying and making out bills for Mr. Reed."

"That is better than being janitor at a dollar a week."

"Yes, but I have to work a good deal harder."

"I am afraid you are working too hard."

"I shouldn't like to keep it up, but it is only for a short time. If I gave up school I should find it easy enough, but I don't want to do that."

"No, I hope you won't; I should miss you, and so would all the boys."

"Including Randolph Duncan?"

"I don't know about that. By the way, I hear that Randolph is spending a good deal of his time at Tony Denton's billiard saloon."

"I am sorry to hear it. It hasn't a very good reputation."

One day Luke happened to be at the depot at the time of the arrival of the train from New York. A small, elderly man stepped upon the platform whom Luke immediately recognized as John Armstrong, the owner of the missing box of bonds. He was surprised to see him, having supposed that he was still in Europe. Mr. Armstrong, as already stated, had boarded for several weeks during the preceding summer at Groveton.

He looked at Luke with a half-glance of recognition.

"Haven't I seen you before?" he said. "What is your name?"

"My name is Luke Larkin. I saw you several times last summer."

"Then you know me?"

"Yes, sir, you are Mr. Armstrong. But I thought you were in Europe."

"So I was till recently. I came home sooner than I expected."

Luke was not surprised. He supposed that intelligence of the robbery had hastened Mr. Armstrong's return.

"I suppose it was the news of your box that hurried you home," Luke ventured to say.

"No, I hadn't heard of it till my arrival in New York Can you tell me anything about the matter? Has the box been found?"

"Not that I have heard, sir."

"Was, or is, anybody suspected?"

"I was suspected," answered Luke, smiling, "but I don't think any one suspects me now."

"You!" exclaimed the capitalist, in evident astonishment. "What could induce any one to suspect a boy like you of robbing a bank?"

"There was some ground for it," said Luke candidly. "A tin box, of the same appearance as the one lost, was seen in our house. I was arrested on suspicion, and tried."

"You don't say so! How did you prove your innocence?"

"The gentleman who gave me the box in charge appeared and testified in my favor. But for that I am afraid I should have fared badly."

"That is curious. Who was the gentleman?"

Luke gave a rapid history of the circumstances already known to the reader.

"I am glad to hear this, being principally interested in the matter. However, I never should have suspected you. I claim to be something of a judge of character and physiognomy, and your appearance is in your favor. Your mother is a widow, I believe?"

"Yes, sir."

"And you are the janitor of the schoolhouse?"

Mr. Armstrong was a close observer, and though having large interests of his own, made himself familiar with the affairs of those whom others in his position would wholly have ignored.

"I was janitor," Luke replied, "but when Mr. Duncan became a member of the school committee he removed me."

"For what reason?" asked Mr. Armstrong quickly.

"I don't think he ever liked me, and his son Randolph and I have never been good friends."

"You mean Mr. Duncan, the president of the bank?"

"Yes, sir?"

"Why are not you and his son friends?"

"I don't know, sir. He has always been in the habit of sneering at me as a poor boy—a working boy—and unworthy to associate with him."

"You don't look like a poor boy. You are better dressed than I was at your age. Besides, you have a watch, I judge from the chain."

"Yes, sir; but all that is only lately. I have found a good friend who has been very kind to me."

"Who is he?"

"Roland Reed, the owner of the tin box I referred to."

"Roland Reed! I never heard the name. Where is he from?"

"From the West, I believe, though at present he is staying in New York."

"How much were you paid as janitor?"

"A dollar a week."

"That is very little. Is the amount important to you?"

"No, sir, not now." And then Luke gave particulars of the good fortune of the family in having secured a profitable boarder, and, furthermore, in obtaining for himself profitable employment.

"This Mr. Reed seems to be a kind-hearted and liberal man. I am glad for your sake. I sympathize with poor boys. Can you guess the reason?"

"Were you a poor boy yourself, sir?"

"I was, and a very poor boy. When I was a boy of thirteen and fourteen I ran around in overalls and bare-footed. But I don't think it did me any harm," the old man added, musingly. "It kept me from squandering money on foolish pleasures, for I had none to spend; it made me industrious and self-reliant, and when I obtained employment it made me anxious to please my employer."

"I hope it will have the same effect on me, sir."

"I hope so, and I think so. What sort of a boy is this son of Mr. Duncan?"

"If his father were not a rich man, I think he would be more agreeable. As it is, he seems to have a high idea of his own importance."

"So his father has the reputation of being a rich man, eh?"

"Yes, sir. We have always considered him so."

"Without knowing much about it?"

"Yes, sir; we judged from his style of living, and from his being president of a bank."

"That amounts to nothing. His salary as president is only moderate."

"I am sorry you should have met with such a loss, Mr. Armstrong."

"So am I, but it won't cripple me. Still, a man doesn't like to lose twenty-five thousand dollars and over."

"Was there as much as that in the box, sir?" asked Luke, in surprise.

"Yes, I don't know why I need make any secret of it. There were twenty-five thousand dollars in government bonds, and these, at present rates, are worth in the neighborhood of thirty thousand dollars."

"That seems to me a great deal of money," said Luke.

"It is, but I can spare it without any diminution of comfort. I don't feel, however, like pocketing the loss without making a strong effort to recover the money. I didn't expect to meet immediately upon arrival the only person hitherto suspected of accomplishing the robbery."

He smiled as he spoke, and Luke saw that, so far as Mr. Armstrong was concerned, he had no occasion to feel himself under suspicion.

"Are you intending to remain long in Groveton, Mr. Armstrong?" he asked.

"I can't say. I have to see Mr. Duncan about the tin box, and concoct some schemes looking to the discovery of the person or persons concerned in its theft. Have there been any suspicious persons in the village during the last few weeks?"

"Not that I know of, sir."

"What is the character of the men employed in the bank, the cashier and teller?"

"They seem to be very steady young men, sir. I don't think they have been suspected."

"The most dangerous enemies are those who are inside, for they have exceptional opportunities for wrongdoing. Moreover, they have the best chance to cover up their tracks."

"I don't think there is anything to charge against Mr. Roper and Mr. Barclay. They are both young married men, and live in a quiet way."

"Never speculate in Wall Street, eh? One of the soberest,

steadiest bank cashiers I ever knew, who lived plainly and frugally, and was considered by all to be a model man, wrecked the man he was connected with—a small country banker—and is now serving a term in State's prison. The cause was Wall Street speculation. This is more dangerous even than extravagant habits of living."

A part of this conversation took place on the platform of the railroad-station, and a part while they were walking in the direction of the hotel. They had now reached the village inn, and, bidding our hero good morning, Mr. Armstrong entered, and registered his name.

Ten minutes later he set out for the house of Prince Duncan.

CHAPTER XXI

THE DREADED INTERVIEW

MR. DUNCAN had been dreading the inevitable interview with Mr. Armstrong. He knew him to be a sharp man of business, clear-sighted and keen, and he felt that this part of the conference would be an awkward and embarrassing one. He had tried to nerve himself for the interview, and thought he had succeeded, but when the servant brought Mr. Armstrong's card he felt a sinking at his heart, and it was in a tone that betrayed nervousness that he said: "Bring the gentleman in."

"My dear sir," he said, extending his hand and vigorously shaking the hand of his new arrival, "this is an unexpected pleasure."

"Unexpected? Didn't you get my letter from London?" said Mr. Armstrong, suffering his hand to be shaken, but not returning the arm pressure.

"Certainly——"

"In which I mentioned my approaching departure?"

"Yes, certainly; but I didn't know on what day to expect you. Pray sit down. It seems pleasant to see you home safe and well."

"Humph!" returned Armstrong, in a tone by no means as cordial. "Have you found my box of bonds?"

"Not yet, but——"

"Permit me to ask you why you allowed me to remain ignorant

of so important a matter? I was indebted to the public prints, to which my attention was directed by an acquaintance, for a piece of news which should have been communicated to me at once."

"My dear sir, I intended to write you as soon as I heard of your arrival. I did not know till this moment that you were in America."

"You might have inferred it from the intimation in my last letter. Why did you not cable me the news?"

"Because," replied Duncan awkwardly, "I did not wish to spoil your pleasure, and thought from day to day that the box would turn up."

"You were very sparing of my feelings," said Armstrong, dryly—"too much so. I am not a child or an old woman, and it was your imperative duty, in a matter so nearly affecting my interests, to apprise me at once."

"I may have erred in judgment," said Duncan meekly, "but I beg you to believe that I acted as I supposed for the best."

"Leaving that out of consideration at present, let me know what steps you have taken to find out how the box was spirited away, or who was concerned in the robbery."

"I think that you will admit that I acted promptly," said the bank president complacently, "when I say that within twenty-four hours I arrested a party on suspicion of being implicated in the robbery, and tried him myself."

"Who was the party?" asked the capitalist, not betraying the knowledge he had already possessed on the subject.

"A boy in the village named Luke Larkin."

"Humph! What led you to think a boy had broken into the bank? That does not strike me as very sharp on your part."

"I had positive evidence that the boy in question had a tin box concealed in his house—in his mother's trunk. His poverty made it impossible that the box could be his, and I accordingly had him arrested."

"Well, what was the result of the trial?"

"I was obliged to let him go, though by no means satisfied of his innocence."

"Why?"

"A man—a stranger—a very suspicious-looking person, presented himself, and swore that the box was his, and that he had committed it to the charge of this boy."

"Well, that seems tolerably satisfactory, doesn't it?—that is, if he furnished evidence confirming his statement. Did he open the box in court?"

"Yes."

"And the bonds were not there?"

"The bonds were not there—only some papers, and what appeared to be certificates of stock."

"Yet you say you are still suspicious of this man and boy."

"Yes."

"Explain your grounds."

"I thought," replied the president, rather meekly, "he might have taken the bonds from the box and put in other papers."

"That was not very probable. Moreover, he would hardly be likely to leave the box in the village in the charge of a boy."

"The boy might have been his confederate."

"What is the boy's reputation in the village? Has he ever been detected in any act of dishonesty?"

"Not that I know of, but there is one suspicious circumstance to which I would like to call your attention."

"Well?"

"Since this nappened Luke has come out in new clothes, and wears a silver watch. The family is very poor, and he could not have had money to buy them unless he obtained some outside aid."

"What, then, do you infer?"

"That he has been handsomely paid for his complicity in the robbery."

"What explanation does he personally give of this unusual expenditure?"

"He admits that they were paid for by this suspicious stranger."

"Has the stranger—what is his name, by the way?"

"Roland Reed, he calls himself, but this, probably, is not his real name."

"Well, has this Reed made his appearance in the village since?"

"If so, he has come during the night, and has not been seen by any of us."

"I can't say I share your suspicion against Mr. Reed. Your theory that he took out the bonds and substituted other papers is far-fetched and improbable. As to the boy, I consider him honest and reliable."

"Do you know Luke Larkin?" asked Mr. Duncan quickly.

"Last summer I observed him somewhat, and never saw anything wrong in him."

"Appearances are deceitful," said the bank president sententiously.

"So I have heard," returned Mr. Armstrong dryly. "But let us go on. What other steps have you taken to discover the lost box?"

"I have had the bank vaults thoroughly searched," answered Duncan, trying to make the best of a weak situation.

"Of course. It is hardly to be supposed that it has been mislaid. Even if it had been it would have turned up before this. Did you discover any traces of the bank being forcibly entered?"

"No; but the burglar may have covered his tracks."

"There would have been something to show an entrance. What is the character of the cashier and teller."

"I know nothing to their disadvantage."

"Then neither have fallen under suspicion?"

"Not as yet," answered the president pointedly.

"It is evident," thought John Armstrong, "that Mr. Duncan is interested in diverting suspicion from some quarter. He is willing that these men should incur suspicion, though it is clear he has none in his own mind."

"Well, what else have you done? Have you employed detectives?" asked Armstrong, impatiently.

"I was about to do so," answered Mr. Duncan, in some embarrassment, "when I heard that you were coming home, and I though I would defer that matter for your consideration."

"Giving time in the meanwhile for the thief or thieves to dispose of their booty? This is very strange conduct, Mr. Duncan."

"I acted for the best," said Prince Duncan.

"You have singular ideas of what is best, then," observed Mr. Armstrong coldly. "It may be too late to remedy your singular neglect, but I will now take the matter out of your hands, and see what I can do."

"Will you employ detectives?" asked Duncan, with evident uneasiness.

Armstrong eyed him sharply, and with growing suspicion.

"I can't say what I will do."

"Have you the numbers of the missing bonds?" asked Duncan anxiously.

"I am not sure. I am afraid I have not."

Was it imagination, or did the bank president look relieved at this statement? John Armstrong made a mental note of this.

After eliciting the particulars of the disappearance of the bonds, John Armstrong rose to go. He intended to return to the city, but he made up his mind to see Luke first. He wanted to inquire the address of Roland Reed.

CHAPTER XXII

LUKE SECURES A NEW FRIEND

LUKE was engaged in copying when Mr. Armstrong called. Though he felt surprised to see his visitor, Luke did not exhibit it in his manner, but welcomed him politely, and invited him into the sitting-room.

"I have called to inquire the address of your friend, Mr. Roland Reed," said Mr. Armstrong. Then, seeing a little uneasiness in Luke's face, he added quickly: "Don't think I have the slightest suspicion of him as regards the loss of the bonds. I wish only to consult him, being myself at a loss what steps to take. He may be able to help me."

Of course, Luke cheerfully complied with his request.

"Has anything been heard yet at the bank?" he asked.

"Nothing whatever. In fact, it does not appear to me that any very serious efforts have been made to trace the robber or robbers. I am left to undertake the task myself."

"If there is anything I can do to help you, Mr. Armstrong, I shall be very glad to do sc," said Luke.

"I will bear that in mind, and may call upon you. As yet, my plans are not arranged. Perhaps Mr. Reed, whom I take to be an experienced man of the world, may be able to offer a suggestion. You seem to be at work," he added, with a look at the table at which Luke had been sitting.

"Yes, sir, I am making out some bills for Mr. Reed."

"Is the work likely to occupy you long?"

"No, sir; I shall probably finish the work this week."

"And then your time will be at your disposal?"

"Yes, sir."

"Pardon me the question, but I take it your means are limited?"

"Yes, sir; till recently they have been very limited—now, thanks to Mr. Reed, who pays a liberal salary for his little girl's board, we are very comfortable, and can get along very well, even if I do not immediately find work."

"I am glad to hear that. If I should hear of any employment likely to please you I will send you word."

"Thank you, sir."

"Would you object to leave home?"

"No, sir; there is little or no prospect in Groveton, and though my mother would miss me, she now has company, and I should feel easier about leaving her."

"If you can spare the time, won't you walk with me to the depot?"

"With great pleasure, sir," and Luke went into the adjoining room to fetch his hat, at the same time apprising his mother that he was going out.

On the way to the depot Mr. Armstrong managed to draw out Luke with a view to getting better acquainted with him, and forming an idea of his traits of character. Luke was quite aware of this, but talked frankly and easily, having nothing to conceal.

"A thoroughly good boy, and a smart boy, too!" said Armstrong to himself. "I must see if I can't give him a chance to rise. He seems absolutely reliable."

On the way to the depot they met Randolph Duncan, who eyed them curiously. He recognized Mr. Armstrong as the owner of the stolen bonds—and was a good deal surprised to see him in such friendly conversation with Luke. Knowing Mr. Armstrong to be a rich man, he determined to claim acquaintance.

"How do you do, Mr. Armstrong?" he said, advancing with an ingratiating smile.

"This is Randolph Duncan," said Luke—whom, by the way, Randolph had not thought it necessary to notice.

"I believe I have met the young gentleman before," said Mr. Armstrong politely, but not cordially.

"Yes, sir, I have seen you at our house," continued Randolph—"my father is president of the Groveton Bank. He will be very glad to see you. Won't you come home with me?"

"I have already called upon your father," said Mr. Armstrong.

"I am very sorry your bonds were stolen, Mr. Armstrong."

"Not more than I am, I assure you," returned Mr. Armstrong, with a quizzical smile.

"Could I speak with you a moment in private, sir?" asked Randolph, with a significant glance at Luke.

"Certainly; Luke, will you cross the road a minute? Now, young man!"

"Probably you don't know that the boy you are walking with was suspected of taking the box from the bank."

"I have heard so; but he was acquitted of the charge, wasn't he?"

"My father still believes that he had something to do with it, and so do I," added Randolph, with an emphatic nod of his head.

"Isn't he a friend of yours?" asked Mr. Armstrong quietly.

"No, indeed; we go to the same school, though father thinks of sending me to an academy out of town soon, but there is no friendship between us. He is only a working boy."

"Humph! That is very much against him," observed Mr. Armstrong, but it was hard to tell from his tone whether he spoke in earnest or ironically.

"Oh, well, he has to work, for the family is very poor. He's come out in new clothes and a silver watch since the robbery. He says the strange man from whom he received a tin box just like yours gave them to him."

"And you think he didn't get them in that way?"

"Yes, I think they were leagued together. I feel sure that man robbed the bank."

"Dear me, it does look suspicious!" remarked Armstrong.

"If Luke was guiding you to the train, I will take his place, sir."

"Thank you, but perhaps I had better keep him with me, and cross-examine him a little. I suppose I can depend upon your keeping your eyes upon him, and letting me know of any suspicious conduct on his part?"

"Yes, sir, I will do it with pleasure," Randolph announced promptly. He felt sure that he had excited Mr. Armstrong's suspicions, and defeated any plans Luke might have cherished of getting in with the capitalist.

"Have you anything more to communicate?" asked Mr. Armstrong, politely.

"No, sir; I thought it best to put you on your guard."

"I quite appreciate your motives, Master Randolph. I shall

keep my eyes open henceforth, and hope in time to discover the real perpetrator of the robbery. Now, Luke."

"I have dished you, young fellow!" thought Randolph, with a triumphant glance at the unconscious Luke. He walked away in high self-satisfaction.

"Luke," said Mr. Armstrong, as they resumed their walk, "Randolph seems a very warm friend of yours."

"I never thought so," said Luke, with an answering smile. "I am glad if he has changed."

"What arrangements do you think I have made with him?"

"I don't know, sir."

"I have asked him to keep his eye on you, and, if he sees anything suspicious, to let me know."

Luke would have been disturbed by this remark, had not the smile on Mr. Armstrong's face belied his words.

"Does he think you are in earnest, sir?"

"Oh, yes, he has no doubt of it. He warned me of your character, and said he was quite sure that you and your friend Mr. Reed were implicated in the bank robbery. I told him I would cross-examine you, and see what I could find out. Randolph told me that you were only a working boy, which I pronounced to be very much against you."

Luke laughed outright.

"I think you are fond of a practical joke, Mr. Armstrong," he said. "You have fooled Randolph very neatly."

"I had an object in it," said Mr. Armstrong quietly. "I may have occasion to employ you in the matter, and if so, it will be well that no arrangement is suspected between us. Randolph will undoubtedly inform his father of what happened this morning."

"As I said before, sir, I am ready to do anything that lies in my power."

Luke could not help feeling curious as to the character of the service he would be called upon to perform. He found it difficult to hazard a conjecture, but one thing at least seemed clear, and this was that Mr. Armstrong was disposed to be his friend, and as he was a rich man his friendship was likely to amount to something.

They had now reached the depot, and in ten minutes the train was due.

"Don't wait if you wish to get to work, Luke," said Mr. Armstrong kindly.

"My work can wait; it is nearly finished," said Luke.

The ten minutes passed rapidly, and with a cordial good-bye, the capitalist entered the train, leaving Luke to return to his modest home in good spirits.

"I have two influential friends, now," he said to himself—"Mr. Reed and Mr. Armstrong. On the whole, Luke Larkin, you are in luck, your prospects look decidedly bright, even if you have lost the janitorship."

CHAPTER XXIII

RANDOLPH AND HIS CREDITOR

THOUGH Randolph was pleased at having, as he thought, put a spoke in Luke's wheel, and filled Mr. Armstrong's mind with suspicion, he was not altogether happy. He had a little private trouble of his own. He had now for some time been a frequenter of Tony Denton's billiard saloon, patronizing both the table and the bar. He had fallen in with a few young men of no social standing, who flattered him, and, therefore, stood in his good graces. With them he played billiards and drank. After a time he found that he was exceeding his allowance, but in the most obliging way Tony Denton had offered him credit.

"Of course, Mr. Duncan"—Randolph felt flattered at being addressed in this way—"of course, Mr. Duncan, your credit is good with me. If you haven't the ready money, and I know most young gentlemen are liable to be short, I will just keep an account, and you can settle at your convenience."

This seemed very obliging, but I am disposed to think that a boy's worst enemy is the one who makes it easy for him to run into debt. Randolph was not wholly without caution, for he said: "But suppose, Tony, I am not able to pay when you want the money?"

"Oh, don't trouble yourself about that, Mr. Duncan," said Tony cordially. "Of course, I know the standing of your family, and I am perfectly safe. Some time you will be a rich man."

"Yes, I suppose I shall," said Randolph, in a consequential tone.

"And it is worth something to me to have my saloon patronized by a young gentleman of your social standing."

Evidently, Tony Denton understood Randolph's weak point,

and played on it skillfully. He assumed an air of extra consequence, as he remarked condescendingly: "You are very obliging, Tony, and I shall not forget it."

Tony Denton laughed in his sleeve at the boy's vanity, but his manner was very respectful, and Randolph looked upon him as an humble friend and admirer.

"He is a sensible man, Tony; he understands what is due to my position," he said to himself.

After Denton's visit to New York with Prince Duncan, and the knowledge which he then acquired about the president of the Groveton Bank, he decided that the time had come to cut short Randolph's credit with him. The day of reckoning always comes in such cases, as I hope my young friends will fully understand. Debt is much more easily contracted than liquidated, and this Randolph found to his cost.

One morning he was about to start on a game of billiards, when Tony Denton called him aside.

"I would like to speak a word to you, Mr. Duncan," he said smoothly.

"All right, Tony," said Randolph, in a patronizing tone. "What can I do for you?"

"My rent comes due to-morrow, Mr. Duncan, and I should be glad if you would pay me a part of your account. It has been running some time——"

Randolph's jaw fell, and he looked blank.

"How much do I owe you?" he asked.

Tony referred to a long ledgerlike account-book, turned to a certain page, and running his fingers down a long series of items, answered, "Twenty-seven dollars and sixty cents."

"It can't be so much!" ejaculated Randolph, in dismay. "Surely you have made a mistake!"

"You can look for yourself," said Tony suavely. "Just reckon it up; I may have made a little mistake in the sum total."

Randolph looked over the items, but he was nervous, and the page swam before his eyes. He was quite incapable of performing the addition, simple as it was, in his then frame of mind.

"I dare say you have added it up all right," he said, after an abortive attempt to reckon it up, "but I can hardly believe that I owe you so much."

"'Many a little makes a mickle,' as we Scotch say," answered Tony cheerfully. "However, twenty-seven dollars is a mere trifle to a young man like you. Come, if you'll pay me to-night, I'll knock off the sixty cents."

"It's quite impossible for me to do it," said Randolph, ill at ease.

"Pay me something on account—say ten dollars."

"I haven't got but a dollar and a quarter in my pocket."

"Oh, well, you know where to go for more money," said Tony, with a wink. "The old gentleman's got plenty."

"I am not so sure about that—I mean that he is willing to pay out. Of course, he's got plenty of money invested," added Randolph, who liked to have it thought that his father was a great financial magnate.

"Well, he can spare some for his son, I am sure."

"Can't you let it go for a little while longer, Tony?" asked Randolph, awkwardly.

"Really, Mr. Duncan, I couldn't. I am a poor man, as you know, and have my bills to pay."

"I take it as very disobliging, Tony; I sha'n't care to patronize your place any longer," said Randolph, trying a new tack.

Tony Denton shrugged his shoulders.

"I only care for patrons who are willing to pay their bills," he answered significantly. "It doesn't pay me to keep my place open free."

"Of course not; but I hope you are not afraid of me?"

"Certainly not. I am sure you will act honorably and pay your bills. If I thought you wouldn't, I would go and see your father about it."

"No, you mustn't do that," said Randolph, alarmed. "He doesn't know I come here."

"And he won't know from me, if you pay what you owe."

Matters were becoming decidedly unpleasant for Randolph. The perspiration gathered on his brow. He didn't know what to do. That his father would not give him money for any such purpose, he very well knew, and he dreaded his finding out where he spent so many of his evenings.

"Oh, don't trouble yourself about a trifle," said Tony smoothly. "Just go up to your father, frankly, and tell him you want the money."

"He wouldn't give me twenty-seven dollars," said Randolph gloomily.

"Then ask for ten, and I'll wait for the balance till next week."

"Can't you put it all off till next week?"

"No; I really couldn't, Mr. Duncan. What does it matter to you this week, or next?"

Randolph wished to put off as long as possible the inevitable moment, though he knew it would do him no good in the end. But Tony Denton was inflexible—and he finally said: "Well, I'll make the attempt, but I know I shall fail."

"That's all right; I knew you would look at it in the right light. Now, go ahead and play your game."

"No, I don't want to increase my debt."

"Oh, I won't charge you for what you play this evening. Tony Denton can be liberal as well as the next man. Only I have to collect money to pay my bills."

Randolph didn't know that all this had been prearranged by the obliging saloon-keeper, and that, in now pressing him, he had his own object in view.

The next morning, Randolph took an opportunity to see his father alone.

"Father," he said, "will you do me a favor?"

"What is it, Randolph?"

"Let me have ten dollars."

His father frowned.

"What do you want with ten dollars?" he asked.

"I don't like to go round without money in my pocket. It doesn't look well for the son of a rich man."

"Who told you I was a rich man?" said his father testily.

"Why, you are, aren't you? Everybody in the village says so."

"I may, or may not, be rich, but I don't care to encourage my son in extravagant habits. You say you have no money. Don't you have your regular allowance?"

"It is only two dollars a week."

"Only two dollars a week!" repeated the father angrily. "Let me tell you, young man, that when I was of your age I didn't have twenty-five cents a week."

"That was long ago. People lived differently from what they do now."

"How did they?"

"They didn't live in any style."

"They didn't spend money foolishly, as they do now. I don't see for my part what you can do with even two dollars a week."

"Oh, it melts away, one way or another. I am your only son,

and people expect me to spend money. It is expected of one in my position."

"So you can. I consider two dollars a week very liberal."

"You'd understand better if you were a young fellow like me how hard it is to get along on that."

"I don't want to understand," returned his father stoutly. "One thing I understand, and that is, that the boys of the present day are foolishly extravagant. Think of Luke Larkin! Do you think he spends two dollars even in a month?"

"I hope you don't mean to compare me with a working boy like Luke?" Randolph said scornfully.

"I am not sure but Luke would suit me better than you in some respects."

"You are speaking of Luke," said Randolph, with a lucky thought. "Well, even he, working boy as he is, has a better watch than I, who am the son of the president of the Groveton Bank."

"Do you want the ten dollars to buy a better watch?" asked Prince Duncan.

"Yes," answered Randolph, ready to seize on any pretext for the sake of getting the money.

"Then wait till I go to New York again, and I will look at some watches. I won't make any promise, but I may buy you one. I don't care about Luke outshining you."

This by no means answered Randolph's purpose.

"Won't you let me go up to the city myself, father?" he asked.

"No, I prefer to rely upon my own judgment in a purchase of that kind."

It had occurred to Randolph that he would go to the city, and pretend on his return that he had bought a watch but had his pocket picked. Of course, his father would give him more than ten dollars for the purpose, and he could privately pay it over to Tony Denton.

But this scheme did not work, and he made up his mind at last that he would have to tell Tony he must wait.

He did so. Tony Denton, who fully expected this, and, for reasons of his own, did not regret it, said very little to Randolph, but decided to go round and see Prince Duncan himself. It would give him a chance to introduce the other and more important matter.

It was about this time that Linton's birthday-party took

place. Randolph knew, of course, that he would meet Luke, but he no longer had the satisfaction of deriding his shabby dress. Our hero wore his best suit, and showed as much ease and self-possession as Randolph himself.

"What airs that boy Luke puts on!" ejaculated Randolph, in disgust. "I believe he thinks he is my equal."

In this Randolph was correct. Luke certainly did consider himself the social equal of the haughty Randolph, and the consciousness of being well dressed made him feel at greater ease than at Florence Grant's party. He had taken additional lessons in dancing from his friend Linton, and, being quick to learn, showed no awkwardness on the floor. Linton's parents, by their kind cordiality, contributed largely to the pleasure of their son's guests, who at the end of the evening unanimously voted the party a success.

CHAPTER XXIV

A COMMISSION FOR LUKE

UPON his return to the city, John Armstrong lost no time in sending for Roland Reed. The latter, though rather surprised at the summons, answered it promptly. When he entered the office of the old merchant he found him sitting at his desk.

"Mr. Armstrong?" he said inquiringly.

"That's my name. You, I take it, are Roland Reed."

"Yes."

"No doubt you wonder why I sent for you," said Mr. Armstrong.

"Is it about the robbery of the Groveton Bank?"

"You have guessed it. You know, I suppose, that I am the owner of the missing box of bonds?"

"So I was told. Have you obtained any clue?"

"I have not had time. I have only just returned from Europe. I have done nothing except visit Groveton."

"What led you to send for me? Pardon my curiosity, but I can't help asking."

"An interview with a protégé of yours, Luke Larkin."

"You know that Luke was arrested on suspicion of being

connected with the robbery, though there are those who pay me the compliment of thinking that I may have had something to do with it."

"I think you had as much to do with it as Luke Larkin," said Armstrong, deliberately.

"I had—just as much," said Reed, with a smile. "Luke is a good boy, Mr. Armstrong."

"I quite agree with you. If I had a son I should like him to resemble Luke."

"Give me your hand on that, Mr. Armstrong," said Roland Reed, impulsively. "Excuse my impetuosity, but I've taken a fancy to that boy."

"There, then, we are agreed. Now, Mr. Reed, I will tell you why I have taken the liberty of sending for you. From what Luke said, I judged that you were a sharp, shrewd man of the world, and might help me in this matter, which I confess puzzles me. You know the particulars, and therefore, without preamble, I am going to ask you whether you have any theory as regards this robbery. The box hasn't walked off without help. Now, who took it from the bank?"

"If I should tell you my suspicion you might laugh at me."

"I will promise not to do that."

"Then I believe that Prince Duncan, president of the Groveton Bank, could tell you, if he chose, what has become of the box."

"Extraordinary!" ejaculated John Armstrong.

"I supposed you would be surprised—probably indignant, if you are a friend of Duncan—but, nevertheless, I adhere to my statement."

"You mistake the meaning of my exclamation. I spoke of it as extraordinary, because the same suspicion has entered my mind, though, I admit, without a special reason."

"I have a reason."

"May I inquire what it is?"

"I knew Prince Duncan when he was a young man, though he does not know me now. In fact, I may as well admit that I was then known by another name. He wronged me deeply at that time, being guilty of a crime which he successfully laid upon my shoulders. No one in Groveton—no one of his recent associates—knows the real nature of the man as well as I do."

"You prefer not to go into particulars?"

Not at present."

"At all events you can give me your advice. To suspect amounts to little. We must bring home the crime to him. It is here that I need your advice."

"I understand that the box contained government bonds."

"Yes."

"What were the denominations?"

"One ten thousand dollar bond, one five, and ten of one thousand each."

"It seems to me they ought to be traced. I suppose, of course, they were coupon, not registered."

"You are right. Had they been registered, I should have been at no trouble, nor would the thief have reaped any advantage."

"If coupon, they are, of course, numbered. Won't that serve as a clue, supposing an attempt is made to dispose of them?"

"You touch the weak point of my position. They are numbered, and I had a list of the numbers, but that list has disappeared. It is either lost or mislaid. Of course, I can't identify them."

"That is awkward. Wouldn't the banker of whom you bought them be able to give you the numbers?"

"Yes, but I don't know where they were bought. I had at the time in my employ a clerk and book-keeper, a steady-going and methodical man of fifty-odd, who made the purchase, and no doubt has a list of the numbers of the bonds."

"Then where is your difficulty?" asked Roland Reed, in surprise. "Go to the clerk and put the question. What can be simpler?"

"But I don't know where he is."

"Don't know where he is?" echoed Reed, in genuine surprise.

"No; James Harding—this is his name—left my employ a year since, having, through a life of economy, secured a competence, and went out West to join a widowed sister who had for many years made her residence there. Now, the West is a large place, and I don't know where this sister lives, or where James Harding is to be found."

"Yet he must be found. You must send a messenger to look for him."

"But whom shall I send? In a matter of this delicacy I don't want to employ a professional detective. Those men sometimes betray secrets committed to their keeping, and work up a false clue rather than have it supposed they are not earning their money. If, now, some gentleman in whom I had confidence—someone like yourself—would undertake the commission, I should esteem myself fortunate."

"Thank you for the compliment, Mr. Armstrong, more especially as you are putting confidence in a stranger, but I have important work to do that would not permit me to leave New York at present. But I know of someone whom I would employ, if the business were mine."

"Well?"

"Luke Larkin."

"But he is only a boy. He can't be over sixteen."

"He is a sharp boy, however, and would follow instructions."

John Armstrong thought rapidly. He was a man who decided quickly.

"I will take your advice," he said. "As I don't want to have it supposed that he is in my employ, will you oblige me by writing to him and preparing him for a journey? Let it be supposed that he is occupied with a commission for you."

"I will attend to the matter at once."

The next morning Luke received the following letter:

"My dear Luke: I have some work for you which will occupy some time and require a journey. You will be well paid. Bring a supply of underclothing, and assure your mother that she need feel under no apprehensions about you. Unless I am greatly mistaken, you will be able to take care of yourself.

"Your friend,

"Roland Reed."

Luke read the letter with excitement and pleasure. He was to go on a journey, and to a boy of his age a journey of any sort is delightful. He had no idea of the extent of the trip in store for him, but thought he might possibly be sent to Boston, or Philadelphia, and either trip he felt would yield him much pleasure. He quieted the natural apprehensions of his mother, and, satchel in hand, waited upon his patron in the course of a day. By him he was taken over to the office of Mr. Armstrong, from whom he received instructions and a supply of money.

CHAPTER XXV

MR. J. MADISON COLEMAN

LUKE didn't shrink from the long trip before him. He enjoyed the prospect of it, having always longed to travel and see distant places. He felt flattered by Mr. Armstrong's confidence in him, and stoutly resolved to deserve it. He would have been glad if he could have had the company of his friend Linton, but he knew that this was impossible. He must travel alone.

"You have a difficult and perplexing task, Luke," said the capitalist. "You may not succeed."

"I will do my best, Mr. Armstrong."

"That is all I have a right to expect. If you succeed, you will do me a great service, of which I shall show proper appreciation."

He gave Luke some instructions, and it was arranged that our hero should write twice a week, and, if occasion required, oftener, so that his employer might be kept apprised of his movements.

Luke was not to stop short of Chicago. There his search was to begin; and there, if possible, he was to obtain information that might guide his subsequent steps.

It is a long ride to Chicago, as Luke found. He spent a part of the time in reading, and a part in looking out of the window at the scenery, but still, at times, he felt lonely.

"I wish Linton Tomkins were with me," he reflected. "What a jolly time we would have!"

But Linton didn't even know what had become of his friend. Luke's absence was an occasion for wonder at Groveton, and many questions were asked of his mother.

"He was sent for by Mr. Reed," answered the widow. "He is at work for him."

"Mr. Reed is in New York, isn't he?"

"Yes."

It was concluded, therefore, that Luke was in New York, and one or two persons proposed to call upon him there, but his mother professed ignorance of his exact residence. She knew that he was traveling, but even she was kept in the dark as to where he was, nor did she know that Mr. Armstrong, and not Mr. Reed, was his employer.

Some half dozen hours before reaching Chicago, a young man of twenty-five, or thereabouts, sauntered along the aisle, and sat down in the vacant seat beside Luke.

"Nice day," he said, affably.

"Very nice," responded Luke.

"I suppose you are bound to Chicago?"

"Yes, I expect to stay there awhile."

"Going farther?"

"I can't tell yet."

"Going to school out there?"

"No."

"Perhaps you are traveling for some business firm, though you look pretty young for that."

"No, I'm not a drummer, if that's what you mean. Still, I have a commisison from a New York business man."

"A commission—of what kind?" drawled the newcomer.

"It is of a confidential character," said Luke.

"Ha! close-mouthed," thought the young man. "Well, I'll get it out of him after awhile."

He didn't press the question, not wishing to arouse suspicion or mistrust.

"Just so," he replied. "You are right to keep it to yourself, though you wouldn't mind trusting me if you knew me better. Is this your first visit to Chicago?"

"Yes, sir."

"Suppose we exchange cards. This is mine."

He handed Luke a card, bearing this name:

J. MADISON COLEMAN

At the bottom of the card he wrote in pencil, "representing H. B. Claflin & Co."

"Of course you've heard of our firm," he said.

"Certainly."

"I don't have the firm name printed on my card, for Claflin won't allow it. You will notice that I am called for old President Madison. He was an old friend of my grandfather. In fact, grandfather held a prominent office under his administration—collector of the port of New York."

"I have no card with me," responded Luke. "But my name is Luke Larkin."

"Good name. Do you live in New York?"

"No; a few miles in the country."

"And whom do you represent?"

"Myself for the most part," answered Luke, with a smile.

"Good! No one has a better right to. I see there's something in you, Luke."

"You've found it out pretty quick," thought Luke.

"And I hope we will get better acquainted. If you're not permanently employed by this party, whose name you don't give, I will get you into the employ of Claflin & Co., if you would like it."

"Thank you," answered Luke, who thought it quite possible that he might like to obtain a position with so eminent a firm. "How long have you been with them?"

"Ten years—ever since I was of your age," promptly answered Mr. Coleman.

"Is promotion rapid?" Luke asked, with interest.

"Well, that depends on a man's capacity. I have been pushed right along. I went there as a boy, on four dollars a week; now I'm a traveling salesman—drummer as it is called—and I make about four thousand a year."

"That's a fine salary," said Luke, feeling that his new acquaintance must be possessed of extra ability to occupy so desirable a position.

"Yes, but I expect next year to get five thousand—Claflin knows I am worth it, and as he is a liberal man, I guess he will give it sooner than let me go."

"I suppose many do not get on so well, Mr. Coleman."

"I should say so! Now, there is a young fellow went there the same time that I did—his name is Frank Bolton. We were schoolfellows together, and just the same age, that is, nearly—he was born in April, and I in May. Well, we began at the same time on the same salary. Now I get sixty dollars a week and he only twelve—and he is glad to get that, too."

"I suppose he hasn't much business capacity."

"That's where you've struck it, Luke. He knows about enough to be clerk in a country store—and I suppose he'll fetch up there some day. You know what that means—selling sugar, and tea, and dried apples to old ladies, and occasionally measuring off a yard of calico, or selling a spool of cotton. If I couldn't do better than that I'd hire out as a farm laborer."

Luke smiled at the enumeration of the duties of a country salesman. It was clear that Mr. Coleman, though he looked city-bred, must at some time in the past have lived in the country.

"Perhaps that is the way I should turn out," he said. "I might not rise any higher than your friend Mr. Bolton."

"Oh, yes, you would. You're smart enough, I'll guarantee. You might not get on so fast as I have, for it isn't every young man of twenty-six that can command four thousand dollars a year, but you would rise to a handsome income, I am sure."

"I should be satisfied with two thousand a year at your age."

"I would be willing to guarantee you that," asserted Mr. Coleman, confidently. "By the way, where do you propose to put up in Chicago?"

"I have not decided yet."

"You'd better go with me to the Ottawa House."

"Is it a good house?"

"They'll feed you well there, and only charge two dollars a day."

"Is it centrally located?"

"It isn't as central as the Palmer, or Sherman, or Tremont, but it is convenient to everything."

I ought to say here that I have chosen to give a fictitious name to the hotel designated by Mr. Coleman.

"Come, what do you say?"

"I have no objection," answered Luke, after a slight pause for reflection.

Indeed, it was rather pleasant to him to think that he would have a companion on his first visit to Chicago who was well acquainted with the city, and could serve as his guide. Though he should not feel justified in imparting to Mr. Coleman his special business, he meant to see something of the city, and would find his new friend a pleasant companion.

"That's good," said Coleman, well pleased. "I shall be glad to have your company. I expected to meet a friend on the train, but something must have delayed him, and so I should have been left alone."

"I suppose a part of your time will be given to business?" suggested Luke.

"Yes, but I take things easy; when I work, I work. I can

accomplish as much in a couple of hours as many would do in a whole day. You see, I understand my customers. When soft sawder is wanted, I am soft sawder. When I am dealing with a plain, businesslike man, I talk in a plain, businesslike way. I study my man, and generally I succeed in striking him for an order, even if times are hard and he is already well stocked."

"He certainly knows how to talk," thought Luke. In fact, he was rather disposed to accept Mr. Coleman at his own valuation, though that was a very high one.

"Do you smoke?"

"Not at all."

"Not even a cigarette?"

"Not even a cigarette."

"I was intending to ask you to go with me into the smoking-car for a short time. I smoke a good deal; it is my only vice. You know we must all have some vices."

Luke didn't see the necessity, but he assented, because it seemed to be expected.

"I won't be gone long. You'd better come along, too, and smoke a cigarette. It is time you began to smoke. Most boys begin much earlier."

Luke shook his head.

"I don't care to learn," he said.

"Oh, you're a good boy--one of the Sunday-school kind," said Coleman, with a slight sneer. "You'll get over that after a while. You'll be here when I come back?"

Luke promised that he would, and for the next half hour he was left alone. As his friend Mr. Coleman left the car, he followed him with his glance, and surveyed him more attentively than he had hitherto done. The commercial traveler was attired in a suit of fashionable plaid, wore a showy necktie, from the center of which blazed a diamond scarfpin. A showy chain crossed his vest, and to it was appended a large and showy watch, which looked valuable, though appearances are sometimes deceitful.

"He must spend a good deal of money," thought Luke. "I wonder that he should be willing to go to a two-dollar-a-day hotel."

Luke, for his own part, was quite willing to go to the Ottawa House. He had never fared luxuriously, and he had no doubt that even at the Ottawa House he should live better than at home.

It was nearer an hour than half an hour before Coleman came back.

"I stayed away longer than I intended," he said. "I smoked three cigars, instead of one, seeing you wasn't with me to keep me company. I found some social fellows, and we had a chat."

Mr. Coleman absented himself once or twice more. Finally, the train ran into the depot, and the conductor called out, "Chicago!"

"Come along, Luke!" said Coleman.

The two left the car in company. Coleman hailed a cab—gave the order, Ottawa House—and in less than five minutes they were rattling over the pavements toward their hotel.

CHAPTER XXVI

THE OTTAWA HOUSE

THERE was one little circumstance that led Luke to think favorably of his new companion. As the hackman closed the door of the carriage, Luke asked: "How much is the fare?"

"Fifty cents apiece, gentlemen," answered cabby.

Luke was about to put his hand into his pocket for the money, when Coleman touching him on the arm, said: "Never mind, Luke, I have the money," and before our hero could expostulate he had thrust a dollar into the cab-driver's hand.

"All right, thanks," said the driver, and slammed to the door.

"You must let me repay you my part of the fare, Mr. Coleman," said Luke, again feeling for his pocketbook.

"Oh, it's a mere trifle!" said Coleman. "I'll let you pay next time, but don't be so ceremonious with a friend."

"But I would rather pay for myself," objected Luke.

"Oh, say no more about it, I beg. Claflin provides liberally for my expenses. It's all right."

"But I don't want Claflin to pay for me."

"Then I assure you I'll get it out of you before we part. Will that content you?"

Luke let the matter drop, but he didn't altogether like to find himself under obligations to a stranger, notwithstanding his assurance, which he took for a joke. He would have been surprised and startled if he had known how thoroughly Coleman meant what he said about getting even. The fifty cents he had with such apparent generosity paid out for Luke he meant to get back a hundred-fold. His object was to gain Luke's entire confidence, and remove any suspicion he might possibly entertain. In this respect he was successful. Luke had read about designing strangers, but he certainly could not suspect a man who insisted on paying his hack fare.

"I hope you will not be disappointed in the Ottawa House," observed Mr. Coleman, as they rattled through the paved streets. "It isn't a stylish hotel."

"I am not used to stylish living," said Luke, frankly. "I have always been used to living in a very plain way."

"When I first went on the road I used to stop at the tip-top houses, such as the Palmer at Chicago, the Russell House in Detroit, etc., but it's useless extravagance. Claflin allows me a generous sum for hotels, and if I go to a cheap one, I put the difference into my own pocket."

"Is that expected?" asked Luke, doubtfully.

"It's allowed, at any rate. No one can complain if I choose to live a little plainer. When it pays in the way of business to stop at a big hotel, I do so. Of course, your boss pays your expenses?"

"Yes."

"Then you'd better do as I do—put the difference in your own pocket."

"I shouldn't like to do that."

"Why not? It is evident you are a new traveler, or you would know that it is a regular thing."

Luke did not answer, but he adhered to his own view. He meant to keep a careful account of his disbursements and report to Mr. Armstrong, without the addition of a single penny. He had no doubt that he should be paid liberally for his time, and he didn't care to make anything by extra means.

The Ottawa House was nearly a mile and a half distant. It was on one of the lower streets, near the lake. It was a plain building with accommodations for perhaps a hundred and fifty guests. This would be large for a country town or small city, but it indicated a hotel of the third class in Chicago. I may as well say here, however, that it was a perfectly respectable and honestly conducted hotel, notwithstanding it was selected by Mr. Coleman, who could not with truth be complimented so highly. I will also add that Mr. Coleman's selection of the Ottawa, in place of a more pretentious hotel, arose from the fear that in the latter he might meet someone who knew him, and who would warn Luke of his undesirable reputation.

Jumping out of the hack, J. Madison Coleman led the way into the hotel, and, taking pen in hand, recorded his name in large, flourishing letters—as from New York.

Then he handed the pen to Luke, who registered himself also from New York.

"Give us a room together," he said to the clerk.

Luke did not altogether like this arrangement, but hardly felt like objecting. He did not wish to hurt the feelings of J. Madison Coleman, yet he considered that, having known him only six hours, it was somewhat imprudent to allow such intimacy. But he who hesitates is lost, and before Luke had made up his mind whether to object or not, he was already part way upstairs—there was no elevator—following the bellboy, who carried his luggage.

The room, which was on the fourth floor, was of good size, and contained two beds. So far so good. After the ride he wished to wash and put on clean clothes. Mr. Coleman did not think this necessary, and saying to Luke that he would find him downstairs, he left our hero alone.

"I wish I had a room alone," thought Luke. "I should like it much better, but I don't want to offend Coleman. I've got eighty dollars in my pocketbook, and though, of course, he is all right, I don't want to take any risks."

On the door he read the regulations of the hotel. One item attracted his attention. It was this:

"The proprietors wish distinctly to state that they will not be responsible for money or valuables unless left with the clerk to be deposited in the safe."

Luke had not been accustomed to stopping at hotels, and did not know that this was the usual custom. It struck him, however, as an excellent arrangement, and he resolved to avail himself of it.

When he went downstairs he didn't see Mr. Coleman.

"Your friend has gone out," said the clerk. "He wished me to say that he would be back in half an hour."

"All right," answered Luke. "Can I leave my pocketbook with you?"

"Certainly."

The clerk wrapped it up in a piece of brown paper and put it away in the safe at the rear of the office, marking it with Luke's name and the number of his room.

"There, that's safe!" thought Luke, with a feeling of relief. He had reserved about three dollars, as he might have occasion to spend a little money in the course of the evening. If he were robbed of this small amount it would not much matter.

A newsboy came in with an evening paper. Luke bought a copy and sat down on a bench in the office, near a window. He was reading busily, when someone tapped him on the shoulder. Looking up, he saw that it was his roommate, J. Madison Coleman.

"I've just been taking a little walk," he said, "and now I am ready for dinner. If you are, too, let us go into the dining-room."

Luke was glad to accept this proposal, his long journey having given him a good appetite.

CHAPTER XXVII

COLEMAN ACTS SUSPICIOUSLY

AFTER dinner, Coleman suggested a game of billiards, but as this was a game with which Luke was not familiar, he declined the invitation, but went into the billiard-room and watched a game between his new acquaintance and a stranger. Coleman proved to be a very good player, and won the game. After the first game Coleman called for drinks, and invited Luke to join them.

"Thank you," answered Luke, "but I never drink."

"Oh, I forgot; you're a good boy," said Coleman. "Well, I'm no Puritan. Whisky straight for me."

Luke was not in the least troubled by the sneer conveyed in Coleman's words. He was not altogether entitled to credit for refusing to drink, having not the slightest taste for strong drink of any kind.

About half-past seven Coleman put up his cue, saying: "That'll do for me. Now, Luke, suppose we take a walk."

Luke was quite ready, not having seen anything of Chicago as yet. They strolled out, and walked for an hour. Coleman, to do him justice, proved an excellent guide, and pointed out whatever they passed which was likely to interest his young companion. But at last he seemed to be tired.

"It's only half-past eight," he said, referring to his watch. "I'll drop into some theater. It is the best way to finish up the evening."

"Then I'll go back to the hotel," said Luke. "I feel tired, and mean to go to bed early."

"You'd better spend an hour or two in the theater with me."

"No, I believe not. I prefer a good night's rest."

"Do you mind my leaving you?"

"Not at all."

"Can you find your way back to the hotel alone?"

"If you'll direct me, I think I can find it."

The direction was given, and Coleman was turning off, when, as if it had just occurred to him, he said: "By the way, can you lend me a five? I've nothing less than a fifty-dollar bill with me, and I don't want to break that."

Luke congratulated himself now that he had left the greater part of his money at the hotel.

"I can let you have a dollar," he said.

Coleman shrugged his shoulders, but answered: "All right; let me have the one."

Luke did so, and felt now that he had more than repaid the fifty cents his companion had paid for hack fare. Though Coleman had professed to have nothing less than fifty, Luke knew that he had changed a five-dollar bill at the hotel in paying for the drinks, and must have over four dollars with him in small bills and change.

"Why, then," thought he, "did Coleman want to borrow five dollars of me?"

If Luke had known more of the world he would have understood that it was only one of the tricks to which men like Coleman resort to obtain a loan, or rather a gift, from an unsuspecting acquaintance.

"I suppose I shall not see my money back," thought Luke. "Well, it will be the last that he will get out of me."

He was already becoming tired of his companion, and doubted whether he would not find the acquaintance an expensive one. He was sorry that they were to share the same room. However, it was for one night only, and to-morrow he was quite resolved to part company.

Shortly after nine o'clock Luke went to bed, and being fatigued with his long journey, was soon asleep. He was still sleeping at twelve o'clock, when Coleman came home.

Coleman came up to his bed and watched him attentively.

"The kid's asleep," he soliloquized. "He's one of the good Sunday-school boys. I can imagine how shocked he would be if he knew that, instead of being a traveler for H. B. Claflin, I have been living by my wits for the last half-dozen years. He seems to be half asleep. I think I can venture to explore a little."

He took Luke's trousers from the chair on which he had laid them, and thrust his fingers into the pockets, but brought forth only a penknife and a few pennies.

"He keeps his money somewhere else, it seems," said Coleman.

Next he turned to the vest, and from the inside vest pocket drew out Luke's modest pocketbook.

"Oh, here we have it," thought Coleman, with a smile. "Cunning boy; he thought nobody would think of looking in his vest pocket. Well, let us see how much he has got."

He opened the pocketbook, and frowned with disappointment when he discovered only a two-dollar bill.

"What does it mean? Surely he hasn't come to Chicago with only this paltry sum!" exclaimed Coleman. "He must be more cunning than I thought."

He looked in the coat pockets, the shoes, and even the socks of his young companion, but found nothing, except the silver watch, which Luke had left in one of his vest pockets.

"Confound the boy! He's foiled me this time!" muttered Coleman. "Shall I take the watch? No; it might expose me, and I could not raise much on it at the pawnbroker's. He must have left his money with the clerk downstairs. He wouldn't think of it himself, but probably he was advised to do so before he left home. I'll get up early, and see if I can't get in ahead of my young friend."

Coleman did not venture to take the two-dollar bill, as that would have induced suspicion on the part of Luke, and would have interfered with his intention of securing the much larger sum of money, which, as he concluded rightly, was in the safe in the office.

He undressed and got into bed, but not without observation. As he was bending over Luke's clothes, examining them, our hero's eyes suddenly opened, and he saw what was going on. It flashed upon him at once what kind of a companion he had fallen in with, but he had the wisdom and self-control to close his eyes again immediately. He reflected that there was not much that Coleman could take, and if he took the watch he resolved to charge him openly with it. To make a disturbance there and then might be dangerous, as Coleman, who was much stronger than he, might ill-treat and abuse him, without his being able to offer any effectual resistance.

CHAPTER XXVIII

COLEMAN'S LITTLE PLAN

THOUGH Coleman went to bed late, he awoke early. He had the power of awaking at almost any hour that he might fix. He was still quite fatigued, but having an object in view, overcame his tendency to lie longer, and swiftly dressing himself, went downstairs. Luke was still sleeping, and did not awaken while his companion was dressing.

Coleman went downstairs and strolled up to the clerk's desk.

"You're up early," said that official.

"Yes, it's a great nuisance, but I have a little business to attend to with a man who leaves Chicago by an early train. I tried to find him last night, but he had probably gone to some theater. That is what has forced me to get up so early this morning."

"I am always up early," said the clerk.

"Then you are used to it, and don't mind it. It is different with me."

Coleman bought a cigar, and while he was lighting it, remarked, as if incidentally:

"By the way, did my young friend leave my money with you last evening?"

"He left a package of money with me, but he didn't mention it was yours."

"Forgot to, I suppose. I told him to leave it here, as I was going out to the theater, and was afraid I might have my pocket picked. Smart fellows, those pickpockets. I claim to be rather smart myself, but there are some of them smart enough to get ahead of me.

"I was relieved of my pocketbook containing over two hundred dollars in money once. By Jove! I was mad enough to knock the fellow's head off, if I had caught him."

"It is rather provoking."

"I think I'll trouble you to hand me the money the boy left with you, as I have to use some this morning."

Mr. Coleman spoke in an easy, off-hand way, that might have taken in some persons, but hotel clerks are made smart by their positions.

"I am sorry, Mr. Coleman," said the clerk, "but I can only give it back to the boy."

"I commend your caution, my friend," said Coleman, "but I can assure you that it's all right. I sent it back by Luke when I was going to the theater, and I meant, of course, to have him give my name with it. However, he is not used to business, and so forgot it."

"When did you hand it to him?" asked the clerk, with new-born suspicion.

"About eight o'clock. No doubt he handed it in as soon as he came back to the hotel."

"How much was there?"

This question posed Mr. Coleman, as he had no idea how much money Luke had with him.

"I can't say exactly," he answered. "I didn't count it. There might have been seventy-five dollars, though perhaps the sum fell a little short of that."

"I can't give you the money, Mr. Coleman," said the clerk, briefly. "I have no evidence that it is yours."

"Really, that's ludicrous," said Coleman, with a forced laugh. "You don't mean to doubt me, I hope," and Madison Coleman drew himself up haughtily.

"That has nothing to do with it. The rule of this office is to return money only to the person who deposited it with us. If we adopted any other rule, we should get into no end of trouble."

"But, my friend," said Coleman, frowning, "you are putting me to great inconvenience. I must meet my friend in twenty minutes and pay him a part of this money."

"I have nothing to do with that," said the clerk.

"You absolutely refuse, then?"

"I do," answered the clerk, firmly. "However, you can easily overcome the difficulty by bringing the boy down here to authorize me to hand you the money."

"It seems to me that you have plenty of red tape here," said

Coleman, shrugging his shoulders. "However, I must do as you require."

Coleman had a bright thought, which he proceeded to carry into execution.

He left the office and went upstairs. He was absent long enough to visit the chamber which he and Luke had occupied together. Then he reported to the office again.

"The boy is not dressed," he said, cheerfully. "However, he has given me an order for the money, which, of course, will do as well."

He handed a paper, the loose leaf of a memorandum book, on which were written in pencil these words:

"Give my guardian, Mr. Coleman, the money I left on deposit at the office. LUKE LARKIN."

"That makes it all right, doesn't it?" asked Coleman, jauntily. "Now, if you'll be kind enough to hand me my money at once, I'll be off."

"It won't do, Mr. Coleman," said the clerk. "How am I to know that the boy wrote this?"

"Don't you see his signature?"

The clerk turned to the hotel register, where Luke had enrolled his name.

"The handwriting is not the same," he said, coldly.

"Oh, confound it!" exclaimed Coleman, testily. "Can't you understand that writing with a pencil makes a difference?"

"I understand," said the clerk, "that you are trying to get money that does not belong to you. The money was deposited a couple of hours sooner than the time you claim to have handed it to the boy—just after you and the boy arrived."

"You're right," said Coleman, unabashed. "I made a mistake."

"You cannot have the money."

"You have no right to keep it from me," said Coleman, wrathfully.

"Bring the boy to the office and it shall be delivered to him; then, if he chooses to give it to you, I have nothing to say."

"But I tell you he is not dressed."

"He seems to be," said the clerk, quietly, with a glance at the door, through which Luke was just entering.

Coleman's countenance changed. He was now puzzled for

a moment. Then a bold plan suggested itself. He would charge Luke with having stolen the money from him.

CHAPTER XXIX

MR. COLEMAN IS FOILED IN HIS ATTEMPT

LUKE looked from Coleman to the clerk in some surprise. He saw from their looks that they were discussing some matter which concerned him.

"You left some money in my charge yesterday, Mr. Larkin," said the clerk.

"Yes."

"Your friend here claims it. Am I to give it to him?"

Luke's eyes lighted up indignantly.

"What does this mean, Mr. Coleman?" he demanded, sternly.

"It means," answered Coleman, throwing off the mask, "that the money is mine, and that you have no right to it."

If Luke had not witnessed Coleman's search of his pockets during the night, he would have been very much astonished at this brazen statement. As it was, he had already come to the conclusion that his railroad acquaintance was a sharper.

"I will trouble you to prove your claim to it," said Luke, not at all disturbed by Coleman's impudent assertion.

"I gave it to you yesterday to place in the safe. I did not expect you would put it in in your own name," continued Coleman, with brazen hardihood.

"When did you hand it to me?" asked Luke, calmly.

"When we first went up into the room."

This change in his original charge Coleman made in consequence of learning the time of the deposit.

"This is an utter falsehood!" exclaimed Luke, indignantly.

"Take care, young fellow!" blustered Coleman. "Your reputation for honesty isn't of the best. I don't like to expose you, but a boy who has served a three months' term in the penitentiary had better be careful how he acts."

Luke's breath was quite taken away by this unexpected attack. The clerk began to eye him with suspicion, so confident was Coleman's tone.

"Mr. Lawrence," said Luke, for he had learned the clerk's name, "will you allow me a word in private?"

"I object to this," said Coleman, in a blustering tone. "Whatever you have to say you can say before me."

"Yes," answered the clerk, who did not like Coleman's bullying tone, "I will hear what you have to say."

He led the way into an adjoining room, and assumed an air of attention.

"This man is a stranger to me," Luke commenced. "I saw him yesterday afternoon for the first time in my life."

"But he says he is your guardian."

"He is no more my guardian than you are. Indeed, I would much sooner select you."

"How did you get acquainted?"

"He introduced himself to me as a traveler for H. B. Claflin, of New York. I did not doubt his statement at the time, but now I do, especially after what happened in the night."

"What was that?" asked the clerk, pricking up his ears.

Luke went on to describe Coleman's search of his pockets.

"Did you say anything?"

"No. I wished to see what he was after. As I had left nearly all my money with you, I was not afraid of being robbed."

"I presume your story is correct. In fact, I detected him in a misstatement as to the time of giving you the money. But I don't want to get into trouble."

"Ask him how much money I deposited with you," suggested Luke. "He has no idea, and will have to guess."

"I have asked him the question once, but will do so again."

The clerk returned to the office with Luke. Coleman eyed them uneasily, as if he suspected them of having been engaged in a conspiracy against him.

"Well," he said, "are you going to give me my money?"

"State the amount," said the clerk, in a businesslike manner.

"I have already told you that I can't state exactly. I handed the money to Luke without counting it."

"You must have some idea, at any rate," said the clerk.

"Of course I have. There was somewhere around seventy-five dollars."

This he said with a confidence which he did not feel, for it was, of course, a mere guess.

"You are quite out in your estimate, Mr. Coleman. It is

evident to me that you have made a false claim. You will oblige me by settling your bill and leaving the hotel."

"Do you think I will submit to such treatment?" demanded Coleman, furiously.

"I think you'll have to," returned the clerk, quietly. "You can go in to breakfast, if you like, but you must afterward leave the hotel. John," this to a bellboy, "go up to number forty-seven and bring down this gentleman's luggage."

"You and the boy are in a conspiracy against me!" exclaimed Coleman, angrily. "I have a great mind to have you both arrested!"

"I advise you not to attempt it. You may get into trouble."

Coleman apparently did think better of it. Half an hour later he left the hotel, and Luke found himself alone. He decided that he must be more circumspect hereafter.

CHAPTER XXX

A DISCOVERY

LUKE was in Chicago, but what to do next he did not know. He might have advertised in one or more of the Chicago papers for James Harding, formerly in the employ of John Armstrong, of New York, but if this should come to the knowledge of the party who had appropriated the bonds, it might be a revelation of the weakness of the case against them. Again, he might apply to a private detective, but if he did so, the case would pass out of his hands.

Luke had this piece of information to start upon. He had been informed that Harding left Mr. Armstrong's employment June 17, 1879, and, as was supposed, at once proceeded West. If he could get hold of a file of some Chicago daily paper for the week succeeding, he might look over the last arrivals, and ascertain at what hotel Harding had stopped. This would be something.

"Where can I examine a file of some Chicago daily paper for 1879, Mr. Lawrence?" he asked of the clerk.

"Right here," answered the clerk. "Mr. Goth, the landlord, has a file of the *Times* for the last ten years."

"Would he let me examine the volume for 1879?" asked Luke, eagerly.

"Certainly. I am busy just now, but this afternoon I will have the papers brought down to the reading-room."

He was as good as his word, and at three o'clock in the afternoon Luke sat down before a formidable pile of papers, and began his task of examination.

He began with the paper bearing date June 19, and examined that and the succeeding papers with great care. At length his search was rewarded. In the paper for June 23 Luke discovered the name of James Harding, and, what was a little singular, he was registered at the Ottawa House.

Luke felt quite exultant at this discovery. It might not lead to anything, to be sure, but still it was an encouragement, and seemed to augur well for his ultimate success.

He went with his discovery to his friend the clerk.

"Were you here in June, 1879, Mr. Lawrence?" he asked.

"Yes. I came here in April of that year."

"Of course, you could hardly be expected to remember a casual guest?"

"I am afraid not. What is his name?"

"James Harding."

"James Harding! Yes, I do remember him, and for a very good reason. He took a very severe cold on the way from New York, and he lay here in the hotel sick for two weeks. He was an elderly man, about fifty-five, I should suppose."

"That answers to the description given me. Do you know where he went to from here?"

"There you have me. I can't give you any information on that point."

Luke began to think that his discovery would lead to nothing.

"Stay, though," said the clerk, after a moment's thought. "I remember picking up a small diary in Mr. Harding's room after he left us. I didn't think it of sufficient value to forward to him, nor indeed did I know exactly where to send."

"Can you show me the diary?" asked Luke, hopefully.

"Yes. I have it upstairs in my chamber. Wait five minutes and I will get it for you."

A little later a small, black-covered diary was put in Luke's hand. He opened it eagerly, and began to examine the items jotted down. It appeared partly to note down daily expenses, but on alternate pages there were occasional memorandums. About the fifteenth of May appeared this sentence: "I have reason to think that my sister, Mrs. Ellen Ransom, is now living in

Franklin, Minnesota. She is probably in poor circumstances, her husband having died in poverty a year since. We two are all that is left of a once large family, and now that I am shortly to retire from business with a modest competence, I feel it will be alike my duty and my pleasure to join her, and do what I can to make her comfortable. She has a boy who must now be about twelve years old."

"Come," said Luke, triumphantly, "I am making progress decidedly. My first step will be to go to Franklin, Minnesota, and look up Mr. Harding and his sister. After all, I ought to be grateful to Mr. Coleman, notwithstanding his attempt to rob me. But for him I should never have come to the Ottawa House, and thus I should have lost an important clue."

Luke sat down immediately and wrote to Mr. Armstrong, detailing the discovery he had made—a letter which pleased his employer, and led him to conclude that he had made a good choice in selecting Luke for this confidential mission.

The next day Luke left Chicago and journeyed by the most direct route to Franklin, Minnesota. He ascertained that it was forty miles distant from St. Paul, a few miles off the railroad. The last part of the journey was performed in a stage, and was somewhat wearisome. He breathed a sigh of relief when the stage stopped before the door of a two-story inn with a swinging sign, bearing the name Franklin House.

Luke entered his name on the register and secured a room. He decided to postpone questions till he had enjoyed a good supper and felt refreshed. Then he went out to the desk and opened a conversation with the landlord, or rather submitted first to answering a series of questions propounded by that gentleman.

"You're rather young to be travelin' alone, my young friend," said the innkeeper.

"Yes, sir."

"Where might you be from?"

"From New York."

"Then you're a long way from home. Travelin' for your health?"

"No," answered Luke, with a smile. "I have no trouble with my health."

"You do look pretty rugged, that's a fact. Goin' to settle down in our State?"

"I think not."

"I reckon you're not travelin' on business? You're too young for a drummer."

"The fact is, I am in search of a family that I have been told lives, or used to live, in Franklin."

"What's the name?"

"The lady is a Mrs. Ransom. I wish to see her brother-in-law, Mr. James Harding."

"Sho! You'll have to go farther to find them."

"Don't they live here now?" asked Luke, disappointed.

"No; they moved away six months ago."

"Do you know where they went?" asked Luke, eagerly.

"Not exactly. You see, there was a great stir about gold being plenty in the Black Hills, and Mr. Harding, though he seemed to be pretty well fixed, thought he wouldn't mind pickin' up a little. He induced his sister to go with him—that is, her boy wanted to go, and so she, not wantin' to be left alone, concluded to go, too."

"So they went to the Black Hills. Do you think it would be hard to find them?"

"No; James Harding is a man that's likely to be known wherever he is. Just go to where the miners are thickest, and I allow you'll find him."

Luke made inquiries, and ascertaining the best way of reaching the Black Hills, started the next day.

"If I don't find James Harding, it's because I can't," he said to himself resolutely.

CHAPTER XXXI

TONY DENTON'S CALL

LEAVING Luke on his way to the Black Hills, we will go back to Groveton, to see how matters are moving on there.

Tony Denton had now the excuse he sought for calling upon Prince Duncan. Ostensibly, his errand related to the debt which Randolph had incurred at his saloon, but really he had something more important to speak of. It may be remarked that Squire Duncan, who had a high idea of his own personal importance, looked upon Denton as a low and insignificant person, and never noticed him when they met casually in the street. It is difficult to play the part of an aristocrat in a country village, but that is the rôle which Prince Duncan assumed. Had he been a prince in reality, as he was by name, he could not have borne himself more loftily when he came face to face with those whom he considered his inferiors.

When, in answer to the bell, the servant at Squire Duncan's found Tony Denton standing on the doorstep, she looked at him in surprise.

"Is the squire at home?" asked the saloon keeper.

"I believe so," said the girl, doubtfully.

"I would like to see him. Say Mr. Denton wishes to see him on important business."

The message was delivered.

"Mr. Denton!" repeated the squire, in surprise. "Is it Tony Denton?"

"Yes, sir."

"What can he wish to see me about?"

"He says it's business of importance, sir."

"Well, bring him in."

Prince Duncan assumed his most important attitude and bearing when his visitor entered his presence.

"Mr.—ahem!—Denton, I believe?" he said, as if he found difficulty in recognizing Tony.

"The same."

"I am—ahem!—surprised to hear that you have any business with me."

"Yet so it is, Squire Duncan," said Tony, not perceptibly overawed by the squire's grand manner.

"Elucidate it!" said Prince Duncan, stiffly.

"You may not be aware, Squire Duncan, that your son Randolph has for some time frequented my billiard saloon and has run up a sum of twenty-seven dollars."

"I was certainly not aware of it. Had I been, I should have forbidden his going there. It is no proper place for my son to frequent."

"Well, I don't know about that. It's respectable enough, I guess. At any rate, he seemed to like it, and at his request, for he was not always provided with money, I trusted him till his bill comes to twenty-seven dollars——"

"You surely don't expect me to pay it!" said the squire, coldly. "He is a minor, as you very well know, and when you trusted him you knew you couldn't legally collect your claim."

"Well, squire, I thought I'd take my chances," said Tony, carelessly. "I didn't think you'd be willing to have him owing bills around the village. You're a gentleman, and I was sure you'd settle the debt."

"Then, sir, you made a very great mistake. Such bills as that I do not feel called upon to pay. Was it all incurred for billiards?"

"No; a part of it was for drinks."

"Worse and worse! How can you have the face to come here, Mr. Denton, and tell me that?"

"I don't think it needs any face, squire. It's an honest debt."

"You deliberately entrapped my son, and lured him into your saloon, where he met low companions, and squandered his money and time in drinking and low amusements."

"Come, squire, you're a little too fast. Billiards ain't low. Did you ever see Schaefer and Vignaux play?"

"No, sir; I take no interest in the game. In coming here you have simply wasted your time. You will get no money from me."

"Then you won't pay your son's debt?" asked Tony Denton.

"No."

Instead of rising to go, Tony Denton kept his seat. He regarded Squire Duncan attentively.

"I am sorry, sir," said Prince Duncan, impatiently. "I shall have to cut short this interview."

"I will detain you only five minutes, sir. Have you ascertained who robbed the bank?"

"I have no time for gossip. No, sir."

"I suppose you would welcome any information on the subject?"

Duncan looked at his visitor now with sharp attention.

"Do you know anything about it?" he asked.

"Well, perhaps I do."

"Were you implicated in it?" was the next question.

Tony Denton smiled a peculiar smile.

"No, I wasn't," he answered. "If I had been, I don't think I should have called upon you about the matter. But—I think I know who robbed the bank."

"Who, then?" demanded the squire, with an uneasy look.

Tony Denton rose from his chair, advanced to the door, which was a little ajar, and closed it. Then he resumed.

"One night late—it was after midnight—I was taking a walk,

having just closed my saloon, when it happened that my steps led by the bank. It was dark—not a soul probably in the village was awake save myself, when I saw the door of the bank open and a muffled figure came out with a tin box under his arm. I came closer, yet unobserved, and peered at the person. I recognized him."

"You recognized him?" repeated the squire, mechanically, his face pale and drawn.

"Yes; do you want to know who it was?"

Prince Duncan stared at him, but did not utter a word.

"It was you, the president of the bank!" continued Denton.

"Nonsense, man!" said Duncan, trying to regain his self-control.

"It is not nonsense. I can swear to it."

"I mean that it is nonsense about the robbery. I visited the bank to withdraw a box of my own."

"Of course you can make that statement before the court?" said Tony Denton, coolly.

"But—but—you won't think of mentioning this circumstance?" muttered the squire.

"Will you pay Randolph's bill?"

"Yes—yes; I'll draw a check at once."

"So far, so good; but it isn't far enough. I want more."

"You want more?" ejaculated the squire.

"Yes; I want a thousand-dollar government bond. It's cheap enough for such a secret."

"But I haven't any bonds."

"You can find me one," said Tony, emphatically, "or I'll tell what I know to the directors. You see, I know more than that."

"What do you know?" asked Duncan, terrified.

"I know that you disposed of a part of the bonds on Wall Street, to Sharp & Ketchum. I stood outside when you were up in their office."

Great beads of perspiration gathered upon the banker's brow. This blow was wholly unexpected, and he was wholly unprepared for it. He made a feeble resistance, but in the end, when Tony Denton left the house he had a thousand-dollar bond carefully stowed away in an inside pocket, and Squire Duncan was in such a state of mental collapse that he left his supper untasted.

Randolph was very much surprised when he learned that his father had paid his bill at the billiard saloon, and still more surprised that the squire made very little fuss about it.

CHAPTER XXXII

ON THE WAY TO THE BLACK HILLS

JUST before Luke started for the Black Hills, he received the following letter from his faithful friend Linton. It was sent to New York to the care of Mr. Reed, and forwarded, it not being considered prudent to have it known at Groveton where he was.

"Dear Luke," the letter commenced, "it seems a long time since I have seen you, and I can truly say that I miss you more than I would any other boy in Groveton. I wonder where you are—your mother does not seem to know. She only knows you are traveling for Mr. Reed.

"There is not much news. Groveton, you know, is a quiet place. I see Randolph every day. He seems very curious to know where you are. I think he is disturbed because you have found employment elsewhere. He professes to think that you are selling newspapers in New York, or tending a peanut stand, adding kindly that it is all you are fit for. I have heard a rumor that he was often to be seen playing billiards at Tony Denton's, but I don't know whether it is true. I sometimes think it would do him good to become a poor boy and have to work for a living.

"We are going to Orchard Beach next summer, as usual, and in the fall mamma may take me to Europe to stay a year to learn the French language. Won't that be fine? I wish you could go with me, but I am afraid you can't sell papers or peanuts enough —which is it?—to pay expenses. How long are you going to be away? I shall be glad to see you back, and so will Florence Grant, and all your other friends, of whom you have many in Groveton. Write soon to your affectionate friend,

"LINTON."

This letter quite cheered up Luke, who, in his first absence from home, naturally felt a little lonely at times.

"Linny is a true friend," he said. "He is just as well off as Randolph, but never puts on airs. He is as popular as Randolph is unpopular. I wish I could go to Europe with him."

Upon the earlier portions of Luke's journey to the Black Hills we need not dwell. The last hundred or hundred and fifty miles had to be traversed in a stage, and this form of traveling Luke found wearisome, yet not without interest. There was a spice of danger, too, which added excitement, if not pleasure, to the trip. The Black Hills stage had on more than one occasion been stopped by highwaymen and the passengers robbed.

The thought that this might happen proved a source of nervous alarm to some, of excitement to others.

Luke's fellow passengers included a large, portly man, a merchant from some Western city; a clergyman with a white necktie, who was sent out by some missionary society to start a church at the Black Hills; two or three laboring men, of farmerlike appearance, who were probably intending to work in the mines; one or two others, who could not be classified, and a genuine dude, as far as appearance went, a slender-waisted, soft-voiced young man, dressed in the latest style, who spoke with a slight lisp. He hailed from the city of New York, and called himself Mortimer Plantagenet Sprague. As next to himself, Luke was the youngest passenger aboard the stage, and sat beside him, the two became quite intimate. In spite of his affected manners and somewhat feminine deportment, Luke got the idea that Mr. Sprague was not wholly destitute of manly traits, if occasion should call for their display.

One day, as they were making three miles an hour over a poor road, the conversation fell upon stage robbers.

"What would you do, Colonel Braddon," one passenger asked of the Western merchant, "if the stage were stopped by a gang of ruffians?"

"Shoot 'em down like dogs, sir," was the prompt reply. "If passengers were not so cowardly, stages would seldom be robbed."

All the passengers regarded the valiant colonel with admiring respect, and congratulated themselves that they had with them so doughty a champion in case of need.

"For my part," said the missionary, "I am a man of peace, and I must perforce submit to these men of violence, if they took from me the modest allowance furnished by the society for traveling expenses."

"No doubt, sir," said Colonel Braddon. "You are a minister, and men of your profession are not expected to fight. As for my friend Mr. Sprague," and he directed the attention of the company derisively to the New York dude, "he would, no doubt, engage the robbers single-handed."

"I don't know," drawled Mortimer Sprague. "I am afraid I couldn't tackle more than two, don't you know."

There was a roar of laughter, which did not seem to disturb Mr. Sprague. He did not seem to be at all aware that his companions were laughing at him.

"Perhaps, with the help of my friend, Mr. Larkin," he added, "I might be a match for three."

There was another burst of laughter, in which Luke could not help joining.

"I am afraid I could not help you much, Mr. Sprague," he said.

"I think, Mr. Sprague," said Colonel Braddon, "that you and I will have to do the fighting if any attack is made. If our friend the minister had one of his sermons with him, perhaps that would scare away the highwaymen."

"It would not be the first time they have had an effect on godless men," answered the missionary, mildly, and there was another laugh, this time at the colonel's expense.

"What takes you to the Black Hills, my young friend?" asked Colonel Braddon, addressing Luke.

Other passengers awaited Luke's reply with interest. It was unusual to find a boy of sixteen traveling alone in that region.

"I hope to make some money," answered Luke, smiling. "I suppose that is what we are all after."

He didn't think it wise to explain his errand fully.

"Are you going to dig for gold, Mr. Larkin?" asked Mortimer Sprague. "It's awfully dirty, don't you know, and must be dreadfully hard on the back."

"Probably I am more used to hard work than you, Mr. Sprague," answered Luke.

"I never worked in my life," admitted the dude. "I really don't know a shovel from a hoe."

"Then, if I may be permitted to ask," said Colonel Braddon, "what leads you to the Black Hills, Mr. Sprague?"

"I thought I'd better see something of the country, you know. Besides, I had a bet with another feller about whether the hills were weally black, or not. I bet him a dozen bottles of champagne that they were not black, after all."

This statement was received with a round of laughter, which seemed to surprise Mr. Sprague, who gazed with mild wonder at his companions, saying: "Weally, I can't see what you fellers are laughing at. I thought I'd better come myself, because the other feller might be color-blind, don't you know."

Here Mr. Sprague rubbed his hands and looked about him to see if his joke was appreciated.

"It seems to me that the expense of your journey will foot up considerably more than a dozen bottles of champagne," said one of the passengers.

"Weally, I didn't think of that. You've got a great head, old fellow. After all, a feller's got to be somewhere, and, by Jove!—— What's that?"

This ejaculation was produced by the sudden sinking of the two left wheels in the mire in such a manner that the ponderous Colonel Braddon was thrown into Mr. Sprague's lap

"You see, I had to go somewhere," said Braddon, humorously.

"Weally, I hope we sha'n't get mixed," gasped Sprague. "If it's all the same to you, I'd rather sit in your lap."

"Just a little incident of travel, my dear sir," said Braddon, laughing, as he resumed his proper seat.

"I should call it rather a large incident," said Mr. Sprague, recovering his breath.

"I suppose," said Braddon, who seemed rather disposed to chaff his slender traveling companion, "if you like the Black Hills, you may buy one of them."

"I may," answered Mr. Sprague, letting his glance rest calmly on his big companion. "Suppose we buy one together."

Colonel Braddon laughed, but felt that his joke had not been successful.

The conversation languished after awhile. It was such hard work riding in a lumbering coach, over the most detestable roads, that the passengers found it hard to be sociable. But a surprise was in store. The coach made a sudden stop. Two horsemen appeared at the window, and a stern voice said: "We'll trouble you to get out, gentlemen. We'll take charge of what money and valuables you have about you."

CHAPTER XXXIII

TWO UNEXPECTED CHAMPIONS

IT MAY well be imagined that there was a commotion among the passengers when this stern summons was heard. The highwaymen were but two in number, but each was armed with a revolver, ready for instant use.

One by one the passengers descended from the stage, and stood trembling and panic-stricken in the presence of the masked robbers. There seems to be something in a mask which inspires added terror, though it makes the wearers neither stronger nor more effective.

Luke certainly felt startled and uncomfortable, for he felt that he must surrender the money he had with him, and this would be inconvenient, though the loss would not be his, but his employer's.

But, singularly enough, the passenger who seemed most nervous and terrified was the stalwart Colonel Braddon, who had boasted most noisily of what he would do in case the stage were attacked. He nervously felt in his pockets for his money, his face pale and ashen, and said, imploringly: "Spare my life, gentlemen; I will give you all I have."

"All right, old man," said one of the stage robbers, as he took the proffered pocketbook. Haven't you any more money?"

"No; on my honor, gentlemen. It will leave me penniless."

"Hand over your watch."

With a groan, Colonel Braddon handed over a gold stem-winder, of Waltham make.

"Couldn't you leave me the watch, gentlemen?" he said, imploringly. "It was a present to me last Christmas."

"Can't spare it. Make your friends give you another."

Next came the turn of Mortimer Sprague, the young dude.

"Hand over your spondulics, young feller," said the second gentleman of the road.

"Weally, I'm afraid I can't, without a good deal of twouble."

"Oh, curse the trouble; do as I bid, or I'll break your silly head."

"You see, gentlemen, I keep my money in my boots, don't you know."

"Take off your boots, then, and be quick about it."

"I can't; that is, without help. They're awfully tight, don't you know."

"Which boot is your money in?" asked the road agent, impatiently.

"The right boot."

"Hold it up, then, and I'll help you."

The road agent stooped over, not suspecting any danger, and in doing so laid down his revolver.

In a flash Mortimer Sprague electrified not only his assailants, but all the stage passengers, by producing a couple of revolvers, which he pointed at the two road agents, and in a stern voice, wholly unlike the affected tones in which he had hitherto spoken, said: "Get out of here, you ruffians, or I'll fire!"

The startled road agent tried to pick up his revolver, but Sprague instantly put his foot on it, and repeated the command.

The other road agent, who was occupied with the minister, turned to assist his comrade, when he, too, received a check from an unexpected source.

The minister, who was an old man, had a stout staff, which he used to guide him in his steps. He raised it and brought it down with emphasis on the arm which held the revolver, exclaiming: "The sword of the Lord and of Gideon! I smite thee, thou bold, bad man, not in anger, but as an instrument of retribution."

"Well done, reverend doctor!" exclaimed Mortimer Sprague. "Between us we will lay the rascals out!"

Luke, who was close at hand, secured the fallen revolver before the road agent's arm had got over tingling with the paralyzing blow dealt by the minister, who, in spite of his advanced age, possessed a muscular arm.

"Now git, you two!" exclaimed Mortimer Sprague. "Git, if you want to escape with whole bones!"

Never, perhaps, did two road agents look more foolish than these who had suffered such a sudden and humiliating discomfiture from those among the passengers whom they had feared least.

The young dude and the old missionary had done battle for the entire stage-load of passengers, and vanquished the masked robbers, before whom the rest trembled.

"Stop!" said Colonel Braddon, with a sudden thought. "One of the rascals has got my pocketbook!"

"Which one?" asked Mortimer.

The colonel pointed him out.

Instantly the dude fired, and a bullet whistled within a few inches of the road agent's head.

"Drop that pocketbook!" he exclaimed, "or I'll send another messenger for it; that was only a warning!"

With an execration the thoroughly terrified robber threw down the pocketbook, and the relieved owner hastened forward to pick it up.

"I thought I'd fetch him, don't you know," said the dude, relapsing into his soft drawl.

By this time both the road agents were at a safe distance, and the rescued passengers breathed more freely.

"Really, Mr. Sprague," said Colonel Braddon, pompously, "you are entitled to a great deal of credit for your gallant behavior; you did what I proposed to do. Of course, I had to submit to losing my pocketbook, but I was just preparing to draw my revolver when you got the start of me."

"If I'd only known it, colonel," drawled Mr. Sprague, "I'd have left the job for you. Weally, it would have saved me a good deal of trouble. But I think the reverend doctor here is entitled to the thanks of the company. I never knew exactly what the sword of the Lord and of Gideon was before, but I see it means a good, stout stick."

"I was speaking figuratively, my young friend," said the missionary. "I am not sure but I have acted unprofessionally, but when I saw those men of violence despoiling us, I felt the natural man rise within me, and I smote him hip and thigh."

"I thought you hit him on the arm, doctor," said Mr. Sprague.

"Again I spoke figuratively, my young friend. I cannot say I regret yielding to the impulse that moved me. I feel that I have helped to foil the plans of the wicked."

"Doctor," said one of the miners, "you've true grit. When you preach at the Black Hills, count me and my friends among the listeners. We're all willing to help along your new church, for you're one of the right sort."

"My friends, I will gladly accept your kind proposal, but I trust it will not be solely because I have used this arm of flesh in your defense. Mr. Sprague and I have but acted as humble instruments in the hands of a Higher Power."

"Well, gentlemen," said Colonel Braddon, "I think we may as well get into the stage again and resume our journey."

"What shall I do with this revolver?" asked Luke, indicating the one he had picked up.

"Keep it," said the colonel. "You'll make better used of it than the rascal who lost it."

"I've got an extra one here," said Mortimer Sprague, raising the one on which he had put his foot. "I don't need it myself, so I will offer it to the reverend doctor."

The missionary shook his head.

"I should not know how to use it," he said, "nor indeed am I sure that I should feel justified in doing so."

"May I have it, sir?" asked one of the miners.

"Certainly, if you want it," said Mr. Sprague.

"I couldn't afford to buy one; but I see that I shall need one out here."

In five minutes the stage was again on its way, and no further adventures were met with. About the middle of the next day the party arrived at Deadwood.

CHAPTER XXXIV

FENTON'S GULCH

DEADWOOD, at the time of Luke's arrival, looked more like a mining camp than a town. The first settlers had neither the time nor the money to build elaborate dwellings. Anything, however rough, that would provide a shelter, was deemed sufficient. Luxury was not dreamed of, and even ordinary comforts were only partially supplied. Luke put up at a rude hotel, and the next morning began to make inquiries for Mr. Harding. He ascertained that the person of whom he was in search had arrived not many weeks previous, accompanied by his sister. The latter, however, soon concluded that Deadwood was no suitable residence for ladies, and had returned to her former home, or some place near by. Mr. Harding remained, with a view of trying his luck at the mines.

The next point to be ascertained was to what mines he had directed his steps. This information was hard to obtain. Finally, a man who had just returned to Deadwood, hearing Luke making inquiries of the hotel clerk, said:

"I say, young chap, is the man you are after an old party over fifty, with gray hair and a long nose?"

"I think that is the right description," said Luke, eagerly. "Can you tell me anything about him?"

"The party I mean, he may be Harding, or may be somebody else, is lying sick at Fenton's Gulch, about a day's journey from here—say twenty miles."

"Sick? What is the matter with him?"

"He took a bad cold, and being an old man, couldn't stand it as well as if he were twenty years younger. I left him in an old cabin lying on a blanket, looking about as miserable as you would want to see. Are you a friend of his?"

"I am not acquainted with him," answered Luke, "but I am sent out by a friend of his in the East. I am quite anxious to find him. Can you give me directions?"

"I can do better. I can guide you there. I only came to Deadwood for some supplies, and I go back to-morrow morning."

"If you will let me accompany you I will be very much obliged."

"You can come with me and welcome. I shall be glad of your company. Are you alone?"

"Yes."

"Seems to me you're rather a young chap to come out here alone."

"I suppose I am," returned Luke, smiling, "but there was no one else to come with me. If I find Mr. Harding, I shall be all right."

"I can promise you that. It ain't likely he has got up from his sick-bed and left the mines. I reckon you'll find him flat on his back, as I left him."

Luke learned that his mining friend was known as Jack Baxter. He seemed a sociable and agreeable man, though rather rough in his outward appearance and manners. The next morning they started in company, and were compelled to travel all day. Toward sunset they reached the place known as Fenton's Gulch. It was a wild and dreary-looking place, but had a good reputation for its yield of gold dust.

"That's where you'll find the man you're after," said Baxter, pointing to a dilapidated cabin, somewhat to the left of the mines.

Luke went up to the cabin, the door of which was open, and looked in.

On a pallet in the corner lay a tall man, pale and emaciated. He heard the slight noise at the door, and without turning his head, said: "Come in, friend, whoever you are."

Upon this, Luke advanced into the cabin.

"Is this Mr. James Harding?" he asked.

The sick man turned his head, and his glance rested with surprise upon the boy of sixteen who addressed him.

"Have I seen you before?" he asked.

"No, sir. I have only just arrived at the Gulch. You are Mr. Harding?"

"Yes, that is my name; but how did you know it?"

"I am here in search of you, Mr. Harding."

"How is that?" asked the sick man, quickly. "Is my sister sick?"

"Not that I know of. I come from Mr. Armstrong, in New York."

"You come from Mr. Armstrong?" repeated the sick man, in evident surprise. "Have you any message for me from him?"

"Yes, but that can wait. I am sorry to find you sick. I hope that it is nothing serious."

"It would not be serious if I were in a settlement where I could obtain a good doctor and proper medicines. Everything is serious here. I have no care or attention, and no medicines."

"Do you feel able to get away from here? It would be better for you to be at Deadwood than here."

"If I had anyone to go with me, I might venture to start for Deadwood."

"I am at your service, Mr. Harding."

The sick man looked at Luke with a puzzled expression.

"You are very kind," he said, after a pause. "What is your name?"

"Luke Larkin."

"And you know Mr. Armstrong?"

"Yes. I am his messenger."

"But how came he to send a boy so far? It is not like him."

Luke laughed.

"No doubt you think him unwise," he said. "The fact was, he took me for lack of a better. Besides, the mission was a confidential one, and he thought he could trust me, young as I am."

"You say you have a message for me?" queried Harding.

"Yes!"

"What is it?"

"First, can I do something for your comfort? Can't I get you some breakfast?"

"The message first."

"I will give it at once. Do you remember purchasing some government bonds for Mr. Armstrong a short time before you left his employment?"

"Yes. What of them?"

"Have you preserved the numbers of the bonds?" Luke inquired, anxiously.

"Why do you ask?"

"Because Mr. Armstrong has lost his list, and they have been stolen. Till he learns the numbers, he will stand no chance of identifying or recovering them."

"I am sure I have the numbers. Feel in the pocket of my coat yonder, and you will find a wallet. Take it out and bring it to me."

Luke obeyed directions.

The sick man opened the wallet and began to examine the contents. Finally he drew out a paper, which he unfolded.

"Here is the list. I was sure I had them."

Luke's eyes lighted up with exultation.

It was clear that he had succeeded in his mission. He felt that he had justified the confidence which Mr. Armstrong had reposed in him, and that the outlay would prove not to have been wasted.

"May I copy them?" he asked.

"Certainly, since you are the agent of Mr. Armstrong—or you may have the original paper."

"I will copy them, so that if that paper is lost, I may still have the numbers. And now, what can I do for you?"

The resources of Fenton's Gulch were limited, but Luke succeeded in getting together materials for a breakfast for the sick man. The latter brightened up when he had eaten a sparing meal. It cheered him, also, to find that there was someone to whom he could look for friendly services.

To make my story short, on the second day he felt able to start with Luke for Deadwood, which he reached without any serious effect, except a considerable degree of fatigue.

Arrived at Deadwood, where there were postal facilities, Luke lost no time in writing a letter to Mr. Armstrong, enclosing a list of the stolen bonds. He gave a brief account of the circumstances under which he had found Mr. Harding, and promised to return as soon as he could get the sick man back to his farm in Minnesota.

When this letter was received, Roland Reed was in the merchant's office.

"Look at that, Mr. Reed," said Armstrong, triumphantly. "That boy is as smart as lightning. Some people might have thought me a fool for trusting so young a boy, but the result has justified me. Now my course is clear. With the help of these numbers I shall soon be able to trace the theft and convict the guilty party."

CHAPTER XXXV

BACK IN GROVETON

MEANWHILE, some things occurred in Groveton which require to be chronicled. Since the visit of Tony Denton, and the knowledge that his secret was known, Prince Duncan had changed in manner and appearance. There was an anxious look upon his face, and a haggard look, which led some of his friends to think that his health was affected. Indeed, this was true, for any mental disturbance is likely to affect the body. By way of diverting attention from the cause of this altered appearance, Mr. Duncan began to complain of overwork, and to hint that he might have to travel for his health. It occurred to him privately that circumstances might arise which would make it necessary for him to go to Canada for a lengthened period.

With his secret in the possession of such a man as Tony Denton, he could not feel safe. Besides, he suspected the keeper of the billiard-room would not feel satisfied with the thousand-dollar bond he had extorted from him, but would, after awhile, call for more.

In this he was right.

Scarcely a week had elapsed since his first visit, when the servant announced one morning that a man wished to see him.

"Do you know who it is, Mary?" asked the squire.

"Yes, sir. It's Tony Denton."

Prince Duncan's face contracted, and his heart sank within him. He would gladly have refused to see his visitor, but knowing the hold that Tony had upon him, he did not dare offend him.

"You may tell him to come in," he said, with a troubled look.

"What can the master have to do with a man like that?" thought Mary, wondering. "I wouldn't let him into the house if I was a squire."

Tony Denton entered the room with an assumption of ease which was very disagreeable to Mr. Duncan.

"I thought I'd call to see you, squire," he said.

"Take a seat, Mr. Denton," said the squire coldly.

Tony did not seem at all put out by the coldness of his reception.

"I s'pose you remember what passed at our last meeting, Mr. Duncan," he said, in a jaunty way.

"Well, sir," responded Prince Duncan, in a forbidding tone.

"We came to a little friendly arrangement, if you remember," continued Denton.

"Well, sir, there is no need to refer to the matter now."

"Pardon me, squire, but I am obliged to keep to it."

"Why?"

"Because I've been unlucky."

"I suppose, Mr. Denton," said the squire haughtily, "you are capable of managing your own business. If you don't manage it well, and meet with losses, I certainly am not responsible, and I cannot understand why you bring the matter to me."

"You see, squire," said Tony, with a grin, "I look upon you as a friend, and so it is natural that I should come to you for advice."

"I wish I dared kick the fellow out of the house," thought Prince Duncan. "He is a low scamp, and I don't like the reputation of having such visitors."

Under ordinary circumstances, and but for the secret which Tony possessed, he would not have been suffered to remain in the squire's study five minutes, but conscience makes cowards of us all, and Mr. Duncan felt that he was no longer his own master.

"I'll tell you about the bad luck, squire," Tony resumed. "You know the bond you gave me the last time I called?"

Mr. Duncan winced, and he did not reply.

"I see you remember it. Well, I thought I might have the luck to double it, so I went up to New York, and went to see one of them Wall Street brokers. I asked his advice, and he told me I'd better buy two hundred shares of some kind of stock, leaving the bond with him as margin. He said I was pretty sure to make a good deal of money, and I thought so myself. But the stock went down, and yesterday I got a letter from him, saying that the margin was all exhausted, and I must give him another, or he would sell out the stock."

"Mr. Denton, you have been a fool!" exclaimed Mr. Duncan irritably. "You might have known that would be the result of your insane folly. You've lost your thousand dollars, and what have you got to show for it?"

"You may be right, squire, but I don't want to let the matter end so. I want you to give me another bond."

"You do, eh?" said Duncan indignantly. "So you want to throw away another thousand dollars, do you?"

"If I make good the margin, the stock'll go up likely, and I won't lose anything."

"You can do as you please, of course, but you will have to go elsewhere for your money."

"Will I?" asked Tony coolly. "There is no one else who would let me have the money."

"I won't let you have another cent, you may rely upon that!" exclaimed Prince Duncan furiously.

"I guess you'll think better of that, squire," said Tony, fixing his keen black eyes on the bank president.

"Why should I?" retorted Duncan, but his heart sank within him, for he understood very well what the answer would be.

"Because you know what the consequences of refusal would be," Denton answered coolly.

"I don't understand you," stammered the squire, but it was evident from his startled look that he did.

"I thought you would," returned Tony Denton quietly. "You know very well that my evidence would convict you, as the person who robbed the bank."

"Hush!" ejaculated Prince Duncan, in nervous alarm.

Tony Denton smiled with a consciousness of power.

"I have no wish to expose you," he said, "if you will stand my friend."

In that moment Prince Duncan bitterly regretted the false step he had taken. To be in the power of such a man was, indeed, a terrible form of retribution.

"Explain your meaning," he said reluctantly.

"I want another government bond for a thousand dollars."

"But when I gave you the first, you promised to preserve silence, and trouble me no more."

"I have been unfortunate, as I already explained to you."

"I don't see how that alters matters. You took the risk voluntarily. Why should I suffer because you were imprudent and lost your money?"

"I can't argue with you, squire," said Tony, with an insolent smile. "You are too smart for me. All I have to say is, that I must have another bond."

"Suppose I should give it to you—what assurance have I that you will not make another demand?"

"I will give you the promise in writing, if you like."

"Knowing that I could not make use of any such paper without betraying myself."

"Well, there is that objection, certainly, but I can't do anything better."

"What do you propose to do with the bond?"

"Deposit it with my broker, as I have already told you."

"I advise you not to do so. Make up your mind to lose the first, and keep the second in your own hands."

"I will consider your advice, squire."

But it was very clear that Tony Denton would not follow it.

All at once Prince Duncan brightened up. He had a happy thought. Should it be discovered that the bonds used by Tony Denton belonged to the contents of the stolen box, might he not succeed in throwing the whole blame on the billiard-saloon keeper, and have him arrested as the thief? The possession and use of the bonds would be very damaging, and Tony's reputation was not such as to protect him. Here seemed to be a rift in the clouds—and it was with comparative cheerfulness that Mr. Duncan placed the second bond in the hands of the visitor.

"Of course," he said, "it will be for your interest not to let any one know from whom you obtained this."

"All right. I understand. Well, good morning, squire; I'm glad things are satisfactory."

"Good morning, Mr. Denton."

When Tony had left the room, Prince Duncan threw himself back in his chair and reflected. His thoughts were busy with the man who had just left him, and he tried to arrange some method of throwing the guilt upon Denton. Yet, perhaps, even that would not be necessary. So far as Mr. Duncan knew, there was no record in Mr. Armstrong's possession of the numbers of the bonds, and in that case they would not be identified.

"If I only knew positively that the numbers would not turn up, I should feel perfectly secure, and could realize on the bonds at any time," he thought. "I will wait awhile, and I may see my way clear."

CHAPTER XXXVI

A LETTER FROM LUKE

"THERE'S a letter for you, Linton," said Henry Wagner, as he met Linton Tomkins near the hotel. "I just saw your name on the list."

In the Groveton post-office, as in many country offices, it was the custom to post a list of those for whom letters had been received.

"It must be from Luke," thought Linton, joyfully, and he bent his steps immediately toward the office. No one in the village, outside of Luke's family, missed him more than Linton. Though Luke was two years and a half older, they had always been intimate friends. Linton's family occupied a higher social position, but there was nothing snobbish about Linton, as there was about Randolph, and it made no difference to him that Luke lived in a small and humble cottage, and, till recently, had been obliged to wear old and shabby clothes. In this democratic spirit, Linton was encouraged by his parents, who, while appreciating the refinement which is apt to be connected with liberal means, were too sensible to undervalue sterling merit and good character.

Linton was right. His letter was from Luke. It read thus:

"DEAR LINNY: I was very glad to receive your letter. It made me homesick for a short time. At any rate, it made me wish that I could be back for an hour in dear old Groveton. I cannot tell you where I am, for that is a secret of my employer. I am a long way from home; I can tell you that much. When I get home, I shall be able to tell you all. You will be glad to know that I have succeeded in the mission on which I was sent, and have received a telegram of thanks from my employer.

"It will not be long now before I am back in Groveton. I wonder if my dear friend Randolph will be glad to see me? You can remember me to him when you see him. It will gratify him to know that I am well and doing well, and that my prospects for the future are excellent.

"Give my regards to your father and mother, who have always been kind to me. I shall come and see you the first thing after I return. If you only knew how hard I find it to refrain from telling you all, where I am and what adventures I have met with, how I came near being robbed twice, and many other things, you would appreciate my self-denial. But you shall know all very soon. I have had a good time—the best time in my life. Let mother read this letter, and believe me, dear Lin,

"Your affectionate friend,

"LUKE LARKIN."

Linton's curiosity was naturally excited by the references in Luke's letter.

"Where can Luke be?" he asked. "I wish he were at liberty to tell."

Linton never dreamed, however, that his friend was two thousand miles away, in the wild West. It would have seemed to him utterly improbable.

He was folding up the letter as he was walking homeward, when he met Randolph Duncan.

"What's that, Linton?" he asked. "A love-letter?"

"Not much; I haven't got so far along. It is a letter from Luke Larkin."

"Oh!" sneered Randolph. "I congratulate you on your correspondent. Is he in New York?"

"The letter is postmarked in New York, but he is traveling."

"Traveling? Where is he traveling?"

"He doesn't say. This letter is forwarded by Mr. Reed."

"The man who robbed the bank?"

"What makes you say that? What proof have you that he robbed the bank?"

"I can't prove it, but my father thinks he is the robber. There was something very supicious about that tin box which he handed to Luke."

"It was opened in court, and proved to contain private papers."

"Oh, that's easily seen through. He took out the bonds, and put in the papers. I suppose he has experience in that sort of thing."

"Does your father think that?"

"Yes, he does. What does Luke say?"

"Wait a minute, and I will read you a paragraph," said Linton, with a mischievous smile. Thereupon he read the paragraph in which Randolph was mentioned.

"What does he mean by calling me his dear friend?" exclaimed Randolph indignantly. "I never was his dear friend, and never want to be."

"I believe you, Randolph. Shall I tell you what he means?"

"Yes."

"He means it for a joke. He knows you don't like him, and he isn't breaking his heart over it."

"It's pretty cheeky in him! Just tell him when you write that he needn't call me his dear friend again."

"You might hurt his feelings," said Linton, gravely.

"That for his feelings!" said Randolph, with a snap of his fingers. "You say he's traveling. Shall I tell you what I think he is doing?"

"If you like."

"I think he is traveling with a blacking-box in his hand. It's just the business for him."

"I don't think you are right. He wouldn't make enough in that way to pay traveling expenses. He says he has twice come near being robbed."

Randolph laughed derisively.

"A thief wouldn't make much robbing him," he said. "If he got twenty-five cents he'd be lucky."

"You forget that he has a nice silver watch?"

Randolph frowned. This with him was a sore reflection. Much as he was disposed to look down upon Luke, he was aware that Luke's watch was better than his, and, though he had importuned his father more than once to buy him a gold watch, he saw no immediate prospect of his wish being granted.

"Oh, well, I've talked enough of Luke Larkin," he said, snappishly. "He isn't worth so many words. I am very much surprised that a gentleman's son like you, Linton, should demean himself by keeping company with such a boy."

"There is no boy in the village whom I would rather associate with," said Linton, with sturdy friendship.

"I don't admire your taste, then," said Randolph. "I don't believe your father and mother like you to keep such company."

"There you are mistaken," said Linton, with spirit. "They have an excellent opinion of Luke, and if he should ever need a friend, I am sure my father would be willing to help him."

"Well, I must be going," said Randolph, by no means pleased with this advocacy of Luke. "Come round and see me soon. You never come to our house."

Linton answered politely, but did not mean to become intimate with Randolph, who was by no means to his taste. He knew that it was only his social position that won him the invitation, and that if his father should suddenly lose his property, Randolph's cordiality would be sensibly diminished. Such friendship, he felt, was not to be valued.

"What are you thinking about? You seem in a brown study," said a pleasant voice.

Looking up, Linton recognized his teacher, Mr. Hooper.

"I was thinking of Luke Larkin," answered Linton.

"By the by, where is Luke? I have not seen him for some time."

"He is traveling for Mr. Reed, I believe."

"The man who committed the tin box to his care?"

"Yes, sir."

"Do you know where he is?"

"No, sir. I have just received a letter from him, but he says he is not at liberty to mention where he is."

"Will he be home soon?"

"Yes, I think so."

"I shall be glad to see him. He is one of the most promising of my pupils."

Linton's expressive face showed the pleasure he felt at this commendation of his friend. He felt more gratified than if Mr. Hooper had directly praised him.

"Luke can stand Randolph's depreciation," he reflected, "with such a friend as Mr. Hooper."

Linton was destined to meet plenty of acquaintances. Scarcely had he parted from Mr. Hooper, when Tony Denton met him. The keeper of the billiard-room was always on the alert to ingratiate himself with the young people of the village, looking upon them as possible patrons of his rooms. He would have been glad to draw in Linton, on account of his father's prominent position in the village.

"Good day, my young friend," he said, with suavity.

"Good day, Mr. Denton," responded Linton, who thought it due to himself to be polite, though he did not fancy Mr. Denton.

"I should be very glad to have you look in at my billiard-room, Mr. Linton," continued Tony.

"Thank you sir, but I don't think my father would like to have me visit a billiard-saloon—at any rate, till I am older."

"Oh, I'll see that you come to no harm. If you don't want to play, you can look on."

"At any rate, I am obliged to you for your polite invitation."

"Oh, I like to have the nice boys of the village around me. Your friend Randolph Duncan often visits me."

"So I have heard," replied Linton.

"Well, I won't keep you, but remember my invitation."

"I am not very likely to accept," thought Linton. "I have heard that Randolph visits the billiard-room too often for his good."

CHAPTER XXXVII

AN INCIDENT ON THE CARS

AS SOON as possible, Luke started on his return to New York. He had enjoyed his journey, but now he felt a longing to see home and friends once more. His journey to Chicago was uneventful. He stayed there a few hours, and then started on his way home. On his trip from Chicago to Detroit he fell in with an old acquaintance unexpectedly.

When about thirty miles from Detroit, having as a seatmate a very large man, who compressed him within uncomfortable limits, he took his satchel, and passing into the car next forward, took a seat a few feet from the door. He had scarcely seated himself when, looking around, he discovered, in the second seat beyond, his old Chicago acquaintance, Mr. J. Madison Coleman. He was as smooth and affable as ever, and was chatting pleasantly with a rough, farmerlike-looking man, who seemed very much taken with his attractive companion.

"I wonder what mischief Coleman is up to now?" thought Luke.

He was so near that he was able to hear the conversation that passed between them.

"Yes, my friend," said Mr. Coleman, "I am well acquainted with Detroit. Business has called me there very often, and it will give me great pleasure to be of service to you in any way."

"What business are you in?" inquired the other.

"I am traveling for H. B. Claflin & Co., of New York. Of course you have heard of them. They are the largest wholesale dry-goods firm in the United States."

"You don't say so!" returned the farmer respectfully. "Do you get pretty good pay?"

"I am not at liberty to tell just what pay I get," said Mr. Coleman, "but I am willing to admit that it is over four thousand dollars."

"You don't say so!" ejaculated the farmer. "My! I think myself pretty lucky when I make a thousand dollars a year."

"Oh, well, my dear sir, your expenses are very light compared to mine. I spend about ten dollars a day on an average."

"Jehu!" ejaculated the farmer. "Well, that is a pile. Do all the men that travel for your firm get as much salary as you?"

"Oh, no; I am one of the principal salesmen, and am paid extra. I am always successful, if I do say it myself, and the firm know it, and pay me accordingly. They know that several other firms are after me, and would get me away if they didn't pay me my price."

"I suppose you know all about investments, being a business man?"

"Yes, I know a great deal about them," answered Mr. Coleman, his eyes sparkling with pleasure at this evidence that his companion had money. "If you have any money to invest, I shall be very glad to advise you."

"Well, you see, I've just had a note for two hundred and fifty dollars paid in by a neighbor who's been owin' it for two years, and I thought I'd go up to Detroit and put it in the savings-bank."

"My good friend, the savings-bank pays but a small rate of interest. I think I know a business man of Detroit who will take your money and pay you ten per cent."

"Ten per cent.!" exclaimed the farmer joyfully. "My! I didn't think I could get over four or six."

"So you can't, in a general way," answered Coleman. "But business men, who are turning over their money once a month, can afford to pay a good deal more."

"But is your friend safe?" he inquired, anxiously.

"Safe as the Bank of England," answered Coleman. "I've lent him a thousand dollars at a time, myself, and always got principal and interest regularly. I generally have a few thousand invested," he added, in a matter-of-course manner.

"I'd be glad to get ten per cent.," said the farmer. "That would be twenty-five dollars a year on my money."

"Exactly. I dare say you didn't get over six per cent. on the note."

"I got seven, but I had to wait for the interest sometimes."

"You'll never have to wait for interest if you lend to my friend. I am only afraid he won't be willing to take so small a sum. Still, I'll speak a good word for you, and he will make an exception in your favor."

"Thank you, sir," said the farmer gratefully. "I guess I'll let him have it."

"You couldn't do better. He's a high-minded, responsible man. I would offer to take the money myself, but I really have no use for it. I have at present two thousand dollars in bank waiting for investment."

"You don't say so!" said the farmer, eying Coleman with the respect due to so large a capitalist.

"Yes, I've got it in the savings-bank for the time being. If my friend can make use of it, I shall let him have it. He's just as safe as a savings-bank."

The farmer's confidence in Mr. Coleman was evidently fully established. The young man talked so smoothly and confidently that he would have imposed upon one who had seen far more of the world than Farmer Jones.

"I'm in luck to fall in with you, Mr.——"

"Coleman," said the drummer, with suavity. "J. Madison Coleman. My grandfather was a cousin of President James Madison, and that accounts for my receiving that name."

The farmer's respect was further increased. It was quite an event to fall in with so near a relative of an illustrious ex-President, and he was flattered to find that a young man of such lineage was disposed to treat him with such friendly familiarity.

"Are you going to stay long in Detroit?" asked the farmer.

"Two or three days. I shall be extremely busy, but I shall find time to attend to your business. In fact, I feel an interest in you, my friend, and shall be glad to do you a service."

"You are very kind, and I'm obleeged to you," said the farmer gratefully.

"Now, if you will excuse me for a few minutes, I will go into the smoking-car and have a smoke."

When he had left the car, Luke immediately left his seat, and went forward to where the farmer was sitting.

"Excuse me," he said, "but I saw you talking to a young man just now."

"Yes," answered the farmer complacently, "he's a relative of President Madison."

"I want to warn you against him. I know him to be a swindler."

"What!" exclaimed the farmer, eying Luke suspiciously. "Who be you? You're nothing but a boy."

"That is true, but I am traveling on business. This Mr. Coleman tried to rob me about a fortnight since, and nearly succeeded. I heard him talking to you about money."

"Yes, he was going to help me invest some money I have with me. He said he could get me ten per cent."

"Take my advice, and put it in a savings-bank. Then it will be safe. No man who offers to pay ten per cent. for money can be relied upon."

"Perhaps you want to rob me yourself?" said the farmer suspiciously.

"Do I look like it?" asked Luke, smiling. "Isn't my advice good, to put the money in a savings-bank? But I will tell you how I fell in with Mr. Coleman, and how he tried to swindle me, and then you can judge for yourself."

This Luke did briefly, and his tone and manner carried conviction. The farmer became extremely indignant at the intended fraud, and promised to have nothing to do with Coleman.

"I will take my old seat, then," said Luke. "I don't want Coleman to know who warned you."

Presently, Coleman came back and was about to resume his seat beside the farmer.

"You see I have come back," he said.

"You needn't have troubled yourself," said the farmer, with a lowering frown. "You nearly took me in with your smooth words, but I've got my money yet, and I mean to keep it. Your friend can't have it."

"What does all this mean, my friend?" asked Coleman, in real amazement. "Is it possible you distrust me? Why, I was going to put myself to inconvenience to do you a service."

"Then you needn't. I know you. You wanted to swindle me out of my two hundred and fifty dollars."

"Sir, you insult me!" exclaimed Coleman, with lofty indignation. "What do I—a rich man—want of your paltry two hundred and fifty dollars?"

"I don't believe you are a rich man. Didn't I tell you, I have been warned against you?"

"Who dared to talk against me?" asked Coleman indignantly. Then, casting his eyes about, he noticed Luke for the first time. Now it was all clear to him.

Striding up to Luke's seat, he said threateningly, "Have you been talking against me, you young jackanapes?"

"Yes, Mr. Coleman, I have," answered Luke steadily. "I thought it my duty to inform this man of your character. I have advised him to put his money into a savings-bank."

"Curse you for an impertinent meddler!" said Coleman wrathfully. "I'll get even with you for this!"

"You can do as you please," said Luke calmly.

Coleman went up to the farmer and said, abruptly, "You've been imposed upon by an unprincipled boy. He's been telling you lies about me."

"He has given me good advice," said the farmer sturdily, "and I shall follow it."

"You are making a fool of yourself!"

"That is better than to be made fool of, and lose my money."

Coleman saw that the game was lost, and left the car. He would gladly have assaulted Luke, but knew that it would only get him into trouble.

CHAPTER XXXVIII

LUKE'S RETURN

MR. ARMSTRONG was sitting in his office one morning when the door opened, and Luke entered, his face flushed with health, and his cheeks browned by exposure.

"You see I've got back, Mr. Armstrong," he said, advancing with a smile.

"Welcome home, Luke!" exclaimed the merchant heartily, grasping our hero's hand cordially.

"I hope you are satisfied with me," said Luke.

"Satisfied! I ought to be. You have done yourself the greatest credit. It is seldom a boy of your age exhibits such good judgment and discretion."

"Thank you, sir," said Luke gratefully. "I was obliged to spend a good deal of money," he added, "and I have arrived in New York with only three dollars and seventy-five cents in my pocket."

"I have no fault to find with your expenses," said Mr. Armstrong promptly. "Nor would I have complained if you had spent twice as much. The main thing was to succeed, and you have succeeded."

"I am glad to hear you speak so," said Luke, relieved. "To me it seemed a great deal of money. You gave me two hundred dollars, and I have less than five dollars left. Here it is!" and Luke drew the sum from his pocket, and tendered it to the merchant.

"I can't take it," said Mr. Armstrong. "You don't owe me any money. It is I who am owing you. Take this on account," and he drew a roll of bills from his pocketbook and handed it to Luke. "Here are a hundred dollars on account," he continued.

"This is too much, Mr. Armstrong," said Luke, quite overwhelmed with the magnitude of the gift.

"Let me be the judge of that," said Mr. Armstrong kindly. "There is only one thing, Luke, that I should have liked to have you do."

"What is that, sir?"

"I should like to have had you bring me a list of the numbers certified to by Mr. Harding."

Luke's answer was to draw from the inside pocket of his vest a paper signed by the old bookkeeper, containing a list of the numbers, regularly subscribed and certified to.

"Is that what you wished, sir?" he asked.

"You are a wonderful boy," said the merchant admiringly. "Was this your idea, or Mr. Harding's?"

"I believe I suggested it to him," said Luke modestly.

"That makes all clear sailing," said Mr. Armstrong. "Here are fifty dollars more. You deserve it for your thoughtfulness."

"You have given me enough already," said Luke, drawing back.

"My dear boy, it is evident that you still have something to learn in the way of business. When a rich old fellow offers you money, which he can well afford, you had better take it."

"That removes all my objections," said Luke. "But I am afraid you will spoil me with your liberality, Mr. Armstrong."

"I will take the risk of it. But here is another of your friends."

The door had just opened, and Roland Reed entered. There was another cordial greeting, and Luke felt that it was pleasant, indeed, to have two such good friends.

"When are you going to Groveton, Luke?" asked Mr. Reed.

"I shall go this afternoon, if there is nothing more you wish me to do. I am anxious to see my mother."

"That is quite right, Luke. Your mother is your best friend, and deserves all the attention you can give her. I shall probably go to Groveton myself to-morrow."

After Luke had left the office, Mr. Reed remained to consult with the merchant as to what was the best thing to do. Both were satisfied that Prince Duncan, the president of the bank, was the real thief who had robbed the bank. There were two courses open—a criminal prosecution, or a private arrangement which should include the return of the stolen property. The latter course was determined upon, but should it prove ineffective, severer measures were to be resorted to.

CHAPTER XXXIX

HOW LUKE WAS RECEIVED

LUKE'S return to Groveton was received with delight by his mother and his true friend Linton. Naturally Randolph displayed the same feelings toward him as ever. It so chanced that he met Luke only an hour after his arrival. He would have passed him by unnoticed but for the curiosity he felt to know where he had been, and what he was intending to do.

"Humph! so you're back again!" he remarked.

"Yes," answered Luke, with a smile. "I hope you haven't missed me much, Randolph."

"Oh, I've managed to live through it," returned Randolph, with what he thought to be cutting sarcasm.

"I am glad of that."

"Where were you?" asked Randolph, abruptly.

"I was in New York a part of the time," said Luke.

"Where were you the rest of the time?"

"I was traveling."

"That sounds large. Perhaps you were traveling with a hand-organ."

"Perhaps I was."

"Well, what are you going to do now?"

"Thank you for your kind interest in me, Randolph. I will tell you as soon as I know."

"Oh, you needn't think I feel interest in you."

"Then I won't."

"You are impertinent," said Randolph, scowling. It dawned upon him that Luke was chaffing him.

"I don't mean to be. If I have been, I apologize. If you know of any situation which will pay me a fair sum, I wish you would mention me."

"I'll see about it," said Randolph, in an important tone. He was pleased at Luke's change of tone. "I don't think you can get back as janitor, for my father doesn't like you."

"Couldn't you intercede for me, Randolph?"

"Why, the fact is, you put on so many airs, for a poor boy,

that I shouldn't feel justified in recommending you. It is your own fault."

"Well, perhaps it is," said Luke.

"I am glad you acknowledge it. I don't know but my father will give you a chance to work round our house, make fires, and run errands."

"What would he pay?" asked Luke, in a businesslike tone.

"He might pay a dollar and a half a week."

"I'm afraid I couldn't support myself on that."

"Oh, well, that's your lookout. It's better than loafing round doing nothing."

"You're right there, Randolph."

"I'll just mention it to father, then."

"No, thank you. I shouldn't wonder if Mr. Reed might find something for me to do."

"Oh, the man that robbed the bank?" said Randolph, turning up his nose.

"It may soon be discovered that some one else robbed the bank."

"I don't believe it."

Here the two boys parted.

"Luke," said Linton, the same day, "have you decided what you are going to do?"

"Not yet; but I have friends who, I think, will look out for me."

"Because my father says he will find you a place if you fail to get one elsewhere."

"Tell your father that I think he is very kind. There is no one to whom I would more willingly be indebted for a favor. If I should find myself unemployed, I will come to him."

"All right! I am going to drive over to Coleraine"—the next town—"this afternoon. Will you go with me?"

"I should like nothing better."

"What a difference there is between Randolph and Linton!" thought Luke.

CHAPTER XL

THE BANK ROBBER IS FOUND

TONY DENTON lost no time in going up to the city with the second bond he had extracted from the fears of Prince Duncan. He went directly to the office of his brokers, Gay & Sears, and announced that he was prepared to deposit additional margin.

The bond was received, and taken to the partners in the back office. Some four minutes elapsed, and the clerk reappeared.

"Mr. Denton, will you step into the back office?" he said.

"Certainly," answered Tony cheerfully.

He found the two brokers within.

"This is Mr. Denton?" said the senior partner.

"Yes, sir."

"You offer this bond as additional margin on the shares we hold in your name?"

"Yes, of course."

"Mr. Denton," said Mr. Gay searchingly, "where did you get this bond?"

"Where did I get it?" repeated Denton nervously. "Why, I bought it."

"How long since?"

"About a year."

The two partners exchanged glances.

"Where do you live, Mr. Denton?"

"In Groveton."

"Ahem! Mr. Sears, will you be kind enough to draw out the necessary papers?"

Tony Denton felt relieved. The trouble seemed to be over.

Mr. Gay at the same time stepped into the main office and gave a direction to one of the clerks.

Mr. Sears drew out a large sheet of foolscap, and began, in very deliberate fashion, to write. He kept on writing for some minutes. Tony Denton wondered why so much writing should be necessary in a transaction of this kind. Five minutes later a young man looked into the office, and said, addressing Mr. Gay: "All right!"

Upon that Mr. Sears suspended writing.

"Mr. Denton," said Mr. Gay, "are you aware that this bond

which you have brought us was stolen from the Groveton Bank?"

"I—don't—believe—it," gasped Denton, turning pale.

"The numbers of the stolen bonds have been sent to all the bankers and brokers in the city. This is one, and the one you brought us not long since is another. Do you persist in saying that you bought this bond a year ago?"

"No, no!" exclaimed Denton, terrified.

"Did you rob the bank?"

"No, I didn't!" ejaculated the terrified man, wiping the perspiration from his brow.

"Where, then, did you get the bonds?"

"I got them both from Prince Duncan, president of the bank."

Both partners looked surprised.

One of them went to the door of the office, and called in Mr. Armstrong, who, as well as a policeman, had been sent for.

Tony Denton's statement was repeated to him.

"I am not surprised," he said. "I expected it."

Tony Denton now made a clean breast of the whole affair, and his words were taken down.

"Are you willing to go to Groveton with me, and repeat this in presence of Mr. Duncan?" asked Mr. Armstrong.

"Yes."

"Will you not have him arrested?" asked Mr. Gay.

"No, he has every reason to keep faith with me."

It was rather late in the day when Mr. Armstrong, accompanied by Tony Denton, made their appearance at the house of Prince Duncan. When the banker's eyes rested on the strangely assorted pair, his heart sank within him. He had a suspicion of what it meant.

"We have called on you, Mr. Duncan, on a matter of importance," said Mr. Armstrong.

"Very well," answered Duncan faintly.

"It is useless to mince matters. I have evidence outside of this man's to show that it was you who robbed the bank of which you are president, and appropriated to your own use the bonds which it contained."

"This is a strange charge to bring against a man in my position. Where is your proof?" demanded Duncan, attempting to bluster.

"I have Mr. Denton's evidence that he obtained two thousand-dollar bonds of you."

"Very well, suppose I did sell him two such bonds?"

"They were among the bonds stolen."

"It is not true. They were bonds I have had for five years."

"Your denial is useless. The numbers betray you."

"You did not have the numbers of the bonds."

"So you think, but I have obtained them from an old bookkeeper of mine, now at the West. I sent a special messenger out to obtain the list from him. Would you like to know who the messenger was?"

"Who was it?"

"Luke Larkin."

"That boy!" exclaimed Duncan bitterly.

"Yes, that boy supplied me with the necessary proof. And now, I have a word to say; I can send you to prison, but for the sake of your family I would prefer to spare you. But the bonds must be given up."

"I haven't them all in my possession."

"Then you must pay me the market price of those you have used. The last one given to this man is safe."

"It will reduce me to poverty," said Prince Duncan in great agitation.

"Nevertheless, it must be done!" said Mr. Armstrong sternly. "Moreover, you must resign your position as president of the bank, and on that condition you will be allowed to go free, and I will not expose you."

Of course, Squire Duncan was compelled to accept these terms. He saved a small sum out of the wreck of his fortune, and with his family removed to the West, where they were obliged to adopt a very different style of living. Randolph is now an office boy at a salary of four dollars a week, and is no longer able to swagger and boast as he has done hitherto. Mr. Tomkins, Linton's father, was elected president of the Groveton Bank in place of Mr. Duncan, much to the satisfaction of Luke.

Roland Reed, much to the suprise of Luke, revealed himself as a cousin of Mr. Larkin, who for twenty-five years had been lost sight of. He had changed his name, on account of some trouble into which he had been betrayed by Prince Duncan, and thus had not been recognized.

"You need be under no anxiety about Luke and his prospects," he said to Mrs. Larkin. "I shall make over to him ten thousand dollars at once, constituting myself his guardian, and will see that he is well started in business. My friend Mr. Armstrong proposes to take him into his office, if you do not object, at a liberal salary."

"I shall miss him very much," said Mrs. Larkin, "though I am thankful that he is to be so well provided for."

"He can come home every Saturday night, and stay until Monday morning," said Mr. Reed, who, by the way, chose to retain his name in place of his old one. "Will that satisfy you?"

"It ought to, surely, and I am grateful to Providence for all the blessings which it has showered upon me and mine."

There was another change. Mr. Reed built a neat and commodious house in the pleasantest part of the village and there Mrs. Larkin removed with his little daughter, of whom she still had the charge. No one rejoiced more sincerely at Luke's good fortune than Linton, who throughout had been a true and faithful friend. He is at present visiting Europe with his mother, and has written an earnest letter, asking Luke to join him. But Luke feels that he cannot leave a good business position, and must postpone the pleasure of traveling till he is older.

Mr. J. Madison Coleman, the enterprising drummer, has got into trouble, and is at present an inmate of the State penitentiary at Joliet, Illinois. It is fortunate for the traveling public, so many of whom he has swindled, that he is for a time placed where he can do no more mischief.

So closes an eventful passage in the life of Luke Larkin. He has struggled upward from a boyhood of privation and self-denial into a youth and manhood of prosperity and honor. There has been some luck about it, I admit, but after all he is indebted for most of his good fortune to his own good qualities.

THE END